C

By

To Bobbie, Jennifer, and Jonathan.

Table of Contents

Chapter 1 Leaving Earth

It was bright and sunny outside this morning. Smiling people walked cheerfully past me. Why did they all have to look so happy? I cursed them. I could feel nothing but the crushing darkness of my impending doom. How was I going to survive? How had my life come to this? I glanced down at Demetrious. "I'm doing this for you," I said, trying to reassure myself. If only there was another way, but I knew there wasn't.

The sun beat down on us. It was already getting hot even though it was still a few hours before noon. And it was humid, god it was humid. My clothes stuck to my body. I was a sticky, sweaty mess as I walked slowly, nervously into the spaceport in Brownsville, Texas. I knew from now on I'd be Tesla Miller, my new identity. I wondered if I would ever get used to that name. Probably, eventually, although, getting used a new name was the least of my worries. In a few hours I was going to be blasted off into space along with my infant son. That sucks. I don't even like flying. Why did I think I could do this? I cursed Alex for putting me in this position. Yet even this was not my biggest problem, not by a long shot.

The double doors to the facility swooshed open as they sensed our approach. I took a deep breath and walked through holding my son Demetrious and my purse in one arm while pulling my suitcase with the other. It was brightly lit and blessedly cool inside. It looked kind of like a small airport. There were two counters straight ahead and a single security line off to the right. The information from the resort said that while space travel was now routine, the number of customers traveling to space was still tiny compared to the number of people that traveled by air each day. It said there was only one flight to Sky City each week so be sure not to miss it. My flight was scheduled for 1:00 pm.

At the security checkpoint I awkwardly struggled to hold my disposable phone up to the scanner while also trying to hold Demetrious with the same arm. Security here seemed more intense than a typical airport. I watched as robots examined every article in my checked luggage and my purse. They looked to be very thorough and fast. They didn't seem to get bored either. I kicked off my shoes, struggled to bend over to pick them up so I could put them through the x-ray thing, then walked through the full-body scanner while still holding Demetrious.

On the other side, I grabbed my shoes and purse and carried everything the short walk to the gate. I found an open seat in the boarding area next to a man who looked to be in his late twenties or early thirties. I sat down without saying say a word, which is unusual for me. Under normal circumstances I delighted in striking up conversations with strangers. I kind of had a knack for that, but not today.

The stress of the events over the last two weeks along with the dreadfully scary proposition of being blasted into space was crushing me. I could feel my breathing getting shallower. My chest started hurting again. The world was closing in on me. Shit, I can't do this. How do I get out of this? I stared at Demetrious hoping his sweet face could help me calm down...Nope. I closed my eyes. I felt my heart racing. I don't want to die today! "I can't breathe," I blurted out loud in a panic.

"What?" said the man sitting next to me. "Are you okay?"

"I can't breathe!" I said again, gasping for air. "I have to get out of here!"

"Look at me," said the man.

"What?"

"Look at me,"

I turned and looked at him. He had the bluest eyes I had ever seen.

"Now, just breathe with me," he said taking my hands. "That's it, just breathe in slowly and then exhale."

After a few minutes of breathing this way with this total stranger, I started to calm down. Eventually I was able to talk more or less normally. "Thank you."

"You're welcome," he said, letting go of my hands. "I think you just had a panic attack. I see that a lot. Is this your first time going into space?"

"Yes." I smiled sheepishly, trying to hid my deeper anguish. "Does it show?"

"Is space big?" he grinned.

"I'm kind of afraid flying. And apparently I'm especially afraid of flying into space." I took another deep breath. "I take it you've flow to space before?" I had a hard time not staring at his blue eyes.

"Yes, many times."

"And you weren't afraid, even the first time?

"Na, even the first time I thought it was exhilarating." There was something calm and comforting in the way he spoke.

"How many times have you done this?"

"I don't actually know exactly. Maybe a few dozen I guess. Anyway, It's no big deal, so you don't need to be nervous."

I smiled somewhat more naturally this time. "Easy for you to say." Talking seemed to help my anxiety. "Why have you gone so many times?"

"It's for work." He paused for a moment, then pointed at my shoes and said, "By the way, you won't be needing those. You should probably just leave them here."

2

I stared at him. What the hell? Why is this stranger telling me to get rid of my shoes? Who does that? Finally, I managed to reply with somewhat more attitude in my voice than intended, "What are you talking about? I like these shoes."

"You're going to Sky City, right?"

"Yes."

"So, you don't need shoes there. Nothing to walk on, right?"

"Everybody knows that," I replied, "but don't people still where shoes?"

"Socks actually, just to keep your feet warm. Or to hide them, I guess, if you have ugly feet." A wry smile crept onto his face.

"You think I have ugly feet?" I saw him look down at my feet.

"Definitely not."

"So you work in space?" I asked trying to change the subject as I slipped my shoes discretely into my carry-on bag. "I'm going to work there too. My name is… uh, Tesla Miller and little guy here is my son Demetrious."

He stood up, turned to face us, extended his hand toward me and replied, "Pleased to meet you Tesla and Demetrious. I'm Marc Elliott."

I shook his hand as I stared again, and probably a little too long, into those incredible blue eyes. He had a firm, but gentle grip and incredibly soft hands. He held my hand for just the right length of time.

"How old is he?" He nodded toward Demetrious.

"He just turned six months."

"Well, at least you don't seem to be nervous flying into space," Marc said to Demetrious.

"Yeah, I wish I could be more like him," I said.

"Well, talking to beautiful women makes me nervous," replied Mark smiling, "so I guess we'll just have to be nervous together."

I will take that as a compliment, I thought. He seems like such a nice person. But then so did Alex when I first met him. There's no way I can get involved with anyone right now, so just keep it cool. "You don't seem very nervous to me." I smiled. "What kind of work do you do in space?"

Marc hesitated momentarily as if searching for the right thing to say, "Well, I kind of help out with the resort. You know, making sure things are running okay. Seems like there's always things to fix or adjust. Plus, I'm working on a new project up there as well. What are you going to do at Sky City?"

It was a simple, innocent, question, but as soon as he said it all my problems came rushing back into my consciousness with a vengeance. Shit, how do you tell someone you're going be a space hooker?...God, I hate my life, I hate Alex. I wish, as I did a million times over the past

3

week, that there was some other way. But I knew there wasn't. Everything else was worse, much worse.

"So what are you going to do there?" Marc repeated politely, pretending that I didn't hear him the first time.

If he's working there, he'll find out sooner or later, so I might as well tell him. "I'll be working at the Three Dolphins Club," I finally said with obvious embarrassment.

"I see," Marc said with little emotion. "Please excuse me."

I watched as he got up and walked over to the flight attendant. Well shit, that didn't go over very well; not that I expected any better. Still, I couldn't help but notice that he was a litter shorter and slimmer than Alex. Maybe about five feet eleven and probably not more than a hundred seventy five pounds. His straight brown hair and those blue eyes were quite different from Alex's dark wavy hair and dark brown eyes.

After a brief conversation with the flight attendant, and much to my surprise, Marc returned.

We continued to talk until it was time to board the flight. The time came too soon. "Well, shit, here's goes nothing," I said as I stood up, trying to sound brave. I swallowed hard, grabbed Demetrious and repeated to myself, you can do this. I tried not to let Marc see that my whole body was shaking as I started walking toward the gangway, but he wasn't following us. I felt my breathing get shallower again and my chest start pounding as I walked onto the spaceplane with Demetrious. It helped just a little that it was a lot like boarding a regular airplane, although it looked smaller inside. The seats were arranged with one seat, an aisle, then two seats in about ten rows.

I somehow managed to get us to our assigned seats. I sat on the aisle and put Demetrious in the seat next to me in an infant carrier provided by the space line. I noticed that there were no windows in the spaceplane which added to that feeling that the world was closing in on me again. Up front was a large screen displaying what appeared to be a view of the outside looking forward, but it didn't help much.

I tensely alternated between looking at Demetrious and staring at the monitor, my heart was beating rapidly even though I was sitting still. I was sweating again. I glanced around the cabin and noticed every seat was now taken except for the one directly across the aisle from me. As the door closed for departure, Marc came in and took that seat.

"Hi, Marc," I managed to say with a tense smile, as I tried hard, but unsuccessfully to hide how scared I was.

"Still nervous, right?"

"Does it show?" Dear god, it felt like I was going to pass out. Maybe talking to Marc will help like it did before. "So how does this thing work.

4

Aren't rockets launched straight up. Shouldn't we be lying on our backs or something?" The questions came spilling out in rapid fire.

"Easy, there. You're going to be okay." Marc smiled calmly at me as he leaned across the aisle. "There are some passenger systems that still launch that way, but not this one. In our case, we're in a rocket plane that is slung underneath the belly of a much larger carrier vehicle. The carrier vehicle will take the rocket plane up to forty-nine thousand feet and then release it. From there, the rocket plane will fire its engines, taking us to space, and the carrier vehicle will fly back to the launch site to be used again."

He paused for a moment, I think it was to see if I was following him. I tried to smile politely, but I think it came across as just more nervousness. Fortunately, Mark continued.

"What most people don't realize is that space is actually not that far away—it starts at an altitude of about a hundred miles. So if you go straight up for a hundred miles you're in space. Now, it's three-hundred eighty miles from Los Angeles to San Francisco, so if you're in Los Angeles, you're actually closer to space than you are to San Francisco, right?"

Okay, he's definitely on the nerdy side. It's funny, when I was in high school, I wouldn't have given him the time of day, but now... I pushed the thought from my mind. My life was already more fucked up than I could stand. The last thing I needed was another relationship. Just keep it to small talk. "So, how long will it take us to get there?" I asked.

Marc was now clearly enjoying himself, "It's about a six-hour trip up to Sky City." He paused for a moment and then continued. "You know, it used to take over two days for the Russian Soyuz capsule to rendezvous with the international space station, can you believe that? Now we routinely go up to Sky City in just six hours. All the burns, course corrections, and navigation are routine and automated. No need for a pilot really, but people feel more comfortable if there's one on board, right? So we have one, well two actually."

"Six hours? If space is only a hundred miles away, why does it take so long to get there?"

That must have been a good question because Marc seemed somewhat surprised and pleased by it.

"That's a very good question. While space is not very far away, it's actually quite hard to get to. That's because to get there and stay there you have to go really, really fast, just over seventeen thousand miles per hour. On top of that, we have to catch up with the resort that is also going really fast. It's that catching up process that takes time."

"How do we do that?" I asked. It was only partially working, listening to Marc answer my questions helped me take my mind off my impending doom, but not entirely. Marc went into this long winded explanation about how this thing works, but I found it nearly impossible to concentrate believing that I was going to die in a few minutes "Got it," I said, when he finally finished, even though I really didn't. I looked at Demetrious who looked like he didn't have a care in the world. Why can't I be like that?

During Marc's long explanation, we must have pushed back from the gate. I realized I was gripping the armrests so tightly my hands started to hurt. I felt the tightness in my chest return. I felt like I couldn't get a good breath.

The takeoff was surprisingly smooth. That's not so bad, just like an airplane. I wondered what was going to happen next. I wish I could remember what Marc said.

After about an hour the captain announced we had reached the drop altitude of forty-nine thousand feet and would be making the separation in sixty seconds. The lone flight attendant directed us to make sure our seat belts and shoulder harnesses were securely fastened and to secure all loose items.

I looked at the monitor up front. It didn't look any different from flying on a regular airplane. That changed in an instant when with a loud CLANG we started to fall. I felt my stomach trying to escape from my body through my mouth. I stared at Marc and urgently gasped out, "What's happening?"

Just as calm as ever, Marc smiled and said, "We just separated from the carrier vehicle, now the fun begins, right?"

Fun my ass! All I could think about was that I was going to die right now in this stupid rocket plane as it plummeted toward the Earth. I looked at Demetrious and cried, "I'm sorry." I gasped for air.

The main engines roared to life throwing me back hard against my seat. The vehicle groaned and creaked as it responded to the thrust. The rocket plane's acceleration, according to the screen at the front of the cabin, increased rapidly before leveling off at three gees. The roar of the engines made it extremely noisy in the cabin, much louder than in an airplane. I tried to scream, but couldn't. I couldn't even move my arms. I involuntarily squeezed the armrests even tighter, digging my fingernails deeper into the fabric, certain the rocket plane was shaking itself apart. With significant effort I turned my head toward Demetrious. He was plastered against his seat, but not crying. I forced my head back the other way and saw Marc grinning from ear-to-ear. Seriously?

Then, just as suddenly as they started, the main engines shut down. Was that supposed to happen? What's going on? Are we going to crash? My mind was racing with questions. It was so quiet now, no vibration, no noise, just my heart pounding.

I can't feel the seat against my back. I'm floating! Is that what Marc said would happen? This is so cool! Demetrious! How's he doing? Oh look, he's floating too, and he's smiling! Demetrious was still in his infant seat of course, but he was clearly no longer plastered against the padding. His arms were floating in front of him.

I looked at the screen up front. "Oh my god, we're in space!" I cried out loud. I couldn't help but smile. I'm in space and I'm still alive! I turned toward Marc, smiled broadly and exclaimed with giddy excitement, "We're in space!"

"Of course we are," Marc replied calmly, flashing those blue eyes at me. "To get to space you only have to be brave for eight minutes, right? But we're just barely there. This baby's still got more work to do, at least one more burn or we're going back down, three more to get to Sky City."

I nodded, grinning from ear to ear. In the screen up front I saw the curvature of the Earth for the first time. That's spectacular! The bright blue Earth was in sharp contrast to the jet black sky. It looked like we were upside down, but it didn't feel that way. Forty-five minutes of weightlessness went by quickly, then the main engines roared to life again, throwing us back into our seats. This time Demetrious started crying, but stopped as soon as the engines cut off and he was weightless again. He repeated this for the remaining two burns making me laugh.

After completing all of the major burns, Marc said we had two more hours before we would dock with Sky City. By now, I had to pee really bad. We had all been these given super absorbent adult diapers before takeoff, except Demetrious, who of course, had his usual diaper.

At first I didn't want to put it on, but now I was glad I did since there was no toilet on the rocket plane. Really? Who's stupid idea was that? Anyway, I just hope this thing is as absorbent and leak proof as they said. Okay, here goes nothing. Ahh, what a relief. Yeah, no leaks! I don't even feel wet!

"See that wasn't so bad now was it?" said Marc as he leaned over toward me.

What?! Shit. How did he know? God I'm so embarrassed.

Getting no response from me, Marc repeated, "The ride to space, it wasn't so bad, was it? See, you had nothing to be afraid of, right?"

Ha! He was just talking about the launch. "No," I responded with relief. I smiled broadly at Marc and looked into those eyes. "It was much better than I expected. It was actually kind of fun, at least the parts where, you know, I wasn't positive I was going to die." Now I understood the ear-to-ear grin I had seen on Marc's face during the launch. "Thanks for helping me get through it."

"Anytime."

Chapter 2 Arrival

The rocket plane neared Sky City and I could see the resort in the screen for the first time.

"Is that Sky City?" I asked Marc. "It doesn't look anything like I thought it would. It's ugly." There was more than a little tension in my voice. I knew I as was going to be living there for the next six months. I thought this place was supposed to be a luxury resort. It looks like a piece of shit.

"Ugly?" replied Marc, a touch defensively. "I think it's beautiful. Why do you think it's ugly?

"I was expecting to see a large rotating thing, you know, like a big wheel, with lights and stuff. Something that looks like a space station. But this doesn't look anything like that. All I see are four big round disks and what looks like some big ugly, dark tubes. Where are the lights? Where are the rooms? Where are the windows?"

Marc laughed. "I see your point. Those big round disks you see are the solar panels. They provide electrical power to the resort. You don't see any lights because all the living areas in Sky City are surrounded by asteroid dirt to provide radiation shielding. There are almost no real windows in the resort."

"What do you mean there are no windows? I thought the view was one of the main attractions. How can you have no windows?"

Marc gave me a reassuring look. "Don't worry, when you get there you'll see that the view is truly out of this world."

I couldn't tell if he was serious or not.

The rocket plane docked to the resort with a gentle thud. It was one of four docking ports at Sky City according to Marc. We had now been weightless for the better part of six hours, although we had been strapped into our seats the whole time. Now it was time to leave the rocket plane and enter the resort. Seven and a half hours ago, I walked onto this rocket plane back at Earth and now I was going to be floating off. How cool is that?!

Each seat along the aisle had a handhold. Exiting the plane was supposedly a simple process of just going hand over hand floating down the aisle. I undid my seat belt and shoulder harness and then took Demetrious out of his infant seat. I let go of him momentarily and he just floated right there in front of me smiling. That's amazing! It's possible that I might actually like this. I grabbed Demetrious and pushed off the handhold to start us down the aisle. I must have pushed too hard because we crashed headfirst into the ceiling.

Marc, who was behind us, grabbed me and pulled us back down. "Are you okay? Best to take it nice and easy."

"I'm okay, just hurt my pride." Nice and easy, I said to myself. I pushed off again. Dammit we crashed into the ceiling again! I looked at Mark. "Guess I don't know my own strength," I said with a sheepish grid as he once again had to pull us down from the ceiling of the rocket plane.

"Don't worry, you'll get the hang of it," Marc replied clearly trying not to laugh.

After that I had no problem carefully, gently gliding down the aisle. I used my left hand to grab the hand hold on the back of the every other seat while holding on to Demetrious with my right. The series of handholds continued through the exit from the rocket plane. Demetrious and I glided past the exit and entered a rectangular corridor. The flight attendant directed us to go down the corridor toward the Sky City lobby.

"I've never seen such a well-behaved baby," said the flight attendant as we floated by. "Usually babies are crying like mad by now."

I smiled at Demetrious.

The corridor was rectangular and decorated so that there was a clear ceiling and floor. Marc pointed out that all the lights were located in the "ceiling." He said that this made it easier for guests who were new to zero-g and who unconsciously expected to know where "up" was. I guess it worked. It never occurred to me that it was even unusual for a corridor in space to have a defined "up" and "down." It just looked like a corridor. Demetrious and I continued our slow glide down the passageway following the other passengers. All I had to do was grab a handhold here and there as needed. It was so very easy to move around in space. This place is delightful!

I was feeling good. I was loving weightless. I was smiling ear-to-ear as we approached the entrance to the lobby. Then it hit me. It was not at all what I expected. Even before entering the lobby I noticed the smell! Incredibly, it smelled like flowers, Plumerias to be exact. I couldn't believe I was smelling flowers. I guess I was expecting it to smell like the space plane, that awful smell of dry mechanically filtered air that reeked of machinery. But this, this was different. This was wonderful. What a pleasant surprise. It reminded me of when my mom and dad took us to Hawaii when I was little. The airport in Honolulu smelled just like this, where the warm humid air was thick with the smell of flowers from the vendors selling leis. Now I'm in space and smelling the same thing, can it get any weirder that this?

I had no idea.

The Sky City lobby was a large room with so much more to see than inside the rocket plane or the connecting corridor. It was decorated like the lobby of a fancy hotel, which in fact, it was. The room looked like it

9

was constructed from a cylinder maybe thirty feet in diameter and thirty feet long. The "floor" appeared to be located about five feet below the centerline of the cylinder so the ceiling was something like twenty feet above the floor at its highest point and curved all the way down to meet the floor. Just like in the corridor, all the lights in the lobby were located in the ceiling, indicating this was "up."

Amazingly, there were four large palm trees in the lobby, one in each corner of the room. The palm trees were located where the ceiling was maybe fifteen feet high and they nearly reached the ceiling. Jesus, they have trees in space! I wondered what it must have cost to bring those up from Earth. It was clear from the trees which direction was up. This seemed perfectly normal to me. This was the way it should be. This was normal.

Then I realized something was wrong. We were entering the lobby head first through the ceiling! The floor of the lobby was oriented ninety degrees from the floor of the corridor. Oddly, I had no fear of falling even though my head was nearly twenty feet above the floor and pointed straight at it. The weird thing was that I simply thought it was the lobby that was upside down, not me.

The flight attendant instructed us to rotate ourselves around and point our feet at the lobby floor. I grabbed a handrail and flipped my body around so that my feet were now pointing at the floor. Hey, now the room was right side up! That's super weird.

A long polished aluminum pole directed us "down" to the floor of the lobby. Following the other passengers, I grabbed the pole and used it to guide myself and Demetrious toward the floor. At the floor, the pole curved and became a railing directing us to the registration desk. Since there were from the spaceplane in line ahead and behind us I figured we must be in the right place. Marc seemed to have wandered off somewhere. Oh well, I guess we just have to wait in line here to check in.

While waiting I noticed that nobody's feet were touching the floor. I was in a line of floating people! How often do you see that on Earth? Weird, weird, weird. Everything's so strange here and yet so cool. I felt myself smiling all the time.

I looked up at the curved ceiling. It was covered in row after row of tropical flowers, most of which I didn't recognize except for the Plumerias. I asked my phone which said that in addition to the Plumerias, there were red and blue Gingers, Anthuriums, Hawaiian Orchids, Bird of Paradise, Heliconia's, and Oleanders. It was like being in a tropical garden. I looked again at the palm trees and this time noticed how strange they looked, I mean besides, you known, the fact that they were palm trees in space. There was something odd about them, but I couldn't figure out exactly what. Finally, it hit me, the palm branches weren't right. On

10

Earth, I remember, palm branches curve gracefully downward, I guess under the pull of gravity. Here, without gravity the branches were straight. It made them look stiff and fake.

I looked down at my feet floating above the floor. The floor looked like highly polished marble. In the comments section of the Sky City website, I remember that someone said that this wasn't real marble; because no one ever walked on it, it didn't need to be durable. It was just for show because that's what people expected to see in the lobby of a fancy resort. Amazingly, there was almost no furniture, no chairs, no sofas, nothing at all to sit on. This made the lobby look more spacious than it was. There were, however, lots of small tables that people started gathering around.

Looking straight ahead I could see the registration desk located approximately in the middle at one end of the lobby. Beyond that was a sign pointing toward the guest suites. The website said the suites were twice as large as the regular guest rooms. I bet those are expensive.

Looking to my left, I could see the entrance to the Sky City Casino, and over my left shoulder behind me, I saw the entrance to the regular guest rooms. I turned my head all the way around to the right. On the wall opposite from the casino entrance was the entrance to the Sports Arena. That sounds like fun. I wonder what kind of things you can do in there.

Suddenly and without warning, a wave of nausea washed over me. Uh oh, what's happening? I felt sick, really sick. I'm going to barf! I let go of Demetrious and scrambled to open the airsickness bag they gave each of us as we exited the rocket plane. Oh god, please let me get it open in time. I doubled over in an involuntary spasm and threw "up" into the airsickness bag. I closed my eyes. I couldn't move. I didn't open them again until I felt my head hit something hard. I was up at the ceiling! I must have drifted through the lobby after I closed my eyes. Some part of my brain realized that this was the third time I crashed into a ceiling since I got here, but mostly I was too sick to give a shit. I closed my eyes again and I didn't care that I was continuing to tumble slowly, aimlessly through the lobby. After a minute or so, I forced my eyes open briefly and saw that I was heading back toward the center of the lobby and the line of people.

It was at that exact moment, in my nausea-induced misery, that I realized I made a terrible mistake. There was no way I could do this. What was I thinking? What was I doing here? How was I going to get out of this? I threw up again. That sucked. I managed to open my eyes again briefly and saw Marc Elliott heading right toward me.

"You have space adaptation syndrome," he said sympathetically to a question I didn't ask. "What the tourist call the space barfs. It affects more than half of the people who fly into space."

I don't give a shit, I thought. Just go away and leave me to die alone.

"Don't worry, it usually goes away in a few days as your brain adapts to weightlessness," he said with annoying cheerfulness. "The best thing to do is to just keep your eyes closed."

No shit. I kept my eyes closed. I didn't really help. I felt him grab ahold of me. I think he stopped me from crashing into the line of people, but I was too weak to care. After another minute or so, I tried opening my eyes again. This was a mistake. Marc was hanging there in front of me upside down. That just messed with my head and made me sicker. The nausea was overwhelming.

"Poor thing, I'll go get some help."

I glimpsed him gliding away as I threw up for the third time. I was hating life. The smile that I thought was permanently stuck on my face was now replaced by seemingly permanent misery.

Sometime later—I don't know how long because I was too miserable to care— I felt someone grab me and then say cheerfully, "Hi, I'm Jennifer from the Three Dolphins Club. Remember me, we spoke on the phone? I'm here to take you to your living quarters."

I didn't answer. Yes, Jennifer from the Three Dolphins Club, I remember. God, is everyone so annoyingly cheerful here? The only thing I wanted to do was lay down and die somewhere. I opened my eyes. Crap, we were back near the ceiling of the lobby again.

"As you know, you'll be sharing the apartment with two other employees, Sasha and Yuri. They're great, you'll love them."

I nodded weakly.

Disoriented and miserable from the nausea I was barely aware that Jennifer was towing me along. I tried opening my eyes again momentarily and through my nausea-induced dizziness, I caught a glimpse of what appeared to be wings. Does she have wings? Why does she have wings? I don't care. Just get me to a bed so I can lie down and be left alone.

"Here we are!"

As we entered the apartment I forced my eyes open once more. It didn't look anything like I expected. Where's the bed? That can't be right. Please god, just let me lie down. I closed my eyes again. I hate this place.

"I'm going to give you something to make you feel better," Jennifer said.

"What? Ouch! What was that?"

"I just gave you a shot of Phenergan, an anti-nausea drug."

The effect was nearly instantaneous. "This is wonderful," I exclaimed in amazement. "Oh my god, my nausea just disappeared! Thank you so much!" I hugged her.

"You're welcome." Jennifer smiled. "We get that a lot."

Now that I felt better, I remembered Demetrious.

"Where's Demetrious?" I said with some urgency.

"He's right here," replied Jennifer. "I grabbed him in the lobby. He seems to enjoy floating."

I turned around to see him floating upside down next to me with a big smile on his face. I grabbed him, turned him around and gave him a big hug too. Now that I wasn't so miserable I notice that Jennifer was about my height, looked to be in her mid-twenties, and had short green hair. "I like your hair," I said.

"Thank you. I think it gives me a more outer space look, don't you think?"

I really didn't think so, I mean, how should I know. I just got here. So I smiled and just said, "Sure."

"This is your apartment. As you can see, there's no bed and no chairs. That's not a mistake. They simply aren't needed in here in space."

"Really,? But where do we sleep?" The room looked really small. "Are you sure we're all going to fit in here?"

"Yes, of course. You'll see. In zero-g, you can make use of the entire volume of the room, not just the floor space as on Earth." Jennifer waved her hands around the room. "And you sleep right here against this rope net."

I looked at the rope net strung from floor to ceiling. You can't be serious. "How do we sleep on a rope net?"

"It's easy and actually quite delightful. You'll see. The airflow in the room will push you gently against the net and it will also keep you cool while you're sleeping. The bathroom is over there," Jennifer said motioning to her right. "There are instructions on how to use the toilet and bath."

I looked at her with a puzzled expression. "Instructions, what do you mean instructions? Why are there instructions on how to use the toilet?"

"Things are a little different here, but it's not hard to get used to. This resort has the latest in zero-g bathroom facilities."

I poked my head into the bathroom and looked around. It looked strange and complicated. I was afraid to touch anything.

"Mr. Abruzzo has asked that you report to the Three Dolphins Club tomorrow at 10 am for orientation," Jennifer continued. "There's a map of the resort on the computer."

"Where's the computer?

"Sky City, open the curtains, please," Jennifer said. What looked like curtains on the far wall disappeared revealing a wall-to-wall window providing a stunning view outside.

"Holy shit!" I blurted out. Marc Elliott was right. The view is spectacular. I silently stared in awe at the brilliant blue and white Earth that filled the top half of the window and an unbelievable number of stars below. Eventually, I managed to say, "I don't understand, someone told me there are no windows in the resort."

"It's actually an ultrahigh definition display. Right now it's showing a live view from outside the resort."

"That's amazing! I'd swear I was looking out a window."

"This was Marc Elliott's idea. He tells me that this is the latest in high-definition displays. It's called a Picture Window Display. It was invented by a Japanese company for use in windowless, ultra-small apartments in Japan. It gives you the impression that you're looking outside though an ordinary window. Spectacular, isn't it?"

"Damn, you're not kidding," I said in amazement, my eyes glued to the view.

Jennifer smiled knowingly. "To address the computer simply start with 'Sky City'. Remember, 10 am tomorrow at the Club."

"Got it, 10 am tomorrow." I stared at the display up close. What an incredible view. Just how the hell did I wind up here?

As Jennifer turned to leave, I caught a glimpse of her wings out of the corner of my eye and said, "Wait!"

Jennifer pivoted in midair, "What?"

"You have wings. Why do you have wings?"

"It's how we get around her. You'll see. Tomorrow it will all be explained," she said with a smile and left.

As she floated away, I thought she looked like a large bird, no like an angel.

Chapter 3 Zero-g

Demetrious and I were alone in our new apartment. I looked around and realized that it had just two rooms, a living room and a bathroom. Seems more like a small hotel room than an apartment, and it's shaped like a wedge! How weird is that? Can we really fit three adults and a baby in here?

The high-definition display was square shaped and covered the entire wall at the big end of the room. I'd guess it was maybe ten feet on a side and what an awesome view it provided. I still can't believe it's not a window. It made the room feel much bigger than it was. Since it's not a window…, "Sky City, what other views are there?"

The computer responded, "Here are the six different views from outside the resort." It scrolled through each one.

"Sky City, stop." The display now showed a view that had just stars, an unbelievable number of stars. Is that for real? "Sky City, why not just use a real window instead?"

"The PWD is a much better solution than a window," replied the computer. "It automatically mutes the harsh glare from the sun when the sun is up and it adjusts its brightness based on the lighting in the room. Importantly, it is much safer than a window enabling the walls to be much stronger and thicker than if there was an actual window. There are six feet of asteroid dirt on the other side of the display that provide radiation protection. The—,"

"Sky City, stop." That's enough of that.

The wall on the small side of the wedge-shaped room, opposite from the display, was roughly forty inches high by ten feet wide. The front entry door, and only entry door as far as I could see, was located on one end of this wall and opened by sliding sideways. The entrance to the bathroom was on the funny-shaped side wall farthest from the entry door to the apartment. Trapezoid, that's it, the wall is shaped like a trapezoid. Weird that could I remember that from my geometry class. Par for the course, I guess, since a lot of weird things have been happening to me lately. Anyway, it looks like the distance from the entry door to the display is also about ten feet. This is definitely a strange room.

I grabbed Demetrious and said, "Let's go check out the bathroom." We glided over to the bathroom and went in. It had the same wedge shape as the main room. Two trapezoidally-shaped walls separated by a distance of about forty inches. At the small end of the bathroom the wall was a square roughly forty inches on a side. At the large end the wall was a rectangle forty inches by ten feet. Jennifer said the bathroom had the latest in zero-g amenities with a zero-g toilet, a zero-g sink, and a full zero-g shower with real running water. It was all so complicated and I was still afraid to touch anything. I'll just deal with it when I have to. The shower was located at the big end of the bathroom.

We went back into the main living room and continued to explore our tiny apartment. I noticed there were no provisions for cooking except for what looked like a small microwave oven embedded on the common wall shared with the bathroom and a strange looking coffee maker thing located "beneath" it. Well, at least I think it was a coffee maker, mostly because it said Mr. Coffee on it. Pullout drawers nearly covered the wall opposite the bathroom. I opened one and found it full of clothes. Obviously, these belong to one of my new roommates. I guess you can't hang up anything in space; just more weirdness. It freaks me out that there's no furniture. On the other hand, now that I didn't feel sick anymore, that delightful feeling of being weightless and floating around was back. I think I could get used to this. A smile crept back onto my face.

I found that the lighting in the apartment was embedded in all of the walls and was selectable by voice command. The square high-definition display, what did the computer call it? Oh yeah, the PWD. Anyway, it was viewable from any orientation. There was nothing in the room that said, this is up. I was surprised that this didn't bother me. I realized that "up" and "down" were just choices I could make. Isn't that strange? I discovered that "down" was simply where my feet were. If I turned myself "upside down," the new "down" was still in the direction of my feet. It was a kind of an Alice-in-Wonderland feeling. It was charming. I could control space! I am the space commander!

Just like Jennifer said, everything in the room was controlled by voice command. The room temperature, the display, the doors, microwave oven, and coffee maker were all controlled by the computer. I found a small refrigerator, which I had missed before. It was embedded in the same wall as the microwave oven.

I poked my head outside our room and looked down the hall. Unlike the corridor from the rocket plane to the resort lobby, and the resort lobby itself, there was no obvious up or down in this corridor. The hall had eight sides, like a stop sign on Earth. There were seven other doors located on the seven other sides of the stop-sign shaped hall near my door. This pattern of doors repeated several times down the hall.

I went back inside and said, "Sky City, tell me about the resort." My sister kept telling me that I should read-up on this place before moving here, but I didn't listen to her. I never was much on reading. But, now that I was actually here I found that I wanted to know everything I could about the resort.

The computer responded, "Sky City Resort and Casino is the largest space structure ever built. It is three hundred forty feet long and two hundred twenty feet wide at its widest point, with a total pressurized volume of forty-three thousand three hundred cubic meters. The resort is laid out like a cross when viewed from above with the long part of the cross housing the guest rooms, the lobby, the guest suites, the crew quarters, and the engineering section all in a line. At the end opposite engineering is the main dining room. The "horizontal" part of the cross is attached at the lobby and includes the Sport Arena, the Carnival Game Room, and the Fitness center on one side and the Casino and Three Dolphins Club on the other. The resort has sixty-four regular guest rooms and eight suites. The suites are twice the size of the regular rooms. With double occupancy the resort can accommodate a maximum of one hundred forty-four guests. There are seventy full time employees and two hundred robots. Most of the robots are basketball-sized, spherically-shaped machines that do routine cleaning and maintenance. The resort was—"

Demetrious started to cry.

"Sky City, stop." Turning toward Demetrious I said, "You must be hungry." After he finished eating I looked at him and said, "Well what do you think of our new home? Pretty strange, uh? I'm kind of tired since I didn't sleep much last night, how about you? What do you say we just hang out here for a while and relax, okay?"

Demetrious looked at me and smiled. He really did seem to like it here, I thought, just before I fell asleep. An hour later I woke up and felt like I was getting a cold. It's weird, but I also felt different in other hard-to-describe ways. I turned on the camera in my phone so I could see my face. What the heck? My face looked puffy. I quickly checked Demetrious, he looked normal. What's going on? "Sky City, what's happening to me?"

The computer responded, "In weightlessness, all the effects of gravity vanish. Your body, which is approximately sixty percent water, is adapting to its new environment. Normally gravity pulls this water down into your legs. In zero-g this force is gone leaving the water free to re-distribute itself inside your body. Much of it is now migrating toward your head and chest making your face puffy and causing your sinuses to begin to close. The resulting nasal congestion makes you feel like you're getting a head cold."

"That's exactly how I feel. Please go on."

The computer continued, "During your life on Earth, gravity pulled on your arms and shoulders. Strong muscles in your neck were used to keep your head upright under its relentless pull. Gravity pulled on your hair and on your internal organs. It pulled on your heart, on your stomach, on your large and small intestines, bladder and uterus. At Sky City all this is gone. Not only are you floating, but your organs are floating inside you."

I looked at my arms, they were just floating in front of me. I couldn't feel the weight of my hair. There was no pressure on my feet. I didn't feel my bra straps pulling on my shoulders. If I relaxed, I found that my body tended to curl up into a fetal position. It was an oddly wonderful sensation. I felt freed of something I had never been aware of before. It was almost like being born again.

Then suddenly and without warning, I had an extremely urgent need to pee. I hadn't felt it at all before, not a single hint. Now it was overwhelming. I had to go RIGHT NOW! I grabbed the nearest handhold and shot myself through the circular opening to the bathroom. I was moving really fast and immediately knew it was a mistake. I was going so fast I couldn't grab onto anything as I flew into the bathroom. I crashed shoulder-first into the far wall of the bathroom. I bounced off the wall and careened back into the living room. After bouncing back and forth in the living room two more times I finally managed to grab a handhold. My bladder was still screaming.

Breathing heavily and feeling a throbbing pain in my shoulder where I hit the wall, I forced myself to calm down. Okay, let's try this again nice and easy, as Marc would say. Holding on to one handle, I reached for the next one closer to the bathroom. I could barely reach it and had to straighten my body to stretch for it. This made my bladder complain even louder. Finally, I floated slowly into the bathroom more or less under control and curled up in a fetal position. I panicked as I looked again at the complicated toilet.

Now what? Whatever you do, you'd better do it fast! I spotted a tube that had an end fitting that looked like it should fit over my anatomy. I grabbed it, pulled "down" my pants, and got it in place just in time. Unfortunately, I didn't have time to read the directions and therefore I didn't know to press the big green "on" button next to the toilet. Pee started leaking out everywhere. Large yellow blobs, small droplets, and everything in between filled the bathroom. I stared at the pulsating blobs of pee which fascinated and grossed me out at the same time. As I stared at them, one broke on my hand. The warm pee quickly spread itself uniformly over my hand. I instinctively, but unsuccessfully, tried to shake it off.

The computer announced that the bathroom's environmental control system detected a "fluid leak" and sprang into action. A strong airflow blasted out of the wall to my right, startling me. It directed all of the pee blobs toward the wall to my left. It turns out that these walls were not solid, but porous. As the blobs of pee broke on the wall's surface they were sucked into the wall. Two spherical robots, each about the size of a basketball, came off the wall above my head. I watched as they scrubbed down and disinfected every surface in the bathroom except for me. Evidently, they could tell the difference between me and the bathroom surfaces.

I looked around for a sink, but couldn't find one. How the heck do you wash your hands around here? There must be a way. Then I saw a glass box attached to the wall with two openings. I put my hands in and the openings sealed around my forearms, but nothing else happened. Oh, right, voice controlled.

"Water, please," I said. Still nothing. "Sky City, water please," and lukewarm water sprayed onto my hands. "Sky City, off. Soap please." The water stopped and liquid soap sprayed on my hands. I rubbed my hands together for a minute, then said, "Sky City, water," and rinsed my hands in the spray. The water turned off automatically. A strong blast of air dried my hands as I pulled them out.

That was pretty cool. I better see to Demetrious. I checked his diaper. Looks like somebody needs to be changed. Better do this in the bathroom. I took off his wet diaper and left him hanging motionless in the air while I figured out where to dispose of his diaper. While I was doing this, Demetrious did what baby boys often do when their diapers are removed, he started to pee. Like a little rocket motor, this started propelling him across the room and made him rotate him head over heels as well. I looked up just in time to see pee spraying across the room and Demetrious about to crash into the wall. I yelled and laughed at the same. Demetrious hit the wall, but not very hard and bounced back toward me. I caught him while blobs of pee again filled the room.

"Gotcha, you little stinker. Let's get another diaper on you. That was a pretty good trick, but let's not do that again, okay?"

The environmental control system kicked in again and cleaned up the mess with the help of the robots.

I looked down at my pee-soaked clothes. I wonder how you take a shower? Looking around the bathroom, I noticed a glass door on what appeared to be the ceiling given my current orientation. I rotated my body around and viola, the glass door was now on the wall. I smiled. I am the space commander.

I opened the shower door and looked in. At the "top" I saw three concentric rings of small holes like you'd see in a shower head on Earth, at the "bottom" I could see the entire surface was a grid with larger holes. Clearly, this is the drain. The shower looked big enough for two people.

I took off my wet, pee-soaked clothes. Not knowing what to do with them, I just let them go. One of the spherical robots came off the wall again and grabbed the clothes.

"Are these to be washed?" a voice came from the room.

Startled again, I said, "Yes."

A drawer in the wall opened and the robots placed the clothes in the drawer. When opened, I could hear a whoosh of air as the drawer drew air in from the room along with the clothes. The drawer closed automatically and the robots went back to their places on the wall.

That's cool.

I entered the shower and closed the door. "Sky City, water, please," The center set of holes started spraying lukewarm water. I shrieked and flailed around frantically trying to get out of the stream of cold water. Finally, I yelled, "Sky City, off!" and water stopped.

I eventually figured out that I had failed to say what water temperature I wanted so the computer erred on the side of safety and provided lukewarm water, which felt cold on my skin. Even though the water had stopped, I felt a strong flow of warm air coming from the showerhead.

"Sky City, warm water, please," I said, trying again. Better, but still too cold, "warmer, please." The computer increased the water temperature in small amounts. After a few tries, I got to the temperature I liked. The computer informed me that it would remember this setting.

The combination of the water hitting me and the continuous airflow pushed me gently toward the drain causing me to have to "stand" very lightly on my feet. The shower felt fantastically luxurious. The airflow kept the space around my head remarkably free of floating water droplets. I could get used to this. Who knew you could take a shower in space?

I finished the shower and said, "Sky City, off," stopping the water, but not the airflow. Now how do I dry off? I don't see any towels out there. I opened the shower door and said, "Sky City, towel, please." Another drawer opened accompanied by the now familiar whoosh of air. I grabbed a towel and said "thank you," and the drawer closed. I dried myself off and then let go of the towel. One of the spherical robots came off the wall, grabbed it and attached it to the wall. The computer informed me that the towel would "hang" there until it was dry. Then the robots would fold it up and put it back into the drawer.

Still naked, I floated back into the living room. Demetrious was asleep floating against the rope net. The airflow in the room held him there. I looked around and thought, That's odd, I don't see any mirrors. Then I realized that the display probably had a mirror mode. "Sky City, mirror mode please," and the PWD became a wall-to-wall mirror.

I stared in amazement at my body. My face was puffy and round looking, my breasts, which had always been firm, thank you very much, looked fuller and higher. My long damp hair floated wildly around my head. I gasped when I looked at my legs. Chicken legs, I've got chicken

20

legs. Now what's happening to me? I checked Demetrious, his legs looked normal. I guess it's just me. I hope I'm not dying.

I pulled my wet hair into a ponytail, got dressed, looked at Demetrious, who was now awake, and said, "Well, what would you like to do?" I no sooner finished saying that when two people entered the apartment. I immediately recognized them as Sasha and Yuri. Sasha came in first followed closely by Yuri. Wow, she's even more beautiful in person. Sasha was tall, thin with short blond hair and brilliant hazel eyes. Yuri was also extremely good looking. He was of Chinese heritage with short dark hair, muscular, and very well groomed. They looked like they had just finished working out at the athletic center.

"Hi, I'm Tesla and this is my son Demetrious."

"I'm Sasha and this sweaty person is Yuri," replied Sasha motioning with her right hand toward Yuri. "When did ya'll get in? We've been expecting you."

"It's very nice to meet both of you." I shook Sasha's hand first and then Yuri's. "We got in a couple of hours ago and have been struggling to get used to zero-g ever since…Actually, I've been struggling— Demetrious here appears to be loving it."

"He's adorable," replied Sasha as she gently pinched Demetrious's cheek. "How old is he?"

"He just turned six months."

"That's a great age for babies," said Sasha. "They're old enough to be fun to play with, but they can't talk back yet."

I just smiled.

"You're going to really like living here," continued Sasha. "Everyone does. That is, once you get used to the chicken legs and peeing on a schedule. I sure you'll find that living here is quite delightful.

"It's the most fun you can have with your clothes on," Yuri quipped.

"Take it down a notch," said Sasha.

Yuri pretended to be hurt.

"Actually, I already really like it," I said. "Well, that is after Jennifer gave me a shot that got rid of my nausea. And I did have a little problem with peeing and the toilet. Other than that and my head cold, I just love floating around, and I love being able to flip a room by just looking at it differently."

"It's not a cold," said Yuri, trying to be helpful. "Just excess fluid in your head."

I nodded. "So how long have you guys been living here?" I asked.

"We both got here four months ago, when it first opened," replied Yuri.

"So, you've been here right from the start. Where are you guys from originally?" I asked with genuine interest.

"As ya'll can probably tell from my accent, I'm from the south," replied Sasha. "I grew up in Atlanta."

"And I'm from Texas," added Yuri with no hint of an accent. "Houston to be specific. My father worked at the Johnson Space Center there. He was the stereo typical space nerd. He always wanted his only son to be an astronaut; he even named me after Yuri Gagarin, the first person to go into space. But I was never very good at math and science. I'm more of a people person."

"How did you guys wind up here? I mean, you know, working at the Three Dolphins Club? I've never done anything like this before and I'm not sure and can do it. So I' really appreciate any advice you can give me."

Sasha and Yuri looked at me and then at each other as if they didn't know what to make of me. Finally Sasha started, "Well, I guess I'm here 'cause my mom died when I was young and my dad worked all the time, so me and my two brothers were kind of left to raise ourselves. I guess I was what you might call a wild child. I never cared much for school and we never had much money. When I was in high school a friend of mine knew a photographer who took topless photographs of women for a living. I thought it sounded exciting so I did that first photoshoot. It was a very erotic experience. After that, I would get steady offers from people who wanted to take nude pictures of me for money. It was pretty good money, or so I thought at the time. Eventually someone recruited me for a softcore porn movie. I guess I'm rather extroverted so I figured, what the hell, why not."

"Sounds like you had a tough childhood," I replied, somewhat taken back by her frankness. "But how did you wind up here?"

"No, I had a great childhood. I came here because it's a new frontier. I thought it would be an adventure. I felt it would be a place where I could express my sexuality and be supported in ways that weren't possible on Earth, a place where I didn't have to worry about some asshole pimp controlling my life. I believed it would be a new journey for me physically, emotionally, and spiritually. I wanted to help people experience sex in a whole new way."

I didn't say anything for a while as I tried to process what Sasha said. Eventually I asked, "What's it like working here. I mean, is it what you expected it would be?"

Sasha hesitated just long enough to glance and Yuri and then said, "Actually, it's been better than I expected, primarily because George is so protective of us and treats us with such respect."

Yuri nodded in agreement, and then added, "My story's pretty much exactly the same as Sasha's. Well, except for the parts about growing up poor in Atlanta, posing for nude photos, and doing softcore porn."

22

"Hey!" It was Sasha's turn to pretend to be offended.

"Actually, I have always been fascinated by space exploration and people living in space. You can't help but have your parents rub off on you I guess. Anyway, as I said, I was never very good at math and science, but I'm very good with people. I like to think of myself as providing a public service, you know, teaching people how to have sex in zero-g. The pay at the Three Dolphins Club doesn't hurt either, along with the fact that it's legal here."

This time Sasha nodded in agreement.

After what seemed like a long silence, Sasha looked at me and said, "So what about you? How did you get here?"

I'm not sure why, but I immediately felt a bond with Sasha and Yuri. Maybe it was because I felt so alone up here and needed friends, or maybe it was because we were all doing the same fucked-up job at the Three Dolphins Club. Whatever the reason I felt I could trust them. Maybe it was a stupid thing to do, but I said, "Okay, here's my story, but please don't tell anyone else. You'll understand after you hear it."

"Oh honey," replied Sasha, "we all have secrets up here. Yours, whatever it is, is safe with us."

Yuri nodded.

"At least you guys knew your dads," I started. "My dad left us when I was four and I have only the vaguest memories of him. My mom said he contributed the Hispanic and Caucasian parts of my heritage. He was a software developer in Silicon Valley before he abandoned us for another woman, leaving my mom to raise me and my sister alone. My mom was a vibrant, strong-willed, determined woman. She was half Japanese and half Chinese, making me the mixed-race mutt that I am."

"Well, you're a very beautiful mutt," interrupted Yuri.

"Yes, that combination of genes definitely combined in a way that makes you stunningly beautiful," added Sasha.

"Thanks, but with my puffy face and chicken legs, I'm not sure that's true anymore." I paused momentarily. "Anyway, as I said, my mom was an extremely capable woman, that is, until her stroke. That stroke transformed her overnight into someone who needed around the clock care. I was devastated. On top of that, my marriage was not the fairytale story I expected. My husband, Alex, was incredibly good looking and charming. He had this tremendously charismatic personality; people were just naturally attracted to him, especially me. I thought he was the love of my life. It was great at first, really great. Our troubles began when Alex started drinking. He was a mean drunk. Our marriage was effectively over the night he came home very late from work and admitted that he was having an affair with his assistant. We had a big fight. I grabbed Demetrious and left in the middle of the night. I knew Alex would try to

23

find me. I had no money and nowhere to go so I took this job up here knowing that Alex would never think of looking for me here. He knows I'm afraid of flying.

"So you took a job as an escort up here to get away from your scum-bag cheating husband," interjected Yuri.

"Yes," I looked down. "That's basically it."

"Sounds about right," added Sasha.

We spent the rest of the evening talking. Still tired after a long day's flight into space I finally asked, "So uh, where does everyone sleep?"

"You just sleep right here, up against the rope wall," replied Sasha, confirming what Jennifer said. "Yuri and I are going to get ready and go out to the bar."

After Sasha and Yuri left, I looked at Demetrious and said, "Well, I guess Jennifer was right, we really do sleep right here." Then I said to the computer, "Sky City, exterior view." The monitor displayed a spectacular view of the Earth with the sun just starting to rise. No, that's not going to do if we're going to sleep. Better change the view. "Sky City, night sky view." The computer switched the display to a different camera on the resort, one that always looked at deep space.

I stared again in disbelief. The number of stars was overwhelming. I grew up in California and was used to seeing only a handful of stars at night under the best of conditions. Is this for real? Are there really that many stars? I had no idea. And they have colors! Who knew stars came in different colors? Lots of white ones, but I see blue ones and red ones, and they seem to go on forever. Floating there, staring off into space, I imagined I was laying on my back in a field far from city lights staring up at the night sky. But this was better. There was no pressure from the hard ground on my back or head and the view was far more spectacular than any view possible from Earth. How exactly did I wind up in this wonderland again? It seemed unreal.

It had been a long, stressful day and I quickly drifted off to sleep again. It was an unusually delightful sleep. I didn't toss and turn as I often did on Earth. My back didn't ache. My knees which always hurt from running too much didn't hurt either. I didn't drool on my pillow— probably because I didn't have a pillow. And yes, I did drool on my pillow sometimes on Earth. Here I slept floating, bathed in the soft warm breeze that pushed me up against the net. It was so nice to be away from Alex. I imagined this must be what sleeping in heaven felt like.

Chapter 4 Sky City

I woke up feeling really good. I looked at my watch. That's weird, I slept just six hours, but I feel great. It was the most restful sleep I ever had. Through the dim light of the multiple electronic gadgets in the apartment I saw that Demetrious was already awake. He was right there in front of me, floating sideway and smiling as always. Such a good baby. I rotated myself around and just like that, Demetrious was right side up. I smiled. It was a continuous surprise to me how delightful life was in zero-g.

I queried my wristband which informed me that my heart rate was thirty-four beats per minute. Wait, what?! That can't be right. As a runner, I was used to keeping track of my heart rate and I knew my resting heart rate should be around fifty-three beats per minute. Why is it only thirty-four beats per minute? What's happening to me? I could think of only one explanation. I AM dying! I knew it! Funny how your mind works when you're in a strange place.

I saw that my two roommates had returned sometime during the night and were sound asleep. I've got to tell them I need help! I reached over and shook Sasha somewhat urgently.

With her eyes still closed, she said, "Unless you're tall, dark, handsome… and rich leave me alone."

"Sasha, it's me Tesla. My heart rate is only thirty-four beats per minute. I think I'm dying."

"I'm tall, dark, and handsome," interrupted Yuri, who was evidently a light sleeper.

"What about the rich part?" replied Sasha, with her eyes still closed.

"I'm rich in spirit."

"Yeah well, you're also gay. So while you know I love you, you're not exactly the man of my dreams."

"Picky, picky, picky."

"Hey, people, what about me," I interrupted. "I think I'm dying here."

"Relax honey, you're not dying," replied Sasha. "That's just what happens up here. Your heart rate goes down. It doesn't have to work as hard—got no gravity to fight. Now if ya'll don't mind, I'm going back to sleep"

Well that's a relief I guess. Even though I didn't really understand why, it was good to know I was probably not going to die, at least not immediately. Having gotten over that hurdle, now I felt hungry. I whispered to Demetrious, "Let's see what we have to eat. They said they would put something in the refrigerator for us." I floated over to the refrigerator, but before I could open the door my bladder started screaming at me again. God, that's annoying. A little warning would be nice. At least I knew what to do this time and I headed to the bathroom under control.

After eating, I fed and changed Demetrious, and got myself dressed. I put on shorts and a blouse, and took out my shoes. These were the ones Marc Elliott said I didn't need. I wonder what he's doing? I bent over to put on my shoes. It was surprisingly difficult to reach my feet. Why is this so hard? Must be because there was no gravity to help me bend over. It felt like my stomach muscles were doing all the work. After exerting much more effort than I expected, I was finally able to fasten the small buckle on the side of each shoe. My stomach ached. Everything's so odd here, even little things like this.

I looked at my feet. They were floating above the floor mocking me. Or was it above the wall? What's the difference? More importantly, did it make any sense that I had shoes on?... No, and I took them off. I guess Marc was right.

…

As we were about to leave for my 10 am meeting with Mr. Abruzzo, Sasha got up and said, "What are ya'll fixing to do with Demetrious?"

"I have an appointment with George Abruzzo at ten," I replied. "I was going to take him with me."

"Living here certainly seems to agree with him," said Sasha. "Me and Yuri can watch him if you like. How long ya'll going to be gone?"

I can barely take care of myself up here, I thought. It would be a huge help if they watched Demetrious, and it's not like they can kidnap him or anything. "I'm not sure how long the meeting will take. It would be wonderful if you could watch him. Are you sure it's not too much trouble? Don't you want to ask Yuri?"

"Na, he's a sweetie. He'll be fine with it, and we're not working till this evening."

"Thank you so much. You'll find everything you need for him in that bag over there attached to the wall. One more thing, how do I get to the Three Dolphins Club?"

"Sky City, map please," said Sasha. A map of the Sky City Resort filled the display at the end of the room. "We're here." Sasha pointed to the section of the resort reserved for the employees. "And ya'll need to go here. So go out the door and turn right down the hall. The hall ends at the lobby. Go to the middle of the lobby and turn right again. You'll see the entrance to the Sky City Casino. At the far end of the casino is the entrance to the Three Dolphins Club. George will be in the Lupanar room."

"Okay, thanks." I kissed Demetrious good-bye, headed out the door and made my way down the eight-sided corridor and past the suites using the occasional handrail to move myself along. I floated into the lobby having let go of the last handrail in the hall and immediately realized that was a mistake. I slowly drifted into the lobby with no way to stop or even change direction. I tried to grab the vertical pole that we used yesterday when we first entered the lobby, but missed.

Well shit. Here are I am helplessly drifting through the lobby again. How embarrassing. I guess I'll just slowly float along until I hit the top of that palm tree. It felt like it took forever, but eventually I did a slow-motion crash into the palm tree and just barely managed to hold on to a branch. From there I realized I could see the entrance to the Casino. I knew just what to do. I pushed off the branch and launched myself in the direction of the Casino.

Oh crap. The stupid branch bent when I pushed off of it. This sent me off in the wrong direction and going much slower than I intended. So here I was yet again drifting out of control and slowly tumbling head over heels through the lobby. On one rotation I caught a glimpse of the receptionist smiling at me. She must think I'm a complete idiot. On another rotation I saw the wall I was slowly drifting toward and would reach eventually. On my next rotation I saw that wall had a number of handrails.

Okay, new plan. All I have to do is grab one of those when I get there. I somehow managed to turn my body around and get my arms in front of me just as I crashed into the wall. I grabbed a hand rail and hung on for dear life as my body hit the wall somewhat harder than I expected.

Yes! Okay, let's not do that again. Hand over hand, I carefully guided myself to the entrance of the casino, trying not to look too foolish and always keeping at least one hand on a railing to make sure I didn't go floating off again.

The casino looked and sounded a lot like those back on Earth except that this one looked like it was built inside a large cylinder. I guessed the cylinder to be about the same diameter as the lobby and roughly twice its length. I could only see the top half of the cylinder since there was a flat floor that cut the cylinder in half lengthwise. All the slot machines and virtual-reality games designed to separate you from your money were located on the floor with the cylindrical structure forming the walls and ceiling. As I carefully moved through the casino, still making sure to stay in contact with at least one hand rail at all times, I passed by the usual assortment of table games: blackjack, baccarat, poker, and pai gow. I wondered how they got the cards to stay on the table. I paused a moment to watch, but it was mid-morning and there weren't many people in the casino. No one was at any of these tables so I couldn't see them in action. Well maybe later.

I continued on, gliding past the craps and roulette tables. I'm sure these have been modified to accommodate zero-g, but how? Against the far wall I saw a long bar, but the bar had no stools. How odd. It's going to take me a while to get used to this whole no furniture thing.

The Three Dolphins Club was supposed to be at the end of the casino and there should be three smiling dolphin images decorating the entrance, at least that's what I think the Sasha said. I probably should have listened more carefully. What else did she say? Oh yeah, The club had a split-level design with the "upper" level used as a theater for exotic dancers and the "lower" level divided into eight rooms similar to the resort's guest rooms. Two of these rooms, she said, were used for the private "entertainment" of guests, four were used as offices, and two were combined into a suite where George Abruzzo lived. George and his team used the offices to manage the affairs of the entire resort including the Club. The main office was supposed to have a sign "above" the doorway that said, 'The Lupanar'.

It wasn't hard to find the three smiling dolphins and I tentatively entered the Club. I peered into the dimly lit theater, but couldn't see anyone. "Hello." No one answered. "Hello, anyone there?" Still no answer.

As my eyes adjusted to the low light, I saw the entrance to the Club's other level. It too was dimly lit. I nervously went through the entrance, turned right and glided past the rooms for private entertainment. I eventually came to a sign that said *The Lupanar*. I was a little late due to the time I spent floating helplessly in the lobby. Oh well, can't worry about that now.

I knocked timidly on the door. It slid open revealing a brightly lit office with four people busy working. There was a large, middle-aged, heavyset man facing away from me, talking on the phone. Even with his back to me I immediately recognized him as George Abruzzo. He looked like he would be close to three hundred pounds on Earth. To his left was a petite Asian woman who appeared to be about the same age as Mr. Abruzzo. To his right was Jennifer, with her unmistakable green hair, busy typing on a computer. Further to the right was a young man of obviously east-Indian descent, also typing on a computer.

The office looked like two rooms similar in shape to my apartment, but with the adjoining wall removed. The large high-definition displays were there, covering the ten-foot by ten-foot square ends of what would have been each room. In this case, without the wall separating the rooms, the displays nearly touched each other at an angle. I noticed that the displays provided one continuous image, not two images of the same thing. The effect was dramatic, and created an even more stunning view of space outside the resort. The angle between the two displays gave a wrap-around effect making it seem as if we were surrounded by space. Jennifer and the young man were using two small sections of one of the displays as their computer monitors.

George Abruzzo turned around, smiled broadly and said, "Good morning Tesla. Please, have a seat."

I didn't know how to respond to that since there weren't any chairs, so I just floated there with a confused look on my face.

"It's a joke," said the young man without looking up from his computer. "Just his weird sense of humor."

"Please, call me George," Mr. Abruzzo said looking at me, and then launched into introductions. Gesturing to his right, "This is my lovely wife Leslie." She smiled and nodded at me. George turned to his left. "This is Jennifer Gerbosi, who you met yesterday. Jennifer is our business administrator. I have known her family since before she was born. The wise guy over there is Dr. Thomas Patel. He's the genius who keeps this place running."

"I prefer Tommy."

"Tommy," continued George, "started working for Sky City right out of school. He started a year before the resort opened and was instrumental in getting all of the resort's engineering functions working properly before the first guests arrived."

He looks too young to have done all that. He can't be much older than me.

"Everyone, this is Tesla Isabella Miller," George went on. "She will be joining us as the newest member of the Three Dolphins Club family. As you know, we consider our employees our most valuable assets, so please treat her accordingly."

"I'm very pleased to meet you all," I said.

"Tesla Isabella Miller, T. I. M." Tommy mumbled under his breath. "Or M.I.T if you say it backwards!" he said louder and with a smile.

"What?" said Jennifer.

"M.I.T., her initials backwards are M. I. T.," Tommy said proudly.

"Just because you went to MIT doesn't mean everything revolves around you," Jennifer replied.

"I went to IIT in Bombay, too," replied Tommy smiling.

"Yes, we know, since you never let us forget." Jennifer teased.

"Okay, we've got a lot to cover," said George.

"Well, anyway, I like her already," Tommy whispered.

"First, we're going to go over the rules for living at Sky City and working at the Three Dolphins Club," George said. "Then once we've gotten that out of the way I have arranged for a special tour guide to show you around the resort."

"Okay," I replied, somewhat uneasily. I intended to give a positive and enthusiastic response, but it didn't come out that way.

"First, the rules for living at Sky City. Think of this as a cruise ship. Safety is paramount. We're nearly six hundred miles above the surface of the Earth traveling at over fifteen thousand miles per hour and surrounded by the deadly hard vacuum of space."

"And yet, somehow we haven't lost anyone yet!" interjected Tommy somewhat sarcastically.

"No, and we don't intend to," said George. "We do a muster drill every week on Sunday when the new guests arrive. You'll be responsible for helping make sure passengers get to their muster stations, and that everyone gets scanned in. There are three muster stations at the resort, one in the main restaurant, one in the lobby, and the third in engineering. These correspond to three of the four locations where ships can dock to the resort. You came in through the primary docking station at the lobby. Now, the resort has three lifeboats, one adjacent to each docking station. Each lifeboat can nominally transport a hundred passengers for ten hours, but could fit a hundred twenty passengers in a pinch. We have a maximum occupancy of two-hundred forty people, so in the unlikely case of an emergency that requires complete evacuation of the resort we could get everyone off in just two of the three lifeboats..."

My mind started wandering. George had a booming voice and a way of speaking that made everything sound important. Even so I struggled to pay attention. It was too much information, too fast.

"...The resort does not carry a spacesuit for every passenger and crewmember. In fact, there are only a half dozen spacesuits on board, used mostly for maintenance. The lifeboats do not have the ability to re-enter the Earth's atmosphere. Instead, they provide in-space transportation to neighboring resorts. The Stardust resort is located at our same orbital altitude and inclination and is approximately two-thousand miles ahead of us. The Galaxy resort is ten-thousand miles ahead of us. We have written agreements to provide mutual emergency accommodations for each other should any of the three resorts have to be evacuated."

"This is cheaper and easier than maintaining the ability to get everyone immediately back to Earth in case of a major emergency," Tommy butted in again, "and I'm all about being cheap and easy."

George continued, ignoring Tommy's interruption. "So is that clear so far?"

It wasn't clear at all, but not wanting to appear stupid I said, "Yes, I guess so."

"Good. Sky City is larger than either the Stardust or Galaxy so we would divide up our passengers and crew and send some to each location if we had to evacuate. Now some basics about living in zero-g."

"Technically, it's called micro-gravity," Tommy interjected yet again. "You see—"

"Not now Tommy," George interrupted. "Don't you have work to do?... As I was saying, living in zero-g," George continued, emphasizing the word zero, "is different from living on Earth. You've probably already noticed that your face is fuller, your legs are skinnier, and you feel like you have a cold. The movement of liquids out of your legs toward your head makes your body think you have too much fluid inside, stimulating your kidneys. So you'll find that you have to pee a lot in the beginning, and as you probably have already experienced, you don't get any warning until the urge to pee is overwhelming."

"Yes, I already had the pleasure of that experience." I replied. "Why does that happen?"

"Tommy?" replied George.

"This is one of our many 'benefits' of weightlessness," said Tommy, making air quotes around the word benefits. "On Earth, gravity pulls the urine down to the bottom of your bladder causing it to stretch. Receptors in the bladder sense the stretching and deliver signals that increase in intensity as the volume of urine increases. This doesn't happen in micro-gravity. Without gravity, surface tension forces dominate. These forces cause the urine to adhere to the entire interior surface of the bladder without stretching it. Only when the bladder is completely full do the walls begin to stretch. The result is a sudden, extremely intense urge to pee."

"Thank you, Tommy," said George.

"My pleasure."

"Therefore, we recommend everyone pee at regular time intervals whether you feel like it or not," George continued. "This will minimize the chances of having an accident. I'm old, so my interval is relatively short, probably a lot shorter than yours."

"TMI, TMI," shouted Jennifer from across the room. "That was something we just didn't need to know," she said smiling.

"Just pick a time interval that works for you," said George, ignoring Jennifer. "Equally important is to drink enough fluids so you don't get dehydrated. You probably won't feel thirsty at first, but you must keep up your intake of fluids. The computer in your room can provide you with the recommended fluid intake schedule for someone your size and age. In a few days your stuffy nose should pass. Okay so far?"

I nodded, but my head was spinning from all this information.

"Great," continued George. "Now for some bad news. When you stay in zero-g for months, your bones start to lose mass and get thinner. To counteract this, a regular exercise program is required. Again, the computer has a plan already laid out for you. It's a combination of running and weight-lifting exercises?"

"How do you run in zero-g?" I asked. "And how do you do lift weights if nothing has any weight?"

"When you go on the tour of the facility and get to the fitness center, this will become clear."

"Okay, and how long do I have to exercise for?

"We recommend two hours per day every day you're here. Even so, this isn't enough to eliminate the bone loss entirely. Therefore, we require all employees to take shore leave every six months. Every six months you must go back down to Earth for a minimum of eight weeks. Then you can come back for another six months. Any questions?"

Questions? I have nothing but questions! Exercise for two hours a day?! Is he kidding? I think I'm in pretty good shape, but two hours a day is a lot. Does everyone here really exercise two hours a day? Mr. Abruzzo certainly doesn't look like it. Eventually, I said, "Why did I throw up yesterday? Also, it was extremely comfortable sleeping last night so why does my back hurt today?"

George turned to Tommy and said, "Your turn again. You want to handle these?"

"Sure," Tommy said enthusiastically. "You got sick because your inner ear, which is sensitive to linear acceleration, could no longer tell where 'down' was and started sending confusing signals to your brain. Meanwhile your eyes were telling your brain something different. This conflict made your brain think you were being poisoned and made you to throw up. It happens to more than half the people who come up here. Your back hurts because some of the excess fluid that used to be in your legs migrated up around your back where it was absorbed by the spongy disks between your vertebrae. Because these disks aren't being compressed by the force of gravity, they get thicker as they absorb this fluid, and this pushes the vertebrae apart. The good news is that you'll likely grow taller by about two inches while you're here. Your back ache and nausea should disappear in a couple of days."

"Really?" I said skeptically, now feeling a little bolder. "So let me see if I've got this straight. Living here means I get nauseous, a puffy bloated face, a stuffy nose, chicken legs, a back ache, and bone loss? Please excuse me for asking, but why the heck would anyone want to come here?"

"Don't forget possible visual impairment due to increased intracranial pressure," replied Tommy.

"What?"

"Since weightlessness increases the amount of fluid in your upper body, in some people this increases the intracranial pressure, uh, increases the pressure in your head. This then increases the pressure on the backs of your eyeballs distorting their shape, blurring your vision, and slightly crushing the optic nerve."

"Oh great, and that! So why is it that people want to come here?"

George's face broke out into a big smile. "My turn again," he said looking at Tommy. Then he turned and looked straight at me. "All these effects, nausea, stuffy nose, and back aches are temporary and typically go away in a few days as the body and brain adjust to living in zero-g. Overall, a short stay in zero-g has no ill effects. None. Nada. On the plus side, being in space is fun! You'll see, living in zero-g is really, really fun! The adventure of the space race from the 1960's has been replaced by the pure enjoyment of experiencing life in zero-g. People just love being weightless. Using the lingo of the early internet days, it is the killer app for space tourism. It is the one thing, the only thing, you can't get on Earth, and that alone makes it valuable. After the initial adaptation period, people find that they sleep better in space, no more tossing and turning. Sleeping in a weightless state reduces sleep apnea and snoring, leading to a much more peaceful slumber for you and your partner. It is so restful in fact that most people find they only need to sleep about six hours a night. Their heart rates drop, their blood pressure drops, aches and pains in their joints and back disappear. Many people even lose weight! It's heaven for people with physical disabilities. For the first time many people with such disabilities feel they are on a truly equal footing, no pun intended, with everyone else. It's a liberating experience, which gives rise to our slogan, 'floating is freedom'."

Good sales pitch, this guy is quite the storyteller and has a personality to match his size! "Anything else?"

"Sex!" Tommy added enthusiastically, "Zero-g sex."

"Oh yeah, right."

"And a great view," added George. "That is why people come here. These are our four major attractions: experiencing life in zero-g, sex in zero-g, an unbeatable view, and when they're not doing those things, they can gamble in our casino. These things are the economic engine that drives this place. And, as I said, it doesn't hurt that many people lose weight when they're here too."

"Technically," interjected Tommy, "the second one, sex in zero-g, is just a subset of the first one, living in zero-g. I'm just say'n, if you ain't having sex, you ain't liv'n."

"Don't mind him," Jennifer said smiling. "He's just your typical socially awkward engineer."

33

"Which brings us to our final, and most important subject," said George. "Working at the Three Dolphins Club. This is a high-class establishment that caters to very wealthy clients. Many of our clients are young, newly minted multi-millionaires who made their money in the tech industry. Now they want to enjoy life, and they can afford it. We provide that for them here with our 'Girl Friend' experience. It's the only option we offer. You will be preselected by the client based on your bio. You'll be given a file on the client as well and you will meet him in the lobby when the spaceplane arrives. You will help him check in, show him to his room, and help him get settled. For the first three days you will act as his adoring, but platonic girlfriend. Most clients don't feel up to sex the first few days anyway. We don't want it to be a bad experience, so we use these days to help them adapt to zero-g and build sexual tension. Show your client around the resort, have meals together, go to the fitness center, the carnival game room, the sports arena, take him gambling, have drinks together, see a movie, just no sex. After three days, the platonic period ends, and you can show him the pleasures of sex in zero-g for the remainder of his seven-day visit to the resort. Do you have any questions?"

My mind was still reeling. I had so many questions, I barely knew where to begin. "Why is it called the Three Dolphins Club?"

"Tommy."

"There is an urban legend that back in the 1960's engineers covertly conducted experiments in one of NASA's neutral buoyancy tanks on what it would take to have sex in zero-g," explained Tommy. "The legend claims they discovered it was helpful to have a third person present to push at the right time, if you know what I mean. The legend further claims this is the way dolphins do it, that a third dolphin is always present during the mating process to help out. This isn't actually true for dolphins by the way. But hey, no need to let truth stand in the way of a good story. Anyway, it led to the creation of the idea of a Three Dolphins Club, kind of like the Mile-High Club for people have sex on airplanes. So, since our goal is to help people enjoy sex in zero-g, we adopted the name." Tommy appeared very pleased with that explanation.

"Uh…how do you have sex in zero-g?" I asked rather sheepishly.

George smiled, "Simply use your arms and legs to stay together. The soft rope net in each room is perfect for one or both of you to grab onto as needed. The rest is up to your imagination. The air flow in the rooms will keep you cool in the heat of the action and it will push you toward the net to keep you from banging into the walls."

"That's it? That's your helpful advice?"

"Don't worry, experience is the best teacher," replied George. "In a short time you'll be an expert. One more thing and this is very important.

You must understand that you are in charge. The client will to think that they in charge, but in reality you are. For most of our clients this is a strange, foreign environment. You are their guide to life in this wonderland. But if you have a problem with a client the resort computer is always listening, just call for help. Got it?

"Not really," I said nervously. "One more question."

"Yes?"

"Who will watch my baby when I'm working?"

"My wife Leslie here just loves babies. Don't you dear," George said, turning toward Leslie. "She has volunteered to watch Demetrious,"

"Yes," replied Leslie with a big smile. "Where's the baby now?"

"He's with my roommates."

"Well, make sure you bring him to me next time."

I smiled and nodded.

"Okay, so that's it for now," said George. "It's time for you to learn your way around the resort. I have arranged for a special tour guide." George opened the door. "Come on in Marc. This is Dr. Marc Elliott, Ph.D. from Princeton in aerospace engineering. Marc's the brains behind the design of this resort."

I turned around and saw Marc Elliott floating through the doorway. "Hi Marc," I said smiling broadly. "As you can see I'm not throwing up any more."

"You look much better than you did in the lobby," replied Marc.

"Marc's here this week for a special event, which he can explain to you later if you like. He asked if he could show you around the resort and since he knows everything there is to know about this place, how could I refuse. You'll be in good hands, so enjoy your tour. Oh, and Marc, try not to be too nerdy."

"I am what I am," replied Marc. "Come on, Tesla," he said waving to me as he glided out of the office.

He asked to show me around. I replayed the phrase in my mind and couldn't help but smile as I headed for the door. That thought was shattered as George stopped me and said quietly so only I could hear, "One more thing Ella, I have an important issue I need to discuss with you after your tour. So come back here when you're finished."

Oh my god, did he just call me by my real name? "Uh, okay," I replied sheepishly, as my mind was racing. What does he know? Am I going to get fired before I even get started? What's happening? Shit.

Chapter 5 Exploring

Marc was waiting for me outside George's office with a puzzled look on his face. "There you are" he said. "I thought you were right behind me."

My mind was reeling from the implications of what Abruzzo just told me and it took me a while to respond. Eventually I replied, "Oh, uh, Mr. Abruzzo just had one other thing he wanted to tell me. I have to come back here after the tour."

"Just so you know, George insists on honesty. He's constantly harping on that to the point where it gets kind of annoying sometimes. But he has a point because he knows living here surrounded by literally nothing, that it's critically important to know the truth about what's going on. He even has a plaque on his wall that quotes an engineer from JPL regarding the value of truth, which he turned it into a haiku. The plaque says,

> New information
> Is taken to be good news
> If it's really true."

I smiled at Marc. "Didn't Mr. Abruzzo tell you not to be too nerdy."

"Hey, it's not my plaque."

"Uh huh, but what does it mean exactly?"

"It means that any news, even if it seems like it's bad, should be considered good news if it's actually true. That's because, if it's true, then it can be dealt with. The truth is essential here. The truth keeps us alive. We have to deal with reality. We can't hide from the truth. For example, if a sensor tells us the carbon-dioxide levels in the resort are increasing even though we're doing the same things we've always done, then we can either ignore it and hope it goes away or we can do the work to find out what the problem is and fix it before it becomes deadly. The longer you don't deal with reality, the more severe the correction will be when it comes, and it always comes. Nature, the old saying goes, cannot be fooled. This is why Abruzzo insists on the truth."

"Sheesh, sorry I asked," I said pretending to be bored to death. After a brief pause though, I added enthusiastically, "So where are we going?"

"We're going to start with the Sports Arena, so you can learn how to move in zero-g."

"That would be great. I had a little trouble in the lobby this morning, so learning how to get around here would be awesome."

"What happened in the lobby?"

I didn't want Marc to think I was completely inept. "Well, let's just say it took me longer to get through the lobby that I intended."

Marc grinned knowingly, then launched into one of his now familiar explanations. "The Sports Arena is the largest room in the resort. It is roughly fifty feet in diameter and a hundred feet long. It's an expandable structure whose technical roots trace back to the Bigalow expandable module first launched to the International Space Station in 2016."

As we entered the arena, I could see that it had no features that indicated which way was 'up.'

"This is the largest open volume ever flown in space," Marc said proudly.

"Is that good?"

"Oh yes, it's good." Marc said with a huge smile on his face. "It's very good! You see people need open space. They need space for recreation, room to play, room to just hang out. That's why cities have parks and playgrounds and stuff like that." Then he seemed to get more reflective. "You know, it's an irony of the first forty years or so of human space exploration that, with the exception of Sky Lab in the early 1970's, astronauts who went into space had very little space. They were surrounded by a nearly infinite volume and yet they were jammed into tiny little vehicles. The Sky Lab astronauts were the only ones who had room to play and they liked it so much they recommended all future space stations have large recreational areas like this one. It's just so much fun to play in zero-g when you have a lot of room. Incredibly, nobody paid attention to this recommendation. Until now, that is. The design of the Sky City Resort by yours truly is the first space dwelling in over half a century to embrace the insight that the Sky Lab astronauts provided, hence this Sports Arena."

I found it strange that I was starting to find all this nerdy stuff interesting. Maybe it was just Marc's enthusiasm rubbing off on me. "So what are we going to do here?" I asked eagerly.

"As I said, you're going to learn the basics of moving around in zero-g," Marc replied. "Ready?"

"Ready!"

"First lesson," Marc said as he grabbed my hand.

I reflexively pulled back. Too much history with Alex, I guess.

"It's okay," said Marc. Just relax.

I nodded and extended my hand.

Marc took it in his and said, "Now for the first lesson."

Hmm, that's a more pleasurable sensation than I expected. He's just holding my hand...Wait, what am I doing. The last thing I need is to get involved with someone right now. That would be stupid. I squeezed his hand anyway. I felt a slight increase in the pressure on my hand in response.

Holding onto a railing with one hand Marc pushed me out into the volume of the recreation area, stopped me there, and then let go. I was left hanging motionless in space approximately six feet from the wall.

"Okay, this I'm already familiar with." I tried to swim toward the wall. But I couldn't move. I tried the breaststroke, sidestroke, even the backstroke, but to no avail. With the backstroke, I noticed Marc trying hard not to laugh. I found I could turn my body to face any direction I wanted, but try as I might, I just couldn't get anywhere. "Okay, I'm stuck. I thought you said this was going to be fun,"

Marc looked at me and smiled with a slightly devilish grin, "I'm having fun. So that's your first lesson. Up here you see, Sir Isaac Newton is in charge. Over three hundred years ago he said, a body at rest will remain at rest unless acted on by a force. I placed you at rest relative to the walls of the sports arena and there you stayed because you were unable to create a force to move yourself. Now for lesson number two." More devilish grinning.

Marc reached over, grabbed my hand again and gently spun me around.

"Newton's laws of motion work for rotation too, right? Try pulling in your arms."

I did so. "Hey it's making me spin faster, just like a figure skater."

"Now straighten out your arms."

I straightened out my arms which slowed down how fast I was spinning, but didn't stop it.

Marc reached out and grabbed me to stop me from spinning.

"Lesson number three. The key to moving in zero-g is to know where your center of mass is and how it affects your motion. Your center of mass is located here," Marc said touching my stomach, "just behind your belly-button."

"Where?" I said playfully.

"Here," said Marc, touching my stomach again, but letting his hand linger there for a moment as he glanced up at me. "Any force applied to your body that doesn't go through your belly button will cause you to rotate."

I couldn't help but flirt with this guy. "You're going to apply forces to my body?" I said smiling, knowing full well what he actually meant.

With just a hint of being flustered, Marc continued on. "Uh…right, so to move in a certain direction without rotating you have to push in a line that goes through your belly button. The key at first is to just move slowly, right? So let's try this. Push off the wall with your legs and fly over to that railing on the opposite side. Do it slowly and when you get there grab the handle."

I nodded and pushed off the wall with my feet. But I didn't get it quite right and I started slowly rotating as I glided to the opposite wall. When I got there, my feet were pointed toward the wall instead of my hands as I intended. So I just used my feet to stop, bending my legs at the knees as my feet contacted the wall. I reached down and grabbed the handle. It looked like I intended to do that all along. Feeling pretty pleased with myself, I yelled across the area, "This is easy!"

"Hey, that was good," Marc yelled back. "That maneuver was going to be our next exercise, but I see you've already got the hang of it. Now try this."

Marc pushed off the wall, did one and a half rotations in midair before landing on his feet and grabbing a handle on the wall next to me.

Determined to show him what I could do, I pushed off the wall, but again with more rotation than I intended. I did three and a quarter rotations before hitting the wall with my back and bouncing off back toward Marc. I was laughing as Marc caught me with one arm. I wrapped my arms around him, looked into those incredible blue eyes and said softly, "Maybe I should try that again."

Marc waited a moment and then nodded.

I let go of Marc and pushed off the wall. This time I did two and a half rotations instead of the one and a half I wanted, but still landed on my feet, bent my legs at the knees, and grabbed the handle. Marc applauded.

After several more trips across the diameter of the arena, I found I could now easily control my rotation rate. I could even push off with virtually no rotation if I wanted, yet I could still control my orientation in space and face any direction I wanted as I glided from one side of the arena to the other. "This is awesome," I said excitedly. "It's like flying. I feel like superwoman!" I started pushing off harder and going faster. I had always been rather athletic and I gained more control over my movements with each trip.

"Now let's try the long way." Marc said. We glided over to the end of the arena. "The arena is nearly twice as long as it is wide, just over one hundred feet. This will give you plenty of time for acrobatics along the way."

This turned out to be even better than going across the short way. After making several trips down the length of the arena I called to Marc, "Watch this." I launched herself into the arena and started dancing in midair as I glided toward the opposite end before rotating just in time to land on my feet. Marc seemed impressed and applauded.

"Now that you've got the basics down, let's get to the fun stuff."

"It gets better?" I asked, thinking this is already pretty darn awesome.

"Oh yes," said Marc, "much better. I'll be right back."

Marc left and then returned to the sports arena holding two bags. He opened one and took out a garment and said, "Here, put this on."

"What is it?"

"Zero gravity wings."

"Cool! I saw Jennifer wearing those yesterday."

"Now you're going to learn to fly," Marc grinned. "So far you haven't been flying, you've just been gliding; a slave to Newtonian mechanics. Now we're going to take control." Marc opened the other bag and took out a pair of zero gravity wings for himself. "It goes on like this, put your arms through the sleeves just like putting on a jacket and zipper it up in front. Then grab this flap in back, bring it up between your legs and fasten it in front. That's all there is too it."

I put the wings on and said, "How do I look?"

Marc looked at me, smiled and replied, "Like a giant Dodo bird."

"Hey!" I pretended to be hurt.

"Okay, let's try it. To move forward, hold your arms straight out from your sides with your palms facing your feet. Now move your arms down to your sides, then rotate your arms so your palms are facing forward, then bring your arms back up so they are again straight out from your sides."

Marc made two quick stokes like this and glided away from the wall. He turned around in midair, made two strokes again stopping his motion. Then he turned again to face me, hovering nearly motionlessly in space.

"See, that's all there is to it. Now you try it, and don't push off the wall."

I held my arms straight out from my body and then pushed them down to my sides. To my delight and amazement, I started to glide forward. I rotated my palms and brought my arms back up straight out from my sides. I pushed my arms down again, harder this time, speeding up my motion. This is great. I did three more strokes like this, speeding up my motion each time. I'm a giant bird. I was so intent on getting my arm movements right I forgot about the wall, which was now rapidly approaching. By the time I realized it, there wasn't enough time to turn around and get my feet toward the wall. I just barely managed to get my hands in front of me to cushion the collision as my body crumpled into the wall. I started laughing which made Marc laugh too.

"Not the best landing I've ever seen," said Marc as he flew over to me.

"You ain't seen nothin' yet!" I took off again. I flew over to the opposite wall, this time turning at just the right time and landing on my feet.

"Not bad," Marc said approvingly.

We spent the next two hours flying as Marc showed me how to stop, how to turn without slowing down, how to turn while slowing down, how to start and stop rotating about each of my principle axes—before this I didn't even know I had principle axes—and how to stop tumbling. Learning these techniques came easily to me, and I was having the time of my life.

"This is so awesome! I can fly like a bird!"

Finally, Marc said, "Okay, I think that's enough. Besides, you look like you're already ready for our soccer team."

"Soccer Team?" I asked with interest.

"Every Sunday night we play five-on-five, 3D, zero-g soccer right here. I join them whenever I'm here. We use special, high-performance wings. We have one goalie, two people on defense, and two strikers. It's a blast. We practice early Wednesday mornings. You should come practice with us. We're always looking for new players."

"That sounds like so much fun. Thanks, I'd like that."

"Let's get these wings off and I'll show you the rest of the stuff in this part of the resort."

Marc put away the wings and then we glided into a room we passed through on our way to the sports arena.

"This is the Carnival Game Room," Marc said. "It's full of zero-g adaptations of typical carnival games designed to separate guests from their money."

"Just like the casino, I guess some things never change. Even up here they still try to rip you off."

"You wanna try some of them? The Game Room is not open right now, but I know the guy who runs this place. He won't mind if we try a few of them."

"Uh, okay, sure."

"Come here. This is 3D Whac-a-mole. You go inside this box with your mallet and the moles come out on three sides, the top, and the bottom. So you have to keep turning around. And, of course, every time you hit one it pushes you the other way, so it takes some practice to get good at it. Do you want to try it?"

"Maybe some other time. What else ya got?"

"How about this one, darts. Just like on Earth. Throw the darts and try to pop the balloons."

"Okay, I think can handle that."

"Here's three darts," Marc said handing me the darts. "Put your feet under the loops there to hold yourself in place."

"Thanks."

I took the darts, held two in my left hand and took aim with the one in my right. "Watch this," I said confidently. I was sure I could hit a balloon. I threw the first dart. It traveled in a perfectly straight line and missed the balloon too high. I threw the second dart and it also missed too high.

When I threw the third one with the same result Marc said, "Grounders always aim high."

I turned to look at Marc. "What'd you say?"

"I said, Grounders always aim high"

"What's a grounder?"

"Well, actually, you are." Marc smiled. "That's what we call people who live on Earth."

I narrowed my eyes, "Really? That's not very imaginative."

"Yeah, I know, but some Grounders, I mean tourists, starting calling the people who worked here Floaters, for obvious reasons, so in response the Floaters started referring to anyone who lived on Earth, Grounders. It was supposed to be an insult."

"You sound like a bunch of kids. What did you mean, Grounders always aim high?"

"Well, it's like this. When you live your whole life in one gee, you naturally compensate for it when you throw something. You aim high because you subconsciously expect gravity to pull the trajectory of the object back down. Up here, Grounders can't help but aim high, and since there's no gravity they always miss high. Come, let's try the baseball throw."

Marc handed me three baseballs.

"The goal is to throw the ball through one of three holes in that painted board ten feet away, just like on Earth."

I thought to myself, don't aim high. I'll show him I'm not a complete Grounder. I put my feet into the loops on the "floor" and threw the first ball. In spite of myself, it still missed high. "That's so weird."

"Grounders always aim high," Marc repeated unhelpfully.

I threw the second one. It too was high. Shit

I looked at Marc and together we said, "Grounders always aim high."

On my third attempt, I purposely aimed at a spot below the hole. I threw the ball and it went in! "Yes! Grounders always aim high my ass." I shouted as I punched Marc playfully in the shoulder and went unexpectedly flying off in the opposite direction.

"For every action, there is an equal and opposite reaction," Marc said as he caught my foot before I drifted too far away. "Now, come over here. Here's one you should have no trouble with. It's called Skylab Run. It's named in honor of NASA's Skylab space station where astronauts figured out how to run in zero-g."

"How'd they do that?"

"They had these oxygen tanks, you see, that lined the circumference of the volume 'above' their workshop forming a circular path twenty-one feet in diameter. The Skylab astronauts figured out that they could run continuously on these tanks if they ran fast enough. Unfortunately, when they did this, it disturbed the station's attitude control system so much that NASA told them they couldn't do it anymore. Heaven forbid astronauts should have any fun, right? Anyway, since we're all about having fun in space, we recreated it here with our very own twenty-one-foot diameter circular track. Just go inside and start running."

"But won't it disturb the attitude control thingy?"

"No, don't worry. We have a much better system than Skylab had. So just go in and try it."

I looked at Marc skeptically. "Okay, I'll give it a try. I ran a lot on Earth." I got in and tried to run. I took two awkward steps started to rotate, wound up doing a flip and landed on my back. Fortunately, I continued to rotate around which brought me back to my feet allowing me to start running again, this time a little faster. The added speed helped. I managed to keep my feet underneath me and was able to run all the way around the track. I yelled to Marc, "Hey, this gets easier as you go faster." I sped up.

This is so cool. I'm running in space! I'm running in zero-g! Who knew that was even possible? There's so many new things here, so many new experiences, so much weird shit.

Marc watched me run around and around and around. "I knew you'd be good at this," he said, "Grounders usually are."

I tried to stop running. It was not a very graceful dismount as I landed flat on my back on the track when I tried to slow down. Fortunately, I bounced back up and grabbed a handle. "So how long do you have to be up here before you're no longer a Grounder?"

"Six months, minimum," replied Marc without hesitation. Even so it sounded like he just made that number up.

"Six months? I thought we had to go back to Earth every six months. Does that mean I'll always be a Grounder?"

"I wouldn't worry about it. Had enough of the carnival games? We spent a lot more time here than I had planned. Let's go see the Fitness Room quickly and then go have lunch."

"Okay."

The Fitness Room was adjacent to the Carnival Game Room, so it only took a few seconds to float over to it. "Here we have treadmills with bungee cords to hold you down, exercise bicycles with seat belts, and various resistance machines for those who like weight lifting."

"Just like a cruise ship," I said, "well except for the bungee cords and seatbelts."

"Yeah, I guess so. Although most people don't use the seatbelts anyway. They mostly just get in the way. The main difference, aside from the lack of gravity, is that here you have a spectacular view," Marc said pointing at the high definition displays covering the walls and ceiling."

"Yes, I can't get over the view."

"You know what else they have on cruise ships?

"What?"

"Food! Let's go eat."

"Great! Where are we going?"

"I thought we'd go to the main dining room."

To get there Marc and I left the Fitness Room and traveled the short distance back to the lobby. "Directly beneath the lobby is the First Aid facility where we can take care of minor medical issues," Marc said. "For anything major, you'd have to go back to Earth. Next to that is a beauty salon and spa for guests who like being pampered."

"I like being pampered," I said playfully. Marc appeared to have no reaction. Maybe he didn't hear me.

From the lobby we turned left and entered the long hallway that provided access to the guest rooms. "This hallway is a hundred eighteen feet long," Marc explained, not that anybody asked him. "All sixty-four guest rooms are along this corridor. The rooms are named after of famous astronomers. Here's Carl Sagan, Edwin Hubble, Nancy Grace Roman, Nicolaus Copernicus, Galileo Galilei, Ptolemy, Vera Cooper Rubin, Johannes Kepler, Tycho Brahe, Edmond Halley, Cecilia Payne Gaposchkin, Stephen Hawking, and Carolyn Shoemaker." Marc read off the names as we traveled down the hall.

At the end of the hall, we entered a short connecting tunnel that took us into the main restaurant for the resort. This turned out to be a regular restaurant, not a buffet like you might find on a cruise ship.

"This entire restaurant was built on Earth and delivered here in a single launch," Marc explained. "Like all of the other major parts that make up the resort it is basically a large cylinder, thirty feet in diameter and sixty feet long. The floor cuts the cylindrical volume in half, length wise, with the restaurant in the 'top' half—the half were obviously looking at now—and the kitchen 'underneath'."

It was beautifully decorated and elegant. This room, like the lobby, was decorated to provide a strong sense of where "up" was. By now, I knew this made it easier on Grounders, especially when they were eating. The walls and ceiling were covered in curved high-definition displays that were currently showing a brilliant blue sky with puffy white clouds. Marc said it was a live feed from Earth, from San Francisco to be exact. The effect was stunning. It gave the appearance that you were dining outdoors in San Francisco.

"Hey, I grew up near San Francisco!" I said. "This is so weird!" There were lots of tables, all attached to the 'floor', but no chairs; odd to see a dining room with no chairs.

As if reading my mind Marc went on, "As you can see, there are no chairs. Chairs, like most furniture on Earth are needed to provide support against gravity. Up here, no gravity, no chairs."

"I got it, no gravity, no chairs, no sofas, no stools, no beds."

The receptionist took us over to a table.

"Put your feet through the loops on the floor," Marc said. "On Earth your legs are used to push your body away from the floor. Here your legs are used to pull your body toward the floor."

"So, what's for lunch?" I asked. "I'm starving."

"Sky City, menu please," Marc said.

The table in front of us turned out to also be a computer display, which was now showing today's lunch menu.

"One of the things this resort has worked very hard on is to provide really excellent food for the guests."

"I would guess that the rich customers expect that," I said.

"Quite right and since smell is critical for your enjoyment of food, it is important to serve the food in a way that allows people to smell it, and to present it in a way that is appealing. We didn't want people eating and drinking out of plastic bags like they used to do in the early days of space exploration. George hired some of the best chefs he could and brought them up here to experiment for months on how to prepare and present really excellent food in zero-g. The results are fantastic as you will see and they keep getting better with time.

"Sounds great! Let's eat."

Unfortunately, Marc ignored my exclamation and continued explaining things. "They key is to make all the foods sticky so that they stick to an open plate without floating away. It allows you to smell the food and it sticks to your fork as you bring it to your mouth. Fortunately, making things sticky is not all that hard. Fluids are naturally sticky in zero-g, even water as you may have noticed. This also enables the chefs to create a wide variety of delightful sauces which both taste great and provide the necessary stickiness."

Maybe sarcasm will work. "Are we actually going to eat, or just talk about it?"

Marc got the hint. We ordered the lunch special, ravioli, and two glasses of red wine. When the food arrived, the waitress set the plates on the table. The plates, Marc explained, were slightly magnetic which allowed them to gently stick to the magnetic table, while the sticky sauce kept the ravioli stuck to the plate.

"This ravioli is terrific," I said between bites.

"Yeah, the chef here's pretty damn good, right?"

I tried the wine. "The wine is really good too, but why do the wine glasses look so weird?"

I saw Marc's face light up and knew another long explanation was coming.

"These glasses are specially designed to work in zero-g. If you had a regular wine glass like you'd find on Earth," Marc said as he picked up his glass, "and you tipped it over like this, nothing would happen. See, you couldn't drink from it. The wine would just stay where it was, clinging to the walls of the glass. If the glass was full enough, maybe you could dip your tongue into it, but that's about it, you couldn't drink it."

That's so weird. I never realized that you couldn't drink from a glass in space. Of course, I never actually thought about it before now either.

Marc continued on. "So around 2015 some smart engineers designed a coffee cup that takes advantage of the unusual behavior of liquids in zero-g. Without gravity, capillary forces dominate, and they found if you create a cup with a sharp corner on one side, these capillary forces draw the liquid, coffee in their case, into the corner. So as you sipped the coffee at the lip of the cup at the corner, more would be drawn into the corner to replace what you drank, and you could now drink your coffee in a very familiar way. We simply adopted that approach for wine glasses. The result is these glasses with a corner on one side."

"Well, I still don't really understand how they work, but as long as it lets me drink this really good wine, I'm okay with that."

"I agree, and importantly, these glasses allow you to smell the wine, as well as drink it. Of course they're also slightly magnetic like the plates so they stick to the table. We added the stems to make them look more like wine glasses and, of course, to keep your hand from warming the wine." Marc looked at me and smiled. He was obviously pleased with his explanation.

We enjoyed the lunch and the wine, and then Marc asked, "So why are you here? You seem like a very nice person. Why are you going to be working at the Three Dolphins Club? I know what you told Abruzzo, but why are you really here? What are you running away from?"

I was not ready to share my most personal problems with Marc and wasn't sure if I should, so I stuck to my story and said somewhat unconvincingly, "Why do you think I'm running away from something? As I told Mr. Abruzzo, the pay was too good to pass up. So here I am."

"Everybody here is either running from something or toward something," replied Marc. After several seconds of uncomfortable silence Marc continued, "Well, maybe someday you'll tell me the truth. In the meantime, let me show you one of our most popular attractions, something we call the Celestial Sphere."

"What's that? It's not dangerous is it?"

Marc laughed. "No, it's not dangerous, but it is awesome. I designed it myself. Come let me show you."

Marc grabbed my hand and we and glided together over to the middle of the restaurant where the entrance to the Celestial Sphere was located. The warmth of his hand in mine felt good. His hand was smooth and soft, obviously this guy doesn't do a lot of manual labor.

"The resort flies in a solar inertial attitude and this restaurant is on the anti-sun side," Marc explained.

Well, there's a mood killer. I cocked my head to one side in disbelief. "Do you ever speak English?"

"The resort always points one end toward the sun. This is the opposite end, so it always points away from the sun."

"See, that wasn't so hard," I said with a grin.

Apparently undaunted, Marc went on, "The Celestial Sphere is another idea we borrowed from cruise ships. Some ships include what they call an observation pod on the end of a three hundred foot long mechanical arm. On those ships, the pods typically hold about a dozen people and have glass windows all the way around. The mechanical arm moves the pod above the ship and over the side providing a pretty awesome view of the ship and its surroundings. We've taken that observation pod concept and adapted it here to create the Celestial Sphere. Our pod is a sphere eleven and a half feet in diameter that can accommodate a dozen people. With no need for a floor, the Celestial Sphere is a seamless, all-glass sphere. We extend the Celestial Sphere from the resort on a tether that is approximately a third of a mile long. The effect is…, well, you'll see."

Marc looked like he couldn't wait for me to experience this.

I entered the Celestial Sphere and gasped. The view was already spectacular even though we were still attached to the resort. I was facing away from the resort and could see nothing but a vast expanse of space, an unbelievable number of brilliant stars, the Earth to my right, and nothing else! The glass walls of the sphere were virtually invisible. Marc entered behind me as the operator closed and sealed the door behind us. Marc didn't say a word. It was completely silent.

I felt the Celestial Sphere detach from the resort and moving away from it on the tether. There was a very slight jolt when we got to the end of the tether; we were a full third of a mile from the resort. At this distance, the resort looked tiny. I couldn't see the tether. The glass walls were invisible. Marc turned off all the lights. The effect was stunning. I felt as if I was just floating there in space, suspended in the inky blackness without a space suit, staring off into infinity.

47

Then I felt something I had never felt before. I didn't know what it was and couldn't put it into words. It was just a feeling really, a sense of awe and wonder. My mind searched for an explanation. No, awe and wonder weren't quite right. It was more than that. It felt like I was in touch with the universe. Deep down I felt it was something important, something eternal. I felt at peace. It was…

"This is pretty cool, right?" said Marc, breaking the silence.

And just like that, the feeling was gone. "Yes," I replied, somewhat stunned, but I recovered quickly. "Oh my god, this is the most incredible thing I have ever experienced. I can't put it into words, this feeling, this experience."

"I know, right? Marc said with enthusiasm. "I love coming out here all by myself. Every time I come to the resort I make it a point to take at least one trip out here. It's about as alone as a person can get. Out here it's just you and the cosmos."

"Yes, it's amazing. I don't know what to say. There aren't words for this. Thank you for taking me here."

"You know," said Marc. "Many people experience a spiritual awakening when they come to the resort. Well, not me personally, but I've heard that a lot of people do."

"I can see why. I'm having a hard time keeping up with everything that's been happening to me. Two days ago, I was in Texas having lunch with my sister. Now I'm here with you, floating in space, surrounded by literally nothing or everything. I don't know, it's just so overwhelming. It's unbelievable and wonderful at the same time."

"Yeah, this was one of my better ideas, I think," said Marc. "The sphere receives power from the resort through the tether, but contains its own air supply. It has enough air for twelve people for ten hours, even though the typical duration of a "ride" is just thirty minutes. The fans that circulate the air are extremely quiet, enabling guests to experience the quiet stillness of space. The glass windows, as you can see, are specially treated to be virtually invisible. It makes for a great effect, don't you think?"

I didn't answer, there was no need to.

After an hour, Marc said, "I'm afraid we have to go back."

"Do we have to?" I pleaded. "I rather stay out here…with you."

Marc grabbed my hand and squeezed it. "Yes, we must. But…if you're not busy tomorrow, I'd like to continue our tour and show you the rest of the resort."

"Okay," I replied somewhat distractedly. I was thinking about that feeling I had at the beginning of our ride and wanted to recapture it. But it didn't happen so I reluctantly agreed to return. When we got back to the resort I quipped, "Now *that* was definitely worth the price of admission."

Marc smiled. "It's late in the afternoon. We need get you back to meet with George as he requested."

Mr. Abruzzo, shit, I was having such a good time I completely forgot about that. What am I going to do?

Chapter 6 Truth

I nervously entered Mr. Abruzzo's office alone, Marc did not go with me.

"Did you enjoy the tour of the resort?" George asked casually as if just making small talk.

"It is amazing!" I said enthusiastically. "Truly amazing. But we didn't get through the whole resort. Can we finish tomorrow? That is if I——." I stopped mid-sentence.

"If what?"

"Nothing." If I'm still working here, I thought. Shit, gotta remember to tell the truth. "So, you wanted to see me?" I couldn't stand the suspense and wanted to know if I had a future here.

"Yes. You see I always do a thorough background check on all the people who work here."

Shit…shit, shit, shit.

"I know your name's not Tesla Miller. I know your real name is Ella Markov. You're married to a man named Alex Markov, who works for the Chicago police department, and who is also the father of your son Demetrious. Is that correct?"

"Yes," I said meekly. No sense trying to lie now.

"And I know why you're here. I know why you left him. Didn't I say earlier today that telling the truth is the most important characteristic a person can have here?"

"Yes, but." Well, that's it, I'm going to be fired.

"No buts. The truth is essential here. I insist on it. I must know that you will always tell me the truth. Can you do that?"

"What? I don't understand. You're not going to fire me and send me back?"

"Oh heavens no girl, I wouldn't have brought you up here just to send you back. But," He paused as if for dramatic effect. "If I'm wrong about you, if I can't count on you to always tell me the truth, then I will send you back. So, think about this carefully before you answer, because it's not as easy as it sounds.

I felt an overwhelming relief, like an enormous weight had been lifted off my shoulders. I wouldn't immediately be sent back down to Earth, I wouldn't have to face all my problems there. I wouldn't have to face Alex. "I promise that I will always tell you the truth, regardless of the consequences."

"Good. I'm glad we got that settled."

Mr. Abruzzo seemed pleased.

"Now there's just one more thing," he said. "I want you to sign a five-year contract. I want you to work for me for the next five years. Can you that?"

"What?" I said with a surprising amount of panic in my voice.

"I want you to sign a five-year contract."

Five years! My heart was pounding. What the hell's going on? I clasped my hands together to keep them from shaking. How could I possibly make a commitment that long? It sounded like an eternity. "I very much want to stay here," I finally managed to say, "but five years, I don't know if I can do that. It seems like such a long time. Why?"

"I have my reasons. Let's just say it's my way of protecting you from your past," replied Mr. Abruzzo.

I was reeling, confused, off balance. I haven't even started yet, I don't even know what this is going to be like. What if I can't stand it? How could I survive for five years? What about Demetrious? Are we better off here or on Earth? I felt trapped again. I don't know what to do!

"Well?" said Mr. Abruzzo.

I searched for excuses. "What if I'm no good at this? You'll be stuck with me for five years."

"You're incredibly beautiful. I'm not worried. But if you don't sign, I will send you back for coming here under a false pretenses."

I couldn't go back. I knew going forward was the only way, but I didn't like it. Shit. For the second time in two weeks, I felt trapped with no way out. I hate you Alex for putting me in this position. Thinking of Alex made me realize what I had to do. I looked down at my feet floating above the floor. I gritted my teeth, swallowed hard and said grimly, "Okay. I'll do it. I'll work here for the five years."

"Excellent!" Mr. Abruzzo said as his face broke out into a big smile. He handed me a stack of documents.

I stared at the documents. "What's this?"

"These are for you. I had my people make them up. The documents you provided wouldn't fool anyone. Here's a new social security card, birth certificates for you and Demetrious, passports, a high school diploma, and even a record of a few college credits for a certain Tesla Isabella Miller. We've created an entire history for her, I mean you."

"I... I don't know what to say."

"Welcome aboard, Tesla."

...

I went back to our tiny apartment. Sasha and Yuri were there being entertained by Demetrious. "How did it go today?" asked Sasha as I floated through the doorway.

Sasha sent Demetrious flying slowly through the air to me. I caught him, gave him a big hug and said, "It was really fantastic at first and then really weird. I met Mr. Abruzzo, his wife Leslie, and Tommy. Jennifer was there too, but I met her yesterday. They all seemed very nice. Then I got a tour of the resort from Marc Elliott. He showed me the sports arena and game room. We even had lunch together. Then we took this incredible ride in the Celestial Sphere. Mr. Abruzzo had asked that I see him again after lunch. So we went back to the club. When I got there he was all like I need you to always tell me the truth, can you do that? So what's that all about?"

"Oh, he does that to everybody. It's no big deal," said Yuri.

I looked at Yuri and Sasha, "Then he had me sign a five-year contract."

Sasha's eyes widened as she stared at me.. "What? A five-year contract? That's strange. I've never heard of that. I don't know anybody here who had to sign a five-year contract. Why would he want you to do that?"

"I don't know." A feeling of dread came over me yet again. "Weird things seem to be happening to me all the time lately."

"Come on," said Yuri, "why don't we all go to the bar and you can tell us all about it over a nice bottle of wine."

"That sounds great," I replied. "And I'm afraid I haven't been completely truthful with you. After a glass of wine or two I'll tell what really happened the night Demetrious and I left Alex."

...

The three of us plus Demetrious gathered around a table in the bar in the Casino. After a couple of glasses of wine I said, "OK, here's what really happened. Are you sure you want to hear this?"

"Confession is good for the soul," replied Sasha.

"Okay, but remember, this is just between the three of us."

First of all, my real name is not Tesla Miller. I was born Isabella Vivian Elridge. My friends and family called me Ella. The first twenty years of my life were pretty ordinary until I got unexpectedly pregnant—I know, not too smart. I married the father, Alex, and we moved to Chicago. That's when my life started to get interesting, you know, in that ancient Chinese curse sort of way. 'May you live in interesting times.'

As I said before, my marriage to Alex was not the fairytale story I expected. At first, everything seemed perfect. Did I mention how good looking Alex was? He was also caring and attentive throughout my pregnancy, so I guess I just kind of overlooked his occasional moodiness. Our son, Demetrious, was born on a bright sunny day at the end of October in Chicago. But it wasn't long before the crisp autumn weather changed into an endless string of dreary cold gray Chicago winter days. Alex started to get frustrated by his new job and seemed overwhelmed by the responsibilities of fatherhood. I think some men are just not cut out to be fathers. Our troubles began when Alex started drinking. Alex is a mean drunk. When he drinks, he becomes violent.

Sasha and Yuri exchanged glances.

It was a little less than two weeks ago, shortly after Demetrious turned six months old. Seems like a lifetime ago now; so much has happened to us since then, but every detail is burned into my memory. Alex and I hadn't been getting along ever since Demetrious was born. I was mad when Alex arrived home late from work. "Where the hell have you been?" I yelled as he came through the door from the garage. "I had dinner ready for you hours ago. Why didn't you text me to say you were going to be late? Why didn't you answer any of my texts?"

"Stop nagging me." Alex yelled back. "I don't have to report my every move to you. I went out for a drink after work with the guys, okay?"

I glared at him. "It took you four hours to have a drink?"

"No," Alex said with disdain in his voice. "Stephanie and I went out to dinner too."

"You and your assistant went out to dinner, just the two of you? What about me and Demetrious?"

"Stephanie and I didn't want you there."

I gasped. The words cut me like a knife. I was so angry I could barely see straight.

"What an asshole," Sasha said. Yuri nodded.

I grabbed the plate I had set out to use for Alex's dinner and threw it on the floor shattering it. That must have set him off. Enraged and drunk, Alex stepped forward and slapped me across the face. Stunned, I stumbled backward. Alex took another step forward and threw a wild punch at my head. I felt the wind on my face as his fist flew by smashing into a cabinet.

Alex screamed in pain.

That was too close. I knew I had to get away, but how? My face was stinging from where he slapped me. I hated it when he came home drunk like this. Why did he always have to get so violent? "Shit," I whispered under my breath as he started toward me again. I turned to run, but he grabbed my arm.

"Ow, that hurts!" I yelled. "My arm doesn't bend that way." God, he's so strong and his breath stinks. Somehow, I remembered the self-defense class I took in college. One of the few things I remember from college. I used to spend a lot more time partying than studying. Anyway, the self-defense move on how to free myself came rushing into my head. I turned my body quickly and fell to the floor. It worked! I slipped through his grip, but now I was lying on the floor.

Alex bent over, grabbed my blouse and lifted me off the ground. As he did so, I kicked his left leg right on the knee as hard as I could. Alex had most of his weight on that leg and it buckled beneath him. He let go of me as he yelled in pain and I fell back down onto the tile floor hitting my head. Alex fell too, crashing to the floor, awkwardly banging his head on the tile with a loud thunk.

I scrambled to my feet while Alex was still lying on the floor. I spotted the cast iron frying pan on the stove. As I reached for the pan, I saw Alex out of the corner of my eye staggering to his feet. I grabbed the pan still containing the dinner that he never came home for, turned and swung it at him as hard as I could, spraying the uneaten food around the kitchen. I felt the pan vibrate in my hand as it hit his head. It was a glancing blow, but I can still hear the ringing-bell sound it made. At the same time, I felt my eye exploded in pain as the back of Alex's hand struck the left side of my face.

I fell to the ground again. I could barely see and my whole body was shaking. "Shit," I whispered to myself again. I think that only made him madder. Now what do I do? "Get away from me!" I screamed, as I scrambled back to my feet. "You're such an asshole. I'm leaving you and never coming back!"

"You can't leave me you useless bitch because I'm going to kill you right now!" he screamed back slurring his words. Blood was pouring from the cut over his right eye where the frying pan hit him. He started toward me again.

I threw the pan at him, but it sailed just past his head. Maybe he's so drunk that I can out run him. I used to be a pretty good runner. I ran out of the kitchen and into the dining room with Alex right behind me. He was gaining on me and I knew I wasn't going to make it. I spotted the large candlestick holders we got as a wedding present, perfect. I grabbed the closer one and in one smooth motion spun around with my arm out-stretched. Bam! It struck him right across the side of his head. A direct hit

54

this time. Wow, I must have hit him really hard because he fell like a ton of bricks onto the floor and his head smacked the tile floor again with a much louder thunk.

He stopped moving. Oh my god, did I kill him? I cautiously approached him still clutching the candlestick holder. My heart was pounding so hard it felt like it was going to jump out of my chest. I didn't dare get too close. It looked like he was still breathing. All I could think about was getting out of there. This was my chance. I ran out the front door and down the deserted, dimly lit street as fast as I could. I ran so fast I started getting dizzy. My eye was killing me. I didn't know if he was following me or not. Finally, I dared to glance back. I didn't see anything. Thank god. He's not following me. Now what?

As I started to calm down, my usual thoughts came rushing back. I know he loves me, but why does he have to be so mean? I must provoke him somehow. And what about Demetrious, my sweet Demetrious? I have to go back for him. In the morning, Alex will apologize and everything will be fine again. Yes, everything will be fine in the morning. I kept repeating that to myself, hoping it was true even though, if I was honest with myself, deep down I knew it wasn't.

I knew what I had to do. I had to sneak back in the house and make sure Demetrious was okay, then I'll sleep in his room tonight. When Alex wakes up we'll apologize to each other and things will okay again.

I slowly crept back through the open front door. I didn't hear a thing. That's good. Alex was still lying on the floor, but he was still breathing. I quietly tiptoed past him trying not to make a sound. I held my breath when I thought I saw him move slightly, but I kept going. I made my way down the short hall of our small, one-story home to Demetrious' room. The hinge let out a loud squeak as I slowly opened the door to his room. My heart almost stopped.

Fortunately, Demetrious was still sleeping. I stared at him, he's such a good baby, so sweet. "Come here Demetrious," I said softly. "Come to mommy." I gently picked him up.

A crash came from the living room. God, Alex is awake! I was nearly paralyzed with fear. My body started shaking. At that moment, holding my precious Demetrious, looking into his innocent face, I knew what I had to do. It was then that I made the decision that would change our lives. I knew I had to take him away from all this. I couldn't let him grow up here. It was too violent, it had too much pain. "We have to escape no matter what the cost," I whispered to Demetrious, "If we can just get to the car, we'll go somewhere safe."

I heard Alex yelling. I cracked open the door to Demetrious' room, peaked out. Alex was just outside the front door. I couldn't make out what he was yelling, but he was furious. I ran down the hall away from the front door, toward the garage. Demetrious started crying. I froze momentarily as I heard Alex stop yelling. He's coming back in the house! I made it to the garage, yelled at the car to unlock the doors and jumped in putting Demetrious on the seat next to me.

"Lock the doors," I screamed, and the car obeyed. "Go!" I shouted at the car.

The car responded calmly, "Do you want me to back down the driveway and pull into the street?"

"Yes, yes!" I yelled hysterically, "and hurry."

The self-driving electric car opened the garage door and slowly, carefully, safely, backed down the driveway toward the street.

"Hurry, god dammit," I screamed, almost beside myself. How the fuck do you make this thing go faster? I couldn't remember the right command.

I saw Alex running toward us from the garage carrying a baseball bat. His face still bleeding profusely and he was limping. Yet, in an instant, he was there. The window next to me exploded in a shower of glass. I knew it took a great deal of strength to break one of these windows, but at six feet three inches tall and over two-hundred thirty five pounds, Alex was a large powerful man.

"I'm going to kill you!" he yelled trying to reach into the car. "Get out of the fucking car you worthless bitch!"

I grabbed his hand and bit it as hard as I could.

Alex shrieked in pain, and pulled his arm out of the car as it continued to back carefully down the driveway.

"Get away from me," I screamed. "We're leaving you and never coming back!"

"If you do, I'll find you no matter where you go and I'll kill you. You hear me? I'll find you if it's the last thing I do!"

As the car finally backed into the street, Alex changed his tone.

"I love you," he said softly. "I'm sorry, you know we're meant to be together. This will never happen again. I need you. Please don't leave me. Please don't take my son."

I felt my resolve weakening and I hesitated. I know there's still good in him, I'm sure of it. Then I saw that familiar look of fury behind his eyes. He wound up to take another swing at the car. Fuck!

"Emergency acceleration," I screamed at the car, finally remembering the right command.

The car obeyed, its electric motor whirring to life, rocketing us to safety just as Alex swung the bat at the car as hard as he could. But he missed. The car was no longer where it was an instant ago. The force of the swing caused him to lose his balance and he fell to the ground in a heap. As we sped away I heard him yell, "I'll find you bitch, I'll find you wherever you go!"

My hands were shaking as I reached over to pick up Demetrious who was now crying hysterically. Tears were streaming down my face as I held him tight in a vain attempt to comfort him.

After a few seconds, the car started slowing down. It accelerated away like it was told, but now it didn't know where to go. Neither did I.

"Jesus!" exclaimed Sasha. "So what did you do?"

Chapter 7 Opportunity

Reliving that part of the story brought back a lot of bad memories and I started to cry. The stupid tears wouldn't run down my cheeks, they just filled up my eyes. God, you can't even cry normally in space. I tried to wipe away the tears.

"You don't have to continue if it's too painful," Sasha said.

When I could see again, I looked at the four of us, me and Demetrious, Sasha and Yuri, just floating in our tiny apartment. "No, it's okay," I sniffed. "I'll go on."

Well, I knew I couldn't go to my mom's, the stroke she suffered just two months after Demetrious was born left her incapacitated. God I miss her. She always tried her best to raise me and my sister. When I was little she made us study all the time. On the weekends she took us to museums, aquariums, art galleries. She said it would broaden our horizons. She also dragged me and my sister to church all the time. I didn't get it and when I got to Junior High, I put an end to all that because, you know, I thought I was too cool. I thought it was way more fun to just hang out with my friends. I thought I had it all figured out. I stopped studying because that was for losers. I barely made it through High School. I only went to college because everyone else did and I didn't really have anything else to do. I don't even know how I got into San Jose State, probably my mom arranged it. I chose psychology as my major because I thought it would be easy.

Anyway, as I was sitting in the car trying to figure out what to do, I finally decided to go to the only family I had left. "Take me to Emma's," I commanded. Emma is my younger sister. The car dutifully accelerated up to the speed limit, notified me that it would take thirty-three hours to make the trip to San Diego and asked if that's what I wanted to do. "Do it," I said.

It wasn't long before Demetrious was sound asleep again leaving me alone with my thoughts. I wondered how I wound up in this situation, fleeing my abusive husband with my infant son. This was not the way I planned my life to go. Of course, I hadn't actually planned it. I never planned anything. I lived my life as if I didn't have a care in the world. I'm thinking now that maybe that was a mistake.

Alex was so sweet when we first met. I was a freshman in college and Alex was a junior. We met during the Napa Valley Ragnar relay race. As I said, I was pretty good at running and doing that crazy two hundred-mile relay race sounded like fun when my friends asked me to join their team. Each team got to pick their own name and some of them were pretty funny like, *We run LA*, *My Drinking Team has a Running Problem*, and *Chaffing the Dream*. Our all-girls team was, *Does this Skirt Make My Butt Look Fast*? The race started on a Friday morning, ran all day, all night and finished Saturday afternoon. Everything was going fine until after my second leg at 2 am Saturday morning. The van wasn't there to meet me. I stood there in the dark at the finish line, hot, sweaty, and tired after running about eight miles thinking, now what? I didn't bring my cell phone because this leg was a straight shot between exchanges so there was no chance of getting lost. While I stood there trying to figure out what to do, Alex approached me. Of course he was a stranger at the time. I couldn't believe how good looking he was; tall and very muscular, with dark wavy hair. His t-shirt that announced his team name as, *We've Got the Runs*. He walked over to me and asked if I needed help.

My god he was so cute! How could he look so good during a Ragnar? And there I was sweating like a pig. I told him that my van wasn't there and I didn't have a cell phone to call them. I asked if I could borrow his. As he handed me his phone, I think I managed to say something clever like, "Hi, I'm Ella." When he told me his name, I wanted to give him my phone number right then and there. Instead, I just told him that the van had a flat tire and they were waiting for triple-A to come change it. They said it was a busy night and estimated that it would take over an hour before they could get there.

Alex was so amazing. He immediately said no problem and volunteered to drive me to my van and change the tire. He introduced me to his teammates as I climbed into their van in the middle of the night. Alex and I talked the entire time as his teammates drove to where my van was. He was so charming and made me feel so comfortable, and did I mention he was good looking? He had me at 'can I help you?' He and his friends changed the tire in no time. Before we continued on with the race, we exchanged phone numbers. He called me at the next major exchange and we spent the next five hours together while our teammates were running.

After that we were inseparable. Even though we went to different colleges, we met every weekend. Either he would drive down to San Jose, or I would drive up to Berkeley. I loved those weekends. It was all I could think about during the week. I would even daydream about us getting married someday. Then I got pregnant.

"Naughty girl," Yuri interrupted, trying to lighten the mood.

I stopped reminiscing about Alex and eventually, I fell asleep in the car as it dutifully continued toward my sister's home in San Diego. I woke up with a start when it pulled off the freeway to recharge. It pulled into an open slot at a charging station and the robotic charging cable sensed the presence of the car, commanded the charge port to open, lifted itself up like a large metallic snake, and plugged into the car, all by itself. I picked up Demetrious, ran into the convenience store and bought food and diapers. Fortunately, I had managed to grab my phone when we raced out of the house just ahead of Alex, and my phone was all I needed to buy things. After just fifteen minutes of charging the car was ready to go. We continued on our way, zipping down the freeway past the numerous abandoned hotels and motels made unnecessary by self-driving cars.

Three hours later I woke up again and asked the car to stop so that I could use the bathroom and throw away Demetrious' dirty diapers. When we got back, there was a video message from Alex. As the car played back the message, I watched Alex apologizing profusely.

Yeah, I've heard that before. I'm not falling for that crap again.

"Good for you!" It was Sasha who interrupted this time.

Then he turned on the charm. "I promise that I'll change this time," he said. "I know I've made mistakes, but your leaving has made me realize I have to change, and I can. I'll stop drinking. I'll go to counselling, anything you want. You and Demetrious are the most important things in the world to me. I'll do whatever it takes to win you back. You'll see, we'll be happy again. It'll be just the three of us playing in the park on the weekends, watching movies together at home. We'll watch Demetrious grow up, and you and I will grow old together. We are meant to be together Ella. Please come home. I miss you."

Dammit, he always knew just what to say to melt my heart. Was I doing the right thing? I stared into Demetrious' face and asked, "What do you think we should do? Do you want to go back to Daddy? I know he still loves us. Maybe he'll change." Being six months old, Demetrious of course, didn't say a thing.

"No! Don't do it. You can't believe him," said Yuri.

We continued on. The car sped through the darkness in its drive across the country. Late that night we received another video message from Alex. This time he was drunk again and angry. "You better get back here right now, bitch," he threatened.

Yeah, I've heard that before too.

"If you don't come back right now, I'll hunt you down. You kidnapped my son. If you're not back here tomorrow, I'm filing a police report. Then there will be no place on Earth you can hide from me. Get your ass back here right now! If you don't, I'll stop paying for your damn mother too. They can kick her ass out on the street for all I care!"

"See," said Yuri knowingly.

His speech was slurred and he kept repeating himself, but I got the message. I knew he could do it too, find us that is, no matter where we went. The Chicago police department would see to that. I clutched my hands together to stop them from shaking, but it was no use. "That's it," I said to Demetrious with determination. "There's no way we can go back. It's just going to be just you and me from now on. Are you okay with that?" Demetrious looked at me and smiled. I'll take that as a yes.

"I'm okay with that!" said Sasha.

An hour before our estimated arrival time, the car sent a text message to Emma informing her of our arrival time. Within a minute of our estimated time of arrival, after traveling for thirty-three hours, the car pulled up outside Emma's dorm at U.C. San Diego. Emma was standing outside waiting for us. Two inches shorter than me, petite with long dark brown hair and brown eyes, I knew that she always looked up to me as her older sister.

"Hi Ella!" she said enthusiastically.

I hugged her like I would never let her go.

"Come, let's go inside," Emma said, as she grabbed Demetrious. "Then you can tell me what the heck is going on." The three of us went into Emma's dorm room and sat on down on her bed.

I proceeded to unload the whole sorted tale that was my life. "As you know, when we first moved to Chicago, Alex was great, very loving and caring. We would do everything together and I barely noticed that I was losing touch with my friends back in California. Then Alex started getting frustrated at work. He had big dreams…You know what he's like, always needing to be the center of attention, wanting to be someone important. It didn't take long before he started to realize that his job as a criminal psychologist for the Chicago police department wasn't what he expected. He wanted to help solve important high-profile cases, work his way up to a job in the DA's office, and then move into politics. But it wasn't happening and he was getting angry. The man has no patience. He was feeling trapped in what he now perceived to be a dead-end job, interviewing a seemingly endless stream of low-life murderers to determine if they were sane enough to stand trial."

"Nobody's job turns out to be exactly what they expected," Emma exclaimed unsympathetically. "That's just the way it is."

"I suppose. But the real problems began when Alex started drinking after work. As you know, alcohol and Alex are a bad combination."

"Yeah, the guy's such a violent jerk when he drinks. I can't believe you didn't leave him sooner."

"I don't know. Or maybe I didn't want to know. He would always apologize profusely the next day, saying that he loved me and that it would never happen again. He said that I was the best thing that ever happened to him and that he needed me… He has that way of talking, that charming, adorable way about him that I so wanted to believe him."

"That's your problem," interjected Emma. "You're always looking for the goodness in people and overlooking their flaws."

"Then things got worse, much worse. He even threatened me with a gun he bought. I started to be afraid all the time… Yesterday was the last straw. He was out of control. I really thought he would have killed me if he had the chance… So I grabbed Demetrious and we ran. I didn't know where else to go. So we came here."

Emma hugged me and said, "It's okay, you're safe here." Even though we both knew it wouldn't be long before Alex came here looking for me.

"I don't know what to do." I broke down in sobs. "I just can't go back to Alex. If I do, I know it will only be a matter of time before he kills me. I'm sure of it. But I don't know how to hide from him either. To make things worse he's going to stop paying for mom's care too. What are we going to do? Do you think I should go to a shelter for battered women."

"I don't think that will work," replied Emma. "Since Alex works for the Chicago police department, he'll probably be able to use his connections there to find you, especially if he tells them you kidnapped his son. Sorry."

Finally, after a long pause Emma said, "Hey, why don't you take a nice shower, try to calm down a little and I'll take care of Demetrious. Then we could go get something to eat and try to figure out what to do." She was clearly trying to sound positive, but it wasn't working.

The shower, however, felt wonderful. I got dressed and saw that Emma had given Demetrious a bath too. "He's such a happy baby," she said.

The three of us left the dorm, went across the street and down two blocks to a new pizza place that Emma liked. She said that one of the advantages of living near a university was the availability of really good pizza.

All during lunch we tried to figure out what to do, but there seemed to be no good solution. If I went back to Alex, our lives would be at risk. If I tried to start a new life with Demetrious somewhere else, Alex would find us for sure and I'd be guilty of kidnapping. Even if I tried to leave the country with Demetrious, Alex would probably still find us. A restraining order wasn't an option either since it seemed to provide little actual protection. On top of all this, there's still the problem of what to do with mom once Alex stopped paying for her care facility.

"This really sucks," I moaned with a sense of hopelessness. On the bright side, Emma was right, the pizza was really good. After stuffing ourselves we walked back, but unfortunately, we were no closer to a solution. As we entered the dorm we passed by a large bulletin board. Amid the jumble of flyers about upcoming shows, clubs, protests, hiking trips, and yoga classes, I spotted a help wanted flyer. I stopped suddenly, pulled the flyer off the board and read it. It was from a place called the Sky City Resort and Casino. The flyer claimed that Sky City was the latest in space resorts and it was seeking young energetic employees for a wide variety of jobs. The flyer promised excellent pay.

I don't think so, I said to myself. I don't know the first thing about space. That would be crazy. I don't even like flying. Then I paused for a moment. It does say excellent pay, I wonder what that means. I handed Emma the flyer and asked, "Do you know anything about this?"

"No, but we can get to a computer and find out," she replied.

"Why don't we just use my phone?"

"If you use your phone, Alex will eventually get your records and he'll know what you were looking at."

We made our way over to a kiosk in the basement of the dorm where there were still old community computers for student use. Scrolling through the Sky City website, we saw listings for cooks, maids, receptionists, managers, various kinds of engineers, busboys, casino table game dealers, security guards, and escorts. All the salaries were good, but the highest salary range by far was for escorts.

"That escort salary has to be a mistake," I said. "It can't be that much. Not that it matters. There's no freaking way I'm going to be a space hooker."

"No offense," I said looking at Sasha and Yuri.

"None taken," replied Sasha.

"Maybe I could be a receptionist or even a maid, assuming I was brave enough to get there, which I'm not. Maybe that wouldn't be so bad. One thing's for certain, Alex, sure as hell, would never think of looking for me there."

We continued to look through the website and whatever tiny bit of interest I may have had evaporated. I clicked on the job description for Receptionist and a pop-up appeared that said all of these positions had

63

been filled. I clicked on Maids, same thing. One after another, I clicked on each job category with the same result, until, that is, I got to Engineers.

"Finally," I said, somewhat exasperated. "There are still job openings for engineers. Not that it does me any good."

There was only one job category left. I hesitated momentarily, then thought, what the hell, and clicked on Escorts. "Yes! Wait, no!" I saw that there was one position open. "Well, that's that, I guess. I am definitely not going to be an escort. End of story! We'll just have to figure something else out."

"You know, I think there was a girl here last semester who quit school to go work there," said Emma. "Yes, it was sometime last semester—right when they first opened I believe. I think her name was Madison. I didn't know her very well, but I've heard that she loves it there. She was friends with one of the girls on my floor, Mia. We should go talk to her."

"Yes, Madison is here. I'll introduce you guys," Sasha interjected.
"I'd like that," I said.

I continued with the story.

Emma grabbed Demetrious and the three of us made our way upstairs to Mia's room. An energetic, second-year civil engineering student, Mia Collins shared a triple dorm room with Madison last year. We found Mia in her room studying calculus. She confirmed that her former roommate, Madison Wallace, did indeed take a job at Sky City last November.

"She works for an 'escort' service," Mia said making quotation marks in the air with her hands around the word escort. "She works for some classy club—I can't remember the name, something to do with a fish I think. Anyway, it caters to rich young millionaires, you know the kind that strike it rich in Silicon Valley and then become bored. Madison said that school wasn't for her and now she says she's making a ton of money."

"You mean she's a prostitute," I said.

"That's a crude way to put it. She prefers to think of herself as providing a valuable service—teaching people how to have sex in zero-g"

"Zero-g?"

"Zero-gravity," said Mia.

"Really?" Yuri interrupted incredulously. "You didn't know what zero-g meant? Man you were clueless."

"This is going to take a really long time if you guys keep interrupting me."

"Sorry," Yuri and Sasha said simultaneously.

64

"No problem. Now back to the story."

"Why do people need help having sex in zero-g?" I asked.

I saw Sasha and Yuri look at each other and smile, but neither one said anything.

"Beats me," replied Mia. "Maybe they have a hard time staying together, if you know what I mean. Anyway, she makes good money and loves living in space. Are you thinking of doing that too?"

"I don't know," I replied. "I don't think I could do that."

Mia looked at me and said, "Well, you're certainly pretty enough, especially with those stunning green eyes."

"Thanks, but I still don't think so."

"Thanks Mia," said Emma as we left and returned her room. We sat down on the Emma's bed in silence. Demetrious was sitting on Emma's lap.

After a long silence Emma said, "It's a 'ton' of money," making air quotes with her hands. "You and Demetrious could hide from Alex, and you'd make enough money to take care of mom too."

"Be serious would you?" I replied nervously.

"Yeah, you're right. It's probably better to just go back to Alex," replied Emma sarcastically.

"I just don't think I could do it. I—." Before I could finish my sentence a video message from Alex arrived on my phone, and he was pissed.

"I'm coming for you, you bitch. I know you're at your mother's. I'm gonna be there real soon to get you and my son and bring you back home where you belong. You know you can't hide from me. When I find you, I'll teach you a lesson you'll never forget."

"Shit," I said gritting my teeth. "I guess it wouldn't hurt to just find out a little more about it."

"Okay," replied Emma sympathetically. "And in the meantime, let's not panic. The fact that he thinks you're at mom's is good, that means he's not using his connections at the Chicago police department yet or they would have tracked your car down here. This should give us a little more time. Now, let's borrow Mia's phone and call the number on the flyer…wait, first you'll need a new identity."

"What?"

"You need a new name. You can't use your name or Alex will find you, even up there."

"A new name? I like my name… I don't know about this."

"Come on, just try it. What names have you always liked?"

"I like Ella."

"You're not trying. Okay, remember how mom used to love that old car she had?

"The Tesla?"

"Yes, you could be Tesla something. You know like how girls were sometimes named Mercedes."

"Tesla, hmm… OK, that's not too bad I guess. The ending's similar to Ella."

"Now for the last name. How about something common like Smith or Jones."

"Seriously?"

"Hey, I came up with Tesla, so you pick your last name."

I thought for a moment. "Well, there was this boy in my elementary school that I had a crush on for years. I always thought I was going to marry him. His name was Mathew Miller."

"So you'd be Tesla Miller. I like it! Okay Tesla Miller, let's go borrow that phone and call Sky City." Emma went down the hall and borrowed Mia's cell phone. She handed it to me and said, "Here's to new possibilities."

I stared at the phone and hesitated. What am I getting myself into? I felt sick to my stomach. "I've never heard of an escort having a salary," I said. "So, I maybe the first thing I should do is find out if that's correct and if the salary range is right. What do you think?"

"Sure."

My fingers tightened around the phone. "Oh god, I can't believe I'm doing this."

"It's just a phone call," said Emma, trying to reassure me.

I dialed the number nervously and put it on speakerphone. A cheerful voice answered. "Sky City Resort and Casino. How may I help you?"

"Um, hello, this is, uh…uh, Tesla Miller. I'm calling about a job there. I saw your flyer advertising for help wanted."

"Great!" said the voice. "What position are you interested in?"

I hesitated for a moment, I can't believe I'm doing this. Shit. "Uh, escort, I guess."

"Excellent," replied the receptionist professionally. "What you need to do is fill out an application online. As soon as we get it we'll review it and then contact you."

"Okay…, but before I do that let me ask you this. This a salaried position, right?"

"That's right."

"And is the salary range given on your website correct?"

"Yes, that's correct," the voice replied. "This type of service is legal in space, and the salary range indicated on our website is correct. Is there anything else I can help you with?"

"So, if I'm interested I would just fill out an application on line and then you'll contact me?" I repeated nervously.

"That's right, and if everything looks good on your application, the next step will be an online video interview with the owner Mr. George Abruzzo. He likes to interview everyone himself. If Mr. Abruzzo likes you, and you decide to take the job, then we'll need your social security number and a copy of your Passport."

"Okay, thank you," I said and I hung up the phone. My heart was pounding. "Oh my god! Now what do I do? The money would be more than enough to take care of mom like you said, but I just can't do it." My chest tightened. I couldn't breathe.

"I know," said Emma compassionately. "Just take some time to calm down. Then, let's just fill out an application anyway. Who knows, you probably won't even get the job. There must be lots of girls who would want to make that kind of money."

"Okay, give me a few minutes."

Waiting didn't help. "Screw it," I said. "I guess it won't hurt to just fill out the application."

It didn't seem real and we wound up having a good time filling out the application for Tesla Miller and making stuff up about her life. "Let's make her a student here at UCSD," said Emma. "What do you want to major in?"

"Biology" I replied. "I like animals."

"You mean Tesla has likes animals," replied Emma. "Biology it is. Welcome to UCSD."

We completed the application, hit send, and got an immediate acknowledgment sent to the email account we just set up for Tesla Miller.

I heard a slight buzzing sound coming from Sasha and saw her glance at her watch.

"This is a great story," interrupted Sasha. "But can you wait a minute? I have to go pee."

"No problem." I looked at Yuri. He just shook his head.

"Much better!" said Sasha when she returned. "Please continue."

I received another email from the Resort the next day. This one was about setting up the video interview with Mr. Abruzzo. "We got the interview!" Emma said excitedly, as she read the email over my shoulder. "It says that Mr. Abruzzo is not available until Sunday afternoon our time.

It also says to please have your social security number and a copy of your passport available at that time."

"I can read you know," I said sarcastically. "But where can I get a social security card and passport for Tesla Miller?"

"Well, I might know a guy who knows a guy who makes fake IDs, mostly for students too young to drink, not that I have one or anything," replied Emma with faked innocence.

"Sure you do."

"It usually takes a day or two, or so I've heard," she said smiling.

"Sunday is two days from now. So that should work, but how are we going to stay away from Alex until then?"

"I don't know, we'll think of something. We should tell them yes."

"I still don't know about this." I felt my life continuing to spin out of control.

"I know, but we should just set up the interview. You can always say no later if you actually get the job."

"Easy for you to say."

Emma shrugged her shoulders.

"Okay," I said reluctantly. "Let's say 1 pm on Sunday." I hit the send button and immediately received the phone number to call on Sunday.

"I'm scared," I said. "I'm afraid I'll get the job and wind up actually moving to space to be a call-girl... I'm also afraid I'll mess up the interview and won't get the job and then Alex will find me... God, how did my life get so screwed up?"

"Well, you married that asshole," replied Emma.

Chapter 8 Decision

I paused for a moment, looked at Yuri and Sasha and said, "Are you sure you want me to go on? Now I'm probably boring you to tears."

"Oh no," replied Yuri smiling. "I like the story of anybody whose life is more screwed up than mine."

"Okay." I looked at Sasha and she nodded.

So, Emma called the guy who knew the guy and arranged to purchase a social security card and a U.S. Passport for Tesla Miller. He instructed us to bring two pictures plus a cash advance. We met with the guy Friday night and provided the pictures and money. He said it would take a day to prepare, so if everything went well we could pick the documents up Sunday morning. Now all we had to figure out was how to evade Alex.

"I think I know how we can buy ourselves some time," I said. "We could drive overnight to San Jose. I'll call him from there and say I made a big mistake and we're coming home. The police will know where the call was made from. Then we'll plug in the car in and enable the data exchange so they can see the car is in San Jose too."

"Won't that tell them exactly where we are? asked Emma. "Seems like a bad idea."

"Actually, it will tell them exactly where we were, because immediately after I make that call we'll drive back here. It will re-enforce Alex's belief I'm in San Jose. That should slow him down by a day or so. We may even be able to sneak in a quick visit to see mom while we're there."

"Okay."

So we hopped in my car and had it car drive us to San Jose.

"That was really good," Emma said after I finished recording a video message to Alex. "You almost had me believing it."

"Not bad, huh? Maybe I should become an actress instead of a space hooker. Let's go see mom."

We pulled into the parking lot at mom's care facility around 8 am. My heart started beating rapidly. "What if Alex is already here waiting for me?" We sat in the car for half an hour watching, looking for any signs of Alex. "We should call the facility to see if anyone has come to visit mom this morning."

"Okay." Emma made the call. "Good news," she said. "No one has checked in for her today or yesterday."

"Good. You go in first," I said, "If he catches you, just deny you've seen or heard from me and that you were just up here to visit mom."

Emma walked quickly toward the lobby and disappeared inside. After fifteen long minutes she came back outside and waved to me, indicating that it was safe for me to enter. I got out of the car, picked up Demetrious and started walking cautiously toward the facility. I hadn't taken more than two steps when I saw a car approaching rapidly. My heart was pounding. I wanted to run, but forced myself to continue walking normally. The car was almost upon us. I strained to look through the windshield, but the glare from the sunlight made it impossible. I froze. The car passed without slowing down. God, it was just someone in a hurry.

With my heart was still beating rapidly as I entered the facility and approached the receptionist. The receptionist was Malaya Mendoza, a wonderfully warm and happy woman. She grew up in the Philippines and came to the United States as a young woman to work as a caregiver for the rapidly aging U.S. population. Now middle aged, she had the perfect personality for this line of work—caring, optimistic, happy, and always pleasant to be around. She always seems genuinely pleased to see me. It made me happy to know there were such caring people in the world.

"Hi Malaya," I said. "How's my mom?"

"Hi Ella," said Malaya with a great big smile. "What a cute baby. Your sister's in there with her now. Your mom's such a sweet lady. Please sign in, then you can go in and see her."

As I entered mom's room I said as cheerfully as I could, "Hi mom, it's me Ella. How are you feeling?" I didn't expect an answer. I had long since gotten used to these one-way conversations. I proceeded to tell her about leaving Alex, and then said, "I'm not sure when we'll be able to come back to see you." Fighting back tears, I added, "I love you very much."

After about an hour Emma said, "We'd better get going."

On the way out I saw Malaya and two other nurses who were on call that morning in mom's wing. I gave Malaya a hug and a little thank you card with a thousand dollars in it and asked her to split it with the other two nurses. Emma and I had visited an ATM that morning and I thought, what the heck, might as well spend some of Alex's money while I can. "Please take good care of my mom," I said warmly.

We arrived back in San Diego Saturday night. I told Emma that there were two more things we had to do. First, I needed to leave another message for Alex, then I was going to send the car back to Chicago.

I recorded the video message—"Hi sweetie. I'm sorry again. Seems like I'm always apologizing. Anyway, I decided to come down here to San Diego to see Emma before going back to Chicago. I haven't seen her in a while and thought it would be nice to make a quick trip down here since I was already in California, plus Demetrious has changed a lot since she last saw him. It was nice seeing her, but we're getting in the car right now and will be home as fast as we can."

I pressed send, threw the phone into the car and instructed it to return home. We waved as the empty car departed.

We spent the night in San Diego relatively confident that Alex would see that the car was traveling back toward Chicago and assumed that he would plan to be there when it arrived.

The next morning, after a little incident we had walking through the UCSD campus, we picked up my fake IDs and at 1 pm Sunday afternoon, Emma and I plus Demetrious gathered in Mia's room and sat at Mia's desk in front of her computer. "Okay, here goes nothing," I said as I clicked on the number to start the video interview with Mr. Abruzzo.

"Now try to be likeable," said Emma teasingly, "not your usual boring self."

"Hey, be nice," I replied, pretending to be hurt. "And be quiet."

The image of a woman with green hair appeared on the computer and said, "Hello, this is Jennifer from Sky City."

"Hi, this is, um, Tesla Miller. I'm calling for—"

"Hi Tesla," Jennifer interrupted, "we've been expecting your call. Please wait, I'll get Mr. Abruzzo."

After a minute, Mr. Abruzzo appeared. His large bald head filled the screen.

"Hello Tesla, George Abruzzo," he said. "You can call me George. Your application looks good. Looks like you're currently a student at U.C. San Diego, is that right?

"Yes," I replied, I lied.

"What's your major?"

"Biology," I lied again.

"If you worked at the Three Dolphins Club you'd have to drop out of school. Are you okay with that?"

I looked straight into the camera and said, "Yes, I've decided college really isn't for me." At least that part was true. "I'm not really into all that studying and stuff."

"So tell me, why do you want to work at the Three Dolphins Club as an escort?"

I anticipated this question and had looked up online the various reasons young women become call girls or work in the sex industry, and had rehearsed my answer.

"Well, it's like this. I like sex and instead of giving it away, I thought hell, why not make some money instead. Then when I saw your ad, and looked up what I could make at your club. I thought, holy shit, this is an opportunity too good to pass up." Yep, I should've been an actress.

"What do you know about the Three Dolphins Club?"

71

"I know that you provide a high-class escort service that helps people enjoy the unique experiences of life in zero-g." I had memorized the tag line from the website. I saw Mr. Abruzzo smile.

"Good. If you come to work here, you'll be away from home for six months at a time. Are you okay with that?"

"Yes," I replied without hesitation. That's exactly what I need!

"Won't you miss your family?"

"Well, my Dad left us when I was four and my mom is in a nursing home and doesn't recognize me. So it's just me and my sister."

"I see," replied Mr. Abruzzo.

Then he asked a question I hadn't anticipated.

"What's your biggest dream in life?"

I hesitated, uncertain how to answer this. I never really thought about the future much, except, of course, to get away from Alex. Finally I managed to say, "I just want to be able to raise my son in a happy, safe environment."

"You have a child?" Mr. Abruzzo asked, sounding surprised.

Uh oh. "Uh, yes, I have a son, Demetrious."

"How old is he?"

"He just turned six months last week."

"Do you expect to bring him to Sky City?"

"Well, yes, I can't leave my baby behind."

"One moment please, I'm going to put you on mute," and just like that the screen went blank.

Well, that's it, I thought. I better start figuring out what to do next. I'm sure I'm not going to get this job. Mr. Abruzzo was gone for a long time, or at least it seemed that way. It was long enough for me to play all kinds of different scenarios in my mind about what I was going to do after being turned down for this job. None of them were good and all of them ended with Alex finding me. Shit. Finally, Mr. Abruzzo came back online. He looked grim.

I knew it.

Then he broke into a broad smile that lit up his entire face and said, "Welcome to the Three Dolphins Club Tesla! You've got the job!"

"Really!" I said with enthusiasm that surprised myself. "That's great!...There's just one thing."

"Yes?" said Mr. Abruzzo.

"It's just this is such a big decision for me, can I have a day or two to think it over?"

Mr. Abruzzo hesitated and then replied, "You can have until this time tomorrow. We have a number of other candidates, so we'll need your decision by then."

"Well, we all know what decision you made," Yuri said. "Since you're obviously here. What made you make up your mind?"

"Be patient, Yuri. I'm getting there."

An hour and a half after we sent the car off we heard someone knocking on Emma's door. Emma looked out through the peephole. "Oh my god," she said as she turned toward me. "It's Alex!"

"What? Alex is here? Shit. What should we do?"

"Grab Demetrious and hide! And hide your stuff too!"

Thank god Demetrious was sleeping.

Alex pounded on the door and yelled, "Answer the damn door! I know you're in there?"

"Just a minute," Emma yelled back. "I'm coming."

Emma opened the door slowly and before she could say anything Alex pushed his way in and said loudly, "Where the fuck is she?"

"Nice to see you too," said Emma. "Don't they have any manners in Chicago?"

"Don't give me any of your crap. I get enough of that from your sister. I just flew down from San Jose to bring her and my son back to Chicago with me. Now where are they?" demanded Alex.

"They're on their way back to Chicago, didn't you get her message?" Emma said, trying to keep her voice calm and stern.

"I got it, but I didn't believe it." Alex looked around the apartment, apparently looking for any signs that Ella might still be there. "What time did she leave?"

"Do I look like a clock?" Emma replied sarcastically.

Alex walked into Emma's bedroom.

Demetrious and I were hiding in the closet and I held my breath as I heard Alex enter the room. I stared at Demetrious, praying he wouldn't wake up.

Seeing he was getting nowhere, Alex tried turning on the charm instead. "It's just that I've been so worried about Ella and Demetrious. I flew all the way out here just to make sure they were okay. If anything ever happened to them, I don't know what I'd do. So if you know anything at all that would help, please tell me."

"What a bunch of crap," replied Emma coldly. "Sorry, I already told you they're on their way back to Chicago. Why don't you just run along so you can be there when they get back?"

Alex sat down on Emma's bed looking for clues, waiting for something to happen. I could hear the bed squeaking. Why doesn't he leave already?

"What did you do when Ella and my son were here?" he asked, presumably making small talk as an excuse to stay longer.

"Get off my bed," Emma demanded with false outrage, trying to hide her discomfort. "I've got homework to do, so you need to leave now! Go home and fix things up with my sister."

After what seemed like an eternity, Alex finally got up and strolled slowly toward the door. As he reached the door, he stopped and said, "Okay, I'm leaving, but why are you so anxious to get rid of me?"

"Look, I've got a lot of work to do. Ella and Demetrious are on their way back to Chicago. For reasons that escape me, my sister says she still loves you and wants to make it work. But, if I could keep her from going back to a drunken loser like you, I would."

"Fuck you," Alex said as he slammed the door on his way out.

The noise woke up Demetrious and he started crying. I tried to cover his mouth, but it was no use. This is it! Alex is going to find us any second. Just as I finished that thought the closet doors opened. Cringing, I tried to sink farther back into the closet.

"It's me," Emma said. "Alex is gone." She reached out her hand to help me up off the floor, but I just sat there shaking.

It took several minutes, but eventually I started to calm down and for the second time that day I felt a wave of relief wash over me. "I thought for sure Demetrious was going to give us away. I can't take much more of this."

"Man that guy is scary," said Emma. "I could see this crazy anger in his eyes. Whatever you decide to do Ella, you cannot go back to him. It would be suicide."

After a few minutes, when I had calmed down I told Emma, "I am not going through something like that again." Then I looked at Demetrious' face. He's so innocent, so loving. I can't let him grow up in a place of violence and fear, I won't. I realized what I had already known deep down. I would do anything to keep Demetrious safe, anything! In that instance, I knew that it was more than just words. I really would do anything to keep Demetrious safe, even if it meant moving to Sky City to become an escort.

"Get me Mia's phone," I said with new found determination. I called Sky City and Jennifer answered.

"Hi Jennifer, it's me, Tesla Miller."

"What can I do for you?" She seemed puzzled and was clearly not expecting to hear back from me so soon.

I swallowed hard and said, "I've decided to take the job."

"Excellent," replied Jennifer as she regained her professional demeanor. "I'll email you additional instructions within the hour along with important information about living in space."

After we hung up, I turned to Emma and said, "I'm doing this for Demetrious and for mom."

"I know," said Emma, and she hugged me with tears streaming down her cheeks. "I love you."

An hour later, just as Jennifer promised, the instructions showed up in Tesla Miller's email. "I have to report to the space port in Brownsville, Texas next week," I said as I read the email. "It says I'm going to have two roommates, Sasha White and Yuri Li."

I looked at them and smiled.

They both work at the Three Dolphins Club, and there's a whole bunch of stuff about how to live in zero-g."

"Can I see that?" asked Emma. "Interesting, it recommends that you cut your hair short."

"Why do I have to cut my hair?" I asked. "I like my long hair."

"It's not required, but it says short hair is much easier to take care of in space."

"Okay," I said. "I guess I'd better read this to see what I've gotten myself into. I'll do it later." I closed the email.

The next day the phone rang.

"It's Alex!" Emma said, before answering. She clicked the 'answer' button, put it on speaker and said, "Hello?"

"Where the fuck is Ella?" demanded Alex.

"Who is this?" Emma replied, smiling at me.

"Her car returned empty, where the fuck are they?" shouted Alex.

"How should I know? Leave me alone," Emma shouted back as she hung up the phone.

"He's really mad. The car made it back and, of course, you and Demetrious weren't there."

Alex called back immediately.

Emma just let it ring. "We need to figure out how to keep you away from your creepy husband until you have to leave."

"Okay, I've got a plan?"

"What is it?" asked Emma.

"Pack, we're leaving."

Using the disposable cell phone we got for Tesla, I called for a rental car. Fifteen minutes later, the driverless car pulled up in front of Emma's dorm and sent a text saying it arrived. "It's here," I exclaimed. "Let's get out of here!"

I grabbed my stuff and Demetrious while Emma grabbed her suitcase. We hurried down the stairs. The rental car was parked right out front with its lights on. We quickly piled into the car and I said, "Albuquerque, New Mexico please."

The car backed out of the parking spot and said, "It will take twelve hours to get to Albuquerque, are you sure that's what you want to do?"

"Yes, do it."

"I don't have to report to the space port in Brownsville for another five days, so I thought we'd travel around to various cities and do some sightseeing and shopping, since I left Alex with nothing but the clothes on my back. Might as well have a little fun before I leave this Earth."

"Okay, sounds great."

"Then, when it's time to leave, we'll drive through Brownsville, and stop just long enough for you to drop me and Demetrious off a few blocks from the spaceport. That way, if Alex ever manages to finds this car, he won't be able to tell we actually went to the spaceport."

"Smart," said Emma.

Twelve hours later, we arrived in Albuquerque.

I felt the pressure grow with each passing day. Even so, five days went by quickly and today was the day. I didn't sleep at all that last night as the stress of the unknown became almost unbearable. I could feel the tightness in my chest all night.

That morning it was a beautiful, sunny day in Brownsville, Texas. Not a cloud in the sky. As planned, we stopped at a convenience store near the spaceport. I hugged my sister and we cried together again.

"I'm doing this for my son and mom," I said finally, more to reassure myself than anything else.

"I know," said Emma encouragingly. "I know."

"It's just that, a week ago I was married and living in Chicago, now I'm probably a fugitive from the law and later today I'll be living in space as a call girl. How did this happen?"

"It seems like the best bad option," Emma replied, trying to be supportive. "You'll be able to keep yourself and Demetrious safe and earn enough money to take care of mom. Besides, it will be Tesla Miller doing these things."

"I know, I just wish there was another way…Hey, I've got an idea," I said trying to smile. "Why don't you go to Sky City and be a space call girl and I'll stay here and pretend to be you and go to school!"

"Ha ha, I'm pretty sure Alex can tell the difference between you and me."

"Maybe if he's drunk enough…Well, anyway, I'm sure going to miss you."

"I got this for you," Emma said. "It's a bag with your new initials on it. See, T.I.M. for Tesla Isabella Miller."

"That's too funny. It's going to take me awhile to get used to that name."

"I love you," said Emma.

"Love you too." I hugged Emma one more time and then took off on foot with Demetrious in one arm and dragging my suitcase behind me with the other.

"Bon Voyage!" Emma called out. "Oh wait, what do they say for astronauts? Godspeed, Ella, I mean Tesla. Godspeed."

And that's how I got here.

We all floated there in silence for a while before Sasha finally said, "I think you did the right thing coming here."

Yuri nodded and then added, "You're part of our family now."
I hugged them both.

Chapter 9 Engineering

I was really looking forward to seeing Marc the next morning to continue our tour of the resort, this time with Demetrious. We met in the lobby. Marc was "sitting" at one of the tables when we arrived.

He smiled broadly when he saw us. "Please, have a seat," he said.

I smiled back. "Ha ha, does everyone tell that same joke up here?" Before he could answer I added, "So where are we going today?"

Marc looked at Demetrious. "Hi Demetrious, you look happy today. Would you like to visit the underbelly of the resort? I'm going to take you to see all the things that make this place function; the things that keep everyone here alive, safe, and warm. Sounds like fun, huh?"

Demetrious just stared at him.

"I knew you'd be excited." Marc turned toward me. "But first Tesla, I thought you might like to go to the Salon. By now you've probably found that having long hair here is a real pain in the ass. They've been working on new zero-g hair styles there, or so I'm told, and well, it's up to you."

I thought for a moment. It's true, my long hair is kind of a pain, and I'm tired of keeping it in a ponytail all of the time. It didn't take me long to figure out that when I don't put it in a ponytail I look like a wild woman. Now that it looks like I'm going to be here a while, I guess I'd better embrace the life style. Plus, Alex would pull me around by my hair when he got mad. Maybe this will be a small step in helping me forget. "Okay. What the hell, let's do it."

The three of us floated "underneath" the lobby, past the Medical/First Aid office over to the Salon. A large high-definition display covered one wall and displayed a dozen different hairstyles. The sign said they were created by Claude Dubois specifically for life in zero-g. As we entered the Salon, Marc whispered in my ear that Mr. Abruzzo hired Claude from Hollywood specifically to create stylish new hairdos for their guests. All the cuts had one thing in common. They were all short hairstyles. Just one more step away from my old, familiar world. I haven't had short hair since, well, never. I can't believe I'm doing this. But then, I can't believe most the things I've been doing recently.

Marc introduced us.

"Ah, Tesla, like the car, no?" Claude said with just a hint of a French accent. He looked intensely at my face as if he were mentally trying different hair styles on me.

"Yes, like the car," I replied, accepting my new identity. "My mom loved that old car, and so, here I am, Tesla."

Claude could tell that I was nervous about getting my haircut and said, "Don't worry, we're going to take good care of you and your hair.

You're going to love it! You are such a beautiful girl, we will make you more beautiful, you will see."

"I hope so because I don't feel so beautiful. Since I arrived here, my face has gotten puffy and my legs look like they belong on a chicken. Now you're going to cut off my hair."

"Not to worry. Do you know what style you'd like? You can pick one of those," Claude said motioning to the high-definition display of hair styles, "or I can create one just for you and your beautiful face."

"One just for me? I like the sound of that. Okay, let's try that, but what if…?"

"You'll love it, trust me," interrupted Claude.

He was a hair styling genius, which is why Abruzzo hired him. When he was done, the result was striking. I looked at my face in the high-definition display, it was zoomed in so I appeared about five times bigger than life. "Wow! This is wonderful," I exclaimed. "Thank you so much!" I gave him a big hug, then I turned to Marc and said, "What do you think?"

"Excellent," replied Marc. "You know, you can also get other beauty treatments here, manicures, pedicures, all that stuff. But not today. We've got more important things to see. Are you ready to go?"

"Sure," I said turning towards Demetrious. "Do you like Mommy's new hairdo? What's that? You love it? I thought so." I turned back toward Marc, "So, where are we going now?"

"Engineering."

"Seriously? You really know how to entertain a girl."

The three of us went back into the lobby, turned right and headed down the hall toward engineering. The hall was nearly one hundred feet long. We went past the guest suites and the rooms for the employees before finally arriving at engineering.

"The engineering module is twenty six feet in diameter and sixty feet long," Marc started. "It is the single heaviest module in the resort, and it was launched all in one piece by NASA's Space Launch System or SLS. Abruzzo somehow managed to get a special arrangement with the government to get a cut-rate deal on four SLS launches. These were used to launch the four biggest pieces of the resort: engineering, the casino/bar and restaurant, the main restaurant, and the sports arena. All the other parts were launched by Falcon Heavies from Space X. Engineering here houses all of the life support equipment for the resort. All of the air handling, thermal conditioning, carbon dioxide removal, air purification, and humidity control are done here. We have four separate units to do this. The resort can be safely run on just one, but we normally keep two running at all times, the other two are backups."

I listened intently. I was surprised that I actually found this interesting and that I wanted to know everything about how this place worked. Of course, I wasn't going to let Marc know that I thought this was interesting.

"This module also contains all of the equipment for water handling, purification, and recycling." Marc continued. "We recycle all of the water that the resort uses, which is approximately twenty tons per week, and because we bring up about four tons of food and drinks per week for our guests and employees, most of which is water, we are accumulating an excess of nearly four tons of water every week."

"Four tons of water per week. What the heck do you do with all that water. I'm guessing that you can't just throw it overboard."

"Quite right. We sell it to companies who turn it into rocket fuel and sell it to other customers."

"What?" How do you turn water into rocket fuel? You're kidding right?"

"I never joke about space propulsion," Marc replied in a way that suggested he was clearly not taking himself too seriously. "Anyway, they split the water into hydrogen and oxygen; same propellants that used to power the old Space Shuttles."

"Oh shit, they really do turn water into rocket fuel."

Marc smiled. "Yes, all it takes is electricity. Speaking of electric power, all of the power for the resort goes through engineering as well. The power is generated by huge solar arrays, those big circular fan-shaped things you saw when we approached the resort. There's a large bank of batteries here too that are used to power the resort when our orbit takes us through the Earth's shadow. Thermal control for the entire facility is managed here as well. The solar arrays generate about three megawatts of electrical power and each person generates about a hundred watts of thermal heat, so we have to get rid of all that waste heat or the resort will get too hot. There are two air locks here so we can go outside the resort to do repairs when necessary. Finally, engineering has all the hardware necessary to maintain the attitude of the resort in space. So, that's pretty much it. What do you think?"

"The resort has an attitude? When Demetrious gives me some attitude I tell him to knock it off."

"Very funny. In this case attitude means the orientation of the resort in space."

I looked at Marc and smiled. "Of course it does."

"Come here," he said, grabbing my hand.

I was getting to like Marc's hand in mine... Don't get involved I cautioned myself.

"Beneath engineering is our storage facility."

"I can't wait to see that," I said with just the right touch of sarcasm.

Marc took us out of engineering and through the entrance to the adjacent storage module. "This module is made of two twenty-six-foot diameter by thirty-foot long segments. Together they're the same size as the engineering module. This where we store all the food, drinks, oxygen, water, towels, and other supplies needed by the resort. There's a docking port on the front end so that supply ships can dock there and unload the supplies we need directly into the storage facility."

I wasn't impressed, I mean come on, it was just a big storage room.

"I can see you're not impressed" said Marc, "You're right, it's not that interesting. So let's go see something that is kind of cool."

"Okay! Anything to get out of the storage room." I flashed Marc a warm smile.

"Follow me."

Marc led us to a door at the end of the storage facility. "Sky City, open the service tunnel."

The door opened revealing tunnel that looked to be six or seven feet in diameter. It seemingly went on forever. I couldn't see the end.

"This service tunnel is two hundred sixty feet long and runs 'under' the entire resort from end-to-end. From it, you can get to any location in the resort. Approximately half way down the tunnel there's an intersection where it branches off to the right and left. If you go straight all the way for two hundred sixty feet you'll come up under the kitchen for the main restaurant. If you only go half the length, about a hundred feet, you'll be under the Medical/First Aid office, the salon, and the lobby. Take the left branch and you'll go under the carnival room, fitness room and then the sports arena. Take the right branch instead and you go under the casino and eventually the Three Dolphins Club. This is a safety feature that provides an alternate route through the resort, but mostly we use it to deliver food, drinks, and other supplies to the restaurants and bars without having to go through the halls used by the guests. Want to play a game?"

"Sure!" I said enthusiastically. "What kind of game?"

"Push off here, fly like superman and see if you can get all the way to the other end of the tunnel, two hundred sixty feet away, without touching the walls. When you get there, turn around and land on your feet. Got it?"

"What do I win if I do it? I asked.

"I'll buy you lunch."

"Deal!"

"Here, I'll show you how it's done."

Marc grabbed Demetrious, pushed off smoothly and glided straight down the tunnel, disappearing into the dimly lit tunnel.

"Do it just like that," he yelled down the tunnel.

Still determined to show him that I wasn't a complete Grounder. I carefully positioned myself at the center of the tunnel, took a deep breath, and cautiously pushed off. It was a good start, straight, with little noticeable rotation. I wasn't going very fast, but after a while I realized that two hundred sixty feet is a long way, long enough that by the time I had traveled roughly two thirds of the way I was skimming along just inches from the side and doing my best to control my body to avoid scraping the wall. About thirty feet from the end, I hit the wall. Rubbing against it stopped me completely just sixteen feet from the end.

"Not bad for a Grounder," Marc said grinning. "Much better than my first attempt and close enough. Let's go eat, my treat."

Sweating from the effort to avoid the wall as long as I could, I looked at Marc and smiled, "Thanks!"

...

While we were enjoying another excellent lunch in the main dining room, I looked at Marc and asked, "When we arrived at the resort a few days ago I asked you then why it didn't look like a real space station. You know, like a large rotating wheel or something like that. But you never really answered. So now I was wondering if you could tell me why Sky City isn't like that?"

Marc grinned, but before he could answer, George and Jennifer came over.

"We saw the three of you over here, mind if we join you for lunch?" asked George.

"Not at all," replied Marc, motioning for them to join us.

"Hi Demetrious, you little cutie" said Jennifer. "Do you remember me?" Demetrious smiled at her. "I just love this little boy."

"I was just about to tell Tesla why Sky City isn't a large rotating wheel like you see in old sci-fi movies," Marc said.

"Well by all means please do, I'd like to hear this myself," said George.

"The only reason for having a rotating space station that looks like a big wheel is to create artificial gravity, right?" Marc started, ignoring George's sarcasm. "The higher the level of gravity you want, the bigger the facility has to be or the faster the rotation rate. Creating an artificial gravity equal to that on the Earth isn't easy. It would require a very large structure, something like a mile in diameter, and then you'd have to spin it at about one revolution per minute—equivalent to the second hand on a clock. This would be really hard to design and build. If you did manage to build it, it would be hard to spin up and then hard to maintain.

"What Marc is trying to say is that it would be a lot more expensive," George interjected.

"Quite right," said Marc. "Warning I'm about to nerd out a little here."

"Here we go," said George as he and Jennifer glanced at each other and smiled.

"If the facility is of a more manageable size, say six hundred feet in diameter instead of a mile, the rotation rate would have to be very high to produce 1 g like on Earth. But the resulting artificial gravity would be weird, not at all like what you experience on Earth. You'd get all sorts of downright bizarre effects."

"Like what?" I asked.

"Well, let's see. There was this company, remember George, Space Hotels International—went by the acronym SHI—that built a rotating resort. It was 500 feet in diameter. I know that because it's now a classic example of what not to do, kind of like the Tacoma Narrows bridge. You see, they built this recreation center in the resort complete with a basketball court. They were thinking how awesome it would be to play basketball in space. Anyway, it's an understatement to say that it didn't go as planned. People would stand at the free throw line and shoot at the basket and even though they would throw the ball forward, they were astonished to see that it would reverse direction in midair and land behind them. Of course people posted the videos on line. It wasn't long before people started adding a *T* to end of their acronym. They never recovered from this and went bankrupt in less than a year."

"Yeah, that was hysterical," added George. "You can still find some of those old basketball videos on YouTube."

"To prevent this you've got to make the facility big, as I said, over a mile in diameter, if you want to create a 1-g environment that's similar to Earth's. Rotating facilities are also affected by gyroscopic forces, making them difficult to point where you want, and they are sensitive to the distribution of mass round the facility making it difficult to maintain a stable spin state."

"But a non-rotating facility like Sky City doesn't have any of these problems. Right Marc?" asked George rhetorically.

"That's right. It doesn't need to be nearly as strong because it doesn't have to withstand the mechanical stresses created by rotation. This makes it much simpler to design and build and since the environment is basically the same at all locations inside, essentially zero-g, it enables the use of all of the interior volume."

I just stared at Marc, enjoying his enthusiasm as he rattled off all this technical mumbo-jumbo.

"Therefore," George jumped in again, "it's much less expensive to create and operate non-rotating space facilities."

"And we have proof that this is true," said Marc. "People have been living in space continuously since way back in 2001 and every one of them, with the brief exception of the people on the "SHIT" resort, has lived in a non-rotating space facility," Marc said, making air quotes around SHIT.

"But none of that really matters," George interrupted one more time, "compared to the real reason for not building a rotating space facility."

"And what would that be, George?" Jennifer asked sweetly while trying unsuccessfully to make her well-rehearsed question sound fresh.

"Good question, Jennifer," replied George now in full sales mode. "As Marc said, the whole point of rotating a space facility is to create gravity, which is wacky because you can get plenty of that on Earth. In fact, you can't escape gravity on Earth. Am I right?"

"That's right, George," said Jennifer right on cue.

"Thank you dear," replied George. "So why the hell would you go to all the trouble of building a space facility and then rotate it to create the same gravity that you have on Earth, the same gravity that you fought so hard against to get into space? It makes absolutely no sense. In fact, it's stupid. The absence of gravity is the *only* thing you can get in space that you can't get on Earth. It is the *raison d'etre* for space resorts."

I watched as Marc sat back and smiled. He'd clearly heard this sales pitch many times before.

George continued on, "If you build a rotating space facility with artificial gravity that matches that on Earth all you've done is created a really crappy place to live, a place that has very little to offer and has very serious drawbacks. Compared to living on Earth such a facility would be tiny, cramped, very difficult to get to, subject to very hot temperatures in the sun and extreme cold in the shade. It would be surrounded by the deadly vacuum of space, and would be bathed in dangerous radiation. It would be easier to live in the worst place on Earth than in such a facility."

"What if you take away gravity?" Jennifer continued on script.

"I'm glad you asked, Jennifer. Take away gravity and now you've got something altogether different. Take away gravity and you've got something fantastic, something that makes it worth the trouble of getting to, something that's worth the trouble of dealing with the hard vacuum and the temperature extremes and the radiation. Now you've got a unique resource, a unique place to play, a place of new opportunities, and if you do it right, a paradise. The biggest problem with zero-g facilities like Sky City is the limited imaginations of the minds of Earth-bound designers like Marc. No offense Marc."

"None taken," replied Marc smiling.

"And once you have lots of people living in space," George went on, "they will literally re-invent everything for use in zero-g. Everything that people use, touch, wear, watch, eat, work with, and play with will be re-invented, generating vast new economic opportunities. Add to this the availability of virtually unlimited power from the sun and material resources from near-Earth asteroids and you've got an engine for economic growth unparalleled in human history."

"Zero-g, that's it?" I said skeptically. "You're selling the absence of something?"

"Yes, my dear! But not the absence of just anything, it's the absence of gravity. Gravity permeates every aspect of people's lives. It is so pervasive, and so dominates how people live that most scarcely give it a second thought—which is why falling often comes as such a surprise. People will be drawn to space because of the absence of gravity. This is the foundation of the economic engine that will drive actual settlements in space—the availability of something you can't get anywhere else."

"You believe this too?" I said looking at Marc.

"Yes, definitely. That's why I'm here. I met George when I finished graduate school and he tells me his vision about how space provides this huge economic potential for whichever nation successfully exploits it first, and I was in."

"If it's such a good thing why hasn't anyone done this before?"

Marc looked at me and smiled and nodded in a way that suggested he thought that was a good question.

"Well, for a long time, human spaceflight was something that only governments could afford, and even they struggled with the cost," replied Marc. "The fundamental problem was that after NASA successfully landed people on the Moon no one could figure out why we still had a human spaceflight program or what it was supposed to accomplish. For fifty years no one could articulate why the American people should pay large sums of money to send astronauts to into space. Now, most people knew we didn't want stop doing this because it would look like the United States was pulling back from the space frontier. But NASA's stated goal of sending astronauts to Mars was too expensive. A popular alternative of sending people back to the Moon was also too expensive and suffered from the 'been there, done that' problem. So the compromise was to do the least expensive thing possible while still being able to claim that we still had a human spaceflight program, and that was to send astronauts to low-Earth orbit. And that's exactly what NASA did, send people to low-Earth orbit for fifty years! Then they wondered why there was little excitement for what they were doing. In the meantime, NASA did endless studies on how to send people to Mars. It wasn't until the 2020s that the

U.S. fully embraced the idea that NASA's true mission was to facilitate the economic expansion of the country into space."

"And so, here we are," said George. "This facility wouldn't have been possible without the support of NASA and the U.S. government."

"That's right," added Marc, "You see, NASA built this fantastic rocket, but it was also fantastically expensive so NASA couldn't afford to fly it very often, and couldn't afford to build the payloads it was designed for. So George here managed to convince the government to give him a really good deal on four SLS launches, which we used to launch the four biggest pieces of Sky City."

"I remember you said that earlier. How did you manage that?" I asked turning toward George.

"Well look," replied George. "It's like this. We need science, private industry, and the government all working together to create the best economy. Science discovers new concepts about the way nature works. Government opens up new economic frontiers and provides necessary infrastructure. Private industry combines these to create new products, new markets, and new wealth. The government then taxes the resulting profits to provide safety and security, tame markets from abusing the people they're supposed to serve, and fund new scientific research. Simple! It was 'the government taxes these profits part' that sold them. In any case, a few courageous leaders at NASA recognized the potential economic impact to any nation that could successfully colonize space and so here we are."

"OK, that was a lot more explanation than I was expecting, but thanks." Wow, these guys are really serious about this stuff.

"Have you told her why you're here?" George said to Marc.

"No, but I was going to show her tomorrow. If she's interested," Marc replied, turning his head to look at me.

I smiled broadly and nodded, "I'm interested."

The next day I met Marc in the lobby without Demetrious. Leslie wanted to watch him for the day, which I thought was great. Everyone is so nice up here.

"So what are we doing today?" I asked as I approached Marc. "Haven't we seen pretty much all of Sky City?"

"Yes, we're done with Sky City, so we're leaving."

A combination of confusion and worry crept over my face and I fired questions at Marc in rapid succession. "Leaving? What do you mean were leaving? Where would we go? I can't leave. What about Demetrious?"

"Relax," Marc said calmly. "We're just going next door, sort of. George is already starting on the construction of a much bigger resort and a special event is taking place there today that I insist on being present for."

"A new resort? But didn't this one just open? I thought this was a new resort?

"It is, but George is confident it will be highly profitable and is already working on a bigger and better one."

"The man's got big cojones, I'll give him that. What's the special event?

"You'll see. Follow me, we have to go to engineering, then board a taxi."

"A taxi, really?" I said incredulously. Seems I never know when Marc is kidding or not. "They have taxis here?"

"Come on." Marc took my hand again and started towing me toward engineering.

We made our way through the engineering module, through the docking adapter and into the taxi. Marc said the taxi was a fully automated, in-space transportation vehicle.

"Sky City II, please," Marc commanded once we got in.

The computer recognized Marc's voice and replied, "It's an hour's trip to Sky City II, please confirm that is where you want to go."

"Confirmed," said Marc. The doors closed, first on both the resort side and then on the taxi side.

"Sky City II? Not very original," I teased.

Then nothing happened. Marc said we had to wait as the taxi made all the necessary safety checks. When that was complete I felt the taxi depart from the resort with a small jolt that caused me to grabbed a hold of Marc to steady myself. I looked into those blue eyes and smiled coyly. "Oh, uh sorry," as I took longer to let go of him than was actually necessary.

The taxi looked nothing like the space plane that brought us up from Earth. It was much smaller, maybe just big enough for about six people and there were, of course, no seats. By now I didn't expect there to be any. There were handholds instead. The kind you'd find in subway cars on Earth. The view was spectacular. Marc confirmed that the windows covering the sides and ceiling were actually high definition displays like in my apartment. They sure look like windows though. After forty-five minutes, I could see something in the distance. Fifteen minutes after that we were docked to a single large cylindrical structure.

"This facility is temporarily outfitted to house the construction workers for the new resort," Marc said. "It's fairly short on creature comforts compared to Sky City."

"So what's going on here today that's so special?"

"I glad you asked. This new resort is going to be big, just over ten times the size of Sky City. That means it requires a lot building material most of which is dirt for radiation shielding. You see, space is essentially radioactive. To protect everyone living here from that radiation we need to surround the entire resort with a lot of dirt. When finished, Sky City II will have a mass of just over twenty-five thousand tons, most of it just dirt. Using NASA's best rocket, the SLS, it would take a hundred seventy five years to launch that much dirt into space. So we're obviously not going to do that. Today you're going to see where we get the all the dirt from."

"Woohoo! You brought me out here to see dirt! Be still my beating heart."

Marc put his arm around my waist and pulled me close. "Nothing but the best for you."

He was about to kiss me when the taxi doors opened. He let go and we floated into the facility. As we entered the construction zone, I heard catcalls from the workers, most of whom were men. I took Marc's hand and smiled.

"Knock it off you guys," said Marc. "This is Tesla Miller from Sky City. Be nice to her or you'll find yourself on the wrong side of the airlock."

Tesla Miller from Sky City. I ran the words over in my mind. How fantastic that sounds. I'm no longer Ella Markov from Chicago, now I'm Tesla Miller from Sky City. I actually live in space. I'm from space! When I go back to Earth and people ask me where I'm from, I'll say, I'm Tesla Miller from Sky City. How cool is that?

"Are we on schedule?" Marc asked.

"Yes," replied Robert.

"Tesla, this is Robert Garrison, he's in charge of the operation today."

"Pleased to meet you." He looked like a typical engineer. Flat top hair style from the 1950's, white dress shirt, neatly groomed. He's pretty buff though, and it doesn't look like he smiles much.

"Nice to meet you too," replied Robert somewhat abruptly.

"Robert here is an extremely good engineer with an obsessive-compulsive attention to detail, which is exactly what this activity requires," explained Marc.

"Hey, I'm just thorough," Robert interjected, but clearly not offended.

"Today he's bringing in an asteroid with a mass of just over forty thousand tons," Marc continued. "Robert has brought in other, smaller asteroids before. In fact, they were used to provide the radiation shielding for Sky City, but he has never brought in one that was anywhere near this massive.

"How does he do that?" I said looking at Marc. I surprised myself in that I actually really wanted to know. Weird. Ella Markov wouldn't have cared at all about this.

"We're just going through the final perigee pass right now," said Robert dispassionately. "Then one more burn fifty minutes later and she's ours."

"He's bringing in the near-Earth asteroid that goes by the catchy name *2023 HU2*," said Marc. "It's a one hundred foot diameter carbonaceous chondrite asteroid discovered by NASA's NEOCam spacecraft in 2023."

"Riiight." I said, intentionally drawing out the word. "You want to try that again?"

"As I said, Sky City II needs a lot of dirt for radiation shielding. We can't afford to bring that dirt up from Earth, so we bring it down from deep space. As you might remember from school, located between Mars and Jupiter is the main asteroid belt, which contains millions of asteroids."

Actually, I didn't remember that, but I wasn't about to let Marc know that.

"What you probably didn't learn, however, is that over time, various small forces can change the orbits of these asteroids and some of them occasionally wind up in places where the gravity from Jupiter or Mars messes with their orbits flinging them onto new orbits that bring them into inner solar system close to the Earth. Somewhat uncreatively, planetary scientists have called these asteroids, the ones whose orbits bring them near to the Earth, *near-Earth asteroids*. It was a really big version of one of these objects, by the way, that wiped out the dinosaurs some sixty-five million years ago. Nevertheless, they represent some of the easiest places in the solar system to obtain the dirt we need for radiation shielding. Now maybe you're thinking, Marc, why not just get material from the Moon? It's big, it's close, what's wrong with that?

"Actually, I wasn't thinking that at all," I replied. "I was thinking, dinosaurs? How did dinosaurs get into this conversation?"

"Work with me here," replied Marc smiling. "The problem is that the Moon is too big. It has too much gravity. It's hard to land on and hard to get back off because of its gravity. It turns out that there are something like a hundred twenty thousand near-Earth asteroids bigger than a hundred feet in diameter that are easier to get material from than the surface of the Moon. So, in the year 2022, NASA launched the NEOCam spacecraft designed to hunt for undiscovered asteroids in the space close to Earth. In 2023, this spacecraft discovered the very dark asteroid given the designation *2023 HU2* that identifies when it was discovered. A few years ago we sent a robot spacecraft there to capture it and bring it back here so we could use it for radiation shielding."

"Uh, okay, that was an explanation only an engineer could love. So how do you move an asteroid? Is that even possible?"

"It most definitely is," replied Marc enthusiastically. You see, around 2015 NASA designed, but never launched, an Asteroid Retrieval Vehicle, or ARV for short. NASA's ARV was designed with a high-power ion drive system that would have enabled it to catch up with, capture, and retrieve entire near-Earth asteroids weighing up to about a thousand metric tons. This would have been humanity's first demonstration of how to exploit the material resources of space on a large scale. But, as I said NASA never launched the ARV, so we took the design, scaled it up by a factor of ten and started retrieving asteroids ourselves. Asteroid *2023 HU2* is our latest and greatest catch. It was just the right size for the new resort and was naturally coming back near the Earth at the right time. Importantly, it was coming by slowly enough that our ion drive system could bring it back."

"Ion drive?" I asked, and then almost immediately regretted it.

"Yes, ion drive. The best rocket technology ever developed for moving around in space."

"Exactly what I was thinking," I said sarcastically.

Undeterred, Marc continued. "It's engines fire out beams of positively-charged particles called ions at a very high speed. Shooting out a beam of high-energy ions in one direction pushes the spacecraft in the opposite direction according to Isaac Newton again. Ion engines are ten times more fuel efficient than regular rockets. There's one problem though. These are high-powered electrical devices and like any good electrical circuit they have to be grounded. Only problem is, there's obviously no ground in space—I'm sorry, I'm just rambling on."

I could tell this was important to Marc and I liked his enthusiasm so I replied somewhat untruthfully, "No, this is very interesting. Please go on."

Marc smiled. "Okay, so anyway, this was a major problem when ion thrusters were first invented, it wasn't clear how to ground them in space. So way back in 1964 NASA flew the Space Electric Rocket Test number one specifically designed to test how to electrically ground ion thrusters in space. It showed that it was easy. All you needed was a device that emitted lots negatively-charged electrons into space near the ion thruster, then the positive ions in the beam naturally drew out exactly the right number of electrons to ground itself. Now, because the ion beam theoretically keeps going forever, the engineers who developed this system started thinking that the electrical ground extended out to infinity—you know, out to where god lives—and began, somewhat tongue-in-cheek, calling this 'God's Ground'."

Marc paused again. I tried hard to make my eyes appear to not be completely glazed over. Apparently convinced that I was still paying attention, he continued. "Now, back to asteroid retrieving. Once the ARV gets to the asteroid it deploys a large bag and we literally bag the sucker. At forty thousand tons, though, the asteroid is much, much heavier than our ARV, so it's a little like a dog chasing a car. What does the dog do if actually catches the car? Anyway, to explain how we get the bagged asteroid back, I will now turn the floor over to the always happy Robert Garrison, engineer extraordinaire."

"You know I have work to do, right?" Robert gruffed.

"I'm sure you can spare one minute out of your busy schedule to explain to the lovely Miss Tesla Miller how to retrieve an asteroid that is the mass of a cruise ship."

"If you insist." Robert spoke rapidly, as if he was trying to get this over with as quickly as possible. "Like all transportation systems it's all about power. It takes a lot power to move this much mass and even then the thing is still pretty much just a big pig that is going to go where it wants to go. The ion drive system gently nudges this pig, slowly modifying its trajectory so that it will fly by close to the Moon. Then we use the Moon's gravity to slow it down. The Moon actually does most of the work of slowing the asteroid down so that we can get it into orbit around the Earth and not have it go flying back off into deep space. God gave us the Moon so we can retrieve near-Earth asteroids."

"Apparently god has a lot to do with moving asteroids," I quipped.

Robert flashed a thin smile then paused for a moment. It appeared he was hoping that Marc would pick up the explanation so he could get back to work. When it was clear Marc wasn't going to jump in Robert's smile faded and he continued.

"Now after a few more maneuvers with our fancy-shmancy ion drive system we put the asteroid on a highly-elliptical orbit... um, make that kind of an egg-shaped orbit, with a perigee, sorry, I mean with a low point in its orbit that dips into Earth's upper atmosphere. Now we use the Earth's atmosphere to slow down the asteroid further. Eventually this lowers the high point in its orbit to be where we are, then all that's left is raising the low point up to our orbit. After that's done we just have to dock the ARV, with its asteroid-in-a-bag, to this facility. That's what we're doing now, the docking, that's the last tricky part. I like to think of it like mating with a Brachiosaurus. Now, while I'm sure two Brachiosauruses could do it without injuring themselves, we've had a lot less practice. Any questions?"

Robert looked pleased with himself, but all I could think of why did dinosaurs keep coming up..

Getting no response, Robert went on, "Today's activity is extremely important. The ARV was launched five years ago to retrieve this asteroid. If we can't dock it successfully, we may not be able to utilize the material it has brought back and the Company will have wasted a few hundred million dollars. Or worse yet," Robert said with a wry smile, "if the vehicle crashes into the construction facility we could lose the asteroid, the capital invested in the ARV, the capital invested in the construction facility, and kill everyone on board."

"Perfect," I said sarcastically. Then I floated over closer to Marc and whispered a little nervously, "He's kidding, right?"

"Yes, he's kidding," Marc whispered back. Then he said to Robert, "It's been a while since you killed everyone on board a space station, right?

Robert gruffed.

"Actually," continued Marc, "Robert's the best there is, and in reality, we wouldn't risk the lives of all these people if we didn't think it could be done safely."

"Awe, you're making me blush," said Robert. "Besides the actual docking is automated. I'm just here to hit the abort button in case something goes wrong, so we can try again later. Automated systems are much better at docking than humans."

"Or Brachiosauruses," added Marc.

...

Right on schedule we saw the ARV with its asteroid-in-a-bag approaching the station. The two large circular solar arrays that Marc said powered the ion drive system dominated the image. I was getting used to seeing those. Everything in space, it seemed, was solar powered. The vehicle plus asteroid now filled the display. It appeared to be motionless, just hanging there in space.

"Why isn't it moving?" I asked. "It looks like it's stuck."

"It is moving relative to us, but very slowly," replied Robert. "Slow is good. Slow is very good. We don't want a repeat of the collision that occurred between the Russian Progress vehicle and the MIR space station back in 1997. In that collision the Progress vehicle was coming in too fast, smashed through one of MIR's solar panels then struck a glancing blow to a newly installed science module. The collision cut the power to the space station in half and created an air leak in the science module. Only quick action by the crew saved their lives." Robert paused for a moment and then said cynically, "I'm sure that won't happen to us today."

I flashed a look of concern at Marc again.

"He's the best there is," Marc repeated. Then turning to look at Robert, Marc quipped, "You're the best, right?"

This time Robert had a concerned look on his face.

"What's up?" asked Marc.

"The approach velocity is at the upper limit of what's acceptable. The docking is going to be a little rougher than I'd like," he said as he kept his finger over the abort button. "The ARV plus the asteroid has a combined mass of just over forty thousand tons. This construction facility has a mass of only sixty tons, that's a lot of mass were about to collide with and the speed is at the upper limit of what the docking mechanism can tolerate. Better grab a hold of something."

Robert addressed the crew of the construction facility and informed them of the imminent docking with the ARV. The approach seemed to take forever as the seconds ticked slowly by. It doesn't look like it's approaching very fast. My eyes were fixed on the display. Then suddenly, I heard the sound of scraping metal. It sounded like metal being torn apart.

I shot a more urgent look of concern at Marc and grabbed his hand. "The sound is being conducted through the docking mechanism, into the structure of the construction facility and transmitted through the air," Marc said in reply to a question I hadn't asked.

Then we felt it. The much greater mass of the asteroid pushed the construction facility backward with a jolt. The facility groaned and shuddered under the strain. Robert and Marc stared intently at the display showing the status of the docking mechanism. One by one indicators for each of the six latching mechanisms turned green.

"Piece of cake," Robert said, the relief obvious in his voice. Then, turning on the intercom and doing his best impersonation of Neil Armstrong, he said, "Sky City II here, the Brachiosaurus has landed."

I could hear cheers from all over the facility.

"That wasn't so bad was it?" said Robert.

"I'm sure you'll do better next time," Marc deadpanned.

"So now what happens?" I asked.

"Now we cut it up and turn it into radiation shielding," replied Marc. "This type of asteroid has a significant amount of hydrated minerals making it a good shield against galactic cosmic rays. The asteroid itself is fairly soft and crumbly, kind of like dried mud, so we'll just break it up and bag it to make it easy to attach to the outside of the resort. This is what we did on Sky City only on a smaller scale. We'll process the leftovers to extract useful elements like oxygen, hydrogen, iron, sulfur, and even some rare-earth metals."

"It's like a buffalo for the American Indians," Robert interjected. "We use every part of it."

"Robert even has his own Haiku about it?" said Marc.

"Of course. Another Haiku, why am I not surprised here in nerd city."

"Sky City," Marc corrected without missing a beat. "Oxygen we can breathe, of course. Hydrogen and oxygen make water, the iron will be used for making super-strong structures, and the sulfur we use as rocket fuel."

I must of had a puzzled look on my face, but didn't say anything. All I knew about sulfur was that is smelled like rotten eggs. Later Marc would tell me that even that wasn't exactly right.

Sensing my confusion and appearing more relaxed now that the critical docking maneuver was complete, Robert warmed up to the task of explaining his life's work. "You see moving these massive asteroids takes a lot of fuel. It takes a lot of fuel even when using a highly fuel-efficient ion drive system. Even with this technology, it takes upwards of a hundred tons of fuel. It's way too expensive to lift that much fuel from Earth. To make matters worse, earlier versions of ion drive systems used xenon as the fuel, an expensive and rare noble gas. A hundred tons of xenon would cost around a hundred million dollars even before you payed to launch it into space. So we have a better way. We extract sulfur from the asteroids we retrieve. It turns out there's a fair amount of sulfur in most asteroids. The asteroid we just brought in should contain about two thousand tons of sulfur, enough to retrieve lots of asteroids. Sulfur is a very light atom so it gives us a high exhaust velocity, which further reduces how much fuel we need. Our propulsion system is designed with ion thrusters connected directly to the solar array. This kind of direct-drive system design was originally invented by NASA in the early 1970's, but wasn't flown in space until we picked it up fifteen years ago. Our approach of using sulfur as the fuel in a direct-drive, solar-powered, ion

94

propulsion system gives us the ability to affordably retrieve these asteroids."

"Thanks." This is all so incredibly cool. I just wish I understood it more. I made a vow to myself that I would.

"We better start heading back to Sky City," Marc said.

"OK.," I replied. "Robert, thank you for your time and congratulations on bringing in the asteroid."

"Yeah, and thanks for not killing us," said Marc.

We turned to leave.

"Wait," I said. "What about your Haiku?"

Without saying a word, Robert pointed to the wall where a framed version of the poem in large letters was displayed. It read,

> Near-Earth asteroids
> Retrieved for exploitation
> Like space Buffalo.

Chapter 11 Sex

It was quiet on the ride back to Sky City with just Marc and me in the taxi by ourselves. I stared out the window. I knew it wasn't really a window, but it didn't matter. It felt like looking out a window. Still in awe of my surroundings, I couldn't get enough of the view. My mind was spinning with questions and emotions. Everyone here seemed so smart, so dedicated to their jobs. I never experienced anything like this before. In college, almost everyone I knew was simply there for the fun of it, almost no one took it seriously. It was different here. They were doing things I never dreamed were possible. I glanced over at Marc. His confidence and passion for his work was such a nice change from Alex's moodiness.

Marc glided over next to me. "I never get tired of the view either," he said breaking the silence. "I just love it here."

"You love it in this taxi?" I deadpanned without looking at him.

"Space is humanity's future," replied Marc, ignoring my quip. "I'm sure of it. We're at a turning point in human history. It's weird that most people don't see it yet."

I turned away from the display and looked at Marc. I've never met someone like this. The people I know don't talk this way. I could feel myself falling for him... I knew I couldn't get involved with him. I knew it would complicate my already overly complicated life. I knew it, but I couldn't help the way I felt. "Maybe people are too caught up in the weird things happening in their own lives to see anything beyond that," I said.

"What do you mean?"

"Well, it's just that weird things seem to keep happening to me lately."

Marc looked at me with sincere interest. "Such as?"

"You don't think floating here alone with you in a taxi in space is weird?"

"Okay, I'll grant you that. Although, it's fairly normal for me. Is that it?"

"God, I wish. No, there have been lots of weird things recently. Like just last week, for example, here's what happened..."

...

Me and my sister Emma were walking across the UCSD campus. *It was to pick up my new identity in the form of a new passport and social security card, but I wasn't about to tell Marc that.* It was Sunday morning and there were very few other people on campus. Suddenly we heard a woman screaming."

"Stop him," the woman yelled, "Someone please help me, he stole my purse."

We turned around and saw a young boy, who couldn't have been more than thirteen years old, running away from a middle-aged woman, who apparently had fallen to the ground and was now was pointing at the boy as he ran away. The young boy had a purse in one hand. Then we noticed a young woman, who looked like a college student, chasing after him. She caught him right in front of Emma and me. She tackled him and they both hit the ground hard. The woman stopped moving. The boy scrambled to his feet and took off running again.

Without thinking, I sprinted after him, and tackled him almost immediately. I thought the boy's head must have hit the ground hard because I felt his body go limp. I saw that his head was bleeding. Oh my god, there was a lot of blood and it started pooling underneath his head. There was blood coming from his ears too. I looked over at Emma, horrified at what just happened. I knelt over the boy. I think he was still breathing, but just barely. "Call 911," I said.

Before Emma could call, the young woman who initially tackled the boy. ran up and said, "What happened? Is he dead? I didn't mean to hurt him." She paused for a moment, the blurted out, "It's all my fault. If I hadn't tackled him, this never would have happened, and over a stupid purse."

"What do you think happened here?" Emma asked, confused about what was going on.

"I saw the boy steal this woman's purse. She yelled for help so I ran after the boy and tackled him." I remember falling. I must have I hit my head because that's all I remember. When I got up and came over here, I saw him lying there in a pool of blood." She paused again and then looked directly at me. "Do you think I'll go to jail? I was just trying to help. I didn't mean for this to happen."

By now, a small crowd was starting to gather. Some people were recording the event on their phones. The police showed up a few minutes later. I wondered how they got there so fast, but then dismissed the thought.

The first officer on the scene checked the boy and said, "I don't think he's going to make it, call for an ambulance, quickly!"

After calling for an ambulance, the other officer addressed the crowd, "What happened here?"

The young woman who initially tackled the boy and who was obviously distraught stepped forward and said in a shaky voice, "It's my fault officer. He stole this woman's purse and I ran after him and tackled him. We both fell to the ground and he must of hit his head really hard. God, I didn't mean to kill him!" She starting to cry again. "I didn't mean to kill him over a purse," she sobbed.

"What's your name?" the officer asked.

"Stacy," she said nervously.

"And where is the woman whose purse was stolen?'

"I don't know." Am I under arrest?'

"We're going to have to take you in for questioning," the officer said. Then he turned to the crowd again, "Did anybody else see what happened?"

People looked around shaking their heads, but nobody moved.

Emma turned to me and whispered, "Nobody else saw what happened, if you don't say anything, no one will ever know you were involved." *And Alex will find you immediately if you get taken to a police station. That's what Emma also said, but I left that part out in retelling the story to Marc.*

I whispered back, "I know, but it's not right…Officer—"

"Don't do it," Emma interrupted.

"Officer, that's not exactly what happened," I said, ignoring my sister.

Emma cringed.

"Did you see what happened?" the officer asked.

"Ella, don't," pleaded Emma.

"This woman, Stacy, I saw her tackle the boy. But he got up immediately and started running again. He would have gotten away too, but then I tackled him, and that's when he hit his head. So, it's my fault not hers."

"And what's your name?" the officer asked.

"Tesla," I said. *Actually I said Ella, but I changed it to Tesla for Marc.* "What's going to happen to me?"

"Like I told that other woman, we're going to have to take you down to the station for questioning."

The realization that it would now only be a short time before Alex would find us hit me harder than I expected. I stared crying.

"It's okay," shouted someone from the crowd.

I turned around and saw a young man coming out of the crowd.

"Hi, I'm Ryan Wilson. Don't worry, you're not going down to the police station and you're definitely not going to be arrested."

"What?" I asked between sobs.

"You've just been part of our school project on moral dilemmas. Can I ask you a few questions?"

"Wait, what?" I was obviously confused.

"It's a school project, see no one was hurt," he said pointing behind me.

I turned around and saw the young boy who was supposedly dying, now standing and smiling.

"That's Tyrone, Stacy is Stacy, that's her real name. She's my sister who 'volunteered' to help us with this project."

"This isn't real?" I asked, still trying to figure out what was going on. "What about the police."

"They're in on it too. This is Bryan who was going to arrest you, and that's Dan over there. They're both just students here. In fact, the entire crowd is in on it. They're all my classmates."

Still not completely certain about what was actually going on, I could feel myself calming down just a little.

"It was just a project to collect data on how people react when put into difficult moral situations. Can I ask you a few questions?"

"Sure, I guess so." I was finally realizing it wasn't real. "I'm just glad I don't have to go down to the police station."

"Are you a student here?"

"Yes," *I lied then and I maintained that lie as I told the story to Marc.*

"Did you believe you would have gotten away with it if you didn't say anything?"

"Yes, I think if I didn't say anything, no one would have known."

"Why did you do it then? Why help out a total stranger if you could have just walked away?"

"I don't know, it just wasn't right. I just couldn't let her, uh Stacy, take the blame for something she didn't do. I guess I couldn't live with myself if I did."

"Well, that's very commendable. It would really help us a lot if you could take a few more minutes and fill out this questionnaire."

I took the questionnaire and saw that there were about a dozen questions. I was so relieved that answering a few questions seemed like a minor inconvenience. I did my best to answer them and then handed the questionnaire back to Ryan.

"Thank you for helping us with our study," Ryan said. "We have a gift certificate for you for your troubles. Dinner for two at a nice local restaurant. Thank you very much." And just like that, they left.

As they walked away, I could see Ryan texting someone.

"Well, that was weird," said Emma.

I nodded in agreement.

...

"I see your point," Marc said. "That was weird." He drifted closer to me and asked gently, "So why are you here?"

Uncertain if I should trust him. Uncertain of everything, I didn't respond. I already took a big risk telling the truth about my past to Sasha and Yuri, I wasn't ready to do that with Marc as well.

"Why does a stunningly beautiful woman with a six-month old baby leave her home on Earth and everyone she knows to work as an escort in space?

He thinks I'm beautiful! No! Don't go there. Don't get emotionally involved. Stick to your cover story. "As I told Mr. Abruzzo, the money was just too good to pass up."

"Don't you want anything more than just money? What do you really want?"

What I want is to keep away from my abusive husband. That's what I'd like to say, but I don't dare. After a long pause I said, "I just want a safe place to raise Demetrious."

"So whatever you left behind wasn't safe."

"I didn't say that." Then, I tried to change the subject. "What did you mean humanity will never be the same?"

Marc paused as if caught off guard by my abrupt attempt to change the subject. "What? Oh, uh we're changing the course of history right now," Marc replied tersely, then added, "What was so unsafe that you had to run here to get away from it?"

"I'd rather not talk about it."

"Remember, George doesn't like secrets."

"Mr. Abruzzo already knows."

"Then why can't you tell me?"

"I said I don't want to talk about it!" That came out with a harshness that surprised even me. I turned back and stared out the 'window'.

Marc fell silent. Neither one of us said another word for the rest of the trip.

...

Soon after we got back to Sky City, I picked up Demetrious and made a video call to Mia back at UCSD. Mia answered the call. "Hi Mia, it's Ella. I hate to bother you, but do you think you could find Emma for me? I need to talk to her."

"No problem, I'll just walk down the hall and see if she's there."

A few minutes later Emma's larger-than-life image filled the left half of the wall-to-wall display in my room while the other half still displayed a view from outside the resort.

100

"Hi Ella!" Emma said excitedly. "How are you? Thank goodness you're okay. I've been so worried since we hadn't heard from you."

"Hi Emma. You would not believe what has been happening here. If you could just see what I'm looking at right now, it's indescribable."

"What are you doing?"

"Demetrious and I are in our room floating in front of a wall-to-wall display showing a view of the Earth passing by below. Just fabulous. Demetrious really seems to like it here."

"What about you? Do you like it there?"

I thought for a moment. I did I like it here? I wasn't sure. "Everything is so strange here," I said finally. "But I'm trying to getting used to it. I absolutely love being weightless and floating around. But I got really sick my first day here."

"You got sick? Are you okay? How's Demetrious?"

"I'm fine. They said it was just the space barfs. I guess it happens to a lot of people who come up here."

"How are your roommates? Did you meet them yet?"

"Yes, my two roommates, Sasha and Yuri, are very nice. We've been getting along great. They've even been helping take care of Demetrious. What's the latest regarding you know who?"

"I haven't heard a thing. He hasn't contacted me, neither have the police. And there's been nothing in the news."

"That's weird. I wonder what's going on?"

"I don't know. I'll call from Mia's phone if I hear anything."

"Okay."

"You look and sound good! Love your new hair style!"

"Yeah, they were right. Long hair is a real pain up here so I cut it. Still feels weird to me, I hardly recognized myself."

"I hesitate to ask this, but how's the job? Have you.. you know?"

"I actually haven't started yet. Mr. Abruzzo gives everyone a week to get used to living here. I get my first client on Sunday. I'm really scared about that. I don't know if I can go through with it. I'm trying not to think about it until I have to."

"Just remember, you're doing this for Demetrious and mom," Emma said, trying to be encouraging.

"I met this guy."

"What? You met a guy? What do you mean you met a guy?"

"Well, he's some kind of engineer and he works up here. I thought he was kind of nerdy when I first met him. But now...I don't know, he seems...interesting. But I kind of told him to leave me alone this afternoon, so now I think he hates me."

"Good! The last thing you need is to mess up your life further with another relationship. Technically, you're still married."

"Technically, Ella is still married," I corrected.

"Good point. "We talked for another hour before finally hanging up." It was so nice to talk to her. It helped me feel normal again, if only for a little while.

...

Demetrious and I were alone in our apartment. I turned to look at him and said, "Well, it's Thursday night in Sky City, what do you want to do?" Demetrious stared at me with that cute little smile of his. "Oh, not talking, eh?"

Just then the phone rang and Marc Elliot's larger-than-life image appeared on the display. "Answer with image," I said. The computer made both audio and video connections.

"Hi Marc." I was surprised to hear from him.

"Hi Tesla, Hi Demetrious," Marc said. "I just wanted make sure you were okay. I had a good time today and I hope I didn't offend you this afternoon by asking questions that were too personal. You're right it's none of my business."

"That's okay." He's apologizing, interesting.

"So let me make it up to you. Tomorrow is Friday and I thought, well, if you and Demetrious don't have anything to do that maybe the three of us could go out together."

"What do you mean out?" I teased. "I hope we aren't going to go catch more asteroids"

"No, no, I just meant out, like uh, you know, on a date. Would you and Demetrious like to go out with me tomorrow night?

"Well, I don't know, we'll have to check our busy schedules. What do people do on a Friday night in Sky City?"

"I thought we'd start with dinner, I know this great restaurant at the end of the resort. Then we could try our luck at the casino, and at midnight they turn the sports arena into a movie theater."

"Looks like you're in luck, Demetrious and I just happen to be free tomorrow night. Will you be picking us up in your car, or do we have to walk?"

Marc smiled. "Excellent! How's seven pm?"

"Great. okay, see you then." I smiled as I ended the call. I guess he doesn't hate me after all…Then the little voice in my head asked, what happened to the plan to not get involved with someone right now? Screw that, I responded.

...

Marc arrived at exactly at seven pm. I answered the door wearing one of the new outfits provided by the Three Dolphins Club. It was a skintight shirt and pants outfit. In zero-g, I've learned, clothes don't hang on you like they do on Earth. Instead, they simply float around your body. For clothes to look sexy in space, they have to be tight. These clothes were tight.

"Wow," said Marc when he saw what I was wearing.

"Do you like it?" Of course, I already knew the answer based on the look on his face.

"It's okay," Marc deadpanned with a smile.

The three of us made our way to the restaurant. There were only two restaurants in Sky City, the main one that we were in now and one in the casino, so the restaurant was quite crowded. The hostess showed us to our table and we ordered drinks and dinner.

When our drinks arrived, Marc raised his glass and said, "Here's to living in space, may we live long and prosper."

He looked a little disappointed and said, "You know, Star Trek, live long and prosper?"

I shook my head, smiled at him and said, "Here's to living in space."

Marc Looked around at the crowded restaurant while we were waiting for our food to arrive said, "Would you like to play a game?"

"Sure. What kind of game?"

"It's a game based on Randolph's Razor."

"Randolph's Razor?" Here we go again, what the heck is Randolph's Razor.

"I'm glad you asked," Marc replied with a devilish grin. "You see, there's a well-known scientific principle called Occam's Razor. It says other things being equal, simpler explanations are generally better than more complex ones. This works because for any phenomenon you could make up a nearly infinite number of possible explanations for how it works, so to cut through most of the bullshit, simpler theories are preferable to more complex ones. Okay so far?"

"Not really. But I'm sure that won't stop you."

"Quite right. So Randolph's Razor is just the opposite. It says, for lack of evidence to the contrary, make up the most interesting explanation. I'll show you how it works. See that woman over there to your right having a drink at a table by herself?"

I glanced over to my right. "Yes, I see her."

"One explanation for why she's alone is that she simply arrived at the restaurant early and is waiting for her husband to join her. That would be a perfectly reasonable, but boring explanation."

"And probably the right one," I interrupted.

"Well, see, that's the thing. You don't actually know. So a more interesting explanation would be, uh let's see, that she's alone because she's actually a serial killer who marries wealthy men and then kills them to acquire their money." Marc seemed pleased with this idea and continued. "She's alone now because she's between victims and has decided to treat herself to a 'well deserved' vacation up here with her recently deceased husband's money."

Marc's devilish grin spread to my face. "Or," I jumped in, "she's here looking for her next victim since there are a lot of wealthy men here."

"That's right," said Marc. "Go on."

"Well, she doesn't keep the money for herself. She gives most of it away to charities. She gives the money to organizations that help battered women escape from their abusive husbands because her first husband physically abused her. She sees herself as performing a public service."

Marc stared at me for a moment without saying anything as if wondering whether there was a deeper meaning here. Finally he asked, "Anything else?"

"I think she's got her eye on you," I grinned.

A few minutes later our food arrived. Dinner was excellent as usual.

...

After dinner we went to the casino. As we entered, Marc ever the engineer, explained its design, "The floor here cuts the cylinder that forms the basic structure of the casino into two equal halves. This a two-level design maximizes the floor space in each level. The 'lower' level, relative to our current orientation, is the mirror image of the 'upper level' and both use the same floor. That is, the 'upper' level uses the 'top' side of the floor and the 'lower' level uses the 'bottom' side. Both levels are decorated so that there is a clear 'up' and 'down'. Except that, the 'up' for the 'upper' level is in the opposite direction from the 'up' in the 'lower' level. This is not generally a problem since casino guests can usually only see one level at a time. Only in going from one level to the other is there the possibility for momentary confusion."

We glided over to one of the roulette tables. Marc explained how the table was modified to work in zero-g, something about centrifugal force, I don't know, but it obviously worked. Then he added that the odds for zero-g roulette are identical to those of their Earth-bound cousins. I quickly tired of losing money. "How does the craps table work?" I asked, wanting to try something different.

We glided over to the crowded craps table, squeezed in, and slid our feet under the foot restraints on the floor. The craps table looked almost identical to those on Earth except for the clear covers that slid into place when it was time to throw the dice in order to keep them from escaping. Marc said the dice were made of iron and the table was covered with a thin layer of weak permanent magnets underneath the green felt. Just like on Earth the shooter would throw the dice to the end of the table where they had to bounce off the padded wall before coming to rest on the magnetic surface. He said the chips were also iron, enabling us to place our bets by simply putting them on the table just like on Earth. Craps was a lot more fun than roulette and we played for over an hour, taking turns throwing the dice and holding Demetrious.

We decided to skip the midnight movie. Marc was staying in one of the suites that hadn't been booked that week. He said that Mr. Abruzzo always provided him the best accommodations available. Marc asked me if I'd like to see it.

"Only if I can bring my friend here," I said looking at Demetrious, who had fallen asleep some time ago.

"Yes, of course, that's what I meant," Marc said sheepishly.

The three of us left the casino, traveled through the hotel lobby and turned left into the hall leading to the suites. Not much farther down the hallway, in the same direction, were the staff rooms including mine. We entered Marc's suite and he commanded the display to show a view from the resort looking down at the Earth. He dimmed the room lights and the display dimmed in response. Demetrious was still sound asleep.

Marc and I hung there motionless in space looking at the stunning view of the Earth below. The wrap-around effect of the two large displays was spectacular. It was nighttime on Earth, at least the part that we could currently see and the European continent was brilliantly lit up.

"I never get tired of looking at this," Marc said.

I nodded in silence.

Marc reached out, put his hand on the small of my back, and I felt him give me a very gentle push. This had the effect of causing us to drift slowly towards each other. I looked at Marc and those beautiful blue eyes. What a strange and wonderful feeling. When we got close enough, Marc kissed me. It was a soft, gentle, wonderful kiss and I kissed him back. My heart started racing. I hadn't kissed anyone but Alex for years and this was wonderful. Marc was holding me close now. It was a delightful sensation, I could feel nothing but Marc holding me, just the two of us suspended there in space, floating. He kissed me again. I didn't want this moment to end.

I no sooner finished that thought when Demetrious woke up crying. He was more screaming than crying actually, at a pitch designed to get maximum attention from anyone nearby. I whispered to Marc, "I'm sorry," and turned toward Demetrious. I grabbed him, held him close and patted his back, but he wouldn't stop crying. I looked at Marc who was clearly uncertain about how to deal with a crying baby. "I better take him back to my place," I said.

"Uh okay," replied Mark, and then added with a smile, "Thanks for an almost unforgettable night."

I kissed him goodnight and left with Demetrious still screaming. Once in the hall I looked at Demetrious and said sweetly, "So, you just couldn't have stayed asleep for just one more hour, eh?"

...

The next morning, I told Sasha and Yuri what happened the night before.

Sasha immediately said, "You should call him."

Surprised, I said, "I can't do that. Shouldn't I just wait for him to call me?"

"Look," said Yuri, "Sasha's right. He's a nerdy engineer. I know this type. You could wait forever for him to call again. Besides, he'd be really flattered if you did."

I looked at Sasha for help and said, "Do you really think I should?"

"Absolutely, Yuri knows what he's talking about when it comes to men. Just don't sound too needy. Guys don't like that."

So I called Marc and asked him if he wanted to go workout with me.

Marc replied, "I'm actually on my way over to Sky City II right now, so I can't."

Shit. I glared at Sasha as if to say, he's brushing me off!

"I see." The disappointment was obvious in my voice. "I just thought that since we're supposed to work out for two hours a day we could've done it together."

"I have to work at Sky City II all day today," replied Marc. "But if you and your noisy friend are free this evening, perhaps we could have dinner together again tonight."

"Well, I don't know," I said coyly. "You're not planning on taking us to the same restaurant, are you?"

"I know this great café in the casino. They serve the best sushi you can get above the Earth's atmosphere. I get back about six pm and could pick the two of you up at seven again."

"Sounds great, see you then." I hung up the phone and smiled at Sasha and Yuri. "It worked!"

"Of course," replied Yuri.

...

Marc again arrived right at seven pm to pick us up. I answered the door wearing another skintight outfit.

"God, I love these outfits," Marc said when he saw me. He looked over at Demetrious. "Hi Demetrious, you look happy. You're not going to cry all night tonight are you?"

We made our way down the hall, through the lobby and turned right into the casino. The café was located roughly in the center of the casino on the "upper level" assuming the "up" direction was that indicated by the design of the resort's lobby. George and Leslie happened to be in the restaurant and when George spotted us he waved for us to come over.

"Please join us for dinner," George said.

"How's my precious little boy?" Leslie said to Demetrious as we approached their table.

"He's doing very well," I said. "He really likes floating around here."

"Leslie and I are celebrating our thirtieth wedding anniversary today," said George.

"Oh, in that case, we don't want to impose," protested Marc.

"Nonsense, I insist," said George. "What are you drinking?" George ordered us drinks as we gathered around the table.

Thirty years, wow, that seems like such a long time. They seem so happy together, even though they look so mismatched. George is such a big guy and Leslie is a beautiful, small Asian woman.

"So what have you two been doing today on your anniversary?" I asked.

"I was making sure my shipment of toys and things for our new daycare arrived on time and undamaged," said Leslie.

"Daycare?" I asked with interest.

"Yes," replied Leslie. "Demetrious, of course, is not the only baby that comes up here. We have a lot of rich, young guests at the resort and they have children. So we're opening a daycare facility for them. This way the adults can engage in things that adults like while we take care of their children. It was my idea. I just love children."

"Where will the daycare be located?" asked Marc. "I think maybe we screwed up in not planning for a daycare in the original design of the resort."

"The plan is to use a small part of the sports arena," said Leslie. "They strung up a net this afternoon to section-off a room. This way the kids will have room to play, but won't float away into the rest of the arena."

"And the net can easily be taken down to enable use of the entire sports arena when needed," added George.

"Would you like to see it after dinner?" asked Leslie. "It would be fun to see if Demetrious likes the toys we got."

"Okay, sure." I glanced over at Marc, hoping that was okay with him.

…

After dinner we all made our way to the newly established day care carved out of the sports arena. There as a brand new sign that said in large letters, "Sky Care: Childcare That's Out of this World!" That's appropriately corny for a daycare, I thought. We watched as Demetrious played with a variety of toys. There was one teddy bear he especially seemed to like. We delighted in seeing him let go of the teddy bear, let it drift away and then grab it again. Sometimes it looked like he would intentionally make the bear spin as he let him go. He would always grab it just before it would get out of his reach. One time Demetrious let go of the teddy bear and it just hung there absolutely motionless.

"That's incredible," Marc said. "That must just have been a fluke. It's extremely hard to let something go in zero-g without imparting some residual motion to it. I've never actually been able to do that myself."

After playing for about an hour, Demetrious, started getting fussy. He was both tired and hungry. I fed him and he immediately fell asleep.

With Demetrious asleep, Marc and I said goodbye to George and Leslie and made our way back to Marc's suite. I attached the sound-asleep Demetrious to one corner of the room using a cloth strap that had a magnet on one end. I placed the magnet end of the strap on an iron strip on the wall used for attaching things you didn't want to lose.

Convinced that Demetrious was safely tethered, Marc floated over to the other side of the suite and grabbed a hold of the net used for sleeping. He instructed the computer to dim the lights and to display an external view of deep space. I glided over next to him and we both hung there motionless gazing at the dazzling display of stars.

After a few minutes, Marc moved over to kiss me, but I decided to toy with him. Turing away slightly, I said, "Marc, how many stars are there?"

"Really? You want to talk about cosmology now?"

"I just want to know how many stars there are," I said playfully.

"Okay Tesla, tell you what, let's play strip cosmology," said Marc with that devilish grin again. "I'll name an astronomical object, uh something found in space, and you have to tell me how many things are in it. If you get it right within an order of magnitude, then I'll take something off, and if you're wrong, then you take something off. For example, how many planets are there in the solar system?"

"Oh, I know this! There used to be nine planets, but now there are only eight because Pluto got demoted."

"That's right! So do you want to play?"

"Okay. So you have to take something off, because I got that right!"

"But, we hadn't started yet," Marc protested.

"Come on." I pulled his shirt off over his head. I looked at Marc with his shirt off and said, "I think I like this game." Then I asked, "You said I have to get it right within an order of magnitude, what does that mean?"

"It means you have to be within a factor of ten either high or low. So if the right answer is a hundred and you guessed anything between ten and a thousand, you'd win."

"That's easy! Let's play."

"It gets harder when the numbers are bigger, right? If the correct answer is ten billion then anything between one billion and a hundred billion will work. Okay?"

"Sure whatever. Let's do it."

"Okay, how many stars are there in the Milky Way Galaxy?" asked Marc smiling in a way that suggested he thought this game was finally going to start getting interesting.

That's what I wanted to know in the first place, I thought to myself. I have absolutely no idea, but fortunately for me the last number I had just heard was a hundred billion, so without thinking I immediately blurted out, "A hundred billion."

Crestfallen, Marc replied, "Well, the right answer is about four hundred billion, but a hundred billion is within an order of magnitude, so as much as I hate to admit it you're right." His voice trailed off at the end with obvious disappointment.

"I'm sorry, what did you say?"

"I said, you're r—"

"I'm right!" I interrupted enthusiastically. "Okay, let's have those pants." Marc took off his pants and handed them to me. "This is a great game!" I said as I took his pants.

"OK, next question," said Marc. "How many galaxies are there in our local group?"

"A hundred billion!" I said excitedly, without thinking.

"I'm afraid there are only ten galaxies in our local group. So you were only off by nine orders of magnitude," Marc said smiling. "Your shirt please, ma'am."

I nervously reached my hands across my body grabbing the bottom of my skin-tight shirt with my right hand on the left side of my body and my left hand on the right side. I then slowly pulled my shirt up and over my head, turning it inside out in the process. Smiling shyly, I handed Marc my shirt. I wasn't wearing a bra.

I floated there topless in front of him. He reached out with his left hand, found the small of my back and just as he did the night before, gently pushed me there causing us to float slowly toward each other. It was the most pleasant sensation as my body gently impacted his. To keep us from immediately bouncing away from each other Marc wrapped his arms around me and I did the same to him.

This was even better than last night. All I could feel was Marc's warm embrace. His skin pressing against my chest. His arms wrapped around me. The two of us floating effortlessly as one, suspended in space. I wanted him. I needed him. I could literally taste the desire. My heart was pounding so hard I thought that if I didn't hold on to him the force of my heartbeats would push us apart.

Marc kissed me. I closed my eyes. It was a long soft kiss. I felt his hands gently caressing my back. He kissed me again. This time I felt his right hand slide around my side. I felt him tenderly but firmly squeeze my breast. Excitement shot through my body. A small part of my brain wondered why the feeling was so intense, so pleasurable, but mostly I didn't care, I was more than content with simply enjoying it. We made love for half the night. Afterward we just floated together wrapped in each other's arms, and fortunately, Demetrious slept soundly through the whole thing.

It was the most incredible experience of my life, a perfect combination of lust and warmth, ecstasy and compassion. I had had sex on Earth of course, and usually enjoyed it, at least before Alex started getting weird, but this was different somehow, better. Better in every way. The whole experience was gentler, softer, sexier. There was no weight of someone on top of me, just pressure and sensations in all the right places and only in those places. Not that I was complaining, but I wondered why it was so intensely pleasurable. Was it Marc? Was it being in space? Was it because I hadn't had sex in quite a while. What it all of these things? I had no way of knowing then that weightlessness had sped up my nervous system, something that was first observed on the Sky Lab astronauts. The result was a heightened body sensitivity that magnified the sensations of sex. If this was the way it was for everybody, they're going to make a fortune with this place. It was obvious that Marc enjoyed it as much as I did.

The airflow that kept us cool in the heat of our passion now kept us warm as we floated naked in each other's arms while the computer made the necessary adjustments according to our body temperatures. The airflow also pushed us lightly against the netting and swept away the carbon dioxide we exhaled.

Floating there in Marc's arms afterwards was nearly as pleasurable as the sex. There was no cutting off the circulation of our arms no matter how we held each other. There were no uncomfortable positions. I wondered if this was what heaven was like as I drifted off to sleep.

...

The next morning I woke up and prepared to return to my room with Demetrious. Marc was already awake. I know he knew today was the day I started my job for the Three Dolphins Club. He knew today I would meet my first client in the resort lobby when the spaceplane arrived from Earth that afternoon. He knew my job was to entertain this client in all the ways implied by the Three Dolphins Club. He knew it, and I'm sure he didn't like it.

Marc didn't say anything as I got dressed. Finally, as I left his room and entered the hallway with Demetrious, Marc stopped me and said, "Why don't you quit your job?"

"What?" Even though I half expected something like this, the question, when I actually heard it, still caught me off guard. "I can't do that. Where would I live? Plus, I signed a contract."

"You could quit your job and live with me, right? I'll take care of you and Demetrious."

My heart started pounding again, but not in a good way. Why is he doing this? My mind was racing. It's too much, too fast. It was an incredible night last night, and he's a great person, but I just can't be dependent on someone right now. I just can't. That little voice came back and said I told you not to get involved. What should I tell him? I don't want to lose him, but I just can't make such a commitment, not right now. Finally, I said, "Marc, you're a wonderful person and last night was incredible, but—"

"Forget it," Marc interrupted. "I didn't mean it, right? And about last night? I just did that as part of my job to familiarize you with living and working at Sky City. It didn't mean a thing."

Before I could respond, Marc ducked back into his suite and closed the door.

I hung in the hallway in stunned silence.

Chapter 12 First Client

I cried all way back to my apartment towing Demetrious along behind me. Sasha and Yuri were awake when we entered.

"Look who was out all night and during her first week in space," quipped Yuri. "Why you little—" he stopped in mid-sentence when he saw that I was crying, and then said, "What happened? What's wrong?"

Through my tears, which filled my eyes making it hard to see, I managed to tell Yuri and Sasha the whole story.

"Men are pigs," said Sasha.

"Hey!" Yuri said with faked indignation.

"Present company excepted," said Sasha. "Anyway, that's why I just do my job here without getting emotionally attached to anyone, well, except for Yuri here. Aside from that, I just take care of myself."

"What should I do?" I sobbed.

"You should go with us to the gym and work out," said Yuri. "Maybe it will help you take your mind off that jerk. Then we'll all have to get ready to meet our new clients this afternoon."

Shit, can my life get any worse?

...

When we got to the gym, I went to the Carnival Game Room instead and asked if I could use the Skylab Run. I preferred running for real around the Skylab Run rather than doing it on a treadmill with bungee cords. I ran around in circles for an hour. As I ran, my mind kept replaying the recent bizarre events of my life.

So much has happened to me over the last week that I can scarcely believe it. I'm not sure how much more of this roller coaster of emotions I can take, and now this afternoon I have to meet my first customer. A total stranger that I'm supposed to entertain over the next week, and have sex with. How can I go through with that? How can I have sex with someone I don't even know? What if he's repulsive? The reality of what I had gotten myself into was hitting home with full force. I cursed Alex again for putting me in this position. I've been doing that a lot lately. It took every ounce of courage I had to prepare myself to meet my first client.

...

It was Sunday afternoon, the new guests always arrived Sunday afternoon. Sasha, Yuri, and I put on beautiful, stylish, skin tight outfits provided by the Club. I was wearing an elegant all black outfit with tight pants and matching blouse. My sleeveless blouse was cut low in front with five equally-spaced, one-inch wide bands of material that stretched horizontally across my back. On my arms, between my wrists and elbows, I wore stylish black winglets. These small wings would supposedly give me just enough mobility to traverse the open spaces in the resort. Sasha was dressed in a one-piece skin tight black leather jump suit with a single long zipper down the front. Yuri was wearing tight black dress pants, a very tight black t-shirt, and a fitted black sport coat with a white stripe down each lapel.

I had memorized my client's face and background. His name was Dr. James Homa, but went by Jimmy. He was thirty-five years old, never married, and had a Ph.D. in computer science from the Georgia Institute of Technology. He owned the company he started called Epoch Sports. The file said that Epoch Sports answered the age-old question 'who's the best.' It claims to provide the first believable way to determine what team was the best ever in a particular sport across the ages. For example, the file said, if you wanted to know if the 2014 Super Bowl Champion Seattle Seahawks could beat the 1979 Super Bowl Champion Pittsburg Steelers, Epoch Sports would tell you. Not only that, they would show you. Epoch Sports' computer animation of the players, they claimed, was indistinguishable from the real thing. The result was that you could actually watch the 2014 Seattle Seahawks play the 1979 Pittsburg Steelers and see for yourself who was better. For the past five years, Epoch Sports teamed up with the NFL to host Classic Super Bowl games that matched legendary Super Bowl championship teams from the past. The events drew huge worldwide audiences, helping make Jimmy a billionaire.

I spotted Jimmy immediately as he entered the lobby. He was slightly built, a little over six feet tall and maybe one hundred seventy pounds, with unkempt blond hair that looked like he just climbed out of bed. He was dressed in a white t-shirt and baggy blue jeans. He looked unsure of himself, but smiled when he saw me.

Being new to this, I was momentarily surprised that he recognized me, then I realized, of course he knew me, he selected me from the list of available escorts provided by the Club. I glided up to him, smiled, and said, "Hi I'm Tesla, you must be Jimmy."

"Yes, pleased to meet you," he said shyly without making eye contact.

I helped him through the Sky City registration process, which didn't take long, but by the time we were finished I could tell Jimmy wasn't feeling well.

"I know exactly how you feel," I said sympathetically. "That's how I felt when I first arrived. I'll take you down to First Aid and they'll fix you right up."

Jimmy didn't hear me, he was too busy throwing up. I towed him to First Aid where Doris Chun, the doctor for Sky City was busy treating other new arrivals. Doris was just over five feet tall with short black hair and brown eyes. She gave Jimmy a shot of Phenergan.

"Wow!" exclaimed Jimmy. "That feels wonderful."

"Amazing isn't it?" I said. "Jimmy, this is Doris, a graduate of Harvard Medical School and one of our two doctors. Hopefully, you won't have to see her again during your visit here."

"Thank you Doc," replied Jimmy. "Better living through chemistry."

Doris smiled.

"Let me show you to your room," I said. We made our way back through the lobby, then down the Hall to the guest rooms. Jimmy was staying in the Carl Sagan room. I showed him around the room, how to work the wall-to-wall monitor and how to work the toilet, sink, and shower. Then I said, "I'll give you a little time to relax, wash up, and change your clothes. Then I'll be back at five pm. There's a muster drill at five fifteen. I'll pick you up and we'll go to your muster station together. After that we can have dinner if you like."

Jimmy appeared to be overwhelmed by the view of Earth on the ten-foot screen at the end of his room, but managed to say, "I'd like that."

"OK, I'll see you at five." I left Jimmy's room and the door closed behind me. Well, that wasn't too bad. He seems nice enough, kind of shy and nerdy. I'm kind of getting used to the nerdy part. Seems like everyone is that way up here. I just can't imagine having sex with him. I shuddered at the thought.

...

I arrived back at Jimmy's room right at five pm. When the door opened, I found him exactly as I left him. He clearly hadn't showered or changed his clothes.

"Jimmy, did you spend the last two hours playing with the Sky City computer?" I asked.

"Yes," he replied innocently. "I was figuring out how it worked. Then I checked out all of the available exterior views from the resort. It's just so cool up here, I guess I lost track of time.

I smiled at him. "That's okay Jimmy. I glad you're enjoying yourself."

He nodded.

"Are you ready? We have to get to your muster station in fifteen minutes."

"Aww, do we have to go?" asked Jimmy.

"Yes, it's mandatory. Come on, I'll take you there, then afterward we can go have dinner if you like."

"Alright."

I led him down the hall to his muster station, which also happened to be the main restaurant. The displays covering the walls and ceiling were again showing a scene from Earth, a brilliant blue sky with puffy white clouds. The effect was dramatic as always. It gave you the feeling of being outside on a pleasant spring day on Earth.

Like most passengers, Jimmy barely paid attention to the safety information that included what to do if this happens or that happens, or where to go in the unlikely event it was necessary to evacuate the resort. After the half-hour briefing, Jimmy and I remained in the restaurant to have dinner. Jimmy didn't drink so we both just had water.

Carbonated soft drinks are not available anywhere at Sky City. It wasn't for health reasons I learned. The resort has lots of wines and all types of hard liquor, but no carbonated drinks, no beer, champagne, or soft drinks. This is because the carbonation in these drinks doesn't behave the same as it does on Earth. In zero-g, the dissolved gas doesn't easily separate from the liquid and most of it finds its way into your digestive system. The end result is that any person who drinks a carbonated beverage pays for it by farting hundreds times over the following couple of hours, or at least that what it says in the information package that every guest at Sky City receives; nice.

After we ordered, I tried to keep the conversation flowing. "So Jimmy, tell me, how did you start your business and how does it work exactly?"

"Well, it all started after I took a course in statistical thermodynamics in college. It was an eye-opening experience for me. Here you could calculate all of the thermodynamic properties of a gas, temperature, pressure, etc. just from the statistical behavior of the molecules that made up the gas. So that really got me into statistics and I realized that everything is statistical in nature. Nothing is black and white. Everything that can be measured actually has a distribution of values not a single value. It was a revelation that changed my life."

Oh my god, here we go again. Why does everyone up here talk like this? I wish Marc was here, he would help me understand this. "Right, changed your life," I said, pretending to understand. "Please go on."

"So, I had always been a big sports fan, even though I never played any sports myself. My father, however, was an athlete in college and loved college sports. I guess his love for all kinds of sports rubbed off on me."

"I used to run a lot when I was in college," I interjected.

115

Jimmy went on seemingly unaware that I had said anything. "When I got into statistics, I started looking for data on how well athletes did things. I started with tennis players. I thought this should be the easiest thing to do because there was only one player on each side. I discovered that there was a huge amount of statistical data available for the top players. Percentage of first serves made, how fast each serve was, where the serve was placed, percentage of second serves made, ground stroke percentages and tendencies. How often they hit it cross-court or down the line. How many unforced errors they had. How these data changed in pressure situations. It was amazing how much data was available."

I forced myself to pay attention, but it was very difficult. I smiled sweetly and nodded.

"Now, here's the key," Jimmy said. "I found a way to combine these data to simulate statistically the way a player would play. Then I could match up two players to see who'd win. I'd use actual matches to test the results against. I continued to fine-tune the process until it became very good at predicting past results. It then occurred to me that if I could predict past results, I could predict future results of matches that had not yet taken place. I made a fair amount of money betting on future tennis matches.

"So you made your fortune betting on tennis matches?"

"No, that turned out not to be as easy as I thought. The problem was that the skills of current players are constantly changing, younger players are getting better and the skills of older players are fading. Then I got this brilliant idea, why not concentrate on the past, where the skills are fixed. I figured I could pit legendary players against each other when each was at the height of their skills. The 1974 Jimmy Connors against the 1980 Bjorn Borg, for example. My gambling winnings gave me enough money to purchase a computer animation business. This business was developing the software to produce photo-realistic animations of people. When I saw what they were capable of I realized I could combine their animation with my statistics to recreate matches that never actually took place."

"What do you mean recreate matches that never took place," I asked.

"Well, take Jimmy Connors, for example. He was at the height of his tennis skills in 1974, but for obvious reasons, this version of Jimmy Connors could never have played against the 1980 version of Bjorn Borg, who was at the top of his skills in 1980. Because of the difference in time, this match could have never taken place, but through the magic of Epoch Sports, we could make it happen, and with our photo-realistic animation, you could watch the match. Because the re-creation is statistical in nature, every match is different, but over many matches, the best player would win the majority of them, and because the players were at the top of their games, the matches were very entertaining."

"Is there really a lot of money to be made recreating old tennis players?"

"You'd be surprised how many people love this stuff. Once we got tennis singles down, we started to branch out. We skipped doubles because, of course, nobody cares about doubles in tennis. So we went on to baseball. That was a good test of how to do a team sport. It was slow, so it was easy to animate multiple players and there was an immense amount of statistical information available on baseball players. After that, we tried basketball, but this was difficult because of the rule change to add the three-point shot in 1979. This made it difficult to compare teams before and after this rule change, so we limited basketball to only teams that played after 1979. Our biggest money, however, came from football, American football. Do you like football?"

"I went to a forty-niners game once in San Francisco."

"Well anyway, the key in all these sports is to normalize the capabilities of each player against the other players of his time. This minimizes differences caused by the increase in player's size and speed due to improvements in training, drugs, and equipment. In tennis, it takes out the improvement in tennis rackets. In football, the increase in the size of the players is significant. For example, a three-hundred-pound offensive lineman was average in 2014, but would have been by far the largest player on the field in the 1970s where the average offensive lineman weighed just two hundred twenty five pounds. All else being equal, the normalization makes a three-hundred-pound lineman in 2014 and a two-hundred-twenty-five-pound lineman from 1974 equivalent in the head-to-head competition.

Okay, once again I had no idea what he's talking about, but I continued to pretend to be fascinated by his explanation.

"We've also recently gotten into international football, what Americans call soccer. I think this will turn out to be our biggest moneymaker yet. Just imagine pitting World Cup champions against each other from across history. We expect the interest will be off the charts…" Jimmy paused and looked at me. "I'm sorry, I'm rambling on."

"No, this is great," I lied. "Please go on." I could tell that he was enthusiastic about his business and that enthusiasm was actually kind of contagious. "Are you working on anything that doesn't involve sports?" I immediately regretted asking that because it sounded like a dumb question given that the name of his company was Epoch Sports.

"Why yes," Jimmy responded enthusiastically. "We also do movies. We can photo-realistically animate anybody from the past, which enables us to provide any actor you'd like for a new movie. You want a movie with Marilyn Monroe and Brad Pitt, no problem. The possibilities are endless. But, there's a lot of competition for this, and so far, it turns out more profitable to just fix up current actors. We can add makeup, scars, wounds, make them younger or older, anything you'd like. There's a lot of demand for us to make actors to look younger. It's our digital makeup division."

"Cool!" Finally, something I can relate to. "I love old movies and it would be so cool to see a young Harrison Ford in a new Star Wars movie."

...

I spent the next three days entertaining Jimmy, showing him around the resort, playing in the sports arena, working out in the fitness room, playing in the carnival game room, and gambling in the casino. We ate most meals together except breakfasts. Jimmy didn't eat breakfast. I took him on the Celestial Sphere ride, just the two of us. I was the perfect girlfriend, beautiful (or so Jimmy said), attentive, and flirty, and it was enjoyable for both of us. To my surprise I was genuinely fond of Jimmy and found him interesting, but I wasn't physically attracted to him. I cried myself to sleep every night.

On the fourth day, I knew what was going to happen. I knew Jimmy liked me. I knew what I was expected to do, but I still didn't know if I could go through with it. I had never had sex with a stranger before, well, at least now Jimmy wasn't a total stranger, and I had never had sex for money before. Of course, there would be no actual exchange of money between us, that had already been taken care of. And what about Marc, I wish it were Marc. Why doesn't he call me? Why doesn't he answer my texts?

On the night of the fourth day, I met Jimmy for dinner as usual. I was nervous and didn't know what to expect or how I'd feel during and after. Jimmy looked nervous too. I knew he was a successful businessperson and billionaire, but he looked unsure of himself. He had confided in me that he didn't have a lot of experience with women, and certainly not any intimate experience with someone as beautiful as me, he said.

Jimmy, not unexpectedly, turned out to be rather clumsy in bed. (Okay, there's not actually a bed here, but you get the idea.) I think this resulted from a combination of his lack of experience, nervousness, and the fact that we were in a zero-g environment. His awkwardness made me relax and, much to my surprise, I took control. Afterward, I could tell that the night, from Jimmy's perspective, went very well. It seemed to go very well indeed, as did the next three days.

For me it was a different story, each night after we had sex, I cried, and I cursed Alex. I sobbed quietly to myself so Jimmy wouldn't hear.

I'm a space-whore. I miss Marc. I hate Alex for doing this to me. The shame was almost unbearable.

At the end of the week, I saw Jimmy off as he boarded the Saturday afternoon spaceplane to return to Earth. I kissed him good bye. Jimmy left looking like that was the best vacation he ever had. For me the results were much different. On one hand I knew I had done my job well and now I better understood that my job was to show clients how enjoyable life in space could be. An important part of that was to help them enjoy sex in zero-g, but there was a lot more to it than just that. Still, I couldn't escape the fact I was being paid to have sex. Before now, it was just an abstract idea, now it was real, now I was a space hooker. It was more devastating to my self-esteem than I ever imagined.

When I got back to my room, there was a message from Mr. Abruzzo that said, "Please come see me in my office at four pm this afternoon, it's about your client Jimmy." Oh god, now what?

...

I arrived at the Lupanar room right at four pm. "You wanted to see me Mr. Abruzzo?" I asked as I entered the office.

"Yes, please come in," George replied without looking up. "And call me George."

"Uh, okay, George, you wanted to see me about Jimmy?"

"Yes, your client Jimmy left a message for me before he departed. He—"

"I swear I thought he had a good time here," I interrupted, thinking for some reason Jimmy was unhappy and had complained about me.

"Relax, Tesla," George said smiling. "Jimmy's message said this had been the most incredible experience of his life. It was far beyond his expectations."

"Well, we aim to please."

"There's more. He left you this tip." George brought up the amount on a corner of the high-definition display. The tip was worth a quarter of my annual salary.

I stared at it in disbelief. "He's giving that to me? What's the catch?"

"There's no catch. The money's yours. But…"

"I knew it, there's always a but."

"But, he would like to be a regular client of yours, if you agree, that is," said George.

"That's it? He wants to be a regular client?"

"Only if you agree. He'd like to come up here once a quarter."

"Sure, I guess." Well at least he won't be a total strange next time.

"Okay," said George. "I'll let him know. Tesla…"

"Yes?"

"He also said he was going to tell all of his rich friends to come up here. Well done." George was grinning ear-to-ear.

…

I went back to my room and called Mia as usual. I always did it this way just in case the police were checking Emma's phone records. If they did, they wouldn't see any calls to her from space. If they happened to check Mia's phone they would simply verify the fact that she had a friend who moved to Sky City. "Hi Mia, it's Ella, I hate to bother you, but could you get Emma for me?

"Sure," said Mia. "Hold on."

After a few minutes Emma's larger than life face showed up on my screen. "Hi Ella!" Emma said excitedly. "It's so good to see you!"

"Hi Emma." I started crying immediately. "I have so much to tell you" I sobbed. I told her about my first client Jimmy. "Well, I guess I'm officially a space hooker now. God, I hate my life. I hate what I've become."

"Look," said Emma. "Don't think of yourself that way. You're just doing what you had to do to survive and to take care of the ones you love."

I told her about Marc.

"I can't believe he did that. What a jerk. He could have at least called you. What's his problem?"

"I don't know. I just didn't know this would be so hard emotionally. I don't know if I can do this." Neither one of us said anything for what seemed like a long time. Finally, I said, "There is a bright spot, though. My client Jimmy gave me a tip."

"That's nice," replied Emma.

"No, you don't understand. The tip was equal to three month's salary. Three month's salary for one week of work."

"You cannot be serious," said Emma. "Maybe I should have traded places with you after all."

I tried unsuccessfully to smile. "Well anyway, now we have enough money to move mom to a new care facility. I'll pay for it through Bitcoin, as we discussed, so the payments will be untraceable." We continued to laugh and cry together for another hour.

Chapter 13 Shore Leave

Length of time in space: *six months*

After my whirlwind first two weeks at Sky City, I managed to settle into a routine consisting primarily of working, taking care of Demetrious, playing soccer, late night discussions with George, and weekly phone calls with my sister. The love and support from Sasha and Yuri enabled me to mentally compartmentalize my job as an escort. This made my life bearable and to my amazement, six months went by in the blink of an eye. Unfortunately, I never heard from Marc. He never returned any of my messages and he never came to Sky City even though I heard that he was frequently at the Sky City II construction site. As my sister would say, 'What's his problem?' Fortunately, I never heard about Alex either. Maybe he's given up looking for us by now.

Demetrious was now a year old and has lived half his life in space, a much greater fraction than any person in history, ever. I worried constantly about him growing up here and whether I've ruined his life. But he seemed so happy and he's so adorable. I don't know what I'd do without him.

For the last five months or so, I played on the Three Dolphins 3D soccer team. Our team name was *3D-Squared*. We practiced early Wednesday mornings and had our matches on Sunday nights. This was the best time to play. It was after the previous guests had left and the new guests were typically resting or sick as they adjusted to their new environment.

The soccer "league" had five teams of six players each. In addition to *3D-Squared*, there was the team from the engineering staff known as *Mega-What?*, the team from the kitchen staff called *Cereal Killers*, the team from the casino staff named *The Goods Are Odd*, and finally *Floaters United* from guest services. This evening we were playing *Mega-What?*.

The matches were played with five players on the "field" from each team with one player sitting out as a substitute. The most popular formation typically had two forwards, two defensive players and a goalie, although some defensive minded teams played a three-one formation instead of two-two. Yes, I've been learning a little soccer lingo. I never played soccer on Earth, but it's enormously fun up here.

Like "indoor soccer" on Earth, there was no out of bounds. The cylindrical wall of the Sports Arena formed the side boundary of the playing field. A ball hitting the sidewall was still in play. Each goal was set in from the end of the Sports Arena by six and a half feet. Three feet behind each goal was a transparent wall that created a space for spectators and separated them from the playing field. Also like indoor soccer, there were no off-sides.

We'd wear special wing suits similar to the one Marc showed me how to use during my first week at Sky City. I still missed Marc. Anyway, these suits were specially designed for speed and maneuverability, and they required more arm strength than the normal every-day wings we used for just getting around.

The game was lightning fast, closer to air hockey, I think, than soccer since there isn't anything other than air resistance, to slow the ball down. There were no time outs. Players substituted on the fly just like ice hockey. And like Grounder soccer, you couldn't touch the ball with your hands, arms or wings, okay, well maybe not exactly like Grounder soccer. You could legally touch the ball with any other part of your body. Built into everyone's wing suit were special gloves and sensors that lit up if contacted by the ball. This made it easy for the referee to call handballs.

Besides me, the rest of the *3D-Squared* team members included my roommates Sasha White and Yuri Li, along with Tommy Patel, Jennifer Gerbosi, and George Abruzzo. Marc Elliott no longer played with the team, which I guess was my fault somehow. Nevertheless, I really liked playing on the team even though we'd lost all but one match so far. We generally didn't take the matches too seriously and played just for the fun of it. After each match, we'd all go out to the bar in the casino for drinks and to re-live our on-field exploits.

George and I would often stay up late into the night talking long after the others had left. More than the soccer, I looked forward to those late night conversations with George. We'd talk about everything—life and love, heartbreak, children, and the future. George was very interested in the future, and seemed particularly interested in Demetrious' future. I came to know him as kind and considerate, and very entertaining. He had a bigger-than-life personality with the most amazing stories extracted from a lifetime of experiences both on and off the Earth. I was starting to see him as the father I never knew.

...

Tonight was the last of the regular season matches. *Mega-What?* and my team, *3D Squared*, were in fourth and fifth place in our tiny space-soccer league and we were playing against each other in the early match. The second and third place teams, *Cereal Killers* and *The Goods Are Odd*, would be facing off against each other in the late match. We had never beaten *Mega-What?* so the *Mega-What?* players Keith, Gus, Sanjay, Santiago, Bryan, and Marcus were acting all confident and cocky. But, they were all engineers and while Santiago and Marcus were excellent athletes, Keith, Gus, Sanjay, and Bryan were not. Unfortunately, that didn't stop them from trash talking nonstop. All of us on *3D Squared* pretended we didn't care about winning, but tonight we wanted to beat *Mega-What?* in the worst way just to shut them up.

Doris Chun was tonight's referee. With no off-sides and no out-of-bounds, all she had to do was keep up with the fast pace of the game, call fouls, and keep the game under control.

As the designated home team *Mega-What?* kicked off to start the match as Doris blew her whistle. Sanjay barely tapped the ball forward and then quickly kicked it backward to Bryan before heading toward the goal. Bryan stopped the ball with his chest, flapped his wings slightly to move his body "up" so that the ball was now at his feet. He kicked the ball forward as hard as he could angling it toward the wall. The ball bounced off the wall at just the right angle and headed directly to Sanjay, who had moved to a position right in front of our goal. Sanjay easily deflected the fast moving ball past George, who was playing goalie as usual. Just like that it was 1-0 in favor of *Mega-What?* As was their custom after scoring a goal, the *Mega-What?* players chanted, "What? What? What?"

"That's obnoxious," said Tommy.

We kicked off after the goal. Tommy passed the ball to Jennifer who headed it to me at midfield. I kicked the ball has hard as I could directly at the *Mega-What?* goal. Marcus, the *Mega-What?* goalie, had no time to move, all he could do was spread his wings. Fortunately for him, the ball struck his left wing. Still 1-0. Marcus kicked the ball to Gus who tapped it to Sanjay who was near the "top" of the playing volume. Sanjay kicked the ball over our goal. The ball banged off the glass behind the goal and rebounded right back in front where Bryan tapped it passed George, 2-0 *Mega-What?*.

"What? What? What?"

We kicked off for a second time in less than a minute and changed formations to a three-one in the hopes of preventing more easy goals. The three defensive players, Sasha, Yuri, and Tommy lined up in a triangular formation as viewed from the opponent's goal. I was the lone striker. The change worked and despite furious action from both sides, there were no more goals in the first half.

I kicked off to start the second half. I barely tapped the ball, then instead of kicking it backwards to one of my teammates I flew straight "up" to the top of the field, holding the ball between my feet. When I got to the wall, I turned my body sharply so that my feet, still holding the ball, contacted the wall. My momentum compressed my legs into a squat. I pushed off the wall as hard as I could directly at the goal. I had to make a few maneuvers along the way with my wings to avoid the *Mega-What?* players. Then I crashed full-speed, shoulder first into Keith, the *Mega-What?* goalie. My momentum carried us both into the goal and we crashed into the back of the net. I still had the ball squeezed tightly between my feet. Doris signaled a goal.

Keith complained bitterly, but it turned out that there was no rule against what I just did. No rule against holding the ball with your feet. No rule about carrying it into the goal with your feet. And with that, I had inadvertently transformed 3D soccer into a combination of soccer and rugby.

Marcus scored the tying goal by accident. He was attempting to pass the ball back to his own goalie, but kicked it a little too hard and not very accurately. It sailed just out of Keith's reach into the goal, making it 2-2.

With time running out I moved in front of the *Mega-What?* goal. Sanjay had the ball between his feet and was barreling full speed toward our goal. Yuri launched himself feet first toward Sanjay. The ensuing collision knocked the ball free and sent Sanjay and Yuri crashing into the wall. Sasha retrieved the ball and passed it forward to me. Sanjay flew over to Doris and started yelling at her that Yuri deserved a yellow card for crashing into him that way. While Doris was distracted by Sanjay, I saw the ball headed my way. I tried to get to it but I could tell that it was going to go over my head. I instinctively reached up and stopped the ball with my hand. For some reason the handball-violation lights in my suit didn't light up. I flipped myself head-over-heals and in one smooth motion kicked the ball into the goal. Doris looked up just in time to see the ball sail into the net. She looked at me, didn't see any penalty light and signaled goal. Doris looked at her watch and blew the whistle indicating that the match was over, 3-2 in favor of *3D-Squared*!

My teammates mobbed me in celebration.

The *Mega-What?* players were yelling handball, handball!

I extracted myself from my teammates and made my way over to Doris.

"Doris," I said. "*Mega-What?* is right. It was a handball. I don't know why my suit didn't light up."

"Are you sure?" asked Doris.

"Yes, I'm sure."

"Thank you for letting me know."

The match ended in a tie.

...

Excited after our big come-from-behind tie, our whole *3D-Squared* team headed to the bar in the casino. As the night wore on, one by one everyone left, leaving George and me by ourselves as usual. We stayed, drinking wine and talking late into the night.

We tended to get philosophical late at night and I asked, "George, when you first interviewed me for a job here, you asked me what my biggest dream in life was. I think really didn't have a good answer then. So now I'd like to ask you the same question, what was your biggest dream in life?"

George smiled. "Good question." He appeared deep in thought for a moment and then said, "For me, it's like what General George C. Patton said back in the 20th century. Compared to war, all other forms of human endeavor shrink to insignificance."

Maybe it was all the wine I had, but that didn't make any sense. "You want to make war?"

"Oh heavens no, child." George laughed and then he got serious. He leaned close to me as if he was about to say something important. "Patton was completely wrong. Wars are useless and obsolete." He paused for a moment, probably for dramatic effect. "No, I'd update Patton's quote for the twenty-first century making it, 'Compared to the settlement of space, all other forms of human endeavor shrink to insignificance.' That's my dream. That's a goal worthy of a lifetime." George settled back to his original position and seemed quite pleased.

"But why settle space?" I asked. "What's wrong with Earth? I like Earth."

George straightened up again, spread his arms wide, smiled broadly. "Don't you like it here?"

This time I hesitated a moment and then said, "Yes, actually I do." I felt my face break into a big smile. "I do. I really do like living here and, more importantly, Demetrious really likes it too."

"That's it then."

"What?"

"That's why people will settle space."

"Just because they like it?"

"Exactly."

. . .

I went back to my apartment with George's words still ringing in my ears, and wondered, what's my worthy goal? Most of my life I don't think I ever really had a goal. Then I had Demetrious and he became the focus of my life. He definitely gives meaning to my life, but is that all?

After sleeping for just five and a half hours, I got up feeling fully refreshed. I got up early and headed over to the Celestial Sphere. I rode out into the inky blackness hoping that maybe I'd discover my worthy goal out there. Hoping to recapture that feeling I had the first time, that feeling that there was something else, that feeling that I had made contact with something out there in the universe. I spent an hour out there by myself, but it didn't happen. Why can't I get that feeling again? Did I just imagine it? No! I felt it. I know I did, but my doubts kept growing stronger. As always, the view was spectacular view and you can't beat the solitude in the Celestial Sphere, but without that something else, it was also a little bit of a disappointment.

…

The day had finally arrived. I was surprised it came so quickly. Demetrious and I had been at Sky City for just over six months and it was time for us to take our mandatory two-month shore leave. The plan was for us to spend the next two months on Earth living in an apartment in Brownsville, Texas provided by the Three Dolphins Club. We would spend those two months recovering from the effects of zero-g. I had been quite diligent about doing my daily two hours of exercises as required by Sky City. Not everyone at Sky City was as diligent, and Demetrious, who was now only just a year old, obviously did not do two hours of exercises every day, or any day for that matter.

I worried that Alex would be waiting for us when we landed. I worried about how Demetrious would do back on Earth. I wondered what Marc was up to. I wondered if I would ever stop worrying about everything.

As I packed up the things Demetrious and I would need, I came across the shoes that Marc told me I wouldn't need the day we first met, the day we blasted off into space. He was right, of course, I didn't need them, but he was such a jerk for never calling me after that night we spent together. I shrugged my shoulders, threw the shoes into my suitcase, grabbed Demetrious and headed to the lobby where the space plane was docked.

Entering the lobby with my luggage triggered more memories. This was where Demetrious and I first entered Sky City. It was just six months ago, but it seems like a lifetime. Everything was so strange then and now it's so familiar. I remember how weird and wonderful it was to float around and how it made me sick. Now it just seems normal, like people were meant to live their lives floating effortlessly. Floating is freedom, that's what George said. I remember how I crashed into one of these palm trees because I didn't know how to move in a large open space. Now I play on a 3D soccer team. I remember how scared and nervous I was coming here, not knowing what to expect, not knowing how I'd survive. Now I'm actually nervous to leave, if even only for two months. This has become my home. I really am Tesla Miller from Sky City. The thought made me smile.

I looked around and saw that Sasha and Yuri were already in the lobby. I also saw George, Leslie, Jennifer, and Tommy. They were all here to see me off. This group of space dwellers, these Floaters, had become my family. I cried as I hugged each one of them goodbye.

"Take good care of my baby," Leslie said, looking at Demetrious. "You be a good boy, and I'll see you in two months."

"Don't do anything I wouldn't do," said Tommy.

"That's not much of a restriction," quipped Jennifer.

I noticed that George had a worried look on his face. "What's wrong George?" I asked. "Don't worry, I'll be back in two months!"

"Be careful down there," George whispered to me as I hugged him. "Please watch Demetrious closely."

With that, Demetrious and I boarded the spaceplane for our return flight to Earth. The interior looked exactly like the one we rode up in. I was nervous again, but not nearly as nervous as during that initial flight. You shouldn't be nervous at all, I said to myself, after all you're an experienced space traveler now. I took a seat next to the wall this time, strapped Demetrious into his infant carrier, and strapped the carrier to the aisle seat. I wonder what George meant by watching Demetrious closely. He probably just cares about him. That's nice.

The doors to the spaceplane closed and the pilot announced we would be departing from Sky City as soon as he received clearance from space traffic control. I looked around and saw that every seat was filled. It felt weird to be in a seat again, even if I was really still just floating above it. I hadn't sat in a chair for six months.

Departure from Sky City was smooth, just a gentle shove to start us drifting away. An hour later the pilot made an announcement to prepare for the de-orbit burn. I remember that it took us six hours and four major rocket firings to get up to Sky City, but it would take only two hours and one burn to get back. The flight attendant informed us that the de-orbit burn would drop the low-part of our orbit into the Earth's upper atmosphere and the atmosphere would slow us down to a safe landing speed.

Judging from the view provided by the display at the front of the cabin it looked like we were flying upside down and backwards when the de-orbit burn started. The thrust pressed us into our seats. The display said the acceleration was of only a fraction of 1 g, something that would have been trivial six months ago, but now it felt impressively strong. Fortunately, it only lasted two and a half minutes, then we were back to our familiar and comfortable weightlessness.

I looked at Demetrious and said in as cheerful a voice as I could manage, "That wasn't so bad, was it?"

Demetrious, who was just starting to talk said, "'kay mommy."

But it was just the beginning. The spaceplane rotated around to face its belly toward the Earth. Thirty-five minutes later, the pilot said we made contact with the upper atmosphere. The deceleration was gradual at first and then grew stronger and stronger. Demetrious and I were pressed into our seats. The deceleration grew to 1 g. Demetrious was immobilized. He looked like he was trying to cry, but couldn't. It grew to 1.5 g, then peaked at 2.0 g.

It was like an elephant was sitting on my chest. I could barely move my arms or legs. It was hard to turn my head, but I managed to turn it just enough to see Demetrious out of the corner of my eye. Good, he's asleep. Wait, that can't be right, he just got up from a long nap before this flight. Oh no, I started to panic. What if he's passed out? What if this is too much for him? What if it's killing him?! I wanted to reach out to him, but I couldn't move. The artificial gravity of the spaceplane's re-entry pinned me down. Fortunately, the peak g-loading only lasted a few minutes. Unfortunately, it was replaced by the constant 1-g force of Earth's gravity. Now that we were inside the Earth's atmosphere flying like an airplane instead of a spaceplane, we felt the full force of Earth's relentless pull on our bodies.

I think because of my dedication to the required two-hours of daily exercise at Sky City, I found I could manage being back in 1 g reasonably well. Everything felt heavy, but I could move my arms, legs, and head. I turned to look at Demetrious. His eyes were closed. I reached out to touch his face. He did not react to my touch. I tried gently shaking him. Nothing. My panic was growing. I felt his chest. Thank god I could feel his heart beating. He's still breathing, but it seemed shallow. What's happening to him?

Thirty minutes after first making contact with the Earth's atmosphere, and two hours after we departed from Sky City, we landed back where we started, the spaceport at Brownsville, Texas. As the spaceplane was being towed to the terminal, I took Demetrious out of his infant seat. He was still passed out. I started calling hysterically for the flight attendant. When she arrived I pleaded, "Please help me, I don't know what's wrong with him. God please help me!"

"Please calm down," replied the flight attendant. "I'll go tell the captain to alert the medical team." And she left.

Not knowing what else to do, I just sat there rocking Demetrious and sobbing. I knew that everyone returning from space who had been there for longer than a month was automatically given a quick medical evaluation before being allowed to leave the spaceplane. Prior to opening the spaceplane's door the flight attendant instructed everyone to stay in their seats until the medical staff could check them out.

In my panic I ignored this instruction and as soon as the door was opened I stood up and ran with Demetrious to the door. I arrived at the door just as the medical staff was entering. I started to feel dizzy. I knew I was going to faint. Somehow I managed to hand Demetrious off to one of the medical personnel just before collapsing. The last thing I remember was hitting my head on something hard as I fell.

...

I woke up in a bed in a room that was obviously in some kind of medical facility. Where was I? More importantly, where was Demetrious? I've got to find him. I stood up quickly. Shit, my body felt like lead. My head hurt. Uh oh, got that dizzy feeling again. I sat back down, but only for a minute. I've got to find Demetrious. I got up again, more slowly this time. I was able to stand without feeling too dizzy. I took a few cautious steps. Not too bad. Okay, it was time to go. I opened the door to leave and as I did so I came face-to-face with the last person I expected to see.

"Marc Elliott, you asshole!" I said angrily. "What the hell are you doing here? On second thought never mind, I don't care. Just get out of my way. I have to find my son."

Marc didn't move. "I've been here waiting for you to wake up," Marc explained. "Demetrious is having a difficult time. I'll take you to him."

"Oh my god! What's happening?"

We walked down the corridor to another room with Marc holding my arm to steady me as I glared at him. Marc opened the door. I gasped when I saw Demetrious. He was unconscious lying face up in a tub of water with a breathing tube down his throat.

"He was having trouble breathing on his own," Marc said.

"What's wrong with him?" I cried out in shock. "Why is he like this? He was so happy and healthy this morning?"

"It's Earth's gravity, right?" said Marc. "It's too much for him. Demetrious has lived half his life in zero-g. That's a far greater fraction than anyone in history."

"Will he be okay?" I begged. "What should I do? I didn't know. What have I done?"

"He's okay for now. The doctor gave him a sedative to ease the pain and we put him in water to try to partially simulate a zero-g environment."

"What should I do?" I pleaded again. "How long does he have to stay like this?"

"They don't know," replied Marc. "Demetrious is kind of a pioneer, right? But if he were my child, I'd get him back into space as soon as possible."

"How can I do that?" I managed to say between sobs. Tears were rolling down my face. "We have to stay here for two months. Can he survive for two months here?"

"Come with me," Marc said, taking me by the hand. He led us out into the hall away from the medical staff. "The reason I'm here is that George was afraid that this might happen to Demetrious and he asked me to do whatever I could to make sure he was okay."

"What? I don't understand."

"I'm here to help," replied Marc. "While you were unconscious I checked on Demetrious. When I saw his condition, I recommended that they submerge him in water. Then I called George. He authorized the immediate return to Sky City for you and Demetrious. The next flight there is tomorrow afternoon. It will be full of workers for Sky City II, but they've agreed to stop at Sky City and drop us off."

"Us?" I asked.

"Yes, I'm going with you."

I felt off balance in every way possible. After living in zero-g for six months, I knew my brain had long since stopped listening to my inner ear. That was a problem now that I was back on Earth, it was causing me to be unstable. And I was so upset about Demetrious' condition I couldn't think straight. My mind kept flashing to the worst possible outcome. He's dying! It's all my fault. I've killed my son. What have I done?

"Hey," Marc said looking into my eyes. "Are you okay? I said I'm going with you. It's going to be alright."

"I've killed him," I cried. "I've killed my son."

"No, you haven't killed him," Marc said, trying to reassure me. "He'll be just fine once we get him back to Sky City. Except—"

"Except what," I said urgently. "What do you mean *except*. You just said he was going to be fine if we get him back to Sky City."

"Yes, it's just that to get him back there he'll have to endure 3 g during takeoff.

"He did it before," I pleaded. "And he was just a little baby then."

"That was when he was used to living in 1 g. Now his body is adapted to life in zero-g."

I started to cry again.

"On the bright side, he made it through re-entry, which went up to 2 g, so I think he should be able to get through the 3-g ascent back to space," Marc said, still trying to reassure me. But then he went on. "On the not-so-bright-side, you said he blacked out during re-entry. That's not good. The key will be to keep his body in the right orientation relative to the acceleration so the blood doesn't drain out of his head and to make sure he keeps breathing. If we do those things, he should be okay." I could tell Marc was trying to sound optimistic.

I was desperate for help and I would do anything for Demetrious. Without any other options, I said "Okay. Please help us. He'll be alright through the launch, right?"

"Sure," said Marc less convincingly this time. "It's just that..." Marc hesitated.

"What now," I demanded frantically.

"Well, as I said, Demetrious is kind of a pioneer, and pioneering is a tough business. But he's a tough little guy. I know he's going to be okay."

...

I stayed with Demetrious overnight, never leaving his side. It was one of the most miserable nights of my life, and I had my share of miserable nights with Alex. I was weighed down by worry, it was so intense I could barely function. And, of course, I felt literally weighed down by gravity. It made everything extremely uncomfortable. Everything was heavy. Doing even the smallest things took too much effort. My feet hurt, my joints hurt, even my skin hurt, yet I barely noticed. All I could think about was my Demetrious. He looked so helpless laying there. Immobilized by this stupid gravity.

My son was unable to move and barely able to breathe. I hate gravity. What have I done to him? My mind filled with self-doubts again. I'm such a terrible mom. Look what I've done.

Marc stayed with us through the night. He made sure the water Demetrious was in was at the right temperature and that the equipment helping him to breathe was functioning properly. The launch wasn't until noon the next day. Time dragged slowly by. Still, I never left Demetrious's side. I stared at him to make sure he kept breathing, willing him to keep breathing.

Finally, thank god, it was time to board the spaceplane. The nurse removed the breathing tube. Marc helped me get Demetrious from the water bath, dried off, dressed, and into the infant carrier. Demetrious was still lightly sedated. All three of us boarded early so that we could get him setup properly and to make sure that his portable breathing apparatus was secure and functioning.

I barely noticed when the carrier plane took off with the spaceplane slung beneath its wings. An hour later, we were ready for the drop. I knew what this would mean. Seconds after the drop the main engines would start and accelerate the spaceplane for eight minutes.

"Eight minutes," I whispered to Demetrious. "You've just got to make it through eight minutes. Then everything will be okay again. Can you do that? Can you do that for mommy?"

The drop. Weightlessness! But it was short lived as the main engines roared to life. The cabin shook like it was going to come apart. I stared at Demetrious as the spaceplane accelerated. The display in the front of the cabin showed the acceleration in gees along with the time to the end of the burn.

Marc read them off, "one-gee…one-point-five…two." The vehicle kept accelerating. Demetrious' heart rate was increasing and his breathing was getting shallower as his body struggled against the ruthless pull of the artificial gravity. "Two-point-five gees, approaching maximum acceleration."

"How much longer," I shouted over the roar of the engines as I fought my own battle against the gees.

"We're at three gees," Marc yelled. "Two minutes to go!"

I could no longer turn my head to look at Demetrious. The acceleration jammed me into my seat. It was so loud, I couldn't hear him breathing. I didn't know how he was doing and it was killing me. I couldn't even scream. Those last two minutes seemed to take forever... Then suddenly silence! No noise and more importantly no gravity! Fuck you gravity! I quickly looked at Demetrious. "Yes!" I said out loud. "He's still breathing!" His breathing was deeper and his heart rate was slowing down. He's returning to normal! He was still sedated, but he didn't seemed distressed. I felt my body go limp with relief and I cried tears of joy. The tears no longer ran down my cheeks, but simply filled my eyes.

…

Sometime later I turned toward Marc, looked directly at him and yelled, "You asshole!"

"What?" replied Marc.

"You don't call me for six months, you don't return my messages, and then you just show up the day we arrive back on Earth?" I scolded. "What kind of crap is that?"

"I wanted to call you. I really did," pleaded Marc. "I wanted to see you. But—"

"But you didn't 'cause you're a chicken-shit, nerdy engineer." Now that I wasn't so worried about Demetrious, I was pissed.

"I know, but I never stopped thinking about you."

"Then what the hell happened?" I shouted.

"If you stop yelling at me I'll tell you."

"Okay, do it," I said coldly.

"That week we spent together, I felt something I had never felt before. I never felt that way about anyone and I was scared. On top of that, I couldn't deal with your job, right? I didn't know what to do, so I just tried to make the whole thing go away. I tried not to think about you. I thought if I had no contact with you I could just forget about you."

"Is that what you wanted? To forget about me?"

"Yes...no! Well it didn't work anyway. I couldn't stop thinking about you no matter how hard I tried. You're all I've thought about for the last six months. But I didn't have the courage to contact you. I thought I had waited too long. I thought you'd be angry or worse, that you would be indifferent."

"So what changed?" I asked with a little less hostility in my voice.

"It was George. He called and said you were taking your shore leave and asked if I could make sure you were okay because he was worried about Demetrious. I jumped at the opportunity! I thought maybe if I could help, I could get a second chance."

I found myself having a hard time staying mad at Marc. He was extremely helpful back on Earth. I'm not sure what I would have done without him. On the other hand, I didn't want to let him off too easily. "I was really pissed at you. Here I was a stranger in this strange place. I was scared too and lonely. I needed you and you weren't there. Do you have any idea how hard that was for me?"

Marc shook his head.

"Now Sky City is my home and I have a lot of good friends there. I somehow managed to survive without you. I'm happy there now."

Marc looked down. "I'm sorry," he said softly. "Message received. I'll leave you alone and won't bother you anymore."

"Dammit Marc. Where's that cocky engineer I first met? Are you going to give up that easily?"

"What? But you said—"

"Jeez you're dense for a smart guy. I said I survived without you. That doesn't mean I didn't want to be with you. I've really missed you. I thought we had something special."

Marc smiled and said, "I knew you couldn't live without me. I knew it all along. A guy with a Ph.D. in aerospace engineering is like catnip to girls from Sky City."

"There's the Marc I used to know and love." I looked into those deep blue eyes. "And thank you for helping Demetrious. I don't know what I would have done if you weren't there."

"You're welcome. I'm just glad I could help, and I'm glad Demetrious looks like he'll be just fine."

I leaned over Demetrious toward Marc and whispered, "Maybe if you're not busy tonight and not throwing up like a Grounder, I could express my appreciation somehow."

"Yep, like catnip," Marc said smiling as he undid his seat belt. He floated across the aisle, over Demetrious and kissed me. As he did so, the engines roared to life for the second of the four burns to Sky City. The sudden acceleration caught Marc off guard and he landed in the laps of the construction workers in the row behind us. It was a short burn and by the time Marc made it back to his seat, it was over.

After the burn I looked at him, shook my head, smiled and said, "Nice move Grounder." By the time we got to Sky City Demetrious was waking up. Hopefully, the whole thing will just seem like a bad dream to him.

...

The first time we flew to Sky City the spaceplane docked at the Lobby air lock and everyone got off. This time, however, only the three of us left, everyone else continued on to Sky City II. As I floated into the lobby with Demetrious in tow, I couldn't help but think back to our first arrival there. How surprising the smell of Plumerias was. Now it was so familiar, so comfortable. Now it was home.

As soon as we got into Sky City we made a brief visit to Dr. Doris Chun so she could check out Demetrious. Then we went straight to the Three Dolphins Club. As we entered the office, I saw George, Leslie, Jennifer and Tommy, all hard at work. They all looked up when they heard us enter.

"Let me see my precious baby," said Leslie looking at Demetrious.

I gently sent Demetrious floating across the room toward Leslie, knowing she would catch him. "He's still kind of groggy from being sedated, but he seems fine now that he's back home."

"Yes, we're happy to be away from that nasty old gravity aren't we," Leslie said to Demetrious in that goofy way that adults talk to babies.

"George, we need to talk," I said.

"Yes," replied George with a look that suggested he knew what was coming.

"There's no way we're going through that again. I was scared to death that I'd lose Demetrious. I won't do that to him again. So I need us to be exempt from the shore leave policy."

"I figured you'd be requesting that and I'm really happy that Demetrious is going to be okay. The intent of that policy it to do what's best for the employees. In your case, it seems clear to me that what's best for you and Demetrious is to not have to return to Earth every six months. You can, of course, return if you want to, but for you and Demetrious it will no longer be mandatory."

"Thank you George!" I exclaimed as I gave him a big hug. "And thanks for sending Mr. Elliott here to help us."

"So I'm Mr. Elliott now, am I?" said Marc.

"It was mostly Leslie's idea," said George. "She and I were both worried about Demetrious, but she also figured that you and Marc needed a little shove, if you know what I mean."

"Thank you Leslie," I said as I hugged her. "For both things."

"It was my idea to get you on today's spaceplane to Sky City II," interjected Tommy. "I had to do a little finagling to free up three seats. If it wasn't for that you'd still be fighting the gees back on Earth until tomorrow."

"Thank you Tommy," I said, giving him a hug too.

"It was nothing," replied Tommy with fake humility. "I was just being my usual indispensable self."

"Aren't you going to tell her?" Leslie said to George.

"Tell me what?" I asked, looking at George.

"Aren't you going to tell her your dirty little secret?" Leslie persisted.

"It's no big deal," replied George. "We can discuss it tonight at dinner. I'm taking everyone out to dinner tonight in the casino to celebrate the safe return of Tesla and Demetrious Miller. Be there at 8 pm."

...

Marc, Demetrious and I arrived at the restaurant in the casino a few minutes after 8 pm. Jennifer and Tommy were already there. We joined them at the table and ordered drinks. Leslie and George were late. The drinks arrived at the same time they did. "Sorry we're late," said George. "One of us never estimates how long it will take her to get ready."

Leslie slugged him playfully on the arm.

"No problem," said Marc. "We just got some drinks to start the celebration."

Leslie and George took their places at the table and ordered drinks too. When they arrived, George raised his glass and said, "To our returning Floaters, Tesla and Demetrious, floating is freedom!"

"Floating is freedom," everyone repeated.

After a second round of drinks, I said to George, "So what's this big secret you have?"

"It's no big deal," replied George looking at his wife. "Leslie thinks it's a big deal, but it isn't."

"Well, what is it?" I pressed.

George turned back toward me. "Alright, here it is. I don't take the regular shore leave either. I tried it once and it was a pain in the butt, so I stopped doing it."

"And," said Leslie.

"And, I don't do the two hours of exercise every day. I tried that for a while too, but it also was a pain in the butt and it took too much time. So I stopped doing it because, well you know, people are lazy. It's unrealistic to expect them to do what's good for them, especially if it's hard, like exercising for two hours every day."

"And," said Leslie again.

"And Leslie's pissed at me because that means I really can't return to Earth either."

"See, that wasn't so hard, was it George," said Leslie. "Confession is good for the soul."

"I hate to tell you George," said Tommy looking at George's rather large stomach and generally round shape. "But it ain't no secret that you don't exercise two hours a day."

"Plus we never see you down in the fitness center," added Jennifer.

"You're piling on too, Jennifer?" said George pretending to be hurt.

"Well here's to living permanently in space," I said lifting my glass

"To living permanently in space!" they all repeated.

"George, I have a question."

"What is it?"

"Sometimes I feel like I've done a terrible thing to Demetrious. I think I've condemned him to a life in space and he never had a choice. How do we know there will always be settlements here? What if this doesn't work out? Where will he live? How could I have done that to my son? I didn't know. How could I have known?

"Technically that was three statements and five questions," said Tommy.

Ignoring Tommy, George replied, "Children never have a choice, they just go where their parents take them. I can't tell you what the future holds for certain. Will this all work out? I don't know, but I can tell you this. Eventually someone will succeed in doing this, it's inevitable. It will happen because of our one unique resource, the absence of gravity. Making this resource available will ultimately result in successful settlements in space."

"Here here!" Marc chimed in. "People won't be living on other planets or moons because, you know, they literally suck. Just look at the two best options Mars and our Moon. Why fight your way out of the

136

Earth's gravity-well, travel over a hundred forty million miles through space to get to Mars, just to go down into another deep gravity-well? Then once you're there it's bitter cold, you're still bathed in galactic cosmic rays, you can't breathe the air, and you get half the sunlight you get at Earth. With less energy at your disposal, people there will naturally be poorer.

"Mars sucks!" exclaimed Tommy.

"The Moon is worse," Marc continued. "The days are fourteen Earth-days long as are the nights, so the surface is really hot during the day, roughly two hundred degrees Fahrenheit, and very, very cold at night, about two hundred forty degrees below zero. This will likely force any settlements to be at the lunar poles in order to get access to continuous sunlight. This greatly limits the amount of good real estate available, if you could call it that, and of course, there's no atmosphere. To make matters worse, everything gets covered in a fine dust with sharp edges that wreaks havoc on people and machinery."

"The Moon sucks too!" exclaimed Tommy again.

"Now don't get me wrong," Marc went on. "There will almost certainly be small scientific outposts on the Moon and Mars, but larger-scale communities there seem unlikely, at least for a very long time."

"You said people will be poorer on Mars," asked Jennifer. "That would seem to be important, but I don't get it. Why is that?"

"It's because one true measure of a person's wealth is the amount of energy they have at their disposal. Space is flooded with energy from the sun. We're bathed in it here. With so much energy easily available, people living in space will be wealthy. But if you're living on Mars, you only get half the sunlight simply because you're farther from the sun. That means you have to work harder to collect the same amount of energy, or for the same effort you get less energy. And less energy means less wealth."

"It's all about economics," added George. "The Moon and Mars simply don't offer compelling economic cases for settlements. Even the worst place on Earth is a much, much nicer place to live than the nicest places on the Moon or Mars. Look, there are lots of really nice places on Earth where very few people live. Why don't people live there? For example, on my last trip to Earth, Leslie and I were in California and we drove from Los Angeles to Cambria, a little town on the coast just north of San Luis Obispo. We took Green Valley Road from the 101 freeway west to Cambria. That is some of the most beautiful countryside you'd ever want to see. Beautiful green rolling hills, nice weather year round. It's in a state with a booming economy in one of the most stable, safest countries on the planet. Yet very few people live there. Why is that?"

"There's no economic reason to do so," Marc and Tommy said in unison, having heard this speech many times before.

"That's right, George went on. "It's the same reason we don't have settlements under the sea or floating cities on the ocean. Those things are hard and expensive and don't offer any compelling economic reasons to exist, and so they don't. Space is hard and expensive too, but it has a compelling economic engine, tourism like we're doing here. And tourism is driven by our one unique resource, freedom from the tyranny of gravity. Eventually, as more people start living in space, they will literally re-invent everything they use because, you know, Grounders don't know shit about really living in zero-g. People living in space, people that move here originally to take care of the tourists, will create a demand for new products and services, ultimately creating vast new markets and creating a huge new economy. Meeting this demand for new products and services will result in lots of people making lots of money. Combine the availability of plentiful energy with the material resources that Marc here obtains from near-Earth asteroids and you've got everything you need for humanity to settle space and to live richly while doing it. The settlement of space provides huge economic potential for which ever nation exploits it first."

"So I didn't ruin Demetrious' life by bringing him here?" I pleaded.

"Well, there are no guarantees in life," replied Marc. "But there are certainly a lot of children on Earth who live in a lot worse places."

"And a lot more people have been killed by gravity than by the lack of it," quipped Tommy.

Marc laughed, "Good point. So Tesla, I think you did alright bringing him here."

Later that night, as promised, I expressed my appreciation to Marc for helping us on Earth. It was as wonderful, intimate, sexy, and thrilling as our first time, although this time I was much more skilled at making love in zero-g. Skills that I could tell Marc both appreciated and lamented at the same time.

...

A few days later at lunch—Sasha, Yuri and I made it a point to have lunch together at least once a week, something we'd been doing for the past six months—Yuri said, "I haven't seen Marc around since you guys spent the night together. What's up with that?"

"He's just busy," I said, hoping it was true. I actually hadn't heard from him since our 'reunion.'

"Uh huh, sure," replied Yuri.

"What's wrong with that boy?" asked Sasha rhetorically.

"There's nothing wrong with him," I said defensively. I no sooner finished saying that when I received a text. "See, I just got a text from him," I said confidently, holding up my phone.

I read the text out loud, "The other night was incredible. You're incredible." I smiled at Sasha and Yuri as if to say 'told you so' and then kept reading. "But I just can't do this. It's your job, I thought I could deal with it, but just can't. It's not you, it's me." The smile quickly faded from my face.

"Men are pigs," said Yuri with a mouth full of food.

"Why do I have such a hard time with men?" I asked. "Is there something about me that's drawn to men intent on making my life miserable?"

"Just tell him to fuck off," said Sasha.

I was so pissed, I immediately sent back a short text; "Fuck off!"

...

Marc called the next day after getting my "fuck off" text. He apologized profusely and admitted he was wrong. I was not impressed.

Chapter 14 Alex

Chicago, Illinois

Alex was still in shock. It had been six months since his wife left him and took off with their son. He could not let go of the blow to his masculinity that Ella's leaving created. *How could she leave me?* He played this question over in his mind as he had a thousand times. *How could she do this to me? It wasn't supposed to be like this. I'm a smart, likeable person. Why wouldn't she want to be with me? What's wrong with her?*

At first Alex channeled all his anger into finding his wife and son. He also drank heavily in mostly a unsuccessful attempt to ease the pain, but his motivation to find them kept his drinking from getting too out of control. As the months dragged on with no progress, Alex's anger turned to depression and his drinking got worse, much worse. He refused help from his friends and co-workers. He started missing more and more days at work. When he did show up, he was either drunk or hung over. Eventually the Chicago police department had enough and they let Alex go. Before long, he was forcibly evicted from the tiny apartment he had moved into after losing the house they used to own. Penniless and homeless, Alex was now living on the streets of Chicago.

When he was sober enough to think about it, he was amazed at how fast his life had changed. *How the hell did I get here?* he wondered. *What had gone so wrong that I wound up like this?* But mostly he didn't care. Mostly he just tried to drink his troubles away. Lately, even that wasn't enough. He couldn't drink enough to forget. But life on the streets in Chicago offered many solutions to this problem. It wasn't long before Alex was addicted to heroin. It was cheap, it was plentiful, and it did the job. It was also all consuming.

Alex had been living on the streets for the last two months. It seemed like a lifetime. Winter was rapidly approaching and Alex was undernourished. Every penny he got from begging went to support his heroin addiction. Getting high was the only thing he lived for, the only thing that made life worth living, if you could call it living.

It was cold today. An early taste of winter in Chicago. High on heroin, Alex didn't notice the cold as he laid in the basement of an abandoned, unheated building with several other addicts. Alex's new "friends" realized it was too cold to spend the night there and they needed to get to a homeless shelter. They tried to wake Alex, but he was unresponsive. Still, they never considered leaving him there. That wouldn't be right. So they carried him six city blocks to the shelter.

Virgil, who ran the shelter, recognized Alex's distress. He had seen heroin overdoses many times before and immediately called the paramedics. Alex spent the night in Cook County Hospital (which is what the locals still called it even though its official name was The John H. Stroger, Jr. Hospital of Cook County). The next morning, after determining Alex was no longer in danger, and after a hot meal, the hospital returned him to the homeless shelter.

Unbeknownst to Alex, it was Sunday morning. Alex had long since stopped caring what day of the week it was. As he entered the shelter, he heard Virgil making an announcement. "Today we have a guest speaker for our morning church service, Pastor Jamal Young. Pastor Young is visiting us all the way from Texas. He is the head pastor at Purification by Grace Ministries in Austin. Please join us in meeting room A at ten am, that's just ten minutes from now."

Alex glanced at the flyer posted in the shelter which indicated Purification by Grace Ministries was a large church dedicated to helping victims of drug abuse get their lives back together through prayer and financial aid. Their calling was to help people beat their addition to drugs, help them find jobs, and help them become productive members of society again—and to save their souls along the way.

I don't need this shit, Alex thought to himself. *I can take care of myself.* A bitter cold blast of Chicago wind hit Alex as he stepped out the shelter door. *All right, maybe it wouldn't hurt to stay just a little while and listen to the good pastor,* he thought. Alex went back in and took a seat near the back of the meeting room. He looked around the room. It was about half full. *They're probably just like me, just wanting to stay out of the cold a while longer.*

Pastor Young entered the room right on time. He looked to be in his late fifty's, but he had an energetic way about him. When he spoke, Alex was drawn in. Jamal was a gifted speaker, clear, captivating and charming. Even so, Alex had trouble concentrating these days and didn't really listen to the whole sermon, but one part caught his attention.

"...It's not your fault," said Jamal. "You are victims in a cosmic battle of good and evil. A cosmic battle for your soul. You may have lost this battle to the enemy, but you can still win the war. There is still hope. Where there is God, there is always hope. God has a plan for your salvation. With God, you can defeat the enemy, you can banish Satan from your life. All you have to do is accept the sacrifice that Christ Jesus made on the cross two thousand years ago, and then pick up your cross and follow him. That's God's plan for your life."

Like the best speakers, Jamal spoke in a rhythm and with a tone of voice that made everything he said sound important. At the end of this sermon, as he did at the end of every sermon, Jamal invited everyone to accept Jesus as their lord and savior. He said all they had to do was to raise their hand.

He wasn't even sure why he did it, but Alex raised his hand, as did several others.

After the sermon, Jamal came over to talk to each one of them. By the time he got to Alex, Alex was in tears.

"Please help me," pleaded Alex looking down at his feet.

"Jesus will help you if you let him," replied Jamal.

"I don't know what to do?" sobbed Alex.

"What are you addicted to?" asked Jamal. He knew an addict when he saw one.

"Who said I was addicted to anything," Alex said defensively.

"I've seen that look too many times before, my son. My guess is heroin. Is that right?" asked Jamal calmly.

Alex nodded, still looking at the ground.

Jamal put his hand on Alex's shoulder. "Lift up your head my son. There's no shame here, only help. What's your name?"

"Alex…Alex Markov."

"Well Alex, I can help you if you let me."

"Yeah?" Alex said hesitantly. "How?"

"It's easy. You just agree to stay with the program for six months and join us tomorrow for the return trip back to Austin, Texas."

"You mean I have to move to Texas?"

"I'm afraid so."

"Where would I live?" asked Alex, starting to get cold feet. "What would I do?"

"You'd live in our detox facility at no cost to you. All we ask is that you help around the church facility when you're feeling well enough to do so, and that you attend a weekly Bible study and Sunday services. After six months you'll be free and clear of heroin and then we'll help you find a job."

"Why are you doing this?"

"We believe it's God's special calling for our congregation. So if you're interested, please let Virgil know before noon tomorrow. Our bus is leaving tomorrow afternoon for Austin."

"Who's Virgil?"

"He's the guy that runs this shelter. That's him over there," replied Jamal pointing to Virgil across the room.

Alex wasn't so far gone that he knew if he didn't commit now, by tomorrow he'd be high on heroin again and nothing else would matter. No, it was now or never, he thought. It was life or death. This is my only chance if I ever want to see my son again. "I'll do it!" Alex blurted out.

"What?" said Jamal, somewhat surprised.

142

"I said I'll do it. I want to try your program."

"Bless you my son. I'll make arrangements with Virgil for you to stay here tonight and then tomorrow afternoon we'll depart for Texas." Jamal knew from experience he had to keep Alex here. If he let him go, he would never return.

Alex spent the night at the homeless shelter and departed with Pastor Jamal Young and his staff the following afternoon along with several other addicts.

Chapter 15 Propulsion

Length of time in space: *three and a half years*

Three years had passed since our ill-fated trip to Earth. Neither Demetrious nor I had been back to Earth since. I had long since settled into a familiar routine of working, raising Demetrious, and playing soccer. It made those three more years seemingly fly by in an instant. Fortunately, in all this time I heard nothing about Alex and nothing from the police.

My relationship with Marc was…complicated. We had also settled into a routine of sorts. He would apologize to me. We'd get together, make love and things would be good for a while. Then I'd get a new client. This would make Marc crazy, we'd fight and yell at each other. I wouldn't see him for a couple of months. Eventually he'd come back and apologize and we'd start up again. It was exhausting.

Demetrious, now four years old, was about to take a shower (there are, of course, no baths in zero-g) and had taken off all his clothes when I heard him call me.

"Mom! Mom? Come here I want to show you something."

"Not now Demetri," I'm busy.

"Mom, come here. It's important!"

"Okay," I replied, somewhat exacerbated. "What's so important that it couldn't wait until after your bath?" I asked as I entered the bathroom.

"Watch!"

I saw him floating perfectly motionless at one end of the bathroom, and then he started to pee. He was aiming his own personal rocket nozzle and began to accelerate across the room. In mid-flight, he directed his little thruster to the side causing him to rotate. He directed it back the other way and stopped his rotation after turning half-way around so that he was facing the opposite direction. He continued peeing until he came to a complete halt. Floating motionless again, he smiled at me and said, "ain't that cool!"

I stared at him through a haze of pee droplets. God, he looks just like Alex. I wanted to be stern with him. I wanted to tell him I was mad and he would be punished for making such a mess. That's what I wanted to do, but I could see he was so proud of his trick and he was so darn adorable, I just couldn't and, if fact, it was actually pretty impressive. It made me remember when he did this as an infant. I burst out laughing.

Demetrious started laughing too when he realized I wasn't mad. The air handling system quickly removed the pee from the air and the service robots cleaned the bathroom surfaces.

I hugged him. "That was amazing, but don't ever do that again." We both laughed.

...

Later that same day my sister called from Earth. "You have to see this!" she said. She sent me a link to a live video stream. "The bot I setup years ago to search for any mention of Alex just turned this up. It's the first hit in over three years!"

I opened the link and there he was! I could scarcely believe what I was seeing. Alex was sitting on stage in the sanctuary of a church called Purification by Grace Ministries. I watched in fascination as the Pastor, who the website identified as the head Pastor Jamal Young, addressed the congregation, "It's my honor and pleasure to present to you our new youth pastor, Pastor Alex Markov."

"Alex is a youth pastor?" Emma and I said simultaneously with the same tone of astonishment.

The crowd erupted in applause as Alex got up to address the congregation. "Thank you, thank you very much." Alex waited for the applause to die down and then began, "This has been a remarkable journey for me. A remarkable journey of redemption and purification. It is by the grace of God that I stand before you today. It is through the power of Jesus that my life has been completely turned around."

"Thank you Jesus," someone in the crowd yelled.

"As many of you know, it was three years ago that I entered the detox program here as a man beaten down by Satan. Only through the power of Christ was I able to give up all works of the devil, no alcohol, no heroin, no drugs of any kind. In six months I was free, praise God. My old self died to the sins that kept me prisoner and I was born again. I accepted Jesus as my Lord and savior. What else could I do?" Alex asked rhetorically with a smile.

"Praise Jesus," someone yelled.

"Two years ago, I started helping with the young-adult ministry. I could relate to their problems. I understood what they were going through, and I knew I had found my calling. I knew I wanted to be a pastor. I wanted to serve God. And now here I am. Isn't God great? We truly serve a remarkable God. Who but God could do such works of wonder?" Alex raised both arms and held them out to his side, palms facing upward, his body forming the shape of a cross. He bowed his head slightly and yelled, "Praise Jesus!"

"Praise Jesus," the crowd responded as it erupted in applause.

Alex stood there motionless, basking in the applause.

"Looks like Alex is finally getting the admiration he always desired," said Emma.

"Don't be so cynical. I'm happy for him." I thought for a moment, trying to make sense of this new development. "Plus, if he's a pastor he's probably forgiven me. Isn't that what pastors do? Anyway, I don't think we need to worry about Alex anymore."

"I hope you're right."

...

That night I was in a good mood. Probably because I was no longer worried about Alex finding us. Also, Marc was coming over from Sky City II to see me; and to apologize once again. I decided to wear one of my sexiest but-classy skin-tight outfits when I greeted him as he got off the taxi.

He wasn't smiling. "We need to talk," was how he greeted me.

Shit. "Okay, let's go to the bar, get some drinks and talk."

Neither one of us said a word as we made our way to the bar in the casino and grabbed a table in a relatively quiet location.

"So talk," I said after we ordered.

"I can't do this anymore."

It sounded like the beginning of a rehearsed speech. "Do what?"

"This rollercoaster of our on-again off-again relationship."

"You think this is easy on me?" I asked with rising tension in my voice.

"I think we should stop seeing each other for good." He said it, but it was clear he didn't say it with a lot of conviction.

That was my opening. "Now you look here Marc Elliott," I said sternly. "I love you and I know you love me. So I'm not going to let you just give up on us like that."

"I've tried, it's just that…"

"Look," I interrupted him. "I have less than a year and a half left on my contract. Just stay with me until then. Can you do that?"

Marc didn't move at first and didn't say anything. Eventually he nodded. Then he looked relieved and smiled an uncertain smile at me. I kissed him. He stayed with me that night, but I could see there was still sadness behind those brilliant blue eyes.

Chapter 16 Management

Length of time in space: *five years*

It was hard to believe that we've been at Sky City for five years I said to myself as I was getting dressed. My relationship with Marc over the last year and a half had been rocky at best. God, why do men have to be such a pain in the ass. I remember when I first arrived and George required me to sign that five-year contract that has been the source of so much of our problems. Five years seemed like it was going to be forever then. Now here it was already. Maybe things with Marc will improve now, I hoped.

...

Sasha, Yuri, and I finished getting ready and hurried over to the lobby as usual to wait for our clients. It was Sunday afternoon and the spaceplane with the new guests would be arriving soon. I was meeting one of my regular customers, Jimmy Homa, billionaire owner of Epoch Sports. True to his word, Jimmy had been coming to Sky City every three months for the last five years to see me. He would be my last client. After this, my contract was up. I wasn't sure what I was going to do next, but it wasn't going to be this. I had a lot of money saved up so I wasn't worried.

Sasha and Yuri were both meeting new clients. Sasha said her client was a man named John Smith. She thought it was a mistake at first, just a place holder. But the client's file confirmed his name was indeed John Smith. According to the file, he was a billionaire philanthropist who inherited his money. He was thirty years old with a bachelor's degree from Harvard. This was his first trip to space. As usual, Sasha memorized his picture.

Sasha's guest was the first one off the plane. I could see that she recognized him immediately. She glided over to greet him. Yuri and I were close enough to overhear their conversation.

"Hi I'm Sasha," she said cheerfully.

"I know, I picked you out, remember," Smith said with an air of disdain.

Sasha looked somewhat taken back by this, but seemed determined to maintain a friendly air. "Did you have a good flight up?" she asked cheerfully.

"Look, I don't care to make a lot of small talk, okay. Just do as you're told, do your job, and we'll be fine."

"Look," replied Sasha, sternly this time. "If you don't want me, I'm sure the Club can arrange for someone else to help you during your stay here at Sky City."

"I already told you I picked you, didn't I. What part of that didn't you understand?"

Sasha didn't respond, but looked over at me and Yuri and mouthed the word "trouble."

"What did she say?" I whispered to Yuri.

"I think she said 'trouble'," replied Yuri quietly.

"Do you know what exactly she means by that?"

Yuri pulled me away from Sasha and her client put his lips up close to my ear. "It means she thinks her client is one of those assholes who abuses women," Yuri said quietly. "I know she's met this kind before, back on Earth. They're demanding, arrogant, bullies that treat women badly."

"We better let George know as soon as possible. Since Jimmy and I know each other very well, I'll get him registered quickly, drop him off at his suite as usual, and then go tell George."

"Okay."

I saw Jimmy entering the lobby. "Hi Jimmy. You're looking good! Earth-life must agree with you."

"Hi Tesla, flattery will get you everywhere," replied Jimmy.

"Jimmy, can I ask you a question?" I said quietly as I floated up close to him.

"Yes, of course."

"Do you see that man over there with Sasha?" I said, tilting my head to the left. "Do you know who he is?

Jimmy glanced over my left shoulder and replied, "No, I don't know him. I've never seen him before. Why do you ask?"

"Sasha thinks he's trouble. After we get you settled I'm going to go tell Mr. Abruzzo."

"I can go with you if you like," said Jimmy.

"Thanks Jimmy, but that's okay. We'll get you settled in so you can relax. Then I'll tell George, I mean Mr. Abruzzo."

When we got to the registration desk, Catherine the receptionist whispered to me, "That client with Sasha was the rudest man I have ever met."

"I know," I whispered back. "Sasha thinks he's trouble. I'm going to go tell George as soon as I get Jimmy settled."

"Hey, I know you two are fighting over me," said Jimmy jokingly. "Catherine, I hate to tell you but Tesla is my one true love."

"You're breaking my heart Jimmy," replied Catherine.

I asked Catherine what room Sasha's client, John Smith, was staying in. Immediately after getting Jimmy to his room, I decided to go check on Sasha before heading to the Three Dolphins Club to see George.

I could hear yelling as I approached the room and knocked on the door. As the door opened I saw Sasha's client slap her across the face. I quickly entered the room and yelled, "Back off asshole." I shoved Smith away from Sasha as I called for help. "Sky City, send security to the Carolyn Shoemaker room immediately."

Smith bounced off the display at the end of the room and headed right back at me. Before I could move he punched me in the nose. I could hear the click as my nose broke.

A few seconds later Charlie, the head of security, and two other guards arrived. After a brief struggle, they subdued and handcuffed John Smith. Sasha handed me a towel to soak up the blood coming from my nose.

George and Jennifer arrived a few seconds after that.

"My god, what happened," said George as he saw my bloody face.

"This asshole punched Tesla," replied Sasha with a great deal of hatred in her voice.

George looked at John Smith and gasped. Smith smiled at George.

I stared at George. "Do you know this asshole?" I managed to say, even though it sounded like I had a bad cold.

"Unfortunately, I do," replied George. "He's my son Michael. He's been trouble since the day he was born. Even as a child he always seemed unhappy. Now, he's getting worse. He used to just be generally unpleasant to be around. Now he's vindictive, short tempered and even violent, as you can see."

"I love you too, Dad," said Michael, his voice dripping with sarcasm.

Now that he said it, the resemblance was obvious. He looked to be about thirty years old, kind of portly, losing his hair already, and the spitting image of George. Strange that we didn't notice that before.

George turned to look at his son and said, "I didn't realize you got out of prison already."

"Special early release program to ease prison overcrowding," replied Michael. "Since mine was a non-violent crime, they let me go,"

"Non-violent my ass," said Sasha.

"Do you want me to uncuff him Mr. Abruzzo? asked Charlie.

I had gotten to be quite fond of Charlie. His full name was Charles Fitzpatrick O'Brien, but everyone called him Charlie. He'd been the head of security at Sky City since it first opened. He was a large man who was reportedly ripped in his younger days, but years behind a desk in Chicago produced a more middle-aged body that he has retained to this day. His once red hair was now mostly gray. He was an ex-Chicago police officer who resigned after twenty-five years of service because his whistle-blower case against the department for corruption didn't get the legal protection he expected. When George gave him a chance to be the head of security at Sky City, he jumped at the opportunity. As a result, Charlie was fiercely loyal to George.

"No," replied George. "Take him to the detention area. We'll send him back to Earth on the next available spaceplane."

"What about pressing charges?" Sasha said. She looked at me, "You need to press charges. We can't let him get away with this. We can't let anyone get away with something like this."

I was uncomfortable with pressing charges or anything that had to do with the police back on Earth, even though I wanted to. But George convinced me that the documents he provided for my identity as Tesla Miller would stand up to scrutiny and that I needed to do this. I trusted George completely and agreed to press charges to make sure his son was sent back to prison.

...

Late that night I made sure that Jimmy was okay and apologized in advance that our last week together wouldn't be what he expected for obvious reasons. He was very gracious and understanding as always, and of course, George gave him a full refund.

I then made sure that Demetrious was asleep before heading out to the casino bar hoping that George would be there. I was not disappointed. I saw him at his usual table. "Hi George," I said. "Mind if I join you?"

"Please, I could use the company," replied George without looking up.

"You don't mind being seen with a person who has two black eyes and a broken nose."

George looked up from his glass of whisky and said, "I'm just glad it wasn't worse."

"What happened today has me really shaken up."

"I can imagine, given your history."

"Did you know your son was coming here?"

"No. I asked Tommy to look into how this happened. Evidently, Michael used someone else's picture and name when he made his reservation. Our usual background check didn't pick up anything unusual. Then he exploited a flaw in our system which allows a client to update his picture with a new one if he or she wants to. My son evidently did this and uploaded his real picture. This was the picture that was included in the file we gave Sasha and why Sasha was able to identify him when he arrived. We never go back and compare new pictures with the old ones to see if it's the same person. Tommy is now correcting this vulnerability. If we had known it was him, we would never have allowed him to come here."

"It just reminded me of how fast it can happen, even with our security measures," I said. "We need to do better. I have some suggestions on what we should do that I wanted to discuss with you, but let me ask you this first. How did someone like your son come from such wonderful people as you and Leslie?"

George shook his head. "Good question. We ask ourselves that all the time. What did we do wrong? What should we have done differently? Maybe we spoiled him when he was little. I don't know. I have a feeling that he was just born this way." George paused for a moment, seemingly lost in his thoughts. Then his face noticeably brightened. "But we also tell each other that you're like the daughter we never had. You have been such a pleasure to have here. I cherish our late-night discussions after the soccer matches and I value your opinions and suggestions on how to improve the Club. It's clear that you have made the club a much better place to work and a much better business at the same time, and that's not an easy thing to do."

I grabbed his hand. "Well, you took a chance on me and Demetrious when we were desperate."

"Yes," replied George softly. "As you know, your five-year contract will be up very soon. I was going to ask you to see me at the office tomorrow, but we might as well do it right now."

"Do what?"

George squeezed my hand, "I wanted to let you know that I won't be running the Three Dolphin's Club forever."

"You're not leaving are you?" I asked with more than a little concern. "You can't leave."

"Oh, I'm not leaving, but I am getting older, and I need time to concentrate on Sky City II. You have learned so much since you first arrived. It's amazing to me to see how much you've grown. How you've changed from that frightened, uncertain person who first arrived here to the smart, confident person I see in front of me today." He paused for a moment and then added, "Well, except for the black eyes and swollen nose."

"Is there a point to all of this flattery?"

"Yes, I want you to take over the day-to-day operations of the club after you recover from your injuries. I have thought a lot about this. I've seen how you deal with people and I'm certain that you're the best person for the job. Tommy will take over the operation of the rest of the resort, but I want you to run the Three Dolphins Club."

"I don't know what to say.
"Say yes. We can work out the details tomorrow."
"Yes!"

...

That night as I floated in "bed" sleep did not come easily. My mind was racing, replaying the events of the day. How quickly someone could turn violent. How powerless we were to stop it. The violence jolted me out of the comfortable, seemingly safe life I had grown accustom to at Sky City. I hadn't experienced such violence since I left Alex five years ago. Why did some men have to get so violent? I wondered if Alex ever thought about us.

George always took such good care of the employees of the Three Dolphins Club. He treated us like family. Now I'm going to be in charge. I hope I can do as well... I'm going to be running a multi-million dollar business. How cool is that? And it's so bizarre. The business is in space, and it's a brothel! How did I come to run a legal prostitution business in space? Life is weird.

I would have tossed and turned all night if I had been on Earth, but here there was no tossing and turning here, just floating. On the bright side, I didn't have to lay my sore, swollen face down on a pillow. Eventually sleep overtook me, but my mind continued on as if only part of my brain was sleeping and part was still awake processing the day's events.

The next morning I was up early. In spite of my worries and injuries, it was still very restful to sleep in zero-g. I went in early to the Club. I wanted to learn everything I could from George about how to run the Club before he left for Sky City II.

Later that morning, all of the employees of the Club gathered in the Sports Arena and asked me to meet them there. As I joined them, uncertain about what was going on, Yuri came forward, smiled at me and said, "Geeze Tesla, you look terrible." He waited for the laughter to subside and then continued. "I all seriousness Tesla, we've known each other for a long time, in fact ever since you first came to Sky City. I knew you when you were that scared girl who couldn't stop throwing up in the lobby, the one who didn't know how to work the toilet, the one who thought she was dying because her heart rate was too low, and you know I love you. So I've been elected to speak on behalf of all of us. George told us what his plans are and while we're all sad to see George leave the Club, we think he couldn't have chosen a better person to take his place. We just wanted to let you know that we believe in you."

"Thank you Yuri," I replied with tears welling up in my eyes. "I love you too. I love all of you. You are like my family here and I will do my very best to continue to run the Club the way that George did."

…

Later that morning I called Marc about the incident and my promotion. I knew he was at Sky City II. He immediately scheduled a taxi to Sky City for that evening to be with me.

I met him as he got off the taxi in engineering. I was dressed casually, not in one of the skin-tight outfits from the Club. I was rewarded with the biggest, brightest smile from Marc that I had seen in a long time.

"You look fantastic," he said as I floated toward him.

"Liar," I responded playfully, knowing that I looked awful with my black eyes and broken nose. But it was a nice lie. He kissed me very gently as my body impacted his. We spent the night together. Since I was obviously in no condition for sex, we just held on to each other all night. It was very romantic.

…

A month later we heard that a judge did indeed send Michael Abruzzo back to prison on assault and parole violations.

By now my black eyes had gone away and my nose was no longer swollen. Marc came over to finish the celebration over my new job. I asked Leslie Abruzzo if she would watch Demetrious for the night. That night was the best sex we had in years. My whole body shuddered with ecstasy. Afterwards, as we floated naked in each other's arms, all I could think of was that this must be what heaven was like. This was heaven. Just before drifting off to sleep, my mind flashed to Alex. In a weird way I had Alex to thank for all this.

…

The next morning after Marc left, I got call from Emma. "It's happening again," she said excitedly. "There's another live-stream about Alex. Here's the link."

I opened the video link. There was Alex sitting on stage again as Pastor Jamal Young prepared to address his congregation. Alex looked out at the crowd, which the scrolling text at the bottom of the screen indicated was in excess of fifty thousand people. The text also indicated that Purification by Grace Ministries was now the second largest congregation in the United States and was still growing rapidly. The website said it already had several assistant pastors, but it needed still more to manage the fruits of its rapid growth.

Alex sat quietly on stage as Pastor Jamal introduced him. "Today it is my great pleasure to introduce you to our newest assistant Pastor. A man many of you have come to know well these past few years. Alex's charismatic personality and the needs of our rapidly growing church have propelled Alex's swift, God-driven rise into the upper ranks of our church family. Please join me in giving a warm welcome to Pastor Alex Markov."

Alex stood as the crowd roared its approval. "Thank you," yelled Alex over the crowd noise. "Thank you." He motioned for the crowd to be quiet.

He looks older, I thought, and it looks like he's put on some weight since we last saw him.

When crowd finally did settle down, he began. "It is by the grace of God that I stand before you today. God saved me from addiction and despair. God took a hold of me when no one else would and forgave me when I had no right to expect forgiveness. Now I have dedicated my life to paying this forward. It is with great honor and humility that I accept this position to become your assistant pastor today. I will use this opportunity to show others how to follow after God, and I am going to start with those who have been forgotten by society. Today, it is my pleasure to announce the initiation of our new prison ministry, because if God can save me, I know he can save those poor souls that society has discarded." Alex paused for a moment, apparently to let those words soak into the crowd, then he shouted, "Praise Jesus!"

The crowd erupted in applause with people shouting back, "Praise Jesus. Praise God."

Alex looked thoroughly pleased with himself as basked in the thundering applause that rocked the arena that morning. He almost had a look of arrogance about him. Maybe it's just my past with him that's tainting my current perception. "Is it just me, or does he look like he's enjoying this a little too much?" I asked Emma.

"Oh, he's definitely creepy," she replied without hesitation.

"But the people sure seem to love him," I replied. "I think we have to give him the benefit of the doubt."

Chapter 17 Negative g's

Length of time in space: *seven years.*

Two years had passed since I took over the Three Dolphins Club. I had everything running smoothly if I do say so myself. Business was good both at the Club and at the resort as a whole. Tommy kept the resort running efficiently. I still frequently consulted with George for advice and guidance even though he was living at Sky City II full time now while managing its development. Nevertheless, he found time to come to Sky City regularly and still played on our soccer team. George and I continued our late-night after-soccer talks.

I was pleasantly surprised at how easy I found it was to manage the business. In fact, everything it seemed just came easier to me now. Things that I used to think were complicated no longer seem difficult. I'm not complaining, it's just weird.

Demetrious was now seven and a half years old and just completed fourth grade online. My relationship Marc was excellent. He was much happier since I was no longer one of the Club's escorts. We had no trouble sustaining our ultimate long-distance relationship with Marc living on Earth and me living up here. We saw each other at every opportunity during Marc's frequent trips to space for work.

Early every Sunday morning I'd still go out in the Celestial Sphere by myself, still hoping to recapture the experience I felt that first time so many years ago. This morning, as I hung there suspended in space with Earth hovering above me and the deep black expanse beneath my feet, I couldn't help but wonder how my life had turned out so well. My son was healthy and happy, I was the successful manager of a thriving business, and I was in a committed, stable relationship with a smart, funny, and caring man. Life was good.

...

The very next day we heard that Michael Abruzzo was released from prison. I was visiting George in his office at Sky City II when his phone rang. George put it on speaker, but no video.

"Dad, it's me, Michael!"

"Yes," replied George cautiously, with a decidedly unhappy look on his face

"Dad, I just got out and you're the first person I wanted to call. I had a lot of time to think in there and I wanted to let you know that I'm ready to change. I'm ready to be a better person. I just need a chance to show you."

"Michael, we've had this conversation before," replied George sternly. There was a tiredness in his voice that I rarely heard. "We've given you lots of chances already. I don't think giving you one more chance will make any difference."

"Dad, this time is different. They released me on parole with time off for good behavior. I've changed dad and I want to prove it to you."

"Michael, I don't…"

"No really, I'm a changed man," Michael interrupted, "I realized, with some help from the people there, that I couldn't continue living the way I was. So I figured that if I could just come to Sky City II, I could help you with the construction. You know, really work hard."

George knew from bitter experience that Michael could not be trusted, and it was obvious he wasn't buying his, 'I've changed' routine.

"I don't think so Michael," replied George.

"How can I prove to you that I've changed?" begged Michael.

"Look Michael, I don't think that there's anything you could do that would convince me." I could tell that it pained George deeply to say that.

"How about I get a job here, keep my nose clean for six months? Then can I come to Sky City II?"

Michael was George and Leslie's only child and George had a soft spot in his heart for him in spite of all the trouble he caused them. They still loved him as only parents could. George knew there was no way Michael could successfully hold a real job for six months, so maybe he thought this would be good way to keep him from coming up here without hurting him further. "Okay, okay," George replied reluctantly. It was clear that this was going against his better judgement. "If you can keep a real job for six months and stay out of trouble, then you can come up here to work. But, and I can't stress this strongly enough, if you do come up here and cause even the slightest bit of trouble I'll send you back down immediately, got it?"

"Got it, Dad. You won't regret it."

"This is a bad idea," George said to me immediately after hanging up. His face displayed an uneasiness nagging at the back of his mind. I knew he always had a hard time saying no to Michael.

…

Six months later the phone call that George was dreading arrived. "Dad, it's me Michael."

"Yes Michael," replied George unenthusiastically.

"Just as I promised, I've had a job for the last six months and I haven't been in any trouble."

"Yes, I'm aware of that. I had some of my people keeping an eye on you. I've been expecting your call."

"So can I come to Sky City II now?" asked Michael. "I'd really like to work there and show you that I've changed. I want to make you proud of me."

"Look son, I'm still not buying your 'I've changed,' routine, so give it a rest," said George, "But I did make a promise. I have a job lined up for you and will make arrangements for your transportation here when you are ready. Just be aware that I will be keeping a very close eye on you. Any screw up and you'll be back on Earth so fast your head will spin.

"What kind of job is it?" asked Michael without saying thank you.

"You'll start at the bottom. The job is to run ALARA. It's our machine that takes in asteroid material and it turns it into packaged radiation shielding. Your job will be to keep the machine running. It's a hard, dirty job because the asteroid dust causes the machine to break down frequently so that it needs to be cleaned and repaired regularly."

"Great Dad. I can be ready to leave next week," Michael said with exaggerated enthusiasm.

...

Michael arrived on the Sunday afternoon spaceplane to Sky City II. This was a different flight from the one used to deliver guests to the Sky City resort on Sunday afternoons. This was mostly a cargo ship that could also accommodate few construction workers for the ongoing construction. The resort was just six months away from its scheduled completion date.

The foreman met Michael and the other new workers upon their arrival at Sky City II, but George, who usually meets with all the new employees, was not there this time. As they got off the spaceplane, they were automatically given a shot of Phenergan to keep them from throwing up. Then they were given directions to the mess hall, shown the location of the head (no private bathrooms for the construction crew), and finally taken to their quarters. The foreman instructed them to report for work first thing the next morning. There was no "grace period" for the arrival of new construction workers. They were expected to start work immediately.

Michael showed up on time for work the next day as he did every day for the next two months, just biding his time and making himself look responsible. He thought of himself more as a person in charge rather than a common laborer and had no intention of doing this dirty, boring job for very long. *I hate this work. It's beneath me*, he thought. *But it won't be long now*, he kept telling himself. *I just need to wait for the right opportunity.*

...

I was in my office at the Three Dolphin's Club screening the passengers arriving at Sky City as I always did when Michael's larger-than-life face showed up on my display. I turned to Jennifer and said, "What's that asshole doing here?"

Jennifer quickly looked up his file. "Evidently he's been working at Sky City II for the last two months. After two months of being a model employee, it says, he earned a day off. I guess he decided to spend it here like the other construction workers, drinking and gambling in the casino.

"Shit," I replied. "Why didn't George tell me?" I left the office to confront George's son in the lobby while trying to figure out how to get him out of Sky City before he caused any trouble. Michael didn't see me approaching him until I was literally in his face.

"What the hell are you doing here?" I said sternly but quietly, so as to not cause a disturbance.

"Nice to see you too, Tesla" replied Michael snidely, "And don't give me any of your shit. I've paid my debt to society."

"What are you doing in my resort?" I persisted. Even though I only ran the Three Dolphins Club, I took it upon myself to know what went on in the entire resort and I did whatever I could to help Tommy keep it running smoothly.

"Your resort?" snorted Michael. "That's a laugh. Soon this entire resort will be mine, including the Three Dolphins Club, and you'll be the one in prison. So you better watch that mouth of yours. How's your nose, by the way?"

"I'll be watching your every move," I replied forcefully. "Step out of line and I'll have you hogtied and shipped back to Sky City II immediately." I called security while hovering right in front of Michael's face. "Security, this is Tesla, there is a Michael Abruzzo in the lobby. I'd like you to assign someone to follow him around the facility to make sure he doesn't become a problem. Jennifer will send you his file."

"That's a waste of time," said Michael. "Don't you know I'm a model employee."

...

That afternoon Michael went to the Fitness Center to lift weights. It was a habit he picked up in prison. As he entered the Fitness Center, he

158

heard laughter coming from the Sports Arena and went to check it out. He saw a young boy about eight years old entertaining a group of younger children with his flying acrobatics. Michael recognized the young boy immediately, *Demetrious.*

Judging by their clumsiness in zero-g, the kids were probably all Grounders Michael surmised. *Spoiled, pre-school aged kids of rich guests at the resort,* he thought. Michael watched Demetrious fly rapidly directly at the children. At the last minute he rotated his body, opened his wings like a large bird, and with one powerful stroke of his wings stopped on a dime directly in front of them. The blast of wind from Demetrious' wings sent the kids flying off, tumbling head-over-heals, making them squeal with delight. They bounced off the walls and floated out into the middle of the arena. Demetrious then collected them one-by-one as they floated helplessly around the Arena giggling. He flew over to each one, grabbed them with his legs, brought them back to where they started, and lined them up in a row facing the long way down the Arena. Demetrious then flew over in front of them, turned to face them, closed his eyes and floated motionlessly, as only a Floater can.

When they saw that Demetrious wasn't moving, all the kids yelled in unison, "AGAIN!" and Demetrious opened his eyes, took off and repeated the process. After doing this several times Demetrious was clearly tired and Michael watched as he took the kids one-by-one back to the daycare section of the Sports Arena. When all the kids were back in the daycare, Demetrious returned to the larger section of the Arena, closed his eyes and again floated motionlessly in the large open space.

Michael was clinging to the wall of the Arena and said, "That was quite a show you put on. You must be Demetrious Miller."

Demetrious opened his eyes, took one look at Michael and said, "And you're the asshole who beat up my mom."

"Such talk from a child. Didn't your mother teach you any manners?" scolded Michael. "Oh, that's right, your mother doesn't have any manners."

"Asshole," Demetrious muttered under his breath.

"Maybe I should teach both you and your mother some manners," threatened Michael. "I can't have such bad behavior here when I take over. I especially can't have foul-mouthed, skinny freaks like you hanging around. I should put you over my knee right now and give you a spanking, you disrespectful piece-of-shit."

Michael's anger was getting the better of him. He pushed off the wall intending to fly over and grab Demetrious, but Demetrious easily moved out of the way. Michael, who wasn't wearing a wing suit, floated helplessly across the Arena. The security guard assigned to watch Michael had seen enough and started after him, but Demetrious was closer.

159

"This guy's such an asshole," Demetrious mumbled to himself. "I hate jerk wads like this." After easily out maneuvering Michael, Demetrious flew over to him, grabbed his foot and spun him around so that he was spinning the way a person rotates when they do a cartwheel, around an axis going from your back to your stomach through your bellybutton. If you were an airplane, it would be called a flat spin.

"Have fun spinning," Demetrious said. "This is what I do to the Grounder kids that pick on me. Although I never tried it on an grownup before. Lucky you."

Michael outweighed Demetrious by two hundred pounds, but Demetrious was so skilled in how to move in zero-g that it made little difference. Demetrious' brain had developed in zero-g. He naturally understood Newton's laws of motion in a deeper way than any Grounder ever could. And so it was easy for Demetrious to grab Michael by the foot as he was flying by and transfer his linear motion into Michael's spinning motion putting him into a flat spin at about one rotation per second. Michael spun around completely once every second. This spin rate, for a person of Michael's size, caused a loading of approximately negative 3 g at his head.

Technically speaking, Michael was now spinning around an axis corresponding to his body's maximum moment of inertia. Without intervention, he would stay spinning like this for a very long time. If he crunched up his body into a ball, he would just spin faster, like a figure skater pulling in his arms. Unfortunately for Michael, spinning like this for adults causes their head to experience a significant level of negative g's. Negative g's are the opposite of the more familiar positive g's which try to pull blood out of your head. Positive g's are why pilots black out if they experience them at too high a level for too long. Negative g's have the opposite effect. They try to push blood into your head. The human body is much more tolerant of positive g's and a typical Grounder can withstand four to five positive g's, but a sustained level of more than three negative g's could kill you.

It all happened so fast that the security guard was unable to intervene but he did marvel at Demetrious' skills.

"That's a pretty cool trick kid," he said.

"Thanks," replied Demetrious. "He deserved it."

"Help me!" Michael groaned.

"Okay, okay, I'm coming," replied the security guard. "Hold your horses." The security guard flew over and grabbed a hold of Michael. The combination of their two bodies now had significantly different moments of inertia causing Michael's stable spinning motion to change into a complex tumbling one.

"Grab onto me," the security guard instructed. Michael complied. This freed up the guard's arms enabling him to use his wings to stop their motion. "You okay?" the guard asked Michael. "You don't look so good."

"I feel sick," Michael said weakly.

"I better take you to Medical."

Michael was in no condition to argue.

The guard took Michael the short distance to Medical. There Doris took his temperature, blood pressure, and heart rate.

Then she looked at his eyes and said, "That's interesting," and typed into the computer *subconjunctival hemorrhages*.

"What is it?" asked Michael irritably.

"You have bleeding that occurs when tiny blood vessels break just underneath the clear surface of your eyes. Have you been straining, vomiting, or rubbing your eyes roughly?"

"No. Why? What the fuck's going on?" snarled Michael.

"Demetrious gave him a spin in the Sports Arena," said the guard. "Could that have done this?"

"It's possible," said Doris. "But he'd have to spin him pretty fast. Two to three negative g's could burst the fine blood vessels in your eyes or brain. How fast was he spinning?"

"I don't know, maybe once per second," replied the guard.

Doris addressed the computer, "Sky City, how fast would a six foot tall man have to rotate to create negative three g's at his head?"

The computer responded immediately, "A rotation rate of one hertz about an axis normal to the long dimension of a six-foot tall man would produce negative three g's at the person's head."

"How long was he spinning like that," asked Doris.

"Ten maybe fifteen seconds at the most," replied the guard.

Doris turned to look at Michael, "Well that's probably it. This shouldn't be a problem and your eyes will clear up in a week or two."

"That little bastard," said Michael. "I'll fix him. What about my headache?"

"You'll be fine. You should just be glad he didn't spin you faster or longer," said Doris.

"What the fuck do you mean?" asked Michael angrily.

"Well, subconjunctival hemorrhages are also observed in child abuse cases, in what is known as shaken-baby syndrome. If he had spun you rapidly enough to create four to five negative gees, that would have caused you to lose consciousness. Sustain that long enough and it could cause permanent brain damage or even death."

"I'm going to kill him, I swear," replied Michael.

"You're not killing anyone," said the guard. "You're coming with me. We're putting you on the next taxi back to Sky City II."

The guard addressed the computer, "Sky City, get me Tesla."

"Tesla here."

"It's me, you better come to Medical, we've had an incident involving Michael."

...

I arrived at Medical in less than a minute and immediately addressed the guard. "Did that asshole beat up someone again?"

The guard chuckled, "No, he was the beat-ee this time."

"What?" I wasn't expecting that. "What happened? And why is Demetrious here?"

"I'll show you," said the guard. "Sky City replay the last ten minutes from the Sports Arena."

After watching the video replay, I had to laugh.

"That's it?" I said looking at Michael. "You physically threaten an eight-year-old and then get beat up by him? You're pathetic."

"Whatever," said Michael. "You're going to regret this day. I promise you."

"Take him away," I said to the guard.

The guard took him to the docking port in engineering where they waited for the next taxi to Sky City II.

I went back to my office and called George.

"Hi Tesla," George said as he answered the phone.

"George, I'm sending your son back on the next taxi with a security officer."

"What happened this time?" asked George.

I explained what happened and then added, "George, I'm afraid for your safety. Michael is mentally unstable and I don't trust him. You shouldn't either."

"Don't worry Tesla," replied George trying to sound positive even though deep down I'm sure he knew I was right. "I'll take care of Michael. I told him that if he got into any trouble that I'd send him back to Earth. So that's what I'm going to do."

"Good," I said feeling a little relieved. "When's the next spaceplane back to Earth from there?"

"Tomorrow afternoon."

"Okay, you be careful until then," I said.

"Don't worry about me."

"I do worry about you. You're like my family here. Be safe and call me when he's on the plane," I insisted.

...

Two hours later Michael and the guard arrived at Sky City II. Per instructions from Tesla, the guard took Michael directly to see George Abruzzo. As they entered George's room, George shook his head and said, "Michael, trouble just seems to follow you around, doesn't it?"

"It wasn't my fault," replied Michael defensively. "It was that damn kid. Look at my eyes! He did that, and my fucking head is killing me!"

"Quit being so dramatic. The nurse says you're going to be fine. And you'll be even better once you're back on Earth."

"What, you can't—"

"Yes I can," said George interrupting him. "And I will. I told you any trouble and I'd send you back immediately. Well, this is it. You're going to be on tomorrow's spaceplane back to Earth."

"It wasn't my fault," replied Michael practically shouting. "You don't give a shit about me. You never have. All you ever cared about were these damn space hotels."

"Calm down, Michael," George said quietly but firmly. "You're leaving tomorrow and that's it."

"Can we at least have dinner together tonight and discuss it?" pleaded Michael.

"My mind's made up."

"It's just dinner," insisted Michael.

"All right," said George, exasperated.

The guard took Michael back to his tiny apartment in the section reserved for construction workers and remained outside the apartment, effective placing Michael under house arrest. Michael made a call back to Earth.

…

That evening the guard escorted Michael to the only restaurant in Sky City II to have dinner with his father. The temporary restaurant, built to meet the needs of the construction workers, had lots of basic, hearty food and plenty to drink. All three of them ordered the beef stew. Michael and George also ordered red wine. The guard just had water. The thick beef stew arrived in open bowls just like on Earth.

Michael grabbed his wine and said, "A toast…to new beginnings."

"To your departure," replied George raising his glass.

"I wish it didn't have to be this way," said Michael.

"Me too. But if you stay out of trouble on Earth, perhaps we can try it again someday."

"I don't think I can wait for someday," replied Michael, putting down his glass.

"Well, I'm afraid you'll just have to."

163

Michael smiled an evil kind of smile and thought, *Nope, I don't think I can wait, and I don't intend to*. He grabbed his napkin and pretended to sneeze. It was a loud, slightly exaggerated sneeze. His exaggerated motion covered up the fact that as he sneezed, he threw a very tiny pill in the direction of his father's stew, a motion he practiced numerous times since his arrival at Sky City II two months ago. The practice payed off. The tiny pill, invisible to the security cameras, followed a straight line, landing undetected in the George's stew. Michael sneezed again just for show. "Sorry," said Michael, after the second sneeze. "Must be dust from the construction."

All through dinner Michael kept a close eye on his father, looking for any signs that it was working. Near the end of dinner he was getting nervous. *Why isn't this working*, he wondered.

Finally, as they finished eating, George said, "I don't feel very good."

Michael breathed a sigh of relief as the drug he put in his father's stew was starting to take effect. It was the latest in illegal date-rape drugs, a derivative of flunitrazepam, more powerful, and virtually undetectable.

Michael told the guard that they better take George back to his room. By the time they got there, George was incoherent and barely conscious.

Wow, they were right, thought Michael, this stuff really works. Now, to finish the job. "I'm really worried about my dad," Michael said to the guard. "You better run and get medical help. I'll stay here with him."

"Right," replied the guard. "I'll be back with help as soon as I can." And he left.

Michael knew that he had about four minutes before the guard would be back. It would have to be enough. Sky City II was still under construction and the security and communications infrastructure was not in yet place in this section of the facility.

As soon as they were inside the apartment, Michael grabbed George and tried to spin him like a propeller blade about his belly button just the way Demetrious did to him. Much to Michael's surprise, it wasn't as easy as he thought. He knew he had to spin him faster than one rotation every second, but that proved to be very difficult. Every time he spun George's body, it quickly drifted away and collided with the wall, stopping the spin. Michael tried again and again with the same result.

Why is this so fucking hard? Michael said to himself. *That kid made it look so easy*. Michael didn't appreciate that it came naturally to Demetrious because he had lived essentially his entire life in space.

I only have a few minutes left to do this before the guard gets back. If dad wakes ups, he'll figure out that I drugged him and I'll be screwed! I can't just suffocate him or they'll know it was murder. This is the only way. They told me it would look like he had a stroke.

Motivated by fear Michael grabbed George again, wrapped his own feet tightly into the rope mesh wall behind him and spun George's body as hard as he could. To his surprise, he somehow managed to spin George without imparting any translational motion. George just hung there in front of him spinning.

Holy shit! But was he spinning fast enough? Michael compared George's rotation with the digital time displayed on the wall. He counted how many rotations George did in ten seconds. Nineteen! It was nineteen rotations in ten seconds, almost two per second. *How long should I keep him spinning this way?*, Michael wondered. *Longer is probably better.* He had only about three minutes left. He decided to let him go until he heard the guard knock on the door. Air resistance was slowing George's rotation rate, but only very slightly.

Two and a half minutes later, Michael heard a knock on the door. He grabbed George to stop him, but forgot to lock his feet into the rope mesh. He and George immediately started tumbling. They were tumbling together in the middle of the room. Michael was unable to reach anything to stop their motion. So they continued to tumble.

For a split second, Michael thought they'd have to stay that way until the airflow slowly pushed them against the rope mesh. But then Michael instinctively pushed George away from him. This caused them to move in opposite directions until they both impacted the walls on opposite sides of the room. Michael hit the rope mesh and grabbed it. He waited there for George to bounce off the far wall and head back toward him. This time when George's tumbling body arrived Michael made sure he kept one hand on the rope mesh while he grabbed George with the other. Now having secured George's body, he told the computer to open the door.

"Thank god you're here," said Michael. "He's right over there. He passed out and I can't wake him up. I think he's still breathing. What's wrong with him?" *I hope that spin was enough*, he thought.

The medics transported George to Medical and then called Leslie.

...

As soon as Leslie got to Medical and saw George's condition she called me.

"Hi Leslie," I said cheerfully.

"Tesla, I've got some bad news," she managed to say through her sobs. "George is unconscious. He's in Medical now, but so far is unresponsive."

"What?" I said urgently. "What happened? Is he going to be okay?" My hands started shaking.

"I don't know, Tesla. I don't know what happened. I don't know what to do? I'm so afraid. What if he—"

"Don't think like that," I interrupted. "He'll be fine," I said, trying to sound confident. "I'll be there as soon as I can. Don't worry." I arranged for a special taxi for me and Doris Chun. We arrived two hours later at Sky City II. During the ride over, I called the nurse and Security at Sky City II and found out what little they knew about what happened. I found out, much to my dismay, that security monitoring had not yet been set up in George's apartment. Consequently, there was no video record of what happened, they didn't even have the usual data on the variation in heat loads or atmospheric gases with time from his apartment, since these weren't recorded either.

What they did know from the temporary security cameras in the hall was that Michael, George, and the guard entered George's apartment at seven minutes past five pm that afternoon and George was conscious, but something was definitely wrong with him. The guard left one minute later and returned at five twelve pm with an emergency medical technician. They brought George out of his apartment at five fifteen pm, and George was now clearly unconscious. They rushed him to Medical.

Michael did it, I concluded immediately. I don't know what he did to him or how he did it, but I'm sure that asshole did it. When Doris and I arrived at Sky City II we immediately went to see George. Leslie was at his side.

"How's he doing?" I asked the nurse. "Any change in his condition?"

"I'm afraid it doesn't look good," the nurse said. "His brain activity is decreasing. The machines are the only things keeping him alive."

"What happened to him?" I pleaded with the nurse for an explanation. "I talked to him earlier today and he seemed just fine, now this. What could cause this?"

Doris examined George. "It's possible that he had a massive stroke," Doris finally said. "Or—," she hesitated.

"Or what?" I asked. "What is it?"

"Murder."

"I knew it! Explain!"

"George has symptoms of shaken-baby syndrome. Just like Michael had, but much worse. The blood vessels in his eyes are broken and the decreasing brain activity is consistent with severe brain damage."

"Michael did it. I know it," I hissed, now seething with rage. "But how can we prove it?"

...

166

I came to visit George every day and every day I pleaded with him to wake up. "George, you have to wake up. We all need you. I need you. I don't know what I'll do without you. You have meant more to me than you can possibly know."

George's condition continued to deteriorate. After seven days, hope for George's recovery was fading rapidly. I leaned over him, kissed him on the cheek and whispered in his ear, "We know who did this to you. I'll make sure he pays for it. I promise you."

George died a few hours later.

...

Following George's death I was so distraught I couldn't function. I just stayed in our apartment for days with the lights off. I didn't want to see or talk to anyone. After a week, Sasha had had enough, she grabbed me by the shoulders and said, "Tesla, you've got to stop this. You can't live like this. We all loved George and we're all sad that he's gone, but you're still alive. You have to live your life."

I didn't say anything. I just gave her a blank stare.

"Come on, why don't ya'll take a shower, get dressed and then we can all go out for dinner; you, me, Demetrious, and Yuri?"

"I can't…"

"Yes, you can." Sasha pulled me close and hugged me. "You're the strongest person I know."

I cried in her arms. This made Sasha do something I had never seen her do before in the seven years that I've known her. She cried too.

Exhausted and emotionally spent, I relented. "Okay, I'll get ready and join you for dinner."

Sasha smiled. "One more thing. I brought you this to help motivate you to get back into the world." She showed me a report on her phone.

"This is bullshit," I said as I read the report on the murder investigation. "It said there was insufficient evidence to arrest Michael who claimed he did everything he could to save his father. What a bunch of crap. I'm going to make him pay for this!"

"That's my girl. Now go get ready."

...

Without George to send him back to Earth, Michael stayed at Sky City II. A funeral service was held a week later at the resort. Hundreds of people gathered for the service, which was held in the newly completed Sports Arena at Sky City II. The arena was the only facility that was big enough to accommodate several hundred people at once. Almost all the employees from Sky City were there along with some regular guests, leaving only a skeleton crew at the resort to make sure the remaining guests were safe. Many of George's business acquaintances from Earth were there as well. By far the majority of the people in attendance were the construction workers, engineers, designers, and other employees from Sky City II. All of the employees from the Three Dolphins Club were there.

George's wife Leslie asked me to give the main eulogy and I reluctantly agreed. My reluctance was not because I didn't care about George, but because, I'm not much of a public speaker. But George had been too important to me, too big a part of my life for me to say no.

On the day of the service, the Sports Arena was beautifully decorated with fresh flowers from Earth. The cylindrical walls of the Arena were covered all the way around, all the way down the entire length of the Arena with seamless ultra-high definition displays. The displays were showing the view from outside the resort. It gave the appearance that everyone in the Arena along with the beautiful extensive flower arrangements were floating freely in space.

Fighting back tears I began the eulogy. "It has been my great pleasure to have known George Abruzzo these past seven years. I never really knew my own father, but in these seven years George became like a father to me. He gave me a job, treated me with remarkable love and kindness, and brought out the best in me. He was an amazing person. The kind of person you hope to meet sometime in your life. The kind of person you'd like to be yourself, if only you could. The kind of person who makes you a better person just because you're around them. It's not just that he was kind and caring—he was definitely those things—but because he was that way and so much more. His many, many amazing accomplishments made the fact that he was so kind and so caring that much more remarkable. Seven years ago, he took a chance on a frightened young girl and her baby, and he changed our lives forever,"—I paused for a moment as I started to cry, after a few seconds I pushed on—"just as he impacted the lives of so many people here and at Sky City. As you know, George was a visionary. His vision, his overarching goal in life, was the human settlement of space, and he was brilliant enough to make it happen—we here today are proof of that. He made a ton of money on Earth, but instead of sitting back and enjoying his wealth, he embarked on this crazy vision, his crazy vision. A vision for humanity to live and work happily in space. A vision where people would create vast new wealth. A vision where people would work together to make life better for everyone. This vision began with the creation of the Sky City Resort and Casino. It was a huge gamble. Many people, maybe most people, just knew that it would never work; they knew he'd go broke. But they were wrong. They were wrong because George knew what people liked. He knew what would draw them to the resort, and he knew that if he treated people fairly and with respect, that they would bust their butts in return and turn his vision into a reality. It wasn't easy, but he had this way with people that drew them in, that made them believers. He brought out the best in everyone. It was infectious, and it worked. The fact that I'm here in front of you now is proof that it worked. How can you thank someone who has had such an impact on your life? How do you honor them? There are no words for this; only our actions matter. Therefore, I will dedicate myself to living up to George's legacy. To living up to his way of dealing with people, to his constant, tireless work to make this a better place for everyone. We will work to extend George's vision here to Sky City II, a place where not just a few hundred people will live and work together, but where thousands will, and eventually millions. This is George's vision. This is now my vision. This is now our vision. Thank you George, we will miss you dearly. I will miss you dearly."

...

Michael Abruzzo hovered in the back of the crowd listening to the eulogy and thought, *such a nice speech, but so naive, it's almost a pity that she has no idea what's coming.*

Chapter 18 Xenon

Length of time in space: *seven and a half years.*

The morning after George's funeral service, Michael showed up at Sky City and called us all together, all the employees of the Three Dolphins Club.

"Good morning," Michael began in a most unfriendly tone. "I summoned you all here today to tell you how it's going to be now that my father is no longer with us. My father's Will left his controlling stake in the entire Sky City Resort and Casino to me. That includes the Three Dolphins Club. Therefore, I am the new owner of this Club, and now that I'm in charge, there are going to be a few changes around here." He paused as if to let that sink in.

Then he continued. "First, I will be taking over the day-to-day management of the Club's activities. Tesla, you'll go back to being a fucking escort." He laughed at his own stupid little joke. He was the only one. "Second, effective immediately, there will be a new salary structure in which the Club's share will be twice what it was previously."

Everyone started looking at each other in disbelief.

"Third, there will be a new fee structure, also effective immediately. There will be new fees on your rooms, on your food, and on your drinks. Fourth, I will expect all of you to take on more clients. I think we can double the number of clients we service per week. To do this we're going to do away with this whole stupid girlfriend experience. It's a fucking waste of time. There'll no more waiting three days before having sex with the client. If the customer wants sex right away then that's just what you're going to do. Oh, and if you don't like it, feel free to go back to Earth. I can always find plenty more where you came from. Now go do your god damned jobs." Michael turned and went to his office leaving everyone in stunned silence.

As we were left there floating in shock, Yuri whispered to me, "Do something!"

"What should I do?" I whispered back.

"I don't know. Go talk to him," replied Yuri. "You can't let him treat us like this."

"Yeah, this is ridiculous," said Sasha who was nearby. "He's treating us like a bunch of whores. What an asshole."

"Alright, I'll go talk to him." I didn't have a clue what I could say to him that would change his mind. He was just a nasty, evil person, who didn't care about anyone but himself. He even killed his own father for god's sake. I know he did, but I couldn't prove it, yet. Anybody who could do what Michael did to his own father was capable of anything, so I knew I'd have to be very careful.

I approached Michael's office, the office that had been mine up until a few minutes ago, still not knowing what I was going to say. I went in and closed the door.

…

Less than two minutes later the door opened again as Michael screamed, "Get the fuck out!" He grabbed me and physically pushed me out of the office. As soon as I flew through the door, I used my wings to stop. I looked back just in time to see Michael smack his head into a cabinet with a loud thump. I knew exactly what happened. The equal and opposite force from shoving me out of his office caused Michael to fly off in the other direction. He stopped only when his head hit the cabinet.

"Stupid Grounder," exclaimed Yuri.

"Yeah, the guy's such an asshole," I said after the office door closed. "How could he possibly be George and Leslie's son?"

"Maybe they dropped him on his head when he was little," Yuri said. "I take it, it didn't go well in there.

"No."

So what are we going to do now?"

"I don't know," I replied. "We'll have to do what he says for a while. Maybe it won't be as bad as we think." I tried to make my voice sound optimistic, but nobody was buying it.

…

Just over a week later, Sasha woke me up in the middle of the night.

"What is it?" I said groggily, as she turned on the light.

I looked at Sasha and gasped. Her face was covered in blood and her left eye was swollen shut.

"Who did this?" I demanded, but Sasha couldn't speak. We would find out later that her jaw was broken. "Did Michael do this?"

Sasha nodded, but she wasn't crying.

"We need to get you to Medical immediately. Don't worry, you're going to be okay and we're going to put an end to this. I promise you."

Sasha wasn't the first girl Michael beat up over the past week, but she was the most seriously injured. It started the day I went into his office to talk. Not only did he physically throw me out of his office, but he had slapped me hard across the face before doing so. Not as bad as when he punched me and broke my nose, but it brought back bitter memories of Alex from so long ago. A few days after that Madison came to me saying that Michael had punched her in the stomach because she dared to talk back to him. Then he spent an hour verbally abusing Jessica because she caught the flu from her client, and he slapped her across the face when sh said she was too sick to go back to work. Now Sasha. This was the last straw.

I called my long-time client and friend Jimmy Homa for help.

"Jimmy, this is Tesla. I need your help."

"You know I'd do anything for you," replied Jimmy.

I went on to explain what I needed.

"Piece of cake," said Jimmy. "It will take a few days, but it will be completely untraceable and indistinguishable from reality."

"You're the best, Jimmy. Love you."

…

The following week I arranged to meet Michael after closing at the new X-bar in the Three Dolphins Club. The X-bar was the latest fad in th use of mood-altering substances by people both on and off the planet. The X stood for xenon.

Since I had to approve the application for the new X-bar in the club and since I had never even heard of xenon, I did a little research. Things came so easily to me now I found that I had no trouble quickly absorbing this information. Xenon, it turns out, was discovered by British chemists back in 1898. It was a noble gas in the same family as helium, neon, argon, and krypton, only heavier. It was a rare gas that made up a tiny fraction, 0.0000087% to be exact, of Earth's atmosphere. Xenon was odorless, colorless, nontoxic, nonexplosive, environmentally friendly, and chemically inert for all intents and purposes. Its rarity made it expensive until recently. In 1939, it was discovered to have anesthetic properties. In fact, it was discovered to be about one and a half times more effective as an anesthetic than nitrous oxide, more commonly known as laughing gas. Because of its chemically inert properties it would get eliminated from th body quickly after you inhaled some of it. In the 1980's xenon became th propellant of choice for ion engines for space propulsion.

Xenon became affordable for wide spread use as an anesthetic for the first time in the late 2020's because its use as a propellant in high-power ion propulsion systems stimulated chemical companies to significantly ramp up xenon production.

That's interesting, I guess I had heard of xenon before. Marc had referred to it during my first week in space. The time we went to the Sky City II construction site for the retrieval of that asteroid. I guess I had forgotten that. So sue me.

Anyway, the website went on to say that the resulting price drop enabled its use as an affordable anesthetic. This further increased the demand, encouraging producers to increase production capability even more, further reducing its price.

It wasn't long before wealthy, bored teenagers discovered that they could get high on xenon. It was an ideal drug for the rich. You could get high and stay high as long as you liked and then sober up quickly. After you stopped breathing xenon, it was eliminated from your body rapidly—about ninety-five percent of it was exhaled in the first few breaths. There were also no calories in xenon, it didn't give you a hangover, and it wasn't chemically addicting. As a result, xenon bars started springing up all over, including the new X-bar, which I approved, that opened recently in the Three Dolphins Club.

I was already at the X-bar when Michael arrived at three am. We were alone. I knew I was taking a major risk meeting him alone given his violent behavior, but it was a necessary risk. It was still and quiet. The ultra-high definition monitors displayed a stunning star-filled view of deep space, but I didn't much notice or care. I had other things on my mind.

Michael was his usual unpleasant self when he arrived. I knew he had already become a frequent after-hours user of the X-bar and that was probably the only reason he accepted my invitation. But he was a genuinely unhappy person and he made no attempts to hide that fact.

"So why the fuck did you drag me out here in the middle of the night?" Michael barked as he approached me at the bar. "I've got more important things to do than to hang out with the likes of you." The contempt in his voice was clear. Michael didn't like most people and he sure as hell didn't like me.

"Come here," I said pointing to what I knew was Michael's favorite spot at the X-bar. I struggled to keep my voice calm and not show any hint of the fear and apprehension I was feeling. "I have some new information you need to know."

Michael took his usual place at the bar and said in a most condescending voice, "Really? What is it? What could possibly be so important that it couldn't have waited until the morning?"

"You'll see. I'm sure you'll agree it's important," I replied keeping my voice soft and calm.

"Well, what is it? Are you going to keep me here all god dammed night?"

"I found the real Will from your Father."

"Bullshit."

Just for an instant I thought that Michael looked rattled by the news. "It's true," I said, more forcefully this time. "And it says that George left

173

the Three Dolphins Club to me. I'm the rightful owner of the Club." I didn't actually have George's Will, but had asked Jimmy to create one, one that left the Three Dolphins Club to Tesla Miller of Sky City. Since all records were electronic, creating a "new" Will was easy for a man with Jimmy's computer skills.

After his initial surprise, Michael appeared to recover quickly and said, "Even if you think you have such a Will, it doesn't matter. My lawyers will tie this up in court for years. You will be bankrupt before this fight is over, and you will never take ownership of this Club!"

The degree of anger in Michael's voice was shocking even though I thought I was prepared for it. I hung my head down and said softly, "I'm sorry."

"What was that Bitch?" Michael said confidently, smiling now for the first time since he arrived. "I couldn't hear you."

I looked up at him. The hatred in his eyes made me shudder. "I said I'm sorry."

"Well you should be sorry. You're just a sorry, good-for-nothing, piece-of-ass. I should just kill you right now, but that's not the plan. So I guess I'll just have to do what they said. I'm going to fire your ass and send you back down to Earth. As of this moment you're fired. I'll expect you to pack up your stuff, take your obnoxious son, and leave Sky City tomorrow on the first flight back to Earth. If you don't leave, I'll have you arrested for trespassing and drag your ass back to Earth. Then maybe I'll go beat up your little friend Sasha again, you know, just to show everyone who's in charge."

"You better not touch her or I'll—." I could barely contain my anger in spite of my best efforts.

"Or you'll what?" mocked Michael.

"Nothing," I said quietly, barely managing to regain my composure. I wanted to scream at him, but I had to remain calm. I struggled against my raging emotions. My heart was pounding. It's now or never. I have to do this. I have no choice. This for Demetrious, for Sasha, and especially for George. I promised George that Michael wouldn't get away with his murder. I can't let him hurt anyone else.

I stared into his eyes and said, "I'm sorry it has come to this." My voice was clear and calm now.

"Whatever. I don't care what you're sorry for. Now, if you'll excuse me, I think I'll enjoy some of this fine xenon and then call it a day. Looks like this day has turned out pretty good after all."

It's the only way, I repeated to myself.

Michael grabbed the nasal cannula, slipped the rubber tubing over his head and inserted the prongs into his nostrils. He turned on the flow, waited a minute to be sure the tubing was filled with the expected eighty

174

percent/twenty percent xenon/oxygen mix, and then took a deep breath through his nose. Almost immediately, he looked to be light headed.

"Whoa, that hit me much harder than usual," Michael exclaimed in the very low baritone voice typical of a person breathing xenon.

"You're probably just tired," I replied reassuringly.

Michael took another deep breath of the xenon/oxygen mix. He seemed to be having trouble thinking. I smiled at him. It was obvious he was struggling to focus.

"Why the fuck are you smiling at me?"

He started slurring his words.

"It doesn't matter...I...I don't give...I don't give a shit," he said slowly and with difficulty.

I could see Michael trying to concentrate enough to know if it mattered. Then he started to sing as if he didn't have a care in the world. He breathed in more xenon/oxygen gas. I glared at him. I could tell by the look on his face that he now recognized the anger on my face. "Are you mad?" he said smiling. "Oh look, I see stars... aren't they...aren't they...beau..."

He never finished the sentence. I leaned in close to his face and whispered in his ear, "This is for George and Sasha."

"Wha...What?" Michael said with great difficulty, as he breathed in still more of the xenon/oxygen mixture. "Everything's fuzzy...What's happening?" He looked up at me with glassy eyes. "Are...are you giving me the finger?... I don't care...fuck."

I could see him trying to fight through the fog. He breathed in more xenon/oxygen.

"I...I... worried... don't care...nope... don't care about nothin'..."

I moved closer to him and put my left arm around his shoulder.

"Awe... hugging me..."

That was the last thing Michael said before he passed out. I covered his mouth with my right hand. I kept my hand over his mouth for a full five minutes. I wanted to be sure that any last breaths he was still able to take would be of the one hundred percent xenon coming through the nasal cannula. Just before Michael arrived that night, I closed the valve to the oxygen bottle that fed oxygen to the flow mixer at Michael's favorite spot. The result was the delivery of one hundred percent xenon instead of the usual eighty/twenty mix. Once Michael passed out from the lack of oxygen, all I had to do was to make sure that he didn't breathe through his mouth. Michael was dead in less than five minutes. I sent a brief message to Jimmy that simply said, "You're number one in my book."

...

Jimmy got the message and told me later it made him think of his favorite quote from the novel *1984*. '*Who controls the present, controls the past.*'

...

Jennifer found Michael's body early the next morning when she came to work to open the Club. She called security immediately.

The inquiry that followed focused on two video recordings, one from Michael's private suite and the other from the security camera in the Three Dolphins Club that had a view of the X-bar. In reality, both videos were created by Jimmy and they were perfect—indistinguishable from reality—just as he said they would be. Jimmy uploaded them early in the morning after getting my text. I had previously given him access to the Sky City security system. After uploading the videos Jimmy erased his digital tracks from the system.

The video from Michael's suite was a suicide note in which Michael explained that he could no longer live with the guilt of having killed his own father. He was clearly distraught and appeared to be on the verge of an emotional breakdown. The video from the X-bar security camera showed Michael approaching the bar alone at three am, going around to the back of the bar to do something for about thirty seconds, and then coming back around to the front, and taking his favorite spot. He put on the nasal cannula, turned on the xenon, and became motionless in less than a minute. The camera angle was unable to show what Michael did behind the bar, but the logical conclusion, the conclusion that Charlie, the head of Sky City Security, easily reached, was that he had closed the valve to the oxygen bottle in order to end his own life.

"Seems like an open and shut case of suicide," said Charlie. Nobody in the security department cared much for Michael, least of all Charlie, and nobody questioned the conclusion that it was suicide.

...

Before his death Michael's lawyers had successfully stonewalled Leslie Abruzzo's access to George's Will and business records. With his death, Leslie was able to gain access to all of George's records including his real Will. She immediately called me from Earth. Leslie had moved back to Earth after George's death. She, like everyone else was certain that Michael had killed her husband, and she needed to be away from him. When I answered the phone Leslie said excitedly, "Tesla, you're the owner of the Three Dolphins Club! George left the club to you!"

"What? But I thought Michael—"

"Michael was lying," she interrupted. He knew all along that you were the rightful owner. George's Will, bless his heart, is crystal clear on this. You own the Three Dolphins Club and I own a controlling interest in the entire resort."

"Thank you for letting me know," I said softly. I was feeling so guilty over what I did to Michael that what should have been incredibly good news brought me no joy. I couldn't get Michael's last words out of my head. He said, 'So I guess I'll just have to do what they said.' What does that mean?

Chapter 19 Mercy

Length of time in space: *eight years*

In the six months since Michael's apparent suicide, everyone at the Three Dolphins Club kept telling me how much happier they were now that Michael was gone and I was back as the Club's manager. Everyone was happier except me that is. Racked with guilt over what I did and afraid to tell anyone, I felt alone and depressed. The depression was killing me. Just when I thought I was as depressed as I could get, I received a video call from Emma.

"What's wrong Emma?" My sister's image appeared on the screen and it was clear that she was crying.

"Mom passed away last night," she just barely managed to say between sobs.

I started crying too. We both cried without saying a word for several minutes. Finally, I said quietly, "What happened?"

"They think it was another stroke," replied Emma, who had now calmed down enough to be able to speak more clearly. "I just saw her last week and she was fine. Well, you know what I mean. She was the same a always."

"I know. Thank you for always going to visit her. I feel terrible that I could never go see her." We started crying again.

...

I had a harder time than usual sleeping that night. My mind kept me awake with its relentless punishment. My thoughts were tormenting me for what I did to Michael and for not being able to spend time with my mom. I woke tired and depressed. Today was Sunday, and so like every Sunday for the last eight years I forced myself to get up early. I got dressed quietly so as to not wake Demetrious and headed over to the Celestial Sphere.

I rode out into the inky blackness by myself, alone in the infinite universe, alone with my thoughts. Unfortunately, my thoughts were crushing the life out of me. How did I get to be such a terrible person? M mind ran through its usual list of transgressions. I ran away from my husband, kidnapped my son, forced him to live in space so that he could never return to Earth. I'm an adulterer, a prostitute, a pimp, and a murderer. I even abandoned my own mother. God, I'm such a terrible person. How did I get this way? I didn't want to be like this. I always thought I was doing the best thing for the people I loved. I broke down in tears again. "I'm sorry, please forgive me," I sobbed out loud to no one in particular.

...

Fifty thousand years ago, about the last time modern people shared the Earth with another species of intelligent humans, a massive star exploded in a far corner of the Milky Way galaxy. This enormous explosion spewed forth huge amounts of very high-energy particles—what modern humans, fifty thousand years later, would call galactic cosmic rays. These particular cosmic rays traveled for exactly 49,855 years through interstellar space where their paths were bent this way and that by a multitude of magnetic and gravitational fields along the way. For a tiny fraction of these, their journey ended as they passed through the glass walls of the Celestial Sphere, zipped through Tesla's hair, skin, and skull, and struck her optic nerve.

...

"Oh!" I gasped. Lights, tiny little lights. What are they? Where are they coming from? Wow! They keep coming. Brilliant, beautiful flashes of light, like dazzling, little blueish-white diamonds. I closed my eyes. I can still see them! How is that possible? I can see them even with my eyes closed. I delighted in the spectacle.

"Oh!" I gasped again. That feeling...it's back! That same wonderful feeling I felt all those years ago. No, not exactly the same. It seems like somethings different...it's me, I'm different...and now...I know what it is! My mind practically shouted. It's the presence of God! It must be. I know it is. What else could it be? I can feel it down deep into the core of my being. Why am I shaking?...I can't stop shaking... I feel warm, I feel warm all over... and comfortable. No, not comfortable, comforted. I...

"God!" I said out loud. I...I feel forgiven! The relief was almost as unbearable as it was incomprehensible. How could God forgive me for the things I have done? And yet, I was sure I could feel the presence of God, I could feel his forgiveness. I felt dizzy and nearly passed out. I laughed and I cried.

I had never been very religious. Mom had taken me and my little sister to church all the time when we were young, but we stopped going when I got to the seventh grade, so I didn't really know what to do next. I left the Celestial Sphere that morning feeling joy and peace for the first time in a very long time.

179

Chapter 20 Judo

Length of time in space: *eight years two months*

We just completed the move to the new Three Dolphins Club at Sky City II. The new resort complex was roughly ten times the size of the original Sky City and it took significantly longer to complete than George's original plans. His untimely death delayed its completion by at two to three years, depending on whose estimate you believed.

People had been living here for years during its construction and selected guests had been there on and off for months helping to identify and shake out bugs, but today marked the official opening of the resort. It also marked the official end of construction, although there were still thousands of little things to be done.

Marc was arriving this afternoon from Earth for the grand opening ceremony and I was looking forward to his arrival. We attended the ceremony. Marc gave a little speech among many others. Later that evening after the ceremony, Marc and I gave ourselves an unofficial tour of the new resort complex. Sky City II was actually more of a small city than a resort. It could comfortably accommodate three thousand people and was designed to be expandable. It included gardens, farms, and industries to fabricate all manner of things from the raw asteroid material delivered robotically to the complex. As these industries expanded, Sky City II was designed to accommodate the expansion.

As a resort, it was comparable to the finest ocean-going cruise ships. It had several elegant dining rooms, bars, and pastry shops, a five-story atrium/shopping mall, a theater for live shows, multiple sports arenas, a large fitness center for guests and another one for the employees and residents. Compared to Sky City it had larger staterooms with expanded bathrooms, an elegant spa, dance clubs, an expanded carnival game room, and of course, an expanded Three Dolphins Club and X-bar. It had several new features not found in Sky City and Marc and I were approaching one of those now.

"Come, let me show you the latest feature that we just finished," said Marc, taking me by the hand.

"What is it? You know I've been to Sky City II many times already and I've probably seen everything"

"Not everything. You haven't seen this, because it wasn't finished until today."

Marc pushed a button opening a door to what looked like an airlock. After we glided inside he closed the first door and opened another one on the opposite side. This door appeared to open directly to space.

I smiled. "Nice effect," I said calmly. "If I were a Grounder that would have freaked me out. It gives you an effect similar to the Celestial Sphere. The glass is so clear it looks like it's not there."

"Cool, huh?" said Marc as he and I left the airlock-like chamber. The door closed behind us as we moved into the glass entryway. "But that's just the beginning."

I looked around and saw multiple glass tubes roughly six feet in diameter leading away from our location. "Where do they go?"

"These tubes run all over the resort. You can travel along the outside of the resort complex from end-to-end and on either side. You can get a direct view of Earth, or deep space, or whatever you like any time you like, just by coming out here. You can stay out here as long as you like, or as long as you're willing to accept the higher radiation that you get out here compared to inside the resort."

"This is awesome," I yelled as I raced down one of the tubes.

Marc struggled to keep up with me. I started doing barrel rolls with my body as I flew down the tube. I slowed down and allowed Marc to catch up with me. We stopped at another entryway.

"Come, let's go out here," Marc said, trying to catch his breath. "I've got something else to show you that was also just finished."

We went through both doors of the airlock-like system and found ourselves at the entry to the casino. The casino in Sky City II was much larger than the one in Sky City, and in a nod to the casinos in Las Vegas, this one featured an attraction intended to draw in people.

"I know you've been through here many times already, but while you were busy moving into the Three Dolphins Club, the construction team was busy completing this for the casino," explained Marc as he pointed to what looked like a giant glass box roughly twenty feet on a side.

"Yes, I saw people working on it. What is it?" I asked as I examined the large glass cube for clues.

"You're about to find out," replied Marc eagerly.

"I know, it's a glass cage to put you in when you've been naughty."

"Very, funny. Watch this!"

A large, spherical blob of water about twelve feet in diameter appeared at the center of the cube. It floated there pulsating as water does. It inverted the image of objects on the other side.

"Uh, that's nice," I said, trying to sound positive, while thinking, I see that every day when I take a shower.

"I know what you're thinking," said Marc. "You're probably thinking, what's the big deal, I see that every day when I take a shower. And you're right. Now keep watching."

Bright colored lights lit up the water. I heard a low rumbling. Then I saw the sound waves rippling through the water. As the music got louder

181

and more complex, the water responded. "This is incredible!" I said excitedly. I stared at the water gyrating to the music. The sound waves created an amazing variety of complex shapes, illuminated by the colored lights, all moving in time with the music. "I didn't know water could do that. This is so cool!

"I'm sorry you don't like it," Marc deadpanned.

"I love it!" I practically shouted. "I can see music!" Watching the dazzling musical-water display brought back a flood of old memories reminding me of all the wonderful, amazing things I experienced when I first moved to space.

After the three-minute show I asked Marc, "What are they going to do with Sky City? I spent a lot of good years there and Demetrious spent his entire life there. They're not going to destroy it are they?"

"No. They sold it off to a consortium of investors who intend to renovate it and update it to create a few large villas and then offer them to other rich people who want a more private and exclusive space experience."

"I'd like to see that sometime after they've finished the renovation."

"Me too. Come, let me show you one last thing that we're about to open to the public."

"There's more?"

"Yes!"

We went back to the exterior glass tunnels and traveled to another part of the complex.

"It's right over here." Marc said breathlessly as we re-entered the complex.

We made our way over to a large door that I had never seen open before. I always wondered what was behind it, but we were too busy moving to worry about it.

Marc opened the door revealing what looked like a museum of old space stuff. "Come on in, this is my latest creation." We glided into the large room and Marc closed the door behind us.

"A museum?" I asked with a noticeable lack of enthusiasm.

"Cool, right?" replied Marc, undeterred by my apparent lack of interest. "It's a collection of old manned space vehicles. Some are the real thing and some are recreations. I had them brought here so that tourists could experience firsthand how people originally flew in space."

"That ought to get them lining up around the block," I said sarcastically.

Ignoring me Marc said, "Here's the Vostok 1 spacecraft that Yuri Gagarin flew. You should bring Yuri Li here sometime and show him this. Over here is a Mercury capsule like the ones that America's Mercury 7 astronauts flew. Look at how tiny it is! And here's a Gemini capsule.

182

Can you imagine spending two weeks in something that small and cramped? There's so little space in these vehicles that you could barely experience zero-g. Man, people were a lot tougher back then I guess."

I just floated there smiling.

Marc looked at me and said, "What are you smiling about?"

"I just love it when you get all nerdy on me. You're like a kid in a candy store."

"Guilty as charged. Look over here! This is one of my favorites. This is the Soyuz capsule. Amazingly, they used this to ferry astronauts to and from the International Space Station as recently as 2020. Look at how cramped the three astronauts were in there! And they landed in Kazakhstan in kind of a controlled crash that injured about thirty percent of the astronauts that flew in it. Crazy huh?"

"Definitely."

Marc dragged me to another section of the museum. "Over here's a recreation of the crew cabin from the Space Shuttle. They used to cram up to seven people in there."

"Seven people, huh? But there's just the two of us now," I said with a devilish grin. We floated into the Space Shuttle cabin. "I've got an idea. Let's try something I'm pretty sure they never did in this spacecraft."

Marc looked over at me as I was pulled my shirt off over my head and I hear him say softly, "God I love this woman."

...

Length of time in space: *nine and a half years*

The employees of the Three Dolphins Club and I quickly settled into a routine in our new home in Sky City II. We had been living in Sky City II for a year and a half now. I could scarcely believe that I was decorating our apartment for Demetrious' tenth birthday party. How is it possible that he's turning ten? Aside from the first six months of his life, my son has lived his entire life in space. Like Marc said a long time ago, he's a pioneer.

...

That evening long after I cleaned up the mess left by the birthday party, Demetrious came to me asking for help with his math homework. He went to school online and I knew he was smart, but like most ten year olds, he would rather play than study. Sometimes he would simply ask for help rather than put in the effort to figure it out on his own.

I liked math when I was little, but when I entered Junior High and became more interested in being popular than in studying; math became indecipherable to me. Algebra was like a foreign language and I had convinced myself that I really didn't like math. When I was in High School I would tell people I had "math anxiety." So I dreaded those rare occasions when Demetrious would come to me for help with his math homework, like now.

Since Demetrious was ten years old, he should have been in fifth grade. But because he was going to school online, he could go to school at his own pace. The result was that he was now taking the equivalent of a seventh-grade math class, and this meant he was learning algebra. I hated algebra, did I mention I have math anxiety? Well, that's not really correct. You can't hate something that you don't know and I certainly didn't know algebra. Then came the words that parents everywhere dread.

"Mom, I need help with these word problems," said Demetrious.

I tried to brush him off. "I'm sorry honey," I replied. "Mommy's too tired from your birthday party."

"Come on Mom, you're always telling me how important school is."

"Okay," I sighed, hoping by some miracle that I could understand the problems well enough to not sound completely stupid. "Bring it here."

I read the problem out loud. "If train A leaves Station A traveling west toward Station B at nine miles per hour and at the same time train B leaves Station B traveling east toward Station A at sixteen miles per hour and Station A is sixty-two miles from Station B, how far are the trains from Station A when they pass each other?" I felt all of the blood drain from my face. Which is weird because, you know, we're in zero-g.

Trying not to show my panic I paused for a moment and then said to Demetrious, "Okay, uh…let's look back in your book to see what we should do." I spent several minutes looking at the section in the online textbook immediately preceding this set of problems. Finally, I saw something that looked relevant, something called the distance formula that said distance equals rate times time. Then I saw an example in the textbook that looked similar to the problem we were trying to solve. I've got to figure this out. I read through the example three times. My heart started pounding. Oh my god! I was barely able to contain my excitement. I understand this! Remember how I said things seemed to come easier to me now? Evidently this extended to math as well, thank goodness.

I looked at Demetrious and smiled. "Let's look at that problem again. Here's what you have to do." I explained how to do the problem. I was very pleased with myself and somewhat astonished that I actually understood how to do this.

Demetrious had already figured out how to do the problem while I was reading and re-reading the examples, but he didn't tell me. Instead, he simply said, "Thanks Mom," but he didn't go off to finish the rest of his homework.

Now that I was no longer panicked about helping him, I could see that there was something else bothering him. "What's wrong, honey?"

"Nothing," mumbled Demetrious.

"Come on, I know that look. What's bothering you?

After a long pause Demetrious finally said, "The Grounder kids, they all make fun of me. I hate it here."

"What? I thought you liked it here."

"They tease me about being skinny and weak. They say I'm a freak. Why do we have to live here? I hate you for making me live here!"

"Demetrious, when did this start?" I was genuinely surprised by this. "You're not a freak. You are unique! In the entire history of the world, there has never been anyone like you. You are the most special person ever."

"Yeah right, then why are they always picking on me? Why do they make me get into fights?"

"Did you get into a fight today?"

Demetrious looked at his feet and shrugged his shoulders.

That explains the message on my phone from Charlie in security that I hadn't read yet. "What did we say about fighting?"

"You don't understand," complained Demetrious. "They think they're so strong, they're always picking on me."

"Are you okay? Did they hurt you?" I asked like a concerned, protective mom.

"I'm fine. They're strong, but they're really stupid. They don't know how to move. I can easily beat them up."

"What do you mean?"

"They're stupid," Demetrious repeated loudly. "They can't control themselves. They're clumsy and inept; it's so easy to beat them up."

"Demetrious, you can't go around beating up the tourists," I scolded, but I was secretly happy knowing that he could defend himself.

"Whatever, this sucks."

I didn't say anything for a long time as I tried to figure out what to do.

"Hello, space to Mom," Demetrious said losing patience. "Are you still there?"

"Hey, I've got it," I replied with exaggerated enthusiasm. "Why don't we open a zero-g judo school? You know how to move in zero-g better than anyone who has ever lived. You could be the instructor and teach people self-defense in zero-g! Whaddya say?"

"Can I make money?" asked Demetrious, starting to sound interested.

"Yes! So, should we do it? I'll run the business part and you do the instruction. We'll be a team."

"Cool! What should we call it?"

"I don't know. What do you think?

"We could call it Judo for Dummies," said Demetrious laughing.

"I don't think you want to insult your customers. How about Space Judo, or Cosmic Judo, or Zero-g Judo."

"Cosmic Judo, I like that!" said Demetrious.

"Cosmic Judo it is!" I hugged him.

Chapter 21 College

Late that night after Demetrious was asleep, as Marc and I were getting ready for bed, I said, "I've been thinking about going back to college?"

"Really?" replied Marc, somewhat surprised.

"Yes, it's weird, but things come very easily to me now. Today I helped Demetrious with his math homework. It was a word problem. A word problem!" I repeated for emphasis. "I haven't been able to do a word problem since…well, never! Anyway, it was easy! Everything seems easy to me now, and recently, mostly because of Demetrious, I've gotten very interested in how living things adapt to life in zero gravity."

"Microgravity."

"Whatever. So I've been looking into it. Almost all colleges let you earn a degree online. I think I'm ready to go to college now. I know I wasn't before. I want to do more with my life than just run the Three Dolphins Club."

"I think that's a great idea, but can you go to school and run the Club at the same time?"

"No, I don't think so, but I've got it all figured out. I'm going to sell the Club to Sasha and Yuri. I know they'll run it well."

"That's awesome," replied Marc. "That's a big step though. Are you sure this is what you want to do?

"I think so. I've thought about it a lot and I think this is the right thing for me now."

"You never cease to amaze me. What can I do to help? What do you want to major in? I can help you fill out your online applications if you like."

"I've been reading a lot about how they're trying to get plants and animals to better adapt to living here. I find it really fascinating."

"Sounds like Biology," said Marc. "Evolutionary biology, to be more specific."

"Yes, evolutionary biology. That's it," I said.

Marc kissed me.

...

With Marc's help, I filled out several online applications, sent them in, and then waited anxiously for acceptance letters. The wait seemed endless. Every day I would check my email. Finally, the results started coming in. Marc was back on Earth and I called him excitedly. "Marc," I exclaimed. "I got accepted to Berkeley!"

Marc seemed surprised. I think he thought I was smart, but Berkeley was one of the top schools in the country. "That's fantastic!" Marc said enthusiastically. "Welcome to college!"

In the end, I was accepted to just one other school and rejected by all the rest. Since I would have to pay out of state tuition at any of them that was not a discriminator. I selected the University of California, Berkeley, partly because it was close to where I used to live and partly because Marc encouraged me to do so. It's weird, though, because that's where Alex went to school.

...

Length of time in space: *ten years*

Sasha and Yuri glided into my office. I handed them my tablet with the contract displayed.

"Are you sure you want to do this?" asked Sasha as she and Yuri flipped through the contract.

"Yes, I've thought about this a lot. I want you and Yuri to take ownership of the Club. I've made a lot of money from this Club, so I have plenty of money already and with the proceeds from the sale I'll be set for life even after paying for college."

"College? Really," said Yuri. "You're planning on going to college? That's so cool!"

"I'm kind of nervous," I replied. "Last time I tried college it didn't go well."

"You're one of the smartest people I know," said Sasha. "You'll have no problem."

"I agree," added Yuri. "But this deal, it's way too generous. Are you sure you want to do this?"

"You two are my nearest and dearest friends. We have been through a lot together, and I just wanted to make sure that you two got the better end of this deal."

And just like that, with the stroke of a pen, ten years after moving to space to become a high-priced escort, I was no longer in 'the business'.

"This will be a big change to your life," said Yuri. "I hope you know what you're doing."

"I hope so too. God knows I've already had my share of major changes in my life, but I know this is the right thing for me to do." I couldn't shake a nagging feeling of uncertainty. A vague notion that the future would hold even bigger challenges than the past. I tried to push the apprehension out of my mind.

As Ella Elridge, before I got married, I completed one year of college. But that had been so long ago that I didn't remember a thing. My official transcripts, courtesy of George Abruzzo, indicated that Tesla Miller completed one year of college at the University of California, San Diego. But it also was so long ago that none of the fake credits counted.

Determined to do well, I poured myself into my online studies. For the first time since elementary school I worked hard at learning. For the first time ever I was genuinely interested in school. I took algebra and trigonometry classes at the same time per Marc's suggestion. He said I'd need these before taking calculus and that all of my science classes would simply assume that I knew calculus. I groaned at the thought of all those math classes, but half way through the semester things were different. This is easy. I don't know why I thought it was so hard before. I can do this easily!

I took two calculus classes the next semester and aced them both. In fact, I finished two full years of college in just the first year, including the summer. By my second year, I was taking all classes in my major.

Whenever I'd learn something new or interesting I wanted to share it with Marc, and it didn't matter if he was on Earth or at Sky City II. If he was on Earth, I'd just call him. If he was at the resort, then he'd be staying with me like he always did. Marc said he loved my enthusiasm and didn't mind listening to my latest discoveries. I think it didn't hurt that I generally discussed these things with him after Demetrious had gone to sleep and after I had gotten into one of my revealing nightgowns that I wore just for him.

…

Length of time in space: *twelve years.*

By taking classes year round, I finished my bachelor's degree in just two years. This feat evidently did not go unnoticed as I found out when the phone rang.

"Hello," I said, answering the video call in my apartment.

"Hello, this is Professor Nagib from UC Berkeley."

"Yes, Professor, how can I help you?" I replied. Professor Nagib? My mind started racing. THE Professor Hamid Nagib? The Nobel Prize winning biologist? What the heck is Professor Nagib doing calling me?

"I see that you finished your undergraduate degree in just two years. That's quite an accomplishment."

"Thank you Professor," I replied.

"And the quality of your work was outstanding."

"Thank you again." I still didn't know what this call was about and how did he know anything about the quality of my work.

"I have an opening for a Ph.D. student. I'm always on the lookout for new talent and I'm interested in knowing if you're considering graduate school. I think you might be a good candidate."

"I guess I never really thought about it," I replied perhaps a little too honestly.

"Well, you should. I just received notice that my latest proposal to continue investigations into how animals develop and adapt to long-term life in a micro-gravity environment has been funded. The proposed plan is to do the research in space with graduate students making frequent trips there to do the work. The fact that you live in space would be even better. You live in Sky City II, is that correct?"

"Yes, I've lived here since it first opened."

"Excellent. Coincidently, Sky City II is where we are opening our new micro-gravity research lab. It will be a remote branch of the university. So if you're interested, fill out an application online as soon as possible," pressed Nagib. "I have other highly qualified candidates for this position, but none of them live in space."

"I'm interested."

...

I called my sister after getting accepted into the PhD program. Even after all these years, we still talked to each other weekly, and seemed to grow closer with the passage of time, especially now that our mom was gone.

"I can't believe you're going to get a PhD," exclaimed Emma. "You're going to be Doctor Tesla Miller. That's so weird."

"I know, right?"

"So what exactly are you doing your PhD on?" asked Emma.

"Okay, you asked for it," I replied. "People have long known that gravity affects every aspect of animal development, from the physical development of the body, to the development of the brain, to how the body functions. But it's unknown exactly how the absence of gravity affects these developments. How exactly does the lack of gravity impact the physical and cognitive development of animals? How does it affect which genes are expressed, and what are the long-term implications? My research will be on how the absence of gravity affects the evolution of multicellular animals. Specifically, I'll be studying both worms and mice to see how the absence of gravity influences their development and

190

evolution at the genetic level. Both of these animals have been extremely well studied on Earth for all sorts of reasons, so they're good subjects."

"Sheesh, you're starting to sound like all those nerdy guys you hang around with up there."

"Yeah, it must be rubbing off on me."

Austin, Texas

Alex was now nearly as popular as the head Pastor Jamal Young. Together under their joint leadership, Purification by Grace Ministries grew enormously, with a worldwide membership now approaching one hundred thousand.

Jamal was an avid hiker and he and Alex, along with several assistants, were taking a large youth group on a long weekend trip to Yosemite National Park in California. They led the group of teenagers to the top of Half Dome. It was an exhausting hike from the valley floor, and it was raining heavily by the time they reached the top. They waited and rested at the top, hoping the weather would improve. It didn't. Eventually, Jamal indicated they couldn't wait any longer and said it was time to head down.

Alex and Jamal made sure that everyone was heading down before they left. It was raining harder than ever. Nobody saw what happened. Somehow, Jamal lost his footing as he approached the cable. His scream was muffled by the rain as he plummeted six hundred feet to his death.

Alex, the last person to see him alive, claimed he didn't see what happened. Many wondered how such an experienced hiker as Jamal could have slipped and fallen to his death.

The following week the leadership of Purification by Grace Ministries named Alex Markov as their new head Pastor. The next day, as Alex approached the pulpit, he looked out over the crowd of nearly seventy thousand people.

"It is with great humility and even greater sadness that I accept the opportunity to serve you as your head pastor. We all loved Pastor Young, especially me. He literally saved my life. Why God would see it fit to take our beloved Pastor is beyond our comprehension. But we take comfort knowing that he is now in a better place. I know I can never fill his shoes. But we must continue to do the work that Pastor Young was doing, God's work. There is so much to be done. Let us pray."

Sky City II

Length of time in space: *twelve years and a half years.*

Marc was at Sky City II for one of his frequent, routine trips for work and, of course, was staying with me. After our usual roll-in-the-hay, and before Marc could fall asleep, I started telling him in detail about my latest studies.

"This is hard," I said. "There's so much to learn and Nagib is very demanding."

Marc grunted, as if he was hoping he could just go to sleep.

Undeterred, I went on. "And my stupid worms—I got some results back today and it wasn't what I expected. I just stared at the data and all I could think was, 'that's odd.'"

"Worms, right," Marc mumbled, barely conscious.

"Yes, my worms just won't die. You see, I need to get lots of generations to study evolutionary changes, but the stupid things are just living too long. They're supposed to reproduce with a life cycle of about three days, but it's taking more like six."

"Your worms are living too long?" Marc repeated, now apparently starting to get interested.

"Yes! They just keep on living. They're living about twice as long as our control groups back on Earth."

"Go on." Marc was now fully awake.

"We're using a worm known as *Caenorhabditis elegans*, or *C. elegans* for short. It is supposed to have a short lifespan and a rapid generation time making it ideal for studying evolution. It was the first multicellular animal to have its entire genome sequenced. Its relative simplicity, it has only a thousand cells, and the fact that roughly thirty-five percent of its genes share a common ancestor with humans, makes it a popular research subject."

"Okay, but what about them living longer," Marc pressed.

"After getting these weird results, I looked up the old literature about the times that *C. elegans* have flown in space. Incredibly, these papers indicate that when *C. elegans* are in zero-gravity they were found to have decreased expression of several genes that subsequent investigations discovered should increase the worm's lifespan. Cool huh?"

Mark nodded.

"Remarkably, however, no one had ever demonstrated that the worms actually did live longer in space. So now I come along and try to get them to reproduce rapidly like they're supposed to, but their stupid life cycles seem to be significantly extended."

"That's amazing Tesla! Are you sure? How do you know?"

"Yes, I'm sure," I replied with a touch of unintended irritation in my voice. "We took a group of worms on Earth and divided them into two groups at random. One group stayed in the lab at Berkeley and the other was brought up here. The group at Berkeley lived normal lives. They

192

reproduced after about three days and lived for a total of about twenty days. The group brought up here, however, reproduced after about six days and lived for a total of roughly forty days. Everything, it seems, takes nearly twice as long. It's both very frustrating and very interesting."

"Do you know why they are living longer?"

"I think it's to be a pain in my butt."

"Come on."

"Okay, the literature says the work done on the International Space Station suggests the zero-g environment alters the organism's metabolism in a way that delays aging. Specifically, there appears to be a decrease in the accumulation of toxic protein aggregates in the worm's muscles."

"You want to try that again, in English this time?" said Marc.

I couldn't help but smile. "Oh, so now you know how I felt when you used to 'explain' things to me," I replied making air quotes around the word 'explain'. "Sucks when the shoe's on the other foot doesn't it."

Marc laughed.

"Anyway, what it means is that a key feature of the worm's adaptation to zero-g is a change to its muscles. Everyone knows muscles tend to shrink in space. These changes have long been understood to result in increased frailty when returning to Earth. But, now here's the cool part, in space, it turns out, these changes, these shrinking muscles, actually become younger and healthier than those of the worms that stayed behind on Earth. The bottom line is that muscles in space age better than on Earth."

Marc floated there smiling at me without saying a word.

"What are you smiling about?"

"I always knew you were smart," replied Marc. "But you seem different now. Smarter in a way that's hard to define."

"Awe, you're making me blush," I said pretending to be embarrassed.

"So, does this work in humans? asked Marc.

"I don't know." I paused for a moment and then grinned, "Let's see if your muscles are healthy enough for another roll in the hay."

...

At the next weekly video conference call with my advisor, I showed Professor Nagib the data demonstrating the expanded life cycles of the *C. elegans* living in space.

"I expected this would likely be the case. It's outstanding that you confirmed it."

"So...because of this, I was thinking that I'd like to change the focus of my research. I'd like to see if I could determine if this extends to mammals and even to humans," I said enthusiastically.

193

"I think that's a bad idea," replied Nagib. "I have to advise you that I don't think it's possible to do that in a typical Ph.D. time frame. You would have to identify what genes were getting expressed, how they're getting expressed and why. You'd need to identify which genes were being suppressed and why. Then you'd need to determine what the primary effects of these altered gene expressions were and then their secondary effects and third order effect, and so on. You would probably start with the *daf-2*, *age-1*, and *daf-16* genes that control the insulin and insulin-like pathways. It has long been speculated that mutations in these genes affect the lifespan in *C. elegans*. Mammals and especially humans, however, are enormously more complex than these simple worms and therefore, the behavior of these genes and many others are likely to be much, much more complex. Perhaps you could do this in a lifetime of research, maybe, but not for a Ph.D."

I felt deflated. "I'm willing to work hard," I replied, a little less sure of myself.

"I'm sure you are, but if you follow this path, you may never graduate."

His words echoed in my mind. I was about to acquiesce, stick to the original plan, take the easier path. But then I thought, you know, I never dreamed I'd be living in space, that I'd become a space prostitute, or run a multimillion dollar brothel in space, and I certainly never thought I'd finish college let alone attempt to get a Ph.D. I knew what I wanted and it wasn't the easy way, not anymore. "Professor Nagib, I've been through a lot of tough things in my life. You selected me for a reason. You know what I'm capable of. This is the opportunity of a lifetime. You have to let me pursue this work."

"Are you sure?" asked Nagib. "I really don't think it's doable."

"We'll never know unless we try. I'm willing to try, but I'll need your help and support."

"This will be highly controversial. You'll need to make an airtight case if it turns out to be true."

I smiled and nodded.

"This will not be an easy path," Nagib cautioned again. "But, I think if anyone can do it, you can.

"Thank you professor!" I said excitedly.

Nagib smiled broadly now, almost as if this is what he really wanted me to do all along. "I will help you as much as I can," he said. "I have long suspected that living in a micro-gravity environment would result in increased human lifespans. I have thought this ever since those early experiments with *C. elegans* on the ISS and then NASA's twins-study with Mark and Scott Kelly back in 2016. You should pull all the literature

194

on that study which showed during spaceflight Scott Kelly's telomeres grew to be longer than those of his brother who stayed back on Earth."

I knew that telomers were protein caps on the ends of chromosomes that protect them from deterioration. Normally telomers got shorter as people aged. However, after a year in space, Scott's had grown longer. Now I got Professor Nagib to agree to let me try to prove that living in zero-g would result in increased human longevity. My heart was pounding with excitement.

…

I worked extremely hard on my research. Far harder than on anything in my whole life, ever. I came home from the lab every night exhausted. I'd often complain to Marc how hard it was until one night he said it's supposed to be hard. Then he quoted some old movie, *A League of Their Own*, I think, where Tom Hank's character says, "If it wasn't hard, everyone would do it. The hard is what makes it great."

…

Six months after starting my Ph.D. work, I called Emma.

"I did it!" I said excitedly.

"You did what?" replied Emma, trying to sound interested even though my call had woken her up in the middle of the night.

"I passed my Ph.D. qualifying exam!" I practically shouted.

"So are you a doctor now?" asked Emma sleepily.

"Oh no, I still have a long way to go. This was just my first step, but it's an important one. If I didn't pass, they wouldn't let me go on. Sorry to call you so late, but Marc and I have been up half the night celebrating."

"Well congratulations, I guess," said Emma, rubbing the sleep from her eyes. "Oh, by the way, I saw Alex on TV last night. He has his own TV show now. Can you believe that? As you know he's the pastor of that large church in Texas. I just can't get used to him talking about God and all, given how he, well you know."

"Well good for Alex," I said. "I'm happy for him."

"Well, I still don't trust him," replied Emma.

"You need to be more forgiving," I scolded.

"And technically, you're still married to him. Anyway, I think I heard him say something about how people shouldn't be living in space. Something about how God made Earth for man and that's where we're supposed to live. He said the heavens are reserved for God or something like that. I don't know, I wasn't really paying that much attention. You ever hear anything like that?"

"Nope. This is where I came to know God, where I felt his presence. That can't be wrong. You should come up here. You'll see, you'll feel it too."

...

As if going to school full time wasn't enough I, of course, still had Demetrious to take care of.

"Mom," said Demetrious, "some Grounder kids were making fun of me again today." He paused for a minute and then said, "They say I can't go to heaven when I die because I'll be crushed by the gravity there."

"Well, don't listen to them," I replied. "They're just being mean. And don't beat them up either."

"Okay, I won't. But Mom, is there gravity in heaven?"

The question had never occurred to me and I was momentarily at a loss for how to respond. Eventually, I responded with something clever like, "I don't know, honey." Seeing that this response didn't help I added, "But, let me tell you a little story. You see, Grounders don't understand how gravity affects literally everything they do. This is because it is woven into the very fabric of their lives. Its constant existence has affected their brains. It's always there for them and has always been. It is so pervasive that it mostly goes unnoticed and is forgotten. Now you and I live in this wonderful world freed from the relentless pull of gravity. You may never be able to set foot on solid ground, but you have the whole rest of the universe as your home. It will be home for you and your children forever."

"Whatever," said Demetrious irritably. "You still didn't tell me if there is there gravity in heaven"

"Well, look at it this way. Most of the Grounders who come up here say that it's like being in heaven, so I'd have to say that you'll be just fine there."

...

Length of time in space: *Fifteen and a half years.*

It's been three years since I passed my qualifying exam. I pushed myself as hard as I could during these three years. I routinely followed long days in the lab with very late nights studying and I spent almost every weekend on my research. Sometimes it would get to be too much and I would feel like quitting. I felt bad about not spending as much time with Demetrious as I wanted. Marc always encouraged me to continue on

I was at the lab early Saturday morning as usual. I was waiting for the results of the analysis I was running on the super computer at Berkeley. The analysis had been number crunching for a couple of days already and I estimated that it should finish this morning. I spent the last two years eliminating possible gene-expression pathways for humans in zero-g. I had already reduced the number from over a hundred thousand down to about twenty thousand, now with may latest data entered into the simulation software I developed, I was hoping to reduce the number down to a manageable number, say a few dozen. That would enable me to experimentally look in detail at those pathways to determine their effects on human aging. The wait seemed interminable.

It was taking longer than I expected, that's probably not good. Finally, just before noon a two-bell chime on my computer told me the analysis was complete. I nervously opened the file. My heart sank. There were still over two thousand credible pathways identified. That was way too many to investigate. What was I going to do?

...

That night Marc was staying with me and I told him about my latest results. "Maybe Professor Nagib was right," I said. "Maybe this is too difficult. Maybe I don't know what I'm doing. I don't think I'll ever be able to finish this. I feel like I've just wasted the last three years."

Marc hugged me and replied, "Hey, everyone who gets a Ph.D. feels like this at some point in their research. It's just part of the process. What you need is a break. You need to get away from this for a while and maybe get a different perspective on things."

"I don't know. Maybe I just need to work harder."

"Nope. Tomorrow I'm going to make arrangements for you and me to visit a new city complex that's being developed. I've been doing some consulting on it, so I'm sure they'll let us visit. We'll get away from things for a couple of days, just the two of us."

"Okay, I guess."

...

It took Marc a few days to make the necessary arrangements. He said we were going to see New Medina, a city complex currently under construction. We took an autonomous space taxi to the complex. When Marc said it was under construction, he wasn't kidding. The life support system wasn't even operational yet.

"Come on, put these on," said Marc, pointing to the spacesuits that he had loaded into the taxi. I could count on one hand the number of times I had worn a spacesuit in my fifteen years in space.

I put the suit on, turned to face Marc and asked, "How do I look?"

"Like Neil Armstrong."

"Very funny."

We went through the airlock into the facility. The spacesuits had built-in propulsion systems that enabled us to move around the airless interior of the facility. The facility was enormous, even though it was a long way from being finished.

"There's no life support in any part of the facility?" I asked Marc.

"No, it's all like this," Marc said motioning with his hands around the large room we were in.

"Uh, so where are we staying tonight?"

"Well, I thought we'd just kind of camp out in the taxi. I brought some sleeping bags, food and water."

"You really need to work on your luxury vacation skills," I teased.

We spent all day exploring the complex. That night we slept in the taxi. We were several thousand miles from anyone else in space. It was just the two of us. It was very romantic. With nothing to do or worry about I slept extremely well.

My brain, however, was hard at work while I slept. "Backwards!" I said out loud in the early morning. I should start with the end result of the gene expression and work backwards. It seemed so obvious, too obvious, but the problem was nobody had lived long enough in space to see the effect of the changed gene expression. Or was that actually true? Demetrious and I have been in space continuously for fifteen years.

"Marc, get up!" I shook Marc to wake him up. "We have to go back. I know what to do!"

Marc opened one eye, looked at me and then at the time and said, "Couldn't it wait a couple more hours?"

"Okay," but I was too excited to sleep. I could test how cells from Demetrious are expressing the genes in his DNA. I could do the same for mine. Then it might be possible to work backwards to the point where my simulations ended. I could connect the pathways from both ends in the middle.

Fifteen minutes later I shook Marc again. "Can we go now?" I asked.

"You're a pain in the butt, you know that?" Marc said jokingly without opening his eyes.

"Yes, but I'm also lovable."

"And modest. Okay, now that I'm wide away, we might as well pack up and get going."

I kissed him.

198

...

Length of time in space: *Sixteen and a half years.*

I pursued this new approach for a year and it worked! I stared at the results of my latest simulation. It showed definitively how zero gravity affects the expression of certain key genes. This modified gene expression then slowed down the aging process. I felt the mild exhilaration that comes with a new scientific understanding, of knowing something that nobody else knew. Not only that, the aging rate reduction factor was incredible. Remember for *C. elegans* this factor was approximately two. Nagib expected that if this worked for humans the factor would likely be somewhere between one and two. My results were showing that is was more like a factor of three. I could barely contain my excitement. I called Marc to share the news.

"Live long and prosper," was his immediate response.

I smiled. This time I knew the reference since we had watched all the original episodes together.

...

Length of time in space: *Seventeen years.*

I spent the last six months writing and rewriting my thesis. Finally, it was finished. What a relief! I turned it into my committee members for review.

Hamid said it was groundbreaking and brilliant. I guess he liked it. It showed that people born in space could expect a life expectancy of roughly two hundred and sixty years. The implications were staggering. Almost every phase of a person's life would be extended by a factor of three. A person could expect the robust health and vigor of being in their twenties to be extended to the ripe old age of seventy. You would be seventy years old, but you wouldn't actually be old, you'd be as healthy as someone who just turned thirty on Earth!

The news was impossible to contain and bits of information started leaking out. Rumors spread rapidly across the internet, some favorable, most intentionally inflammatory, almost all of them made up. The University started dealing with an increasing number of calls from the news media and ordinary citizens. Very quickly, politicians started calling, demanding information on the behalf of their constituents. I became simultaneously famous and infamous.

To quell the growing demand for information, the University arranged a press conference at their Sky City II branch. The plan called for Hamid to travel to Sky City II to be there in person to give a brief introduction. Then I would summarize my findings followed by a question and answer session.

…

The evening before the press conference Marc Elliott arrived at Sky City II along with an old college friend Rusty Steele. I met Marc and Rusty for dinner at Roy's, one of the best new restaurants at the resort.

"Tesla, I'd like you to meet Rusty Steele," said Marc. "Rusty is an old friend from Princeton."

"Very pleased to meet you," I replied. Rusty was an impressive and imposing figure. He would have been about six feet seven inches tall on Earth and probably weighed over two hundred seventy pounds. He had very dark skin, a shaved head, and looked like he never missed a day at the gym. His eyes lit up his face and he had the intense look of a scholar—the piercing look of a man attempting to extract all of the available information from his surroundings. "Marc has spoken of you often, it's so nice to finally get to meet you in person."

"The pleasure is all mine," replied Rusty in a deep rich voice.

"Rusty has come up here to listen to your press conference in person," said Marc.

"Really? I'm flattered. Marc tells me that you teach religious studies at Princeton Theological Seminary, that you're an expert in the textural criticism of the New Testament. What does that mean exactly?"

"It means I do analysis on the manuscripts of the New Testament to identify and correct copying errors, spelling errors, and other more significant changes in order to attempt to reconstruct the text as it was originally written," explained Rusty.

I glanced at Marc who shrugged and then looked back at Rusty. "Why do you need to do that? I don't understand. I thought the Bible was the Bible?"

"Most people do. The fundamental problem is that the original manuscripts of the New Testament no longer exist. They were lost somewhere along the way."

"I didn't know that."

"What we have are manuscripts that had been copied and recopied by hand over hundreds of years after the original text was written. Over this time period there were numerous copying errors as well as unintentional changes and even numerous intentional modifications and additions. So

200

my job is to try to sort it out to determine what the original manuscripts said."

"That's very interesting. So why would you care about what I have to say?"

"If your work is correct," replied Rusty, "The implications would be enormous. I believe it would be the catalyst for an explosion of people wanting to live in space. It could change the course of human history. It might even change Man's relationship with God. That's why I'm here."

"Well, I don't know about that last point, but I'll go along with the first one and possibly the second," I replied. I am changing the course of history, I thought to myself. How cool is that!

"Marc tells me you're a born-again Christian. Is that true?"

"If Marc said it, it must be true, at least that's what he tells me," I looked over at Marc and smiled. "But, to answer your question, yes, I am a born-again Christian."

"And yet you're getting a PhD in evolutionary biology. How did that happen?" pressed Rusty.

"How did I become a born-again Christian, or how did I get a PhD?" I deadpanned.

"Both. Again, and more to the point, how do you reconcile your faith with your profession?"

"Well first of all, I became a born-again Christian after moving here. Living here in space, experiencing the vastness of the universe, staring out into the infinite, I just felt God's presence. It was undeniable and overwhelming."

"And how do you reconcile that with your profession?" pressed Rusty.

"Do you think God is afraid of science, Rusty?"

He didn't answer, so I continued. "Only men are afraid of science. I believe that you do not have to give up the factual understanding of the physical universe as revealed by science in order to have faith in God."

"I like this woman," Rusty said to Marc before turning back to me. "I only fear that some people will not react well to the changes your results could bring."

"What do you mean," I asked.

"There are radical groups down on Earth even now speaking out against people living in space, and they're starting to attract a lot of attention," replied Rusty.

I looked over a Marc who nodded.

"They're religious fringe groups mostly," continued Rusty. "Typically small organizations, except for one that I know of. It's a large church in Texas called Purification by Grace Ministries, headed by a charismatic pastor named Alex Markov. This pastor has been going around the country, and on the internet, spreading the message that the Heavens belong to God, that people were not meant to live there, and that it's God's will that we immediately stop all settlements in space. He's getting quite a following."

"I don't understand how anyone could think that God would not want people to come here," I replied, pretending that I never heard of Alex Markov.

"Alex Markov?" asked Marc rhetorically. "I met an Alex Markov once, except he wasn't a pastor then, maybe a youth pastor, or something like that."

"What?" I said staring at Marc in disbelief. What in the world is going on. "When did you meet him? How well do you know him? What did you talk about?" I asked in rapid fire, sounding increasingly agitated.

"Hey, take it easy, right?" replied Marc. "What are you so worked up about? Do you know Alex Markov?"

"No." I lied. "When you met him and what did you talked about."

Marc gave me a strange look, but answered my questions anyway. "It was at some kind of community outreach event I think. I don't know, it was several years ago. I was helping out some of my NASA friends in Houston. They were there to encourage kids to study math and science. It was a huge event with lots of organizations. All kinds of sports. Football, yeah, that's right, I remember, lots of football teams."

"Whatever," I interrupted. "What about Markov?"

"I'm getting there. There were faith-based groups there too, encouraging kids to get involved in church. I guess that's why Markov was there. Anyway, we had assigned seating at dinner that night and we wound up sitting next to each other. As we were talking, I mentioned that I had just returned from Sky City, this was before the move to Sky City II. Anyway, I told him I was sad because I just left the most incredible woman. He was easy to talk to and seemed very interested. So I told him about you and how we met. I told him about Demetrious. Now that I think about it, he seemed particularly interested in Demetrious for some reason. He wanted to know how old he was and what he looked like. I just assumed he was interested because he was a youth pastor."

"Then what happened?" I asked trying to suppress the urgency in my voice. My heart was racing.

"That was pretty much it," replied Marc. "After that dinner I never talked to him again."

Questions flooded my mind. Does he know we're here? If so, why hasn't he done anything about it? What is he waiting for? Maybe he doesn't know. Maybe he didn't make the connection. My breathing started to get rapid and shallow. My hands started shaking; my heart was pounding in my chest. He must have figured it out. How could he not?

202

But wait, that was several years ago and he's a pastor now. Wouldn't that mean that he must have forgiven me? Yes, that makes sense. Now that he's a pastor, I'm sure he's forgiven me. That's what pastors do, right? That explains why he hasn't come after us. With that thought, my hands stopped shaking, and my pulse returned to normal. It's going to be okay! He must know about but us, but it doesn't matter. He must have forgiven me. The thought made me happy.

Chapter 22 Life Expectancy

The following day at the start of the press conference, the crowd of reporters fell silent as Professor Hamid Nagib approached the microphone.

"I'd like to welcome everyone here this afternoon," Nagib began. "I welcome those of you who are fortunate enough to be here in person, as well as everyone attending remotely. Since joining my lab with the goal of getting her PhD, Tesla Miller has been one of our shining stars. She has been working in my lab for the past four years where she has been investigating how animals adapt to life in micro-gravity. This work has taken some unexpected turns and produced some surprising results, which Tesla will explain shortly. She first caught our attention by completing her undergraduate degree at Berkeley in just two years. We suspected then that she was something special. Today you'll have the opportunity to judge that for yourselves. Tesla will start by giving you a brief summary of her results, and will then be available to answer your questions. So, without further ado, please join me in welcoming Tesla Miller."

"Thank you Professor," I said as I reached the microphone. And thank you all for attending this afternoon, or whatever time of day it is wherever you are around the world. I'd like to start by telling you a story about some little worms. These are very special worms that scientists have named *Caenorhabditis elegans*, a type of nematode, but for today, we'll just call them worms. These are cool, tiny, transparent little worms only about one millimeter long, but they have made a big impact on science. They were the first multicellular animal to have their complete genome sequenced, all one-hundred-million base pairs, way back at the beginning of this century. This is significant because about thirty-five percent of the genes from these worms have human homologs. A homolog is a gene that is similar in structure and evolutionary origin to a gene in another species, in this case, us. So this means that about thirty-five percent of our worm's genes are similar to genes that we have, which has made them attractive research subjects for decades. They have been studied extensively to understand how the genome affects human health. These worms were also the first worms to fly in space in the 1990s. Experiments onboard the International Space Station along with subsequent ground-based investigations suggested that under the right conditions these worms may live about twice as long in zero-g as their relatives left behind on Earth. That's pretty cool, but it gets better. The really interesting thing is that these experiments also suggested that not only should these worms live longer in space, but that their adaptation to zero-g should result in them living healthier lives with healthier muscles.

Now, this suggestion had been around for decades. But nobody knew for sure if was really true.

So what did we do? Well, the first thing we did was to take a bunch of these little worms, divide them randomly into two groups, one we left behind on Earth and the other we brought up here. We followed them for several generations to see if they really did live longer in space and were they really healthier? What we found was yes and yes. Incredibly, we demonstrated that these little worms really do live about twice as long in zero-g as on the ground and their muscles are indeed healthier. The next step was to determine why these things happened. Our goal was to understand at the genetic level what was happening. Why do they live longer? I won't bore you with the details here; they are all explained in excruciating detail in my thesis, as well as in a paper that Hamid and I wrote that will be coming out shortly in the journal *Nature*."

I paused for a moment to let that sink in and then continued. "But I'm sure you didn't come here to hear me talk about worms, as interesting as I think that would be. What you really want to know is, what does this have to do with people? Well, a lot, it turns out. You see, the same mechanisms that extend the life of our little worms in space also operate in humans, but with a twist. Humans, of course, are not worms. We are much more complicated than a simple worm that only has about a thousand cells, whereas humans have about thirty-seven trillion cells. The bottom line, though, is that the effect first observed in these little worms turns out to be much more complicated, and to our astonishment, also much more effective in humans. We have been able to show conclusively that people living in a micro-gravity environment should expect about a factor of three increase in their lifespan. This is explained in detail in our *Nature* paper as well. With that, I'll entertain any questions. I've been told to ask you to please state your name and institution before asking your question.

A roar erupted in the room as hands shot up. I began calling on people by pointing at them.

"Linda Fletcher, ABC News. So how long will people live in space?"

I replied, "Well, the current life expectancy on Earth is about eighty-seven years, so if you multiply that by three you get two-hundred-sixty-one years. Therefore, assuming you're not killed in an accident, or by someone you know, and assuming you take relatively good care of yourself, you could expect to live that long, approximately two-hundred-sixty years."

"Kate Nguyen, New York Times. I thought that living in zero-g was bad for you, that you lose bone and muscle mass similar to an elderly person on Earth. Are you saying that's not true?"

"Adaptive changes to zero-g definitely make you lose muscle and bone mass and those losses will make you more frail when you return to

Earth. There's no question about that. But, and this is the key point, if you don't return to a one-g environment, then the adaptive changes to micro-gravity are actually beneficial, resulting in healthier muscles, including the heart muscle, healthier cells, healthier genes, and longer life."

"Marvin Reynoso, BBC News. People have been flying in space since the 1960's, why hasn't anyone discovered this before?"

"Spaceflight is stressful," I replied with a smile. "At least it was before the advent of resorts such as this one. Astronauts were under tremendous pressure to not screw up. The living conditions sucked. It was crowed and noisy, making it hard to sleep. There was little privacy, bathrooms were primitive at best, and there were no showers. Sanitation was poor. Significantly, there was no protection from the harsh radiation environment. These factors dominated the human space experience for decades. Once they're fixed, however, the benefits of micro-gravity become evident. But just to be clear, there have been clues in the past. Most significantly there were the longer telomeres observed on Scott Kelly after a year in zero-g compared to his stay-at-home twin brother Mark, that hinted at possible human life extension. Part of the work that Hamid and I did explained why telomeres tended to increase in length in micro-gravity and how this results in improved chromosome health."

"Joel Hunter, Fox News. If your life expectancy is two-hundred-sixty years, won't you just be old for more than two-hundred years? Who wants to be old for two-hundred years?

"Actually no. What we think happens is that you mature to adulthood on a relatively normal schedule, but then the aging process slows down significantly. So that when you're seventy years old, you'd be as healthy as a thirty-year-old on Earth. Let's think about that for a minute. That would mean that you'd enjoy the robust health of a person in their twenties from the age twenty to age seventy, or for about fifty years. You would enjoy your thirties for about forty years from age seventy to about a hundred and ten, and so on."

The buzz in the room grew louder. I called on another reporter.

"Giselle Donovan, AFP. This sounds too good to be true. How do you know this is true? Is there any possibility that you're wrong?"

"The short answer is in both our worms and in humans, spaceflight results in the decreased expression of hundreds of genes that if expressed at a lower level, increase lifespan. The response to spaceflight is an altering in the expression of key metabolic genes, specifically those that affect insulin and insulin-like signaling in a complex process that affects aging. Regarding your second question, while obviously no one has lived for two hundred sixty years in space, there is a very high probability that our conclusions are correct. That means it is not a certainty for humans, but we did demonstrate it for worms."

"Walter Williams, CNN. So does this mean that women living in space will have a much longer time over which they can have children?"

"While we didn't specifically look at this question, I believe this is likely to be correct, that women living here will be able to bear healthy children when they're a hundred years old."

The crowd buzzed with excitement. I waited for the noise to subside before calling on the next reporter.

"Svetlana Boginskaya, MSNBC. Does this work for dogs too? I'd like to keep my dog around much longer." This brought laughter from the crowd.

"We don't know, but it works for worms and it works for humans, my speculation is that it would work for dogs too. The major question is by how much, and that we don't know.

"Jorge Ramos, The Wall Street Journal. Do you have to be born in space to get the benefit of a longer lifespan?"

"No, the adaptive response to micro-gravity begins as soon as you're in this environment and because it impacts the metabolic pathways that affect aging you will get this benefit no matter what age you move to space."

"Cristina Maria, Washington Post. There are rumors that people living in space become smarter too, is that true?"

"Is it true that there are such rumors, or is it true that living in space makes you smarter," I teased before continuing. "Actually, as I'm sure you know, it's virtually impossible to define what you mean by smarter, and this wasn't part of our investigation, but I will say this. We do know that a large fraction of your brain's physical real estate, as well as a large part of its activity, are used to enable you to stand upright against gravity. Without gravity, this real estate and brain activity are unnecessary. It is also well known that neuroplasticity gives your brain the ability to physically change in response to what you do, and what you don't do. Now, because you don't need to stand upright against gravity here, all that brain real estate and activity are freed up to be repurposed. In addition, for reasons that are still poorly understood, your nervous system works faster in zero-g. This has been known since the 1970's and, I might add, has the added benefit of increasing sensual pleasures in space. The end result is that it is certainly within the realm of possibility that some people may become smarter in space, whatever that means." I'm certain it worked for me. The crowd started buzzing again.

"But hold on," I said, trying to speak above the crowd noise. "There's one big caveat, and that is, this only works, if it works at all, if you protect the brain from the damaging radiation in space. It is well known that a particular type of radiation, galactic cosmic rays to be specific, blast apart the synaptic connections in your brain resulting in decreased cognitive functionality, uh, it makes you dumber. But if you protect the brain from these galactic cosmic rays, like we do here at Sky City II, then the cognitive benefits of living in micro-gravity may become evident. With that I think we have time for one more question."

I pointed to a white-haired man floating near the back of the room who seemed particularly anxious to be called on.

"Edgar Whisenant, sent by God... God did not mean for people to live in space," he said forcefully. "The Bible is clear," his voice growing louder, 'The HEAVENS belong to the LORD, but the earth he has given to mankind,' Psalm 115:16."

"Uh, was there a question in there?" I asked.

"You and your kind should not be living here!" he replied, practically shouting now. "It is an offense to God. For this you must DIE BLASPHEMER!" he yelled as he pulled out a gun.

Everyone at the press conference scattered. The Grounders attempted to duck down as they would on Earth, trying to flatten their bodies against the floor, but this was monumentally unsuccessful in space. Instead, they tended to curl up like balls, filling the room and bouncing off each other like atoms in some strange gas. Marc Elliott raced over to me, reaching me just as we heard Whisenant say, "I am the avenging angel of the lord! Death to trespassers!"

Through the jumble of floating bodies we saw Whisenant level the gun at us and fire three rounds in rapid succession from the back of the room, pop, pop, pop. All three sailed just over my head. Marc grabbed me and whisked me out of the room down a long corridor.

"Grounders always aim high." I whispered to Marc,

I looked back and saw that the randomly careening balls of Grounders momentarily blocked Whisenant's line of sight to us, but we heard two more shots fired. I could see blood filling the room. Somebody must have been shot. Spherical robot cleaners came off the walls to start vacuuming up the blood out of the air. I saw Demetrious with Rusty Steel in tow emerging from the resulting chaos. They followed Marc and me down a long corridor toward the city center and caught up to us just as we entered the four-story atrium and shopping complex. As we glided into the center of the large open space we immediately realized that this was a mistake. There was no cover here. We were completely exposed.

Demetrious looked back down the corridor, "He's following us!" he shouted.

"Over here!" I commanded. I led us across the atrium toward an exit.

"Where does this lead?" asked Rusty.

"To the industrial part of the complex," I replied. "Hurry! There should be lots of places there to hide from this mad man until security can subdue him."

As we got to the exit, Demetrious looked back again. "Uh oh, he's entering the atrium," he whispered. "We've got trouble."

"No shit," said Marc sarcastically.

"No, there's three of them now, and they all have guns," replied Demetrious excitedly.

A shot rang out before Marc could apologize. It sailed over our heads. "Grounders always aim high," said Demetrious looking at his me.

"Let's get out of here!" I commanded.

We raced down the wide corridor with Demetrious helping Rusty, who, as a Grounder, could not move in zero-g as easily as the rest of us. Fortunately, Whisenant and his two accomplices were also Grounders and they struggled to get through the large open volume of the atrium quickly.

The four of us eventually made our way into the farming region of Sky City II. Rusty stared in awe at the enormous complex.

Always the engineer, Marc started explaining. "There are several of these farming complexes here. We can grow enough food to sustain a population of two thousand people. Even so, Sky City II is not completely self-sustainable. We still rely on lots of resources from Earth, but it's much farther along that path than any other space complex. The carbon dioxide levels here in the farming areas are artificially high to help accelerate plant growth. The lithium-plasma lighting provides a spectrum nearly identical to the sun and is also controlled to maximize growth."

"Is it safe to be in here?" asked Rusty.

"Safer than where those fucking gunmen are," quipped Demetrious.

"Demetrious!" I said.

"What?"

"Yes," replied Marc to Rusty's question. "The carbon dioxide levels are set to be good for the plants, but not too high to be a problem for people. We should be able to hide out here. There's no way they'll find us in this place, it would take them forever to search this complex."

As I started to relax a little, I realized that Hamid was not with us. "Where's Hamid," I exclaimed. "We've got to go back and get him."

"Hamid didn't make it Mom, I'm sorry," said Demetrious.

"What do you mean?" I replied, fearing the worst.

"When the shooting started, he grabbed me and positioned himself between me and that whack-job shooter. He saved my life, but a bullet hit him right in the head."

"Oh my god!" I started to cry. Marc grabbed me and hugged me. "Why is this happening," I sobbed. "He was such a good man."

"We can't hide here forever," said Demetrious. "Why don't we just call security and see if they've caught them yet?"

Marc and Rusty looked at each other sheepishly.

"Sky City II security, this is Marc Elliott." There was no answer. "That's odd, there's always supposed to be someone on duty at security. Sky City II, why is there no answer from security?" Marc said, this time speaking directly to the computer.

"There is no one present in security," responded the Sky City II computer. Since the computer knew the locations of all the on-duty employees, Marc was about to ask the computer where the head of security was when we heard someone enter the farming complex.

"They're heading right for us," I whispered. "I thought you said they'd never find us here." I stared at Marc.

"They must have taken over security, the computer knows where we are," Marc whispered back."

"What are we going to do?" asked Rusty quietly with more than a little concern in his voice.

"Follow me," I said, drying my eyes. "I've got an idea." I led us through the greenhouse and then through a pair of double doors. The smell hit us like a ton of bricks—manure! The air was heavy with the warm, moist smell of manure.

We stopped momentarily and stared down the central corridor. There were cows as far as the eye could see. It was a bizarre scene really, which must have seemed even more bizarre for a Grounder like Rusty. Around the cylindrical walls of the room there were eight pens with each one holding a single cow such that if you floated in the middle there would be one directly overhead, one beneath your feet, one each to your left and right and four more at forty-five degrees to those four pens. The cows all had their feet toward the cylindrical outer wall, so that their backs were toward the center, making the cow above your head upside down compared to the one beneath your feet. The cows to your right and left appeared to be lying on their sides. The pens were about thirteen feet long, and this arrangement of eight pens and eight cows was repeated twelve times down the length of the room so that there were ninety-six cows in all.

"Jesus, you've got cows in space," exclaimed Rusty. "What are all these cows doing here?"

"Shush!" I commanded. "Keep moving."

"You've heard of Kobe Beef, right?" whispered Marc as we made our way down the center of the chamber.

"Sure," replied Rusty quietly, "It's that beef from Japan that's supposed to be really tender. I read somewhere that those cows are fed beer, massaged by hand, and kept in tiny pens to keep them from getting much exercise."

"That's right," whispered Marc. "So one of our Japanese investors, Mr. Yabusaki, brought two dozen Wagyu cattle here from Japan with the

210

idea that raising them in zero-g would result in even more marbled beef since the animals can just float in their pens. He calls his product Sky Ranch Beef, the Best Beef in the Universe, and sells it mostly to the guests at Sky City II, although recently, I think, he's started exporting it back to Earth."

"Is it?" whispered Rusty.

"Is it what?" replied Marc.

"The best beef in the universe?"

Before Marc could answer, we heard the door to the cattle chamber open.

"Quiet! "They're coming in," I whispered.

"Mom, come here, help me with this," Demetrious said quietly.

Demetrious was busy unhooking one of the cows from its restraint. We pushed the cow into the center of the corridor. Demetrious and I put our feet on the cow's back and started pushing it using our winged-arms. At first the cow barely moved. While it was weightless, it still had a mass of nearly three quarters of a ton. This was a lot of mass to accelerate. Before long, however, we got it moving and continued to accelerate it down the corridor. The cow was between Demetrious and I and the gunmen.

The gunmen looked up and all they could see was this cow flying at them. Their initial reaction was to start shooting at it. To their surprise, the bullets were monumentally ineffective at slowing the cow's momentum. But it did make a bloody mess of things.

Demetrious and I gave the cow one last shove toward the gunmen before ducking for cover. Not accustomed to moving in zero-g, the gunmen had difficulty getting out of the way. The cow smashed squarely into two of the them driving them backward and smashing them into the door of the chamber. It was as if on Earth someone had dropped a fifteen-hundred-pound cow on them from a height of six feet. It knocked the wind out of them, probably broke a couple of their ribs, and knocked them unconscious. It also covered them in cow's blood from the bullet wounds. The cow bounced off the end of the chamber and headed back down the corridor, tumbling head over heels, spraying blood everywhere.

The third gunman received only a glancing blow from the animal, but enough to send him tumbling backward. He bounced awkwardly off the end wall sending him back down the corridor directly toward Demetrious and me. Somehow, he had managed to hold on to his gun, but his tumbling motion made it nearly impossible for him to shoot straight. He fired several wild shots, one of which struck another nearby cow spraying more blood into the chamber.

As the gunman tumbled by, Demetrious pushed hard off the wall of the pen where we were hiding and flew rapidly head first directly toward him. The gunman saw him coming and tried to fire at Demetrious, but missed badly. As Demetrious flew past the gunman, he grabbed him by the foot, turned, and in one smooth motion transferred his relative angular momentum to the gunman causing him to spin rapidly around his belly button while continuing down the corridor.

The gunman fired wildly using up the remaining bullets in his clip without hitting a thing. Demetrious quickly arrested his own residual motion as he watched the gunman spinning down the corridor. The gunman wasn't traveling straight down the center, but was veering off to one side. A few seconds later his head smacked hard against the side of a pen. It made a ringing sound as it struck the steel column, knocking him unconscious.

Unsure if there were more gunmen, Marc and I directed everyone to keep moving. Several spherical robots streamed into the cattle ranch and started cleaning the walls.

"They look like white blood cells in a giant body streaming in to repair an injury," marveled Rusty. The environmental control system started clearing the air of blood.

We led them out of the Sky City Ranch down a corridor and into a smaller room. The room was filled with wooden barrels.

"Whiskey," Marc said before Rusty could even ask. "It ages differently up here, very popular with the tourists."

"But no place to hide," I said. "Let's keep moving."

We left the whisky storage room and entered another large growing complex. This one was for flowers, and they were all in bloom. "Isn't this spectacular," I said. "I always love coming here. It's so beautiful, and it smells so good. The rows and rows of flowers remind me of when my mom used to take us to Lompoc in the spring to see the flowers. I used to love that. But we better keep moving. I know a better place to hide."

The four of us traveled through the fields of flowers to an exit at the far end, through another short corridor, and into yet another large growing complex, this one for corn.

"Now this is a place to hide," said Rusty looking at the rows and rows of nearly fully mature, six foot tall, corn stalks.

"They've been genetically engineered to grow straight and tall in zero-g," I said.

"Okay, let's wait here until we get word that it's safe," said Marc.

As the adrenalin wore off, I started feeling the weight of the events that had taken place and felt a grave sense of responsibility for what happened. "I can't believe I was the target of an assassination attempt, and I'm the reason that Hamid is dead," I lamented. Then I hugged Demetrious and said, "Thank God you're okay!"

Chapter 23 God's Will

Eventually, Security concluded that there was just one other gunman besides the three assailants we subdued at the Sky City Ranch. Robot security guards had quickly captured and restrained the lone gunman who had taken over the security office and human security officers collected the three gunman at the ranch while they were still unconscious, effectively ending the incident. A subsequent investigation revealed that the guns had been smuggled up to the resort by bribing a pilot.

Over the next week, worldwide reaction to my press conference and the ensuing attack ranged from horror and outrage all the way to sympathy for the attacker's cause. But the attack itself was quickly forgotten on Earth, drowned out by headlines that screamed "People Live Three Times Longer in Space," and "Want to Live to be 260? Move to Space," and "Space People are Smarter, Live Longer." They have better sex too, I thought to myself as I read the headlines in my news feed.

I noted that, as usual, the news media couldn't distinguish between the scientific results Hamid and I established demonstrating, to a high degree of confidence, that people lived longer in micro-gravity, and the mere speculation that living here could make you smarter in some sense. More likely, they didn't care as long as it attracted eyeballs. Furthermore, I couldn't help but notice that media outlets of all types made a point of showing my picture as the centerpiece of the story. Yuri said they did that because it helped attract viewers. If so I'm flattered, I guess. Yuri also said that I was now the unofficial face of the new Space Immigration Movement (SIM), an immediate dramatic increase in the number of people wanting to move to space.

Prior to this there was a steady, but small trickle of people moving to space, mostly for jobs, some for the adventure, and a few after retirement to avoid the relentless pull of gravity on their increasingly frail bodies. Now the trickle turned into a deluge. The news media's pastime *de jour* became interviewing people intending to move to space. The media dubbed these people SIMs. I was watching online as a reporter interviewed people from a long line of SIMs waiting to fill out applications in person for apartments in the few existing space resort cities, including Sky City II. The reporter approached a young couple. Hey, I know that reporter. She was at my press conference the day of the shooting.

"Excuse me, I'm Kate Nguyen, New York Times. Could you tell us why you two want to move to space?"

"Sure!" answered the happy young woman who was obviously in love. "We're newly married and we plan to spend the rest of our lives together. We want to be together as long as possible," she said smiling at her husband.

"I see," replied Kate. "So, instead of being married for maybe forty or fifty years, you two could be married for something like two hundred and forty years," said Kate as she turned to face the camera with a feigned look of horror.

"Yes!" answered the young woman. "Isn't it wonderful?"

"Yes, I'm sure it will be," replied Kate. "Thank you for your time." Kate turned back to the camera and said, "There you have it folks, young lovers planning a long, long, life together in space."

Kate next found a middle-aged woman in line by herself. The woman looked up as Kate approached her. "You're in line to apply for an apartment in space, could you share with us why you want to make such a drastic move?"

"I'm fifty years old," replied the woman gruffly. "My back hurts, my knees hurt, I have high blood pressure, I have trouble just getting off the sofa for god's sake. If I stay on Earth, I'm sure I'll be dead in ten years and I'll probably be in pain the whole freaking time. So I want to move to space where I've heard that my knees and back won't hurt. Where I don't have to worry about getting off the damned sofa. Where maybe I could even live for another hundred years. Wouldn't you?"

"I supposed I would," answered Kate smiling at the camera. "Thank you for sharing that with us."

Kate then caught up with a young man who appeared to be by himself. "Excuse me, could you tell us why you want to move to space?"

"I'd be happy to!" replied the young man enthusiastically. "I just finished college and want to go to graduate school in physics. I hear that all the best research papers are now coming from people living in space. People are smarter there you know. So if I'm going to compete with them, I have to move there too. It's as simple as that."

"Do you think you'll be smarter if you live in space?" asked Kate.

"I'm counting on it," replied the young man. "Oh, and that Tesla Miller is hot too! She's a babe! I'm hoping I'll get to meet her too when I'm living there."

Kate looked into the camera and deadpanned, "Yes, I think we can all agree that Tesla Miller is literally out of this world. Thank you."

The reporter moved on to do another interview.

Okay, that's enough of that. I changed the channel.

...

After Professor Nagib's funeral service, Marc, Rusty, Charlie O'Brien, the head of Security, and I made our way to one of the many

214

bars at Sky City II. Charlie felt personally responsible for my safety now and began providing me with my own personal security guard, a job he often fulfilled himself.

The actual funeral service was on Earth, making it impossible for me to be there in person. Marc and Rusty could have gone, but decided to stay with me in case I needed their support. While I could not be there physically, I participated in the funeral service through the latest in live video conferencing. I even gave one of the many eulogies.

"I can't believe it," I said as the four of us took our places around a table at the Cosmos Café. "For the second time since moving here I've had to give a eulogy for someone near and dear to me. First it was George and now Hamid." Then I looked straight at Rusty and said, "You're a man of God, why would God allow this?"

Before Rusty could respond Marc interrupted, trying to change the subject, "Uh, what do we know about the shooters? One of them was named Edgar Whisenant? What have we found out about that?

"We've been checking," replied Charlie, "but there doesn't seem to be any information about him other than that Edgar Whisenant is not his real name. Someone has been able to cover his digital tracks very well. Fingerprints, DNA, dental records, all turn up empty."

"Digital tracks?" I ask rhetorically. "I know someone who might be able to help with that."

...

It took him two days, but Jimmy Homa found what he was looking for and called me.

"Hi Tesla," said Jimmy. "It took some doing, but we got 'em."

"Hi Jimmy," I said warmly. "I knew you could do it. What did you find out?"

"As you suggested, Edgar Whisenant is not his real name. His name is, Buford J. Wellington. Born in Arlington, Virginia; moved to Texas about ten years ago. He took the name Edgar Whisenant when he joined an extremist group that calls itself the Prophets of God. Each member of this group takes the name of someone from the past who predicted when Jesus would return to Earth. The real Edgar Whisenant wrote a book back in the 1980's titled, *88 Reasons Why the Rapture Will Be in 1988*. Interestingly enough, before he wrote that book, Whisenant was a NASA rocket engineer. I knew you couldn't trust those rocket scientists."

"Let's stay focused Jimmy," I chided good-naturedly.

"Sorry. The other members of the Prophets of God include Hippolytus of Rome, Pope Sylvester II, Sandro Botticelli, Thomas Muntzer, Michael Stiflel, William Aspinwall, Henry Archer, and William

Miller—not their real names, of course. Each of these historical figures predicted that Jesus would return within their own generation. The basic philosophy of the Prophets of God is that all of these people were actually right in their predictions of when Jesus was going to return, but that mankind did something that prevented the second coming each time. Now they believe that people living in space are the problem, and that they must cleanse the heavenly realm, or something like that, before Jesus can return. Their goal is to eliminate all human settlements in space."

"That's pretty crazy," I said.

"There's more," said Jimmy. "The Prophets of God split off from a church called Purification by Grace Ministries headquartered in Austin, Texas. This is the church headed by Pastor Alex Markov. He's now strongly promoting the idea that people shouldn't be living in space and is gaining a large following. I'm really worried about what this guy can do. He has headed Purification by Grace Ministries since he became the lead pastor several years ago under suspicious circumstances. Under his leadership, the church has grown from a large one in Austin, Texas, to a megachurch with a worldwide congregation and over a hundred and twenty thousand active members. His sermons are watched by followers literally in every country in the world. He has virtually unlimited resources. I'll send you a link to his latest sermon."

"Thanks Jimmy. You're the best."

The Prophets of God split off from Alex's church! I struggled to make sense of what Jimmy told me. Could Alex be behind all of this. I thought he had forgiven me. What if he's trying to have me killed? Or does he actually believe that living in space is an affront to God. As usual, I had more questions than answers.

...

Later that Marc, Rusty, Charlie and I gathered in my apartment so we could watch Alex's most recent sermon from this past Sunday.

Austin, Texas

"Let us pray," Alex began. "I pray Holy Spirit that you will bless this message. I pray that these words are your words, not mine. I pray that we, your servants, will act according to your will here on Earth. Amen."

Alex paused to create a solemn moment before continuing.

"Jesus is coming soon. Of this, there can be no doubt…Jesus is coming soon…Now, is the time to prepare for his coming…Now, is the time to prepare for his return…Now, is the time to clear the way. The signs are all around us. Jesus said, 'The time has been fulfilled, the kingdom of God is at hand; repent and believe in the good news.' Of course, we don't know exactly when this will happen, Jesus himself made this clear when he said that, 'of that day and hour no one knows, not even the angels of heaven, nor the Son, but the Father alone.' But, we know that it will be soon, it will be very soon and we must be prepared." Alex strode across the stage as he spoke. "We must be ready. But how, my friends, how do we know it will be soon? How can you be so certain Pastor Alex? Truly I tell you, we know from God's own word. For the scriptures tell us when this will happen…It will happen when, 'men will be lovers of self, lovers of money, boastful, arrogant, revilers, disobedient to parents, ungrateful, irreconcilable, malicious gossips, without self-control, brutal, haters of good, treacherous, reckless, conceited, lovers of pleasure rather than lovers of God…' Truly I tell you, who can deny that this describes the condition of society today. It couldn't be more clear. You know it to be so. You know it in your hearts."

"That's some good preaching," Alex said as he paused for effect. "But wait. There's more!" he shouted, and then lowered his voice to just above a whisper. "Jesus said, 'And this gospel of the kingdom will be preached in the whole world as a testimony to all nations, and then the end will come.' Isn't that astonishing?" he said louder now. "Jesus said these words over two thousand years ago and now here I am preaching this message to you. And this message is going out to the whole world. It is reaching every country in the world right now. Isn't God great! We truly serve a great God!" he said practically shouting again.

Alex paused and then said solemnly, "We have a problem my people of God. We have a truly terrible problem. A problem that arises from man's sinful and arrogant ways. Daniel tells us that the end will not come until the cleansing of the heavenly sanctuary is complete."

Speaking louder Alex continued, "Psalm 115:16 says that 'The heavens belong to the LORD, but the earth he has given to mankind…' God said, the heavens belong to him…The heavens belong to the Lord," he repeated for emphasis. "Space is God's ground. And yet my good people, every day we see more and more sinners defying God's word…More and more people leaving Earth to live in the heavens…The arrogance of mankind is breathtaking…God gave the earth to mankind, NOT the heavens," Alex shouted and then paused to let that soak in.

Then quietly again Alex continued, "Recall from Genesis where mankind says, 'Come, let us build ourselves a city, with a tower that reaches to the heavens, so that we may make a name for ourselves;' But the mighty hand of God put a stop to it. Why? Because the earth is where God intends for us to live. God is crystal clear on this. Jesus said, 'You will receive power when the Holy Spirit comes upon you, and you will be

My witnesses in Jerusalem, and in all Judea and Samaria, and to the ends of the EARTH.' Jesus is instructing us to spread his word throughout the earth."

Alex paused. "PERIOD!" he shouted. "Does He say to spread His word throughout the heavens? NO! He certainly does not! He says spread my word to the ends of the EARTH."

Quietly once more, Alex went on, "Paul knew this when he wrote 'If indeed you continue in your faith, established and firm, not moved from the hope of the gospel you heard, which has been proclaimed in all creation under heaven, and of which I, Paul, have become a servant.'"

Louder now Alex said, "Paul says 'in all creation UNDER heaven.' He doesn't say, throughout heaven. He doesn't say, 'to the ends of heaven.' No, he says UNDER heaven. WE ARE DESIGNED BY GOD TO LIVE ON EARTH. PERIOD! WE ARE COMMANDED BY GOD TO LIVE ON EARTH."

Alex paused once again to get ready for the big finish, then shouted, "JESUS WILL NOT RETURN UNTIL THE HEAVENLY SANCTUARY IS CLEANSED…WE MUST CLEANSE THE HEAVENLY SANCTUARY…We, the body of Christ must do this. It is up to us. There is no one else. We are the body of Christ, and Paul tells us, 'The body is a unit, though it is comprised of many parts. And although its parts are many, they all form one body. Now you are the body of Christ, and each of you is a member of it…' We are the body of Christ." Alex repeated. "THE BODY OF CHRIST MUST NOW RISE UP AND CLEANSE THE HEAVENLY SANCTUARY. IT IS GOD'S WILL THAT PEOPLE SHALL NOT LIVE IN SPACE. IT IS GOD'S WILL THAT THESE SINNERS MUST STOP LIVING IN SPACE. It is our duty, as followers of Christ, to stop this blasphemy against God…If you agree with the word of God say amen."

The entire congregation said "amen."

"If you agree with the word of God say amen," Alex repeated louder this time.

And the congregation responded with a louder "amen."

"IF YOU AGREE WITH THE WORD OF GOD SAY AMEN!" Alex shouted.

And the congregation shouted "AMEN!" and erupted into applause.

Alex stood in front of them, arms outstretched with his palms facing up as he looked up, his body again making the shape of a cross. He smiled as he appeared to delight in the applause.

Sky City II

"Well, that's disturbing," said Marc.

"I just don't understand how anyone could say it's blasphemous to live in space," I said. "This is where people find God. How can that be wrong?"

"People fear what they don't understand," replied Rusty. "They think those who live in space are different and therefore something to be feared. Your press conference reinforced this idea that people living in space are freaks who live longer and are smarter. It's a natural response. I'm surprised it didn't happened sooner."

"It's weird, though, right?" said Marc, "because you can't actually make people leave space. Even if you're living on the Earth's surface, you're still in space, because the Earth is in space. So technically, the right perspective is that you can either live down at the bottom of Earth's deep gravity well, under the illusion that you're not in space, or you can live up here free from the constant crush of gravity. In either case you're really just still in space."

"What do you know about Alex Markov," I asked Rusty.

"Well, I've never met him. But I've certainly heard of him and his church. I have a friend though, Gabriel DeJesus, who is the pastor of another megachurch in Texas, in Dallas actually, who knows him quite well."

"We should talk to him, this Gabriel DeJesus," said Charlie. "Find out what he knows about Markov."

"I can tell you this," replied Rusty, "he's not a fan of Pastor Markov."

"I like him already," said Marc.

"What's he like, Pastor DeJesus?" I asked. "Maybe we could invite him up here and talk with him in person."

"He's very personable, as you might expect from a popular pastor of a megachurch," replied Rusty. If you'd like to see for yourself, we could look up one of his recent sermons. His church is called Go Forth Ministries.

Dallas, Texas

Gabriel DeJesus, the charismatic pastor of Go Forth Ministries, saw it as his calling, indeed the principal calling of mankind, to spread the Gospel message. He founded Go Forth Ministries right after graduating from Dallas Theological Seminary with the goal of spreading the Gospel as far and wide as possible.

The Go Forth Ministries website said that Pastor Gabriel DeJesus founded the church fifteen years ago. It said he was fluent in both Spanish and English and could read and write Greek, Latin, Hebrew and Aramaic.

Go Forth Ministries had grown from a few dozen followers to more than fifty thousand under his leadership. I clicked on the button to play his most recent sermon. The video started with Gabriel walking up to the podium to addresses the congregation.

"Good morning. What a great pleasure it is to welcome you all here this morning; those of you who are in the Sanctuary and those of you who are online around the world. You are not here by accident. If you are listening to this message this morning, it is because God intended for you to hear it. Today we're going to start out with a little story."

He looked to be about six feet tall with long dark wavy hair that nearly reached his shoulders. The camera zoomed in on Gabriel's face. And he had beautiful brown eyes.

"One Sunday morning," Gabriel continued, "in a small rural church, the congregation crowded in, filling every seat. They EAGERLY awaited the pastor's sermon. Did I mention that this was a true story?"

Gabriel paused momentarily to let the snickering die down and then continued. "Before the pastor arrived, however, the devil himself appeared. Chaos erupted. People screamed and scrambled for the exits. A few minutes later the devil looked out over the now empty sanctuary and saw one man sitting calmly all by himself. 'Aren't you afraid of me?' the devil snarled. 'Nah,' replied the man. 'I've been married to your sister for twenty years.'"

Gabriel paused again to let the laughter die down before going on. "Today we are going to talk about fear and love, God's love. Let's pray. Come Holy Spirit, bless this message, fill this place with your presence, open the ears and hearts of your people that they may understand. I pray that my voice be diminished and your voice be increased so that the people may know the truth of your message. It is our job as Christians to spread the love of Jesus Christ. We as believers have the privilege and the responsibility to share the gospel. Amen."

"Jesus said, 'Go ye into all the world, and preach the gospel to every creature.' In Matthew, He puts it this way, 'Go ye therefore, and teach all nations, baptizing them in the name of the Father, and of the Son, and of the Holy Ghost.' But Scripture cannot be understood without the help of the Holy Spirt, and therefore, those who do not seek after Him will misunderstand it. In first Corinthians, Paul teaches us that 'The person without the Spirit does not accept the things that come from the Spirit of God, but considers them foolishness, and cannot understand them because they are recognized only through the Spirit.'"

"After much praying and fasting and seeking after God's will, I have come to understand that God created a vast universe filled with space, and God created man with the ability to travel to space, with the ability to live in space, with the ability to work in space. These are not accidents. These are not mistakes, for God does not make mistakes. This we can be sure of for Scripture tells us, 'Great is our Lord and mighty in power; his understanding has no limit.' So my friends, God does not make mistakes. In fact, 'we know that in all things God works for the good of those who love him, who have been called according to his purpose.'

Some say it is blasphemous for people to live in space. Some say that it is against God's will. Some say we should be afraid of those living in space. But those who say these things do not understand the Gospel, and they are afraid of what they do not understand. But I say fear not, for if God is for us, who can be against us? Fear not, for God has commanded us to spread his good news. This is our calling and our privilege. 'The fruit of the righteous is a tree of life; and he that winneth souls is wise.' As the body of Christ, it is our responsibility, it is our destiny to spread God's word throughout the cosmos. As people expand out into the vast unknown, we will be there bringing God's word. As people live and work in space. We will be there. As people laugh and cry in space, as they raise their families, we will be there teaching them about God's word. And when people die, as a natural part of life, we will be there sharing God's love, because love is God's greatest gift. 'So now faith, hope, and love abide, these three; but the greatest of these is love.' But how should we do this pastor, you may well ask? What should we do? The answer is simple my friends. The best way to teach people about God is by loving each other and forgiving each other, just as each of us longs to be loved and forgiven. We live our lives in our relationships with other people, the people in our families, our friends, our co-workers. This is where we experience love. This is where we give love. This is where we find meaning in our lives, by loving others and by being loved. God is love, and we learn about God when we learn about love. The Bible puts it this way 'God is love; whoever abides in love abides in God, and God in him.' Let us pray."

...

It took a month before Gabriel could clear his schedule sufficiently to accept my invitation to visit Sky City II. He arrived on the afternoon shuttle from Brownsville, Texas. Rusty, Marc, Charlie and I, were all there to greet him as he entered through the main spaceport.

"I need a drink!" said Gabriel as floated awkwardly toward Rusty, the only person in the group he recognized.

Wow, Gabriel DeJesus is even better looking in person than he is on his website. His long dark hair was pulled back into a ponytail. He was ruggedly handsome with a dazzling smile. "First trip to space?" I asked. "I thought I was going to throw up a lung when I first arrived here."

"Yes," replied Gabriel. "They gave me a shot of something before I got off the shuttle, so now I feel okay, but the ride up was a little nerve racking."

"Suck it up," said Rusty jokingly. "Gabriel, I'd like to introduce you to Tesla Miller, she's the one who invited you up here; and this is Marc, Tesla's significant other and the principal designer of Sky City II; and finally this is Charlie, head of security. He feels personally responsible for Tesla's safety and has been following her around ever since the shooting several weeks ago."

"Pleased to meet you all," said Gabriel. "You all seem like such nice people, what are you doing hanging around with this disreputable Rusty character," he said smiling.

"He's an old friend of Marc's from school; evidently before Marc was smart enough to know better," I said piling on. "Come, we'll take you to the Cosmos Café for that drink."

The five of us gathered around a table. "Gabriel, what can you tell us about Alex Markov?" I asked.

Gabriel tilted his head slightly to one side and then replied, "Alex Markov is a man with deep pain. He hides it well, but he is deeply troubled by something in his past."

Shit, I thought to myself without reacting.

"Do you know what it is?" asked Charlie.

Gabriel shook his head. "Unfortunately, no. I wish I did. But what I do know is that he is also very charismatic. People are naturally drawn to him."

Yeah, I know that first hand.

"He has used this ability to grow his church from what was already a megachurch to a truly enormous worldwide organization. He seems a little too ambitious for my taste. He has nearly unlimited resources and some of his followers will do anything for him. Such people can be dangerous because there may not be sufficient checks on their behavior. Why the interest in Pastor Markov?"

"You know that shooting here?" Charlie asked. "The people who did it were part of a group that calls itself the Prophets of God. It turns out that group split off from Markov's church a few years ago."

"You think Pastor Markov was involved?" asked Gabriel. "That's hard to believe."

"We're just checking all possibilities," replied Charlie. "But like you said, such men can be dangerous. Do you know any reason why Markov might have something against Tesla?"

"All I know is that he has been preaching against people living in space for the past few years, and a lot of people agree with his message.

222

"But you don't agree with him, right?" asked Marc. "You said in your sermon that it was God's will that mankind spread the Gospel throughout the cosmos. Do you really believe that?

"Yes, most definitely," replied Gabriel.

"I don't get it," said Marc. "Both you and Markov read the same bible and yet you come to completely opposite conclusions. Markov says it's against god's will for people to live in space and you say that it is god's will for people to expand out into space. You can't both be right. How do you explain this?"

"Marc!" I chided. "Don't be rude to our guest."

Gabriel smiled in a calm, understanding way. "It's okay, it's a very good question. People should ask honest questions even if they're hard or uncomfortable."

Marc punched me playfully in the shoulder as if to say 'I told you so.'

Gabriel continued. "I cannot control what others say or do, nor can I judge their actions. But for me, the test of whether something is biblically true depends on whether it benefits people. I believe this is truly a turning point in the history of mankind. God created an enormous universe, most of which is space. God also saw fit to make living in space delightful; he made it like living in heaven. These are not accidents. God does not make mistakes. And when people come here many experience, often for the first time, a strong spiritual connection to God. Why do you suppose that is? I believe that space is God's ground where He intends to plant mankind so that people can go forth and multiply; to fill the cosmos with his love."

"Good answer," said Rusty as he leaned toward Gabriel, "But how can you talk of spreading god's love throughout the cosmos when there's so much pain and suffering on Earth. Doesn't evidence suggest that we are unable to successfully spread god's love on Earth, let alone up here?"

Gabriel flashed that same knowing smile again, as if he's heard all these questions before. "I believe in the basic goodness of Man. I see that goodness every day. Yes, there is evil in the world, no doubt, terrible evil, but there is way more goodness. I see this goodness when I meet with people, when I council them, when they talk about the love they gave and the love they received. I even see goodness when people talk about the love they never received or never gave, but wish they had. I see goodness in people who did not know love in their families, but still know that they should have been loved. All this I believe, because at the most fundamental level, God is love. Wouldn't you agree, Rusty?"

"Don't ask him," Marc interjected. "Rusty has studied the scriptures so hard that he no longer believes in god."

"Oh, I know that," said Gabriel. "I'm just giving my old friend a hard time."

"Is it true?" I asked.

"Yes, it's true," replied Rusty. "You see, it's clear to me that the New Testament scriptures are very human products, written by several different people over a period of several decades. These documents were written by people and for people living in first century Palestine. The result is a multitude of inconsistencies, discrepancies, and theological differences that you'd expect from such a collection of writings. Consequently, I found that I could no longer believe in a personal god who intervenes in the daily affairs of people. But what I do believe, however, and it is in this sense I agree with Gabriel, that if the *idea* of god causes people to act with love toward each other, then in that very real sense god is love."

"And what about you, Tesla?" Gabriel said looking right at me. "Do you believe in God?"

"Yes,"

"And yet you also have a Ph.D. in evolutionary biology. How do you reconcile that?"

"Easy. You see, I am personally convinced that both are true. There's no doubt about the truth of evolution. It's as well established fact as anything in science—but I have also physically felt the presence of God. I don't believe in a literal interpretation of the Bible for many of the reasons Rusty just mentioned. But I have felt God's presence. God is very real to me and I think a belief in God does not require me to ignore factual reality. I think you can enjoy the considerable benefits of religious faith, *and* the considerable advantages that come from a deep understanding of the physical world."

"Here's to the deep understanding of physical reality that enables us to survive and thrive here," interrupted Marc as he raised his glass in an unsuccessful attempt to lighten up the conversation.

"If you don't believe in the scriptures literally, what guides your faith," asked Rusty.

"Love God and love your neighbor as yourself. That's it. Everything else is just preacher talk." I looked over at Gabriel. "No offense."

"None taken," replied Gabriel.

There's that smile again.

"And what exactly do you see as the 'considerable benefits of religious faith'?" asked Rusty, looking at me.

"Cooperation," I replied without hesitation. "Religious faith provides a framework that both enables and in fact encourages people to work together, to help and care for each other. The most amazing thing to me is that religion and evolution have both come to the same conclusion, that we need each other, that we are all in this together.

"What do you mean exactly," Rusty pressed.

"It's clear scientifically that collectively we form a larger organism similar to the way bees function as a colony. Religious faiths of all sorts have known this for a long time. Evolutionary science has only recently come to the party, only recently has it recognized the enormous advantages of cooperation. Science now understands that humans are the latest organism to make the leap from a group of individuals, to a group that functions as a super organism. Christianity glimpses this truth when it refers to the body of Christ. The resulting power enabled by this intimate cooperation among large numbers of people enables humanity to dominate the Earth and even expand out into space.

"So you believe in both religion and science?" asked Gabriel.

"Yes, I believe there are two ways to understand the cosmos. There's the factual understanding as revealed by science through reason, and there's the understanding provided by religion that provides a framework that helps band people together to work cooperatively for the good of the group. It's a powerful combination."

"What about good and evil?" asked Rusty. "Don't science and religion differ wildly on their understanding of good and evil?"

"The Bible is quite clear on this," said Gabriel. "It's clear that all of creation is divided into two parts, the forces of evil and the forces of good."

"Remarkably, science has come to the very similar conclusion," I said. "It is predicted at a very fundamental level by evolutionary theory. The conflict is eternal and encompasses all life on Earth."

"What do you mean good and evil encompass all life on earth?" asked Marc. "Isn't nature indifferent to life's suffering?"

"Yes, but it turns out that there are two basic approaches to evolutionary success," I replied. "One involves exploiting your neighbor to gain success; the other involves working with your neighbor to be successful together. Nature is full of examples of both approaches. Characteristics we consider 'good' like honesty, love, loyalty, and forgiveness enable people to function well together as a group. While behavior we consider 'evil' like selfishness, deceit, hate, and betrayal favor individuals even if their groups suffer. Evil people cheat to benefit themselves at the expense of their group, so you need to protect the group from cheaters and evildoers. This is reflected in first Corinthians where Paul says, 'You must remove the evil person from among you.'"

"But what about organisms that aren't people?" asked Rusty. "How can you say they're good or evil?"

"That just depends on how you look at it. Take, for example, giant redwoods trees. Their magnificent height is awe inspiring, but they are selfish. The reason they grow so tall is to deprive their shorter neighbors of light. They clearly do not 'love thy neighbor.' There are examples

225

where even some of the simplest forms of life, bacteria for example, both cooperate for the good of the group, and yet have individuals that cheat for their own benefit. The battle between good and evil is waged across the full spectrum of life's complexity. It is an inescapable fact of social life. It is the battle between the benefits of working together and the benefits of cheating."

"Cheating bacteria," Marc said. "Who knew?"

"So what does science say you should do? Should you cooperate or cheat?" asked Gabriel. "I know what the Bible says about this."

"Until recently, science had nothing to say," I replied. "But now it's quite clear. Cooperation gives people enormous power, the power to control the entire planet and beyond. But to access this power, people have to exhibit the 'good' characteristics I mentioned above; honesty, loyalty, forgiveness and love. Groups of evil people are unstable because without these characteristics the group will ultimately disintegrate. This instability of evil groups is why Martin Luther King could state, 'The arc of the moral universe is long, but it bends toward justice."

"So, is evolutionary science discovering the nature of reality as already revealed in religious texts or are religious texts actually just a reflection of the way nature evolved naturally?" asked Marc.

Before anyone could respond, an announcement rang throughout the Cosmos Café. "Charlie, please report to security immediately."

The Sky City II computer knew Charlie's location at all times and for urgent matters contacted him every way possible, through the public address system, by text and by email with additional details. Charlie checked his phone as he headed out of the cafe.

"What is it Charlie?" I asked.

"Looks like some kind of disturbance at the main space port. I have to go check it out." Charlie arrived at the spaceport and called me immediately. "You won't believe who's here."

"Who is it," I asked casually.

"It's Alex Markov!" replied Charlie.

"Alex is here?" I exclaimed. I'm sure the panic was clear in my voice. Shit, what is he doing here?

Sensing my distress, Charlie said reassuringly "Don't worry we'll protect you."

I hope you're right. "What does he want?"

"He says he wants to talk to you."

My hands started to shake. God, how can he have such an effect on me even after all these years? Is he here for revenge or forgiveness. I don't know what to do? After a long pause, I finally said, "Tell him I'm not available." Brilliant move, that'll work for about one millisecond.

"Tesla, Charlie again. Two armed police officers just exited the cargo vehicle and joined Markov. They say that they have a warrant for your arrest. Maybe you better come over here and we'll straighten this thing out."

Okay, he's not here for forgiveness. What should I do? They're going to arrest me! How do I get out of this?

Marc looked at me and could tell I was distressed. "What's wrong? Why are you so upset? He's just a crazy pastor. Don't worry, we'll all go with you."

Marc, Rusty, and Gabriel accompanied me to meet with Markov and the two police officers. I didn't say a word as we made our way to the spaceport.

As soon as Markov saw me entering the spaceport he said in his loud booming voice, "Ella, finally! It's been a very long time."

I just stared at him, speechless. Just seeing him again made my skin crawl.

"Ella?" asked Marc, "Whose Ella?"

As we got closer to Markov and the two police officers, Markov said, "Allow me to introduce my wife, Ella Markov. This is Officer Williams and Officer Porter, they are here to arrest you on kidnapping charges."

Officer Williams then said, "Ella Markov, you are under arrest for the crime of kidnapping Demetrious Markov. We're here to take you back to Chicago to stand trial."

I didn't know what to say. I started to back up slightly. I looked at Marc as if pleading for help. Then I heard Charlie's voice from behind me.

"I'm afraid I can't let you do that," said Charlie firmly.

Markov flashed this evil smile. "I'm afraid you don't really have a choice. These fine gentlemen here have all the proper paperwork to make this arrest and bring her back."

"Let me see that," Charlie demanded, reaching for the papers.

While he was examining the papers, the officers took out plastic handcuffs.

"What the hell is going on?" asked Marc. "You can't take her to Chicago, or anywhere else on Earth. The gravity would kill her."

"That's really not my problem now is it," said Markov in a most condescending way. "She has to face justice for what she's done. Put the cuffs on her," he said to the officers and then turned to face me. "You have no idea how long I've waited for this moment. Now you'll finally pay for what you've done. Now you'll pay for kidnapping Demetrious and taking him away from me."

"Tesla, what is he talking about?" asked Marc urgently.

"Marc, I'm so sorry."

"You're not really married to this asshole, are you?" asked Marc.

I lowered my head and replied, "Yes."

"The paperwork looks official," said Charlie, "But I still can't let you take her. She's not going anywhere until I can get to the bottom of this."

"And Demetrious is his son?" Marc continued.

Again, I replied, "Yes."

"And you kidnapped him and brought him here?"

"Yes. But—" I stopped. It didn't seem to matter right now why I did it. For some reason it didn't seem to matter that I thought I was doing the right thing for Demetrious. None of it seemed to matter.

"Oh that's just great, right?" said Marc angrily. "That's just fucking great."

I never heard Marc swear, but I guess it seemed appropriate right now, and then he started laughing.

"What's so funny?" demanded Markov.

Marc looked directly at me. "Everybody thinks they own Demetrious, right? In addition to you and this asshole, we have George Abruzzo, who, I found out just recently, hired you precisely because you had Demetrious. Demetrious was his experimental subject, his guinea pig. He wanted to know how a person would grow up and develop in space. That's why he hired you."

I stared at Marc in disbelief.

"But first, he needed to make sure you were the right kind of person, someone with the right kind of morals if you were going to live in this close community at Sky City for a long time. That's why he arranged for that little ethical experiment you went through at UC San Diego. That's right, George arranged that, it was a test, and you passed. After that, he

228

wanted to make sure you'd stay around, that's why he insisted you sign a five-year contract, right? It was monumentally unethical. I didn't find out about any of this until they started to investigate Professor Nagib's death and turned up all this stuff about George. Did you ever wonder why he so easily caved in on the requirement to return to Earth every six months? He wanted to see what would happen to someone who grew up continuously in zero-g. And then there's Hamid Nagib, he was in on it too. He and George were old college friends and they shared the same burning interest in knowing how people would develop in zero-g. Hamid followed you and Demetrious from the start. That's how you got into Berkeley, Hamid made it happen. Then Hamid offered you that unique graduate school position in his lab. With George gone, he needed a way to keep a close eye on you and Demetrious, right? He needed to continue monitoring their unethical experiment on Demetrious, and they both paid for it with their lives."

My head was spinning. My entire life was unraveling before my eyes. Everyone I trusted, it seemed, had betrayed me. Still, I didn't care what happened to me as long as Demetrious was safe.

"Uncuff her," Charlie demanded. "She's staying here."

Suddenly an announcement came over the public address system, "Charlie, report to security immediately, there are multiple active shooters in the city center."

"Shit," Charlie said under his breath. He looked right at Markov and commanded, "Stay here until I come back." Then he left while rapidly shouting orders into his phone.

As soon as Charlie was out of sight Markov said to the two officers, "Let's go."

"Alex, what are you doing, my friend?" said Gabriel. "You can't take her. It's not right."

"That's right, we won't let you take her," Rusty said as he moved forward and grabbed Alex.

Upon seeing this very large, powerfully-build man grab Alex, Officer Porter pulled out his gun and shot Rusty. A single shot that hit him in the chest on the right side. Rusty cried out in pain and let go of Alex.

Who's next?" the officer shouted.

"Okay, I'll go, just don't shoot anybody else," I yelled. And with that, they hurried me to the cargo ship that had just brought them up to the resort.

. . .

"Gabriel, take Rusty to medical immediately," commanded Marc Just follow the signs. We've only got about ten minutes before that cargo ship will be able to depart."

"Where are you going?"

"They're in a standard cargo ship," replied Marc. "It has two airlocks, one for any passengers that are on board, and one in the back for cargo. I'm going to see if I can get onboard through the cargo airlock."

Less than a minute later Marc arrived at the Sky City II cargo airlock location. Shit, they've already disconnected. "Sky City II," Marc addressed the computer, "are you still connected to the shuttle in docking port three?" The computer recognized his voice and automatically gave him priority access.

"Yes," replied the computer.

"Do you still have the ability to open the shuttle's cargo port?"

"Yes."

Marc glanced over at the spacesuits lining the walls. No time for the four-hour pre-breathing required to use those, they'll be long gone by then. So, I need a different approach. After briefly considering his options, Marc gave detailed instructions to the computer. The timing will have to be just right, he thought. I'll only have about fifteen seconds before I lose consciousness.

The computer estimated five seconds for the emergency decompression of the airlock, four seconds for the jump across the vacuum gap to the shuttle, and twenty seconds to complete the emergency re-pressurization of the ship's airlock.

The cold won't be a problem for that length of time, my body can't radiate its heat away fast enough. Must remember to exhale, fortunately that should feel natural based on my scuba diving experience. I just hope I don't get the bends too bad. Okay, I'm ready, I think. Marc took a deep breath.

"Sky City II, now!"

Marc grasped a handle with both hands and held on tightly as the air lock rapidly decompressed. The roar of the air exploding into the vacuum of space was deafening. Sharp pain stabbed at his ears as the pressure in his head strained against his eardrums. The rushing air tried to drag him out of the air lock, he held on for dear life. He forced himself to exhale and then started to panic when it felt as if his very life was being sucked out of him.

Then, just as quickly as it started, the noise ceased. The air was all gone. He was in the hard vacuum of space without a spacesuit. Marc forced his eyes open momentarily and through blurry vision managed to see that the computer had successfully opened the airlock to shuttle's cargo bay. He jumped as hard as he could and flew through space like superman across the vacuum, hands out in front, eyes shut tight. His mind flashed back to the time he had first shown Tesla how to glide straight down the long service tunnel in the original Sky City resort. He hoped his aim was accurate.

Adrenaline made him jump harder than expected and he crossed the gap in three and a half seconds instead of four. He successfully entered the airlock on the shuttle and crashed into the far wall. He bounced off the wall and headed back toward the still open airlock door. Because his jump took less time than estimated, the computer had not yet closed the door. Marc again opened his eyes briefly and could see that he was heading back toward the open airlock door. He was heading back out into space, to certain death. He started rapidly, wildly moving his arms, trying in vain to stop his motion, but there was no air to push against.

Meanwhile the computer was patiently, slowly, methodically, counting down the required four seconds: three, two, one, zero, and finally commanded the door to close. It was eighty percent closed when Marc crashed into it, sending him back into the middle of the airlock. Rapidly losing consciousness, the last thing his brain registered was the sound of air hissing into the airlock and the feeling of pain in his joints. Then everything went black.

…

Finally Marc woke up. I could tell that his hands, like mine, were handcuffed behind his back. Both of us were also tethered to the wall to keep us in place. "About time you got up," I whispered. "What are you doing here?"

"I'm rescuing you," Marc managed to whisper. "God my joints hurt."

"Great rescue," I whispered back.

"Shut up you two," said Officer Williams.

Just then, Markov came in, "Oh, I see our unwanted guest is awake. That was quite a stunt you pulled," he said looking at Marc. "We didn't anticipate anyone being stupid enough to jump through space without a spacesuit."

"You jumped through space without a spacesuit?" I exclaimed. "What were you thinking?"

"I told you, I'm rescuing you," said Marc, grimacing through the pain in his joints.

"Oh right, I forgot," I replied half-smiling.

"So, you think this is funny Ella?" demanded Markov. "You won't think it's so funny when you find out what's going to happen. You see, I didn't have you arrested to stand trial in Chicago. These aren't even real police officers," he said motioning to his two accomplices. "These guys are actually pilots. They work for me, as do the people who caused the disturbance and disabled the lifeboats back at the resort. No, I brought you here to witness the destruction of Sky City II and the death of your son. The son that you took from me all those years ago, I am now going to take from you."

"Alex, no!" I pleaded. "Do whatever you want with me, but leave my son alone!"

"He's bluffing," said Marc. "Sky City II is nearly a mile long; it's too big to be destroyed by anything except maybe a small nuclear bomb."

"Very good," said Markov. "At this very minute a small nuclear warhead is speeding its way toward Sky City II. It was launched about five minutes ago from Kazakhstan and will arrive in about an hour and a half."

"Bullshit," exclaimed Marc. "How would you get your hands on a nuke?"

"Oh ye of little faith," replied Markov with his preacher's voice. "For with God, all things are possible. The good Lord sought fit to deliver into my worldwide congregation two Russian military officers, and to put into their hearts the calling to cleanse the heavens of man's wicked and sinful presence. It was these officers, these faithful men of God, who knew how to exploit, with a sufficient amount of money of course, the weaknesses in Russia's security apparatus designed to safeguard their stockpile of nuclear weapons. The beauty of this is that they didn't even need to smuggle the weapon out of Russia, really, just transport it through Kazakhstan to the launch site at Baikonur. The Russian government believes it to be a research satellite."

I looked at Marc as if to ask, can this really be true? Marc nodded.

"Even now we are moving into a position that should provide us with a spectacular view," continued Alex. "You will be witnesses to the wrath of God as He destroys your blasphemous sky city and we broadcast the event worldwide. Just like Sodom and Gomorra, after the destruction of Sky City II, the world will know that God does not tolerate blasphemers. It is God's will not mine. Then, we'll send Mr. Elliott here back out into space wearing the same spacesuit he came in with. When our work here is done, we'll return to Earth where you, my dear sweet Ella, will face justice for your crimes. Where you will live out your life in agony, literally crushed by Earth's gravity and by the knowledge that you destroyed everyone you ever loved."

"Please, Alex, I'll do anything you want," I repeated. "Just don't kill Demetrious. You can't kill your son!"

Alex looked at me with that familiar fury behind his eyes. "He's no longer my son. I don't even know him," hissed Markov. "I have waited a very long time for this moment. Now all we have to do is wait a little bit longer, and then watch as everything you love is taken from you, just as you took everything from me."

My heart sank, my hands started shaking. I gasped for air. This couldn't be happening. How could God allow this? He must be punishing me for all the terrible things I've done. But losing everyone I love, losing my dear Demetrious, and Marc, and all the people at Sky City II, it's more than I could bear. I just don't know how to stop it. I strained at the cuffs binding my hands and feet. I never felt so completely helpless. Tears filled my eyes.

Sky City II

Tommy Patel, who used to work at the original Sky City Resort and Casino, was now Robert Garrison's assistant overseeing all engineering operations at Sky City II. He called Garrison and said, "Robert, you better come to the control room. We have an unidentified contact on an intersecting trajectory with us."

Garrison, having completed the initial construction of Sky City II, now headed the ongoing operations of the complex. "I'm on my way," replied Robert calmly. "What is its estimated time of arrival?"

"Ninety minutes."

"Where did it come from?"

"Looks like it was launched from Kazakhstan."

"That's strange. Do we have any scheduled cargo deliveries from Russia?" asked Robert.

"Nothing on the manifest," replied Tommy. "This thing is small, too small to be a cargo ship."

Robert entered the control room.

"What?" said Robert with a little more urgency in his voice. "Contact the FSA; see if they know what this is."

The FSA is the United States Federal Space Administration, the equivalent of the old FAA, responsible for the regulation of flights to and from space.

"I already did. They have been tracking it and confirmed that it's on an impact trajectory with us. They contacted Kazakhstan who said it's a research satellite."

"Then why the hell is it on an impact trajectory with us? Is it off course?"

"It doesn't appear to be," replied Tommy. It looks like it's been heading for us the whole time. It's on an optimized trajectory to intersect with us. This is not an accident."

233

Cargo Ship

"What's the matter, Ella?" Markov taunted. "Not so happy now are we? Now you'll know how I felt. Now you'll understand what you did to me, leaving me and taking my son, you'll see."

"When did you know I was here?" I asked weakly. I couldn't bear to look at him.

"I've known ever since your boyfriend here told me about this girl he met and her son Demetrious. I've been trying to get you back to Earth ever since. First, I sent Michael Abruzzo up here to bring you back, but he was too hot tempered to stick to the plan and failed. Then I sent the one you know as Edgar Whisenant along with some backup support, but they failed too. So now I'm here to do it right."

"You knew Michael Abruzzo?" Now I finally understood what he meant when he said, 'So I guess I'll just have to do what they said.' It was Alex all along.

"Yes, once I knew you were here, I learned everything I could about Sky City. I found out that it was the brainchild of a George Abruzzo, and I learned that he had a troubled son in prison. So I set up a prison ministry and befriended him, it was easy. When he got out of prison I got him a job, took care of him, and gave him a purpose in life. It wasn't long before he would do anything for me, even kill his own father."

George, Hamid, they were both killed by Alex. Now he's going to kill Demetrious and Marc, and I was powerless to stop him.

Sky City II

"It's intentionally on a collision course with us?" repeated Robert. "How can that be?"

"I don't know, but that's what it looks like," replied Tommy. "And it's an intercept trajectory, not a rendezvous trajectory. Whatever it is, it's not planning on a gentle docking with us."

Anna Chin from FSA, who Tommy had talked to earlier, called back. Robert put the video call on the full-wall display so everyone could see it.

"We have reliable reports that a Russian tactical nuclear weapon went missing last year," said Chin. "And there are rumors that it may have fallen into the hands of a radical group that calls itself the Prophets of God."

"That's the same organization responsible for the attack last month," interrupted Jennifer Gerbosi, who had just joined them in the control room.

"Is there any way you can stop it?" asked Robert.

"There's not enough time to intercept it and it's going too high," said Chin. "Missile defense systems are designed to intercept vehicles returning to the atmosphere, not flying up to your altitude."

"OK, Tommy, let's figure out our options," said Robert calmly. "We're too big to get out of its way, so how else can we stop this thing? We've got eighty minutes to figure it out."

Cargo Ship

I felt defeated, helpless to stop the loss of everything I loved. The only thing I could think to do now was pray. Marc was in no shape to help as he was constantly writhing in pain from his decompression bends which caused him to continually bump up against me.

Suddenly I saw a flash of light in my eyes, then another, and another. I closed my eyes. There were lots of them, the brilliant flashes of light, the dazzling blueish-white diamonds were back! I knew immediately what it was and what it meant. We could get out of this! My heart started pounding. Got to free my hands first, but how?

I pulled hard at my handcuffs, as I had done so many times over the last hour, but this time, to my amazement, they came apart! It so startled me that I almost yelled. I looked at Marc who had stopped writhing. Is that a hint of a smile on his face? That wonderful, nerdy engineer has somehow cut me free! God, I love that man. Then I saw him start to writhe again. He must be working on his own straps now.

I started formulating a plan. All I have to do is subdue Alex and the two armed guards by myself. Simple! Okay, back to reality, how the heck am I going to do that? Alex is so strong... Wait a minute. They're all Grounders, this is my turf, and strength doesn't matter much up here. I just have to remember the self-defense things that Demetrious taught me. I looked around, the two fake guards were in the cockpit sitting in the pilot and co-pilot seats. Alex said they weren't really police officers. That's good, they should be less of a threat.

Alex was hovering at the entrance to the cockpit talking with them and had his back to Marc and me. Fortunately, you can travel completely silently here. He won't be expecting anything. I'll just glide over there and grab the gun out of his holster before he even knows what's happening. Okay, here goes nothing.

I pushed off the wall without making a sound and glided toward Alex. My heart was pounding so hard I was sure he could hear it. I got to Alex without him noticing and grabbed the gun, but it didn't come out of the holster cleanly.

Alex turned quickly as he felt something tugging on his hip. As he turned, he swung the back of his hand at me, striking me right across the side of my head. I cried out in pain. It was a glancing blow, but it was enough to cause me to let go of the gun just after I got it free from the holster. The gun went flying across the cabin. I flashed back to the last time Alex struck me across the face all those years ago. How could this be happening again? Alex looked right at me with that rage in his eyes. My hands were shaking. Then I saw how awkwardly he moved. Remember, he's a Grounder. No, he's a fucking Grounder! A confident calm came over me. My hands stopped shaking.

Alex pushed off the wall toward me.

I knew just what to do. I pushed off the opposite wall, not at him, but 'below' him. I glided past him just out of reach as he twisted and turned attempting to grab me. As I passed him, I spread my arms and gave a single strong swish with my wings causing me to turn quickly. As I turned, I grabbed his legs, nearly stopping our combined motion in the middle of the cabin. Nearly, but not entirely. Just as I planned we were still drifting slowly in my original direction of motion. Before Alex could grab me, I pushed off him, just hard enough to stop his motion completely right in the middle of the cabin while I drifted away from him.

Wow! That worked better than I could have hoped. Demetrious would be very proud of me for executing that maneuver. Alex'll be helpless there for a awhile. Unable to get anywhere, he started swearing at me, but I ignored him. Then disaster struck. The gun I dropped when Alex hit me continued to ricochet around the cabin and just happened to strike Alex right in the back, stopping its motion.

Alex turned around to see the gun floating right in front of him and smiled at his good fortune. He grabbed the gun, turned and pointed it at me. "I guess I'm just going to have to kill you right now Ella," Alex said angrily. "You'll just have to die knowing that Demetrious and Marc will die shortly after you."

Marc's timing was perfect. Having cut himself loose, he pushed off from the cabin wall and flew rapidly toward me. He managed to get his body between me and Alex just as Alex fired. I screamed. The bullet struck Marc in the left hipbone, causing Marc to cry out in pain.

Alex watched as blood spurted from Marc's hip while his body continued to travel across the cabin before crumpling into the opposite wall. It was just a momentary lapse in attention.

As Alex was focused on Marc, I launched myself as fast as I could directly toward him. I arrived just as Alex's attention returned to me. I grabbed his arm. He started to bring the gun in his other had around to point it at me. Then I let go of his arm spinning him rapidly. I had perfectly executed another maneuver Demetrious taught me, transferring my linear motion into the spinning motion of another person.

It was clear that Alex was spinning so fast that he couldn't tell where I was. He started firing wildly, apparently hoping to hit something. All but one shot traversed the cargo bay without hitting anything, striking the walls of the ship. The one shot that actually hit something struck the copilot as he entered the cabin to see what all the commotion was about. The bullet hit him right in the head, killing him instantly.

While Alex was still spinning out of control, I flew over and grabbed the dead copilot's gun. I extracted the gun from his holster and gripped it tightly. Alex collided with the far wall of the cargo hold, stopping his spinning motion. As I turned toward Alex, he pointed the gun at me and fired. The shot zinged just over her head.

Grounder always... Never mind, I steadied myself against the wall of the cargo bay. Without thinking, I fired back. Bam, bam, bam. The sound echoed in my ears. Time seemed to slow down as I watched three shots tear into Alex's chest. One shot must have pierced his heart. Alex's body immediately went limp. "Don't ever threaten my family again!" I yelled at him.

Now, where's the pilot. I rapidly scanned around the cargo hold. Fortunately, he had stayed in his seat. I ordered him into the cabin and bound his hands and feet with the plastic cuffs I found on the copilot.

Finally, I turned my attention to Marc. I grabbed the first aid kit that all ships have, and dressed Marc's wound as best I could to stop the bleeding. I gave him a shot of morphine, and kissed him. "Don't you die on me Marc," I said sternly. Marc was clearly in distress and appeared to be on the verge of passing out. I called Sky City II.

"Sky City II here, this is Robert."

"Robert!" I said excitedly. "This is Tesla. We're still on the shuttle. Marc is wounded, Alex and the co-pilot are dead. I've got the pilot tied up."

"Tesla?" replied Robert. "Jesus, are you okay?"

"Yes, but we've got a big problem. There's a nuclear weapon heading your way! Alex sent it. He's gone mad. He's going to destroy Sky City II. Can you get everyone out of the city?"

"We know about the weapon, we've been tracking it. But no, we can't get anyone out of the city. All of our transports have been sabotaged and there's not enough time to get any from the other cities."

"Oh my God!"

"Tesla, we've got a plan," said Robert. "But... Tommy has done the calculations and they've been confirmed by the FSA."

"What is it Robert," I pleaded urgently.

"Gabriel called his friend Abdul Zahir Hakimi, they are just starting the construction of an Islamic city called New Medina, fifteen miles west of Sky City II."

"I know, I've been there," I interrupted.

"They have the city center core structure and radiation shielding in place. More importantly, they just completed installation of the solar panels. This complex now has a hundred megawatts of installed solar array power. It's a huge solar array complex covering a very large area."

"Get to the point," I demanded.

"Hakimi has agreed to help us. He is willing to let us use the complex to try to stop the missile. He said he's willing to sacrifice his unfinished city, which is currently unoccupied, to save the lives of the people of Sky City II."

"Why would he do that?"

"He said the Quran teaches that, 'whoso saveth the life of one, it shall be as if he had saved the life of all mankind.' He said it means we are all in this together. So if we can move New Medina into the path of the missile, we stand a good chance of having the weapon hit the solar panels because of their large area. But there are two problems."

"What?!" I said impatiently. "Tell me!"

"First, there's no propulsion onboard the complex, except that used for attitude control which is too wimpy to move it. And..." Robert hesitated.

"And what?" I practically shouted.

"Well, it just that we think the weapon is likely set to detonate on impact. So if we're successful in getting it to impact the solar arrays, that will likely set it off."

"Okay, so how do we move the complex into the right position?" I asked urgently.

"Unfortunately, you're in the only working vehicle in range," replied Robert as gently as he could. "You would need to dock with New Medina and use the cargo ship's propulsion system to push it into position. It will pretty much take all of the fuel you have on board."

"Let's do it!" I said without hesitation. I'd gladly sacrifice myself to save Demetrious and the people of Sky City II. "Just tell me what to do?"

"Hang on. Tommy will send the instructions to the cargo ship," replied Robert.

"Robert, we've got a problem," said Tommy.

"What is it?" replied Robert.

"They've locked out the remote pilot feature. I can't drive it from here unless they release that lockout."

"OK, I'll tell Tesla."

"Tesla, this is Robert. You need to get the pilot to release the lockout he's put on the remote pilot feature. He can do this by voice command, but it has to be his voice."

"Will do," I replied.

I was in no mood for fooling around with my son's life at stake. I went over to the pilot and said, "Release the remote pilot feature or I'll fire this bullet into your brain."

"Do it," said the pilot. "You can kill me now or kill me when the nuclear bomb goes off. Either way I'm dead."

I shot him in the foot shattering several bones and screamed at him, "Do it now!"

"I forgive you," replied the pilot, grimacing in pain.

"What?" His response shocked and confused me. Finally, I said, "It's no good, Robert. He won't do it."

"That's okay, we've got a backup plan," replied Robert. "You'll have to fly the ship."

"What? Okay, how do I do that?"

"Get in the pilot's seat, Tommy will tell you what to do."

Tommy guided me through the basics of operating the cargo ship and together we drove the ship to New Medina. Fortunately for me, once we got to within three hundred feet of the complex, the automatic docking system came on and took us the rest of the way in autonomously.

"I've got all green docking lights!" I said excitedly. "We're docked to the side of complex."

"Okay, excellent! Good job! Now let's push this thing," said Tommy. "I'll send you the attitude control coordinates for you to enter into the computer. We'll need to start thrusting as soon as possible, at full throttle, and for as long as possible."

I received the coordinates and entered them into the computer following Tommy's instructions. "I think we're all set here."

"On my mark, tell the cargo ship to initiate thrusting," replied Tommy, who then hesitated.

"What's happening?" I said. "I'm ready. What are we waiting for?"

"It's just that... well, if we're successful, you'll be... you know..."

"I know. Come on, let's do it. We're running out of time."

"Initiate," said Tommy quietly.

"We're thrusting!" I confirmed the cargo ship indicated that the engines were at full thrust.

"Thanks," replied Tommy. "Impact in twenty seven minutes...if we're successful."

"God, I hate this," said Robert. "If we're successful, the bomb will most likely impact the solar array because of its extremely large area. If it does, it will explode on impact. The solar array will be vaporized

239

instantly. The intense fireball will generate powerful x-rays that will vaporize and then ionize the asteroid dirt surrounding the resort on the side facing the bomb. The force of the explosion will most likely crush the interior structure of the city. Tesla and Marc will be vaporized."

The synchronized clocks on both the cargo ship and in the Sky City II control room counted down. Nobody wanted to count down the time out loud, everyone just stared at the clock in silence.

…

The clock displayed the last few seconds: 3, 2, 1, 0. Nothing happened.

"I'm still here," I said. "What happened?"

"Maybe we miss—" Tommy stopped mid-sentence as the image from the telescope focused on New Medina changed to bright white and the computer indicted loss of signal from the cargo ship.

Data from the telescope indicated that the bomb impacted the solar array three quarters of the way toward the end of the array, about three hundred feet from the main body of the city on the deep space side.

Nobody in the control room knew how to react. Some started to clap since they were successful in saving Sky City II. Most hung their heads in silence knowing that Tesla and Marc were dead. For several minutes, nobody said anything.

Then they heard the unexpected. "Hey, anybody there? What happened?" I asked.

"Tesla! You're alive!" shouted Robert.

"Tesla! It's wonderful to hear your voice!" exclaimed Jennifer. "Now don't take this the wrong way, but how come you're not vaporized? How is that possible?"

"I don't know! But we're still here!

There was a long silence. Then I heard Tommy's voice.

"I know!" said Tommy excitedly. "It's Lew Allen's balls!"

"Tommy, this is not the time for that," scolded Jennifer.

"No, I'm serious. It's Lew Allen's balls! That's why they're still alive!"

"You want to explain yourself?" said Jennifer sternly.

"Doesn't anyone read history around here?" asked Tommy rhetorically. "General Lew Allen, he was the director of NASA's Jet Propulsion Laboratory during the 1980's, before that he was a four star General in the Air Force, but before that he was a physicist for the Air Force. Way back in the 1950's he did a series of experiments during the atomic weapons testing in Nevada. He would take these steel balls,

240

surround them with a thick layer of graphite, and hang them underneath the towers supporting the nuclear bombs back in the days of above ground testing. What he found was that the balls would actually survive the hundred and fifty-thousand-degree temperature of the nuclear fireball. He figured out that the graphite surrounding the balls would get vaporized and ionized. The resulting dense plasma turned out to be opaque to the intense heat and radiation from the bomb. It was the plasma, it acted like a shield and protected the steel from being vaporized."

"So in our case," interrupted Robert, "New Medina was surrounded by asteroid dirt made mostly of carbon and silicates. The nuclear blast must have vaporized and ionized this material, turning it into a plasma that then protected the cargo ship from the intense heat of the fireball just like the plasma that protected the steel spheres in Lew Allen's tests."

"You mean Lew Allen's balls," said Tommy.

"Yes, we got it Tommy," said Jennifer. "You can stop saying that now."

"But wait, there's more," said Tommy.

"Now what?" said Jennifer somewhat irritably.

"It's just that, while the balls survived the nuclear blasts, they were blown much farther away from the tower than expected," replied Tommy. "This discovery was the basis for the original project Orion in the 1950's. This project was going to launch huge spaceships into orbit using a series of nuclear bombs—bam, bam, bam. One per second until it reached orbit. In our case, if the blast collapsed the superstructure of the city center, it would have absorbed much of the shock, just like the shock-absorbers used in the Orion concept."

"Uh oh," said Robert and Tommy simultaneously as they looked at each other.

"I'm on it," said Tommy.

"I don't understand. What does that mean?" asked Jennifer urgently.

"It means that the blast likely provided a substantial delta-V to the cargo vehicle," said Robert. "That is, the explosion probably pushed the cargo vehicle hard enough to change its orbit significantly. The blast would have vaporized the asteroid material on the side facing the bomb, pushing New Median in the other direction. Since the cargo ship was attached to New Medina, it would have been pushed onto a new orbit as well."

After a few minutes Tommy said, "Got it. And it doesn't look good. They got quite a push from that blast. They are definitely on a re-entry trajectory. No doubt about it, and there's no fuel left to stop it."

"Shit," said Robert. "Tesla can't go back to Earth. She'll be killed by its gravity. I better call her... Tesla? Robert here."

"Hi Robert, I thought you guys forgot about me."

"Tesla, that blast has put you on a re-entry trajectory. Like it or not, you're going to Earth."

"I know, I heard everything. What should I do?"

"The first thing you need to do is to undock from what's left of New Medina. Can you do that?"

"I think that already happened during the blast. I don't see any part of the resort."

"Okay, that's good. Now the cargo ship should be able to land itself, it has a layer of fault protection that can't be overridden and will land the vehicle automatically, so you don't have to worry about that. We just have to hope that your heat shield wasn't damaged in the blast."

"How will I know?"

"Unfortunately, you won't know until it's too late. Either you'll land successfully or…"

"Or I burn up, right?"

"Yes, I'm sorry," replied Robert.

"I've got some good news," said Tommy. "For the trajectory that she's on, her best landing site is the Armstrong Flight Research Center in California. The autopilot should recognize this and make the necessary adjustments."

"Tesla, Robert here. Looks like you're going to California. Here's what you need to do." Robert proceeded to instruct me on how to position my body to best survive the re-entry forces and Earth's gravity.

…

So I'm going back to Earth after all. Okay, I can do this. I'll use this medical tape to fasten these seat cushions to the floor, then I'll lay flat on my back with my legs elevated as Robert suggested. I created two sets of cushions side by side on the floor. One for me and one for Marc. I grabbed Marc, who was unconscious, and positioned him next to me just above one set of cushions. I floated above the other set while holding his hand. It took about thirty minutes before we started to feel the deceleration. I instructed the computer to announce the g-levels during the descent.

"Zero point zero, zero one gee," said the computer.

A hundredth of a gee, I can handle that. No problem. It helps keep us on the cushions.

The deceleration increased rapidly.

"Zero point zero five gees," the computer announced.

Five hundredths of a gee, man, now I'm feeling heavy. I can barely hold my head up. My arms are heavy. I'm such a wimp.

"Zero point one gee."

A tenth of a gee. I was having trouble concentrating. I can't move! My arms are pinned to the ground. This is awful and it's only a tenth of a gee. I can't believe I used to live in one gee.

"Zero point five gees."

I can't breathe. It feels like an elephant is sitting on my chest. The world is closing in on me. I fought to stay conscious.

"One point zero gee"

One gee! Yay! I made—, I blacked out.

Sky City II

"What do we do now?" asked Jennifer.

"Contact Armstrong and let them know what's happening. Then we wait," replied Robert. "We'll know in about ten minutes if the cargo ship survived reentry."

A few minutes went by.

"These ten minutes are taking forever," Jennifer complained

A few minutes after that. "There it is," shouted Tommy. "We have signal acquisition from the cargo ship!" Everyone in the control room cheered.

Shortly afterward, the cargo ship landed safely at Armstrong.

Armstrong Flight Research Center, California

"Let's go people!" shouted Sargent Chomko. "We have two VIP's onboard, both in need of immediate medical attention."

"What a mess!" said Private Collins as they entered the cargo bay.

There was blood everywhere, on the floor, on the walls, and on the ceiling.

"We have two persons alive but unconscious," Chomko reported. "One adult male and one adult female, lying on the floor holding hands. We also have two deceased persons, both adult males, and one person alive, conscious and in handcuffs tied to the wall, with a foot wound. He is very unhappy."

"Hey Sargent, look at these," said Collins as he extended his hand holding bits of metal.

"Hollow-point bullets," Chomko said as he took them examined them in his hand. "Each of these has been flattened into a pancake. Where'd you find these?"

"There all over the place."

243

"Clearly whoever used these planned on killing people since these are extremely good for that purpose. Fortunately, they don't have much penetrating capability on non-fleshy things. I would guess that none of these penetrated the walls of the ship, which explains their flattened shape. If they did, nobody would have survive reentry. Look around just to make sure."

"Yes sir."

Medical personnel rushed in and transported both Tesla and Marc to the base hospital. The handcuffed pilot was arrested and taken to the hospital as well.

In the hospital, the emergency room doctor ordered Tesla to be placed in a g-suit.

"Why a g-suit?" asked the attending nurse. "She's not in a high-g environment."

"We've been informed that this person has spent the last seventeen years living in micro-gravity," replied the ER doctor. "For her, the one gee here on Earth is a high-g environment. She doesn't have enough blood volume to survive here. So, we need to make sure we keep enough blood going to her brain."

"Seventeen years in space, wow!"

Marc underwent emergency surgery.

Sky City II

Meanwhile Jennifer Gerbosi made arrangements to get Tesla on the next ship headed back to Sky City II. The Armstrong staff put her on a special transport plane to Brownsville, Texas.

Tesla remained unconscious through the launch where the added g-loading during the ascent didn't help her condition. She was still unconscious when the ship arrived at Sky City II. Doris Chun and the medical staff took her immediately to the medical center.

"Is she going to be okay," Demetrious pleaded with Doris.

"I don't know dear," replied Doris. "Your mom has lived in space continuously longer than anyone. Well, anyone except you. Anyway, we just don't know what will happen. We'll just have to wait and see…On the bright side, at least here, we don't have to worry about her getting bedsores," Doris said in a way that sounded like she was trying to come up with something positive to say.

Three days later Demetrious, who hadn't left his mother's side, noticed a subtle change in his mom's breathing and whispered to the nurse, "I think she's starting to wake up!" The word spread quickly and people flocked to her room.

...

I slowly started to regain consciousness. Where was I? I had a splitting headache and my head was spinning so I kept my eyes closed as I tried to concentrate. The last thing I remembered I was on the cargo ship. I think we were heading back to Earth. What happened?... Slowly the memories returned. That's right, I remember, we were going to reenter. The explosion pushed us out of orbit. We were going to land on Earth... But this can't be Earth. I feel like I'm floating. Oh my God, the heat shield must have failed. I must be dead! I forced my eyes open. I couldn't focus very well. My head was killing me. I could barely make out some shapes floating in front of me and I think they might have wings. Summoning all my strength I tried to speak and managed to say weakly, "Is this heaven?"

"Yes, Mom," replied Demetrious as he glided over to give me a big hug with tears welling up in his eyes. "This is heaven."

Chapter 25 Homo Spaceians

I held Demetrious like I would never let him go. Slowly I felt the world come back into focus. I looked around the room and smiled as I realized that everyone I cared about was there, Tommy, Jennifer, Robert, Sasha, Yuri, Jimmy, and Leslie. Oh my goodness even Emma was here!

"Emma!" I managed to say weakly but excitedly, "what are you doing here?"

Emma came over, hugged me and said, "About time you woke up!"

"I love you too, sis."

Then I remembered Marc. "Where's Marc?" I said in a panic. "Robert, where's Marc? What happened to him?"

Robert looked rather grim. "Marc got shot remember. He was injured pretty badly. The bullet shattered his left hip. He was in surgery for seven hours back on Earth."

"But he's okay, right?" I said urgently.

"They say he may never walk again," replied Robert softly.

"But he's alive, right? He's going to live?" I repeated.

"Damn right I'm going to live!" said Marc from the video display to my right. "Sorry I can't be there in person. The doctors on Earth said I couldn't leave yet. They said my hip needed to heal more before I could travel into space. Idiots."

"You stupid fool!" I said smiling as I turned toward the monitor. "You jumped through space without a spacesuit! Why would you do that?"

Marc smiled, his bright blue eyes lit up his face, "Because, you are, and always have been, the love of my life."

"I love you, too. And Rusty? What happened to Rusty?"

"I'm over here," came Rusty's deep baritone voice from behind the curtain. "I'm too hooked up to all these damn machines to come over there."

"He'll live," said Doris.

"Thank goodness you're alive, Rusty," I exclaimed. "I thought when you got shot that—"

"It'll take more than a single gunshot to do me in," replied Rusty. "It just broke a rib and punctured my lung. No big deal. Oh, and Tesla, Gabriel is here with me. I'll send him over to your room with someone you should meet."

As they entered my room Gabriel said, "Tesla, this is Abdul Zahir Hakami, owner of New Medina that you blasted to pieces."

"Mr. Hakami, words cannot express my gratitude for what you did. I don't know how I could ever repay you."

"Facilities can be rebuilt, but seeing the faces of the people here at Sky City II is payment enough," replied Abdul.

...

The next day I was released from the medical center. That evening Demetrious, Emma and I gathered in Rusty's room. I looked at Rusty and said, "I've been meaning to ask you why, why did you risk your life for me?"

"Don't you know? replied Rusty smiling. He shrugged his shoulders and said, "We're all in this together,"

"Well, if we're all in this together why do these assholes keep trying to kill us?" asked Demetrious.

"Demetrious!" I reprimanded.

"Well, they are."

"Okay, but some people are just afraid of what they don't understand. Some people on Earth think we're different and that frightens them."

"But we are different," said Demetrious, "Everyone knows that."

"Maybe so, but everyone's a little bit different. No two of us are exactly the same. And you, my son, are the most unique person who ever lived."

"Here we go again," replied Demetrious. "Okay, I'll bite, what do you mean this time, mom?"

"Well, let me explain."

Demetrious rolled his eyes expecting that one of my long-winded explanations was coming.

"You see, living here in the zero-gravity of space is a new environment for mankind. It is an enormously new and different environment. And, as I have so painfully experienced recently, once people live here for a long enough time they cannot return to the Earth. The absence of gravity is a powerful barrier separating everything that lives here from everything that lives on Earth, and it will eventually result in the evolution of all kinds of new species here, including us. Space is where a new species of humans will evolve."

"You should call that new species *Homo spaceians*," quipped Rusty.

I smiled at Rusty before continuing. "You see, my son, you are unique because you are the branching point. You are the last common ancestor between *Homo sapiens* and Rusty's *Homo spaceians*. But, what makes you even more unique is that no living creature has ever known that they were the branching point. In the three and a half billion year history of life's evolution on Earth, you are the only one.

Acknowledgements

I am extremely gratefully for the efforts of the following people who helped enormously to improve the quality of this work including Bobbie Brophy, Jennifer Brophy, Jonathan Brophy, and Brian Caliando, who suffered through the first draft and provided extensive comments and suggestions for improvement. Tom Brophy, Dan Goebel, and Steve Snyder received the (hopefully) improved second draft, and provided numerous additional insightful comments and suggestions of things to change or fix. Finally, Louis Friedman, Emily Pokoik, Tom Jones, Jay Polk, and Darren Sholes reviewed the third draft and provided still more valuable suggestions.

The concepts contained in this novel were drawn, in part, from the outstanding ideas, insights, and information contained in the books and references listed below. This book is entirely fiction. Whatever factual errors exist in the text are completely my responsibility.

The descriptions of life in free fall were drawn primarily from the following three sources: Mary Roach's wonderful book, *Packing for Mars*, Tom Jones' excellent book, *Sky Walking*, about flying on the Space Shuttle, and, *A house in Space*, the outstanding book about life onboard the Skylab space station by Henry Cooper.

The common ground between religion and science was drawn from Dave Sloan Wilson's the terrific book, *Evolution for Everyone*. The description of God's love by the character Gabriel DeJesus was based on the brilliant article by Kerry Egan, "What people talk about before they die." The statement that the character Rusty Steele makes, "But what I believe is that if the idea of God causes people to act with love toward each other, then in that very real sense God is love" is from Karen Armstrong's superb book, *A History of God*.

The description of Lew Allen's balls is taken directly from George Dyson's, *Project Orion, the True Story of the Atomic Spaceship*.

It is a privilege to read the outstanding works of nonfiction listed below and I am grateful that people take the time to share this information in such accessible and entertaining prose. It has been my great pleasure to attempt to weave this information into a hopefully entertaining story.

Armstrong, Karen, *A History of God*, Ballantine Books, 1993, ISBN 0-345-38456-3.

Brand, Stewart, ed., *Space Colonies*, Penguin Books, Ltd., 1977, ISBN 0-14-004805-7.

Carlson, Linda, *Company Towns of the Pacific Northwest*, University of Washington Press, 2003, ISBN 978-0-295-80553-5.

Compton, David W. and Benson, Charles D., *Living and Working in Space—A History of Skylab,* LeClue, Amazon Digital Services LLC, 2008, ASIN: B0017S2H5K.

Cooper, Henry S.F., *A House in Space*, Holt, Rinehart and Winston of Canada, 1976, ISBN 0-03-016686-1.

Dawkins, Richard, *A Devil's Chaplain*, Houghton Mifflin Company, 2003, ISBN 0-618-33540-4.

Dawkins, Richard, *The Blind Watchmaker*, W.W Norton & Company, 1996, ISBN 0-393-31570-3.

Dyson, George, Project Orion, the True Story of the Atomic Spaceship, Henry Holt and Company, LLC, 2002, ISBN 0-8050-5985-7.

Egan, Kerry, "What people talk about before they die," Facebook Live on CNN Health, December 20, 2016.

Ehrman, Bart D., *Jesus, Apocalyptic Prophet of the New Millennium*, Oxford University Press, Inc., 1999, ISBN 0-19-512474-X.

Ehrman, Bart D., *Jesus, Interrupted*, HarperCollins Publishers, 2009, ISBN 978-0-06-117393-6.

Honda, Y., Honda, S., Narici, M., and Szewczyk, N.J., "Spaceflight and Ageing: Reflecting on *Caenorhabditis elegans* in Space," *Gerontology* 2014; 60:138-142.

Howe, A. Scott and Sherwood, Brent, *Out of this World, The New Field of Space Architecture*, American Institute of Aeronautics and Astronautics, Inc., 2009, ISBN 978-1-56347-982-3.

Jones, Tom, *Sky Walking*, HarperCollins Publishers, 2006, ISBN 978-0-06-088436-9.

Jordan, Bryan D. and Wright, Elizabeth Laura, "Xenon as an Anesthetic Agent, *AANA Journal*, October 2010, Vol. 78, No. 5.

Lunau, Kate, *Chris Hadfield,* Rogers Publishing Limited, Amazon Digital Services, LLC, 2013, ASIN B00CRP3DXM.

O'Neill, Gerard K., *The High Frontier*, William Marrow & Company, 1976, ISBN 978-0688031336.

Parihar, Vipan K., et al., "What happens to your brain on the way to Mars," Sci. Adv. 2015;1e1400256, 1 May 2015.

Phillips, Robert W., *Grappling with Gravity*, Springer Science + Business Media, LLC, 2012, ISBN 978-1-4419-6898-2.

Roach, Mary, *Packing for Mars*, W.W Norton & Company, 2010, ISBN 978-0-393-07910-4.

Ross, Jerry, *Space Walker*, Purdue University Press, 2013, ISBN 978-1-55753-631-0.

Sagan, Carl, *Pale Blue Dot*, Random House, Inc., 1994, ISBN 0-679-43841-6.

Sherwood, Brent, "Comparing future options for human space flight," Acta Astronautica 69 (2011) 346-353.

Shubin, Neil, *Your Inner Fish*, Pantheon Books, Inc., 2008, ISBN 978-0-375-42447-2.

Stine, G. Harry, *Living in Space*, M. Evans and Company, Inc., 1997, ISBN 0-87131-841-5.

White, Ronald J., "Weightlessness and the Human Body," *Scientific American*, September 1998.

Wilson, David Sloan, "*Evolution for Everyone*," Random House, Inc., 2007, ISBN 978-0-385-34092-2.

Woodmansee, Laura S., *Sex in Space*, CG Publishing, Inc., 2006, ISBN 1-894959-44-2.

Worden, Al, *Falling to Earth*, Smithsonian Books, 2011, ISBN 978-1-58834-310-9.

Made in the USA
Las Vegas, NV
21 December 2023

83359036R00144